DOGS ARE HUMAN TOO

By
Don Kirk

OTHER BOOKS BY
DON KIRK

AVAILABLE FROM THE PUBLISHER
lulu.com/spotlight/sweetwater
amazon.com
barnes&noble.com

*Welcome to Redrock Canyon Territory:
An Old West Resort, Movie Ranch, Entertainment Park,
and Open-Air Living History Museum*

*Barbed Wire, Windmills, & Six Guns: A Book of Trivia,
Fact, and Folklore About The American West*

Discovery Bay

Erika

Hinsdale: The Summer of '58

Cool Short Stories: Psychodramas With A Twist

My Remembrances Of Life At Tompkins Barracks

The Story of Columbia Coloring Book

Western Art Coloring Book Vol I & Vol II

Iron Horse Art Coloring Book

Sundry Art Coloring Book

DOGS ARE HUMAN TOO

Tall Tails From A Canine's Point-Of-View

By

DON KIRK

Dogs Are Human Too
Tall Tails From A Canine's Point-Of-View
By Don Kirk

Published by
SWEETWATER STAGELINES™
An imprint of
THE OLD WEST COMPANY™
5118 Village Trail Drive
San Antonio, Texas 78218

Tradepaper (ISBN13): 978-0-9898004-3-3
Tradecloth (ISBN-13): 978-0-9898004-2-6
Printed and bound in the United States of America

SWEETWATER STAGELINES™
SAN ANTONIO, TEXAS

R4

Dogs Are Human Too

Tall Tails From A Canine's Point Of View

By Don Kirk

FORWARD

Dogs can sometimes warm your heart better than people can.

What will you find in this compendium? You'll find a few entertaining short stories about our canine friends spiced with humor but intended to reveal the plight of many dogs in America. Many are mistreated and pinned up in small backyards with no exploratory walks through the neighborhood.

You can look into the eyes of a dog and feel their undying love. They look deeply into your soul and wait eagerly for your next directive. "What are we going to do next?" they ask. After all, they discern they are family and want dearly to please us.

In this compilation, you'll find a story told from a young boy's point of view, from a dog detective's perspective, from a man getting a Saturday morning haircut, and from a sad dejected Chihuahua with no home. You'll experience a Dalmatian's adventures at a fire station, a German shepherd "riding shotgun" in a police vehicle, and a Redbone Coonhound traveling with an Old West wagon train. Some of the stories are told from the dog's point of view, yes, from inside their heads as we try to get into the noggins of these compassionate, loving companions that will willingly fight to the death to protect their Masters.

It's been proven that our canine friends all have unique personalities and desires—all dog owners know this—and we find that every breed sees and responds to the world differently with varying motivations. They were bred to have special interests like hunting, herding, guarding, rescuing, various sports, and some are happy quietly cuddled up to their masters. And many love to do specific things like swimming, retrieving, and simply chewing on rawhide bones. Some dogs are personable and others are standoffish, but that's usually a reflection of their owners. Some are sweet as chocolate candy and others won't let you near them; the introduction of some of these standoffish critters is a low-pitched growl with raised lips exposing their incisors. Sounds just like some human characteristics, does it not? A dog's behavior is usually a reflection of their owner's personalities.

Dogs have a sweet spirit and gentle soul. They're compassionate, affectionate, and caring. They convey love and have proven to be quite smart—having the intelligence of a two to three old human child—and they have instinctive feelings and emotions (yes they do, it's been scientifically proven). They have a strong emotional bond with their humans (all caring dog owners know this) and they can gauge a person's emotional state just by looking at their faces. They often have dog buddies, but they prefer to hang out with humans instead of their own kind. Dogs even yawn just like humans and they have a strong willingness to please. They hunt, they guard, they retrieve, they exhibit undying allegiance. The crucial traits required to be a good guard dog are loyalty and being able to remain calm, self-confident, and self-assured. You can't beat that. But when you leave your dog alone at home for the day they exhibit separation anxiety the same as a young child. You are part of their family. You are the pack leader that cares for and feeds them. Scientists have even shown that dogs have a real sense of what's wrong, what's right, and what's fair. Dogs can even smell events months after they have happened, and, of course, they know where every cat hangs out. When in their deep slumber, dogs may even dream about daily events and the joys of chasing cats. Sometimes they toss and turn and grumble as if speaking to those in the dream.

Just like humans, these loving canines are individuals responding markedly to humans based on the inherited skills and interests of the breed. When I look into the eyes of my canines, I see inside a living soul waiting patiently for me to tell them what wild adventure we're going to embark on next.

Take care of your dog. Life is fragile. It's made even more apparent when you see your pooch trying to cross a street and witness it narrowly missed by a car.

Look into those dog's eyes, at their faces, and you'll find they are as expressive as humans. Pay attention to them just as you would a human child. Dogs are quick studies of human behavior and they can adapt to their situations even better than a chimpanzee. Dogs can "read" our movements and they seem to know what we're thinking. They have been loyal, loving companions to humans around the world for thousands of years.

In these pages are a few tall tales starring dogs who use their tails, paws, and snouts to tell you what they're trying to say. I hope these stories will be just plain fun with a few surprises along the way.

Don Turk

Tribute to a Dog

"The one absolutely unselfish friend that man can have in this selfish world, the one that never deserts him, the one that never proves ungrateful or treacherous, is his dog. A man's dog stands by him in prosperity and poverty, in health and sickness. He will sleep on the cold ground where the wintry winds blow and the snow drives fiercely, if only he may be near his master's side. He will kiss the hand that has no food to offer, he will lick the wounds and sores that come with the roughness of the world. He guards the sleep of his pauper master as if he were a prince. When all other friends desert, he remains. When riches take wings and reputation falls to pieces, he is as constant in his love as the sun in its journey through the heavens." —George Graham Vest, 1870

CONTENTS

Happy, a Golden Retriever

1. The Dog Nanny
By Don Kirk

I took in a dog that had lost his way,
Lost his family, had no place to stay.
I gave him a name, for I knew not his,
He wagged his tail, and jumped with bliss.

I walked him twice a day and fed him three,
And took him swimming; a Golden was he.
We played fetch, and I challenged him in games of keep-away,
I taught him tricks—to shake hands, roll over, and stay.

I bathed him, brushed him, and washed his teeth to fight decay.
I gave him tasty treats and the finest toys on his birthday.
I took him wherever I went; in the front seat he sat and grinned,
His head hanging out the window, his ears trailing in the wind.

He followed me into the house and checked his bowl for food.
He sat beside me watching TV, sitting quietly, never rude.
He watched me fix things and watched me as I read,
And always, every night, he slept at the foot of my bed.

He used to follow me through the front door, this canine,
He would wait for his dinner until I'd eaten mine.
He used to come running when I called out his name,
And strolled beside me on our walks; to him it was a game.

But now he leads me about the neighborhood,
And barks at me when I don't keep up, as if I ever could.
He has the gall to drag me to the neighborhood trash dump,
And take me for a swim in the nearest sewer sump.

A Thrilled Golden

He had become a welcome and valued member of our family,
But now he begs for attention and demands petting relentlessly.
And dog gone it, I'm afraid he's become the leader of our pack,
Because he gets half my french fries, and most of my Big Mac.

He's got me sleeping on the living room divan,
And sniffing at aromas, especially those from the trashcan.
He's got me scratching and biting at pesky fleas,
And taking him to visit the neighbor's pedigree.

He's got me treeing squirrels and jumping on unsuspecting
felines.
He's got me lifting my leg to fire hydrants and trumpet vines.
He's got me barking at suspicious noises in the alley,
And frenzied I become hearing two cats fighting ferociously.

I hide under the bed when I hear thunderclaps,
And frightened by anything on four legs, I have mishaps.
And after I've devoured a good steak of my own,
I find myself gnawing pleasurably on the juicy bone.

When it's hot, I lie spread eagle on the cool kitchen flooring,
And I find myself always listening
For the crinkling sound of plastic packaging,
A telltale sign that food is in the offing.

And so, I watch, I listen, I park myself by the front door,
Fearing my family will leave me evermore.
And in the night, by lonely streetlight, I scamper free,
Wandering the quiet streets, looking for that pedigree.

I take worm pills and a monthly flea treatment, as I should,
And I look with disdain, on the cats invading the neighborhood.
For I know—as sure as Romeo loved his Juliet—
These cute fur balls are aliens from another planet.

I scratch, I groom, I lick my feet and legs and posterior,
And other special parts, I care not to mention here.
I find myself curling up when it's cold as winter's hail,
My nose snuggled warmly under my cozy tail.

I find I must bury my leftovers, and crawl around on all fours.
I find myself circling the bed before I lie down to snore,
And circle everyone I meet, and up on strangers I leap,
And happily, with the joy of a dog, I chase cats in my sleep.

—The Dog Nanny

Dakota, a Borador

2. A Hound Dog At Heart
Inside a Dog's Head:
A true story as told by Dakota
(Transcribed by Don Kirk)

1. FORWARD

What do they think? How do they feel? They indeed have emotions. And unlike our human ancestors, the monkeys, they trust humans. You tell them food is over here, or over there, and they believe you. But monkeys, they figure you're trying to fool them. Humanoids, descendants of apes, have apparently inherited that mistrust of other humans.

Try to get into a dog's head. Look into his eyes. He wants to do things with you: play, hunt, and eat. He's a sincere team player. He will happily be a part of the pack and will alert you of attackers. He's willing to sacrifice himself to protect you and he's well aware that you're not even a dog. He greatly appreciates that you feed him and care for him even if you do make him take a bath once in a while.

The canine is much more intelligent than most humans think. How does a dog's "smarts" compare to a human child's intelligence? A veterinarian will tell you that dog's have an intelligence equivalent to a two to three-year-old human! If they had a voice box they could probably speak...and not just say "da-da." Humans created the dog. They took in the curious wolves who hung around for food scraps and taught them to bark if an enemy approached. Yes, that's right, wolves did not bark, humans taught their new partners this horrendous habit.

It turns out, dog intelligence varies with the breed. Some were bred as working breeds to assist humans and so they enjoy, and in fact require, lots of activity. The working breeds are usually the smartest, ranking the highest on the intelligence tests. The Border Collie, German Shepherd, Golden Retriever, Doberman Pinscher, Shetland Sheepdog, Labrador Retriever, and the Papillion, are all sharp and astute, but the Poodle is actually second on the list if you can believe that! The lovable Beagle sits way down on the list—87th—so he enjoys just sitting around next to you and watching television, though he too needs lots of exercise.

The working breed looks into your eyes waiting quietly for your next command and hopes for an adventurous day. Maybe a ride in your car so he can stick his head out the window to sniff out prey, or maybe a free run in the neighborhood, or maybe a visit to a dog park where he can meet others of his kind.

I wanted to get inside the dog's head so I contacted a veterinarian and a neurological surgeon about implanting a microchip of some sort to transmit and record some mental activity. I could later translate and interpret their behavioral thinking during their daily activities. After some months, something similar to a microchip, but larger, was developed to implant at the base of the brain to allow the scanning and recording of the dog's thoughts and then be transmitted to an external device. This would allow us to get a better idea of what the dog was thinking throughout the day. The experiment turned out to be enormously successful, though the brain impulses had to be translated into some sort of English so you the reader could better understand. Here are some of those translations.

This article is written by a dog—a dog's point of view of his world—so here are some of the adventures in Dakota's life as translated by humans from his own barks and facial expressions. So now let's begin; here's the English translation:

2. A RESCUED DOG

I cowered at the back of the cage. I had been impounded for weeks in this lifeless, inhuman place. A big black breed was stranded in the cage beside me and barked all the time. On this day, a man I hadn't seen before came into the animal shelter as so many human types had done before. The black breed jumped wildly and barked at the visitor as it had done to all those stopping by before.

"These two canines are the last we have right now," said the lady human who previously brought me food and water.

"The yellow one there is staying at the back of the cage; she won't even look at us, her head is down," said the visiting human.

"Submissive, been traumatized. She's afraid of people, but she will come around. These are all we have right now, and they will be euthanized in two days. This is Stafford City. We're not like Podunk where they don't allow it. We just don't have the space."

"So she gets the needle in two days?" the visiting human asked.

"That's right."

"But she's so cute."

"She'll make a great companion. She's only one-and-a-half years old, fully grown, a mix."

"Can you bring her out so I can see her?"

"Sure."

They opened the door, connected something to my neck, and pulled me forward.

"Here, she's sweet-natured, a bit reserved right now, but she'll come around."

"She's so attentive."

I looked up at the nice elderly man, but kept my head lowered with only my eyes looking up high in their sockets.

"She's very protective around strangers and strange dogs."

"I can socialize her. I'll take her."

"Great, follow me."

They led me down a long hall so an elderly human could fill out some paperwork. After an uneasy time, they took me outside. The real outdoors again, sunlight, wow! The nice human with the dark-green military cap, baggy cargo pants, and scruffy white beard put me into a large dirty-green transport. I was scared, but he put the window down part way and I dared to stick my head out the window. Wow! Eyebrow-raising winds blew on my face, my ears trailing behind me, my lips flopping wildly. Oh, what I could smell! An awesome thing this was.

Soon, the man came to a stop, led me out of the transport, and took me into a fenced-in yard. He wrapped a red collar around my neck; it was too tight, I snapped at him. He loosened it. He said this to be temporary, he would purchase a better collar with my name on it and a phone number where he could be contacted if I got lost, so not to worry. On the collar hung some kind of chime that rattled when I moved. It bothered me at first, but I got used to it. I found I could tune out noises like the man's television with its yapping human voices and focus on sounds of importance like potential threats or the plastic packaging noises of forthcoming tasty treats.

I felt comfortable in my new digs; it sure beat that confining, wire cage.

I wore "angel's wings" just behind my shoulders, a white mix of hair that's longer-than-the-rest of my coat. My mother told me I was an angel and would be a "good girl" and so I was determined to do my best to show my new pack leader I was indeed a virtuous spirit, full of energy, and ready to work. My bright, focused eyes always waiting for the next command. My master would surely be seduced by my bewitching brown eyes; I could get what I wanted!

3. GOOD MORNING SUNSHINE

My peepers opened. I sat up. My master lay beside me but seemed to be asleep. I looked at this glassy thing and saw the glowing red numbers my master banged down on in the early morning as soon as it screamed a loud shrill sound. I also saw a canine creature looking at me in this glass above the vanity.

Oh, it was me: a medium-sized dog, 18-inches high, 35 pounds, a yellow-orange color, but covered with the white patches inherited from my mother: a white breast, white lower legs, white on the muzzle, and a narrow white strip between my awesome eyeballs. I flaunted fluffy white thighs, and a white tip on my tail. And look at that radiant smile! Yes indeed, I was a sexy girl. Humans called me a "Borador." I wasn't an accidental mix, no-sir-re. A designer breed they said. My father had been a muscular, yellow Labrador Retriever and my mother a pretty Border Collie with long, flowing, black and white hair. The image in the glass was posing and showing off, but then I saw behind me my new master turning over. I moved to get clear of the frantic pounding to come very soon, but hey, why don't I just lick my master's face now and maybe he'd turn it off before it's loud piercing cry...

Master, it's time to get up. A good lick to the face ought to do it. The human stirred and spoke, "Ahhh, not now, it's too early." The human turned over and away from me. I raised my paw to his shoulder. "All right, all right, I'm coming," the human responded.

I jumped off the bed, hitting the floor running, ready for our morning hunt. I yawned big and lowered my front legs and stretched them. I then stretched my hind legs. And I couldn't wait to find a place to leave my mark. I also needed to track down last night's food scraps left outside by my master for the birds. And I sorely wanted to go hunting for cats. In my nostrils already, the scent of them scampering about.

My master, the current head of our pack, crawled slowly and dazedly out of bed and hurried to mark a room he called a "bathroom." I assumed he was making darn sure everyone knew it to be his territory. I had no problem with that; I routinely marked other areas in our vast territory my human called a "neighborhood."

I quietly watched my master get dressed, watched him put on his socks, and then, Wow! Paw coverings. He's putting on his paw things! I jumped in excitement, we were leaving our den.

"Do you want to go for a walk?" my master asked. I was excited. 'A walk', we we're going hunting! My tail wagged high and at great speed. I did three-sixties on two legs. I loved to go on these

"A 'Walk'?"

walks with my nose to the ground to hunt for critters.

"I think that means 'yes'," my master said.

I hurried ahead of him to the door but turned around to see if he intended on coming. He came, but turned away and grabbed his baseball cap and a small plastic bag. I couldn't imagine it's purpose. He finally opened the door and I jumped out in a flash. I ran figure-eights in the yard from one end to the other as fast as I could. Not ovals, but eights, requiring me to quickly turn left and then right and back to the left again. I figured this could be an exercise to stay sharp and agile so I could catch a varmint for my new master. But this particular display of excitement was for him, to show I was happy to be here. I kept it up for some time—my master loving it and trying to stay clear of me—but after a bit, I headed for the water bowl, my pink tongue hanging out.

"Where's your leash?" my master asked. I ran to the gate of the chain-link fence surrounding the front yard. He placed the leash on my collar—I had no idea why—and we went out the gate and down the sidewalk. I led; I was sure he wanted me to do that, to be prepared to fight off any attackers—to be first on a critter.

Off we went. All kinds of interesting smells. Some odors brought me to a halt, me trying to gather more information: droppings from a member of another pack, a ground creature, a lizard maybe, a frog, or some tasty food in the offing. I found no food nearby so I walked on. A fellow canine yapped in the distance, I looked up, then stopped, trying to locate the bark—was it friend or foe?

Some little humans approached on the sidewalk. What were they? One of them tried to pet me. I freaked and backed off. When one of them tried again I growled at her.

"You kids, stay back!" barked my master.

I was happy to see the little humans back away, apparently as afraid of me as I of them.

On another day's walk a little boy playing stickball with another human creature stopped to pet me when his ball landed nearby. That was okay; I let him touch me. He seemed nice but then raised his stick and I freaked! I grabbed his arm; afraid he would hit me. He screamed and ran to his mother at a nearby house. Other humans came running from a house next door, but the mother told them the boy's arm was fine. I didn't understand what I had done wrong.

[It became obvious to the new owner that the Borador had been abused. The dog was afraid of all sounds, even common ones like squawking birds and chattering cicadas. Even passing cars freaked her out. She feared airplanes and barked wildly at them. The new master noted that anytime he threaded his belt into his pants, the dog retreated, cowering in the corner, exposing her belly. She had obviously been beaten with a belt. She wouldn't even let the owner touch her. But after about two weeks, she began to relax and enjoy a regular dish of canned vittles and became familiar with the owner's yard outside. The owner taught her a few basic tricks she loved to do like: sit, stay, come, jump, down, the hand shake, high-five, and even rollover...but more importantly, she picked up commands on her own like stop, wait, okay, don't pull, that's all, and a firm "NO!" And she responded to questions like "Do you want to go for a ride?" after which she would run to the car and wait for the master to open the door. She even understood "Go get your tennis ball?" "Where's your teddy bear?" and "On your mark, get set, go!" whereby—after her leash had been removed in a public park—she would take off running at high speed. But she saved her all-out breakneck speed for chasing cats, those creatures from another planet.]

4. PLAYING OPOSSUM

I saw it waddling around in my neighbor's yard: it was grey with a small white head, long snout, beady-eyes, and a long, thin rat-like tail. I had to get it so I began rapidly digging out the dirt under the neighbor's chain-link fence. I hated these fences found everywhere in the human's neighborhood, such a hindrance to good hunting. I fight for what I believe in. If there's a critter on the other side of a fence, I'm going to dig, and dig, and remove rocks, even bricks, until I get to that confounding creature. It's my job for the master. So I kept digging, faster, and faster. Finally, the hole was big enough. I pushed through, ran after the critter, and grabbed it and shook it. It hissed at me and growled. I tried to bite down on it, but it didn't collapse so easily. It fell quiet, eyes closed and lips drawn back showing its teeth. I pushed on it with my snout, prodded it with my paw, but no movement. I actually won out over it! My master would be pleased. The creature emanated an awful, putrid odor—even I thought so. I came back under the fence to tell him, entered the house through an open door, and scurried through it with blissful excitement as my paws slipped and slid on the floor looking for him. The wild, scratching sound of my claws on the tile floor was awesome, if I do say so myself.

"Yes, Dakota, what is it?"

I jumped with my forelegs onto his lap. I was thrilled; my tail wagged rapidly. The master figured I could paint an entire house in short order with that tail. He said so.

"Okay girl, show me."

I dashed back out of the house well ahead of my master. I couldn't wait to show him my find. And there it was. The critter lay there not moving.

"All right, you got a big momma opossum. You've caught five young opossums already. I sure wish you could leave these nice earth creatures alone; they're cute and not doing us any harm."

I looked down, feeling bad about the master's dissatisfaction with me, but he looked squarely at me and asked, "Where can they be coming from, Dakota?"

I stayed and watched as my master took a plastic bag—the same thing he used to bring home tasty goodies and stored his leftovers—and placed the critter in it and tied it tightly. He put another bag over that one, wrapped it tight with tape, put the bag in the neighbor's trashcan, and knocked on the neighbor's door. I jumped concerned. A female human opened the door, came out.

"Mrs. McGillicutty, Dakota took down another opossum, a big one, the mother or papa; I couldn't tell which. I don't know where they are living—a whole nest of them somewhere nearby—but you have to stop throwing food scraps into your front yard."

"They're for the birds and all the other wonderful creatures in our neighborhood."

"What, like raccoons, opossums, skunks, feral cats, and those scum-eating rats? Dakota can testify that they're all here."

"Rats, hell no! I don't want…okay, okay, I'll stop throwing my scraps out," agreed Mrs. McGillicutty finally. "I'll stop."

"I'll put this opossum in your trash. City trash pickup is tomorrow."

The next morning I watched across the fence as Mrs. McGillicutty came out to put her food scraps in her trashcan. I wished she would let me get my pick of the bounty; some of it was right good eating. She lifted the lid and wow! The giant "dead" opossum jumped out at her. McGillicutty jumped back in terror—leaving the ground by two feet or more—and ran into her house and slammed the door. Wow! The opossum ran off. I tried to go after it, but the hole under the fence slowed me down and I lost sight of the critter. I sniffed the ground. The scent led me back and forth for a while, but I finally took to a hotter scent and moved faster. I came upon a big tree root and saw a hole leading down under it. Down there; I was sure of it. I stuck my head in the hole, but unable to get deep enough, I started digging—my front paws, claws extended, moving with lightning speed. I dug, and dug some more, and found myself under a big tree root but still no critter to lock in my jaws. I lay down and waited. My master will be so happy if I catch it. He gave me food from his catch everyday; it was only fair for me to return the favor.

After a long spell, I got up, retreated to our den, and went to bed.

The next night I surprised the big waddling critter again. He sneered at me, showing all his pointed teeth, but that wasn't going to stop me. I attacked, and quickly took him down. This time I showed no mercy: I bit his body and neck, shook him violently, and then barked for my master. He came quickly, bagged the critter, and threw it into McGillicutty's trashcan again, but this time he put a big, heavy, concrete block on the lid.

5. EATING OUT

I loved riding with my master in his car. He let me stick my head out the window and enjoy an airstream full of odors, cooler and more refreshing than lying in the boring backseat of his car.

My master turned into a parking lot and turned off the engine. Getting out of the car, he spoke firmly, "Hold on, Dakota, stay here a minute. It's lunch time, a coupla Subways."

Lunch time?

He soon came back, climbed into his car, and set a plastic package on the front dashboard. We drove off. A few minutes later he turned into another parking lot, jumped out, and disappeared into a store. I could smell an awfully fresh, tantalizing treat; my nose led me to the dashboard. I grabbed the package with my teeth and pulled it down between the front seats so I could eat it on the center console; the perfect table just for me. I tore into it. Covering the two treats were wax-paper wrappings; I tore one of them open. In it long pieces of bread with...Wow! A gold mine. Delicious cow. Wonderfully great! There's more, I thought, and torn into the other package and, Wow! Turkey or chicken. I took another big soul-satisfying bite. I was finishing the first half of this second food bonanza when my master opened the car door and climbed in. He saw wax paper strewn about in little pieces and...

"Oh no, Dakota, you didn't! That was to be my dinner for the next two days. Well, at least you left me half of one Sub for today's lunch. Looks like you've had your meals for several days."

I barked with pleasure, but hoped my master would give me a big cow bone with vanilla ice cream to top it off.

6. THE CAT CHASE

An intense cat scent held my attention; I rounded the master's transport and stuck my nose into a wheel well. Cat, cat, there's a C-A-T in there! Master, there's a cat! I tried to crawl over the wheel, but couldn't quite make it. The cat moved; I followed, circling the car trying to find a way to her hiding place. I tried to crawl underneath. It was there, I knew it—a fresh hot catch! But it ran. Without hesitation, I backed out and raced after the cat. The prey attempted an escape, but I stayed close behind. It ran into the street and I ran after it, my tail trailing straight back. I could shift my tail side to side to counterbalance any fast turns I might have to make. This was exciting, a thrill; I loved doing this. The cat's tail trailed behind, and was just inches from my snout, but I couldn't quite, couldn't quite...the cat ran into a large field with a gravel road beside it.

Out of the blue, my master's transport came up beside me; he wanted to stop my hunt, I was sure. But he was now racing alongside. I could here him yelling: "Stop Dakota stop, leave that cat alone! Fifteen, twenty, twenty-five miles per hour. Damn, Dakota, you're too dog gone fast!"

I didn't understand what my master was trying to tell me and I couldn't get a bite of the critter's tail. The cat approached a chain-link fence and like whoop—with it's paws spread very far apart—sprung over the barrier in a flash. I came to a quick stop and jumped up and on the fence, but couldn't get over it.

The master's car door opened, "Come on, Dakota, good try but no cigar, climb in..."

I jumped in.

"But you have to stop this, Dakota, all creatures great and small have an equal right on this planet. Well, maybe not all. I know you've got hound-dog blood in you and I'm allergic to cats so I don't much care, but can't you just ignore them?"

I yelped, but I knew the master didn't know if I was in agreement or just frustrated. He didn't yet know the differences in my barks. I hoped he'd learn them soon: when I called up the pack, warn them, or when I wanted to play. I lay down on the back seat and licked my aching paws; that gravel painfully rough. I liked being a dog, I could lick almost every part of my body, including you know what.

7. A LITTLE RAT KILLING

It was afternoon and I made a search of our den for food or anything new and appetizing. And there, I detected something familiar and took a deep thoughtful whiff. It's here, under the bookcase, no it's behind this display cabinet, here, no here; I put my nose close to a small hole. I recognized the odor: it's that small, round, grey, thin-tailed rodent, the crafty little, scavenging rat! I had found one outside just a few days earlier, but now, it's in our den. I must act! A hot, fresh trail, oh boy! My interest peaked, nose twitching, tail at attention showing intense excitement. I knew my master would want me to apprehend it so I stayed on its trail. I tracked the critter down to one room only to have it set up camp in another room where I couldn't get to it, dat burn it! It was under the master's very heavy bookcase, but I couldn't move it. I must get at the critter! I had already torn into a cardboard box where the rat had been earlier, but now I would have to tear into the shelf's base because I knew the rat lay beneath. I chewed viciously into particle board trying to rip it away to make a hole to get at the rat. The bookshelf's corner now completely gone, chips lying all over the floor, and I still couldn't make my way underneath. I lay down, eyes on the big hole, to hang out and wait. The uninvited critter, I was sure, would show. My master will be so happy if I catch it. The long-tailed thing will eventually have to come out to get water. It could eat paper as a food substitute though I did not think that was very healthy even for a rat. But water, no substitute for that; we all need water. I'll get the varmint, just you wait. The bookshelf began to creak and lean forward;

"Rat killin', I'm ready."

books started sliding. I jumped up and backed away as the whole shelf of books came crashing down! I quickly moved to the newly revealed floor where the bookshelf had been and sniffed, and sniffed, but I didn't find the rat.

It was late, and the master had gone to bed. I lay on the cool tile floor by the bedroom door so my master couldn't leave without me, but as I put my head down, I picked up a scratching sound with my very good auditory organs—better than my masters— and dashed frantically to the kitchen; no more than two of my feet on the floor at any given time. My head jerked up, nose twitched, ears were aimed forward, I focused on a cabinet. In there! There the rat must be! I yelled a loud posthaste cry calling out for my master.

"Dakota, what now? Come to bed."

I barked again, and again, until my master came. He finally presented himself with sleepy, half-closed, eyes, "Dakota! What's up?" I raised my right paw at the location of the strongest scent: the top drawer of a kitchen cabinet.

"Is it here, Dakota, is it in here?" my master asked.

I barked firmly, grabbed the handle, and pulled out the top drawer, but he jumped back and his foot landed on my paw; I freaked out and squealed, but I was okay. The rat scurried to the back of the drawer.

"Ah, sorry Dakota," he said, lifting his foot.

I pointed my nose at the second drawer and my master quickly opened it. He jumped again—both feet leaving the floor—and said something I can't repeat here. He had seen the rat run to the back of the drawer. I think he could see what was happening and so pulled out the third drawer—and there, the rat! I pointed to the bottom drawer and the master opened it. I peered in, saw the rat just as it ran to the rear and disappear yet again. I could now attach a specific smell to the critter, the same odor outside days earlier. I was at full alert, very excited, tail straight up. A kill in the offing for my master, but the smell from the rat creature had weakened. I took a sitting position. Unexpectedly, the smell intensified again. I moved to my left and clawed at a nearby cabinet door.

"Ah, Dakota stop! That was a good kitchen cabinet," snapped the master as he pushed me back with open hand flat to my face—I knew what that meant—and opened the cabinet door. I immediately pushed in past him and found great-smelling food and scrumptious treats, but I was after that blasted rat. The master coaxed me to move back so he could remove the cabinet's contents. "Damn," or some such unpleasant words pierced my ears. I tore into the cabinet base with my canines. There was already a nice rat hole; I just made it bigger, but I didn't find the rat; it had made an escape yet again. I rechecked all the cabinet drawers, carefully sniffing each one.

"I'm going to bed, Dakota, it's late, come on. We'll look for that rodent tomorrow."

I followed my master into the bedroom and jumped into bed with him. He turned a light out, but I could still see, I could still smell, I could stay on night watch. Soon, I heard something moving in the house, jumped up, and ran for the kitchen. I clawed open the cabinet door below the kitchen sink and, with paws and jaws, pulled and tugged on the paper towels, rags, brushes, and chemicals. I pulled them all out, working my way to the back. The critter was there; I knew it. I reached up, reaching for the rat; I clawed and wrapped my choppers around a water supply tube, and wrenched, tore into it, but, without warning, a huge force of water drenched me. I backed out; I wanted no bath tonight. I returned to my master's bed, my feet sloppy wet, the floor a river of water, and peered over the edge of the bed, quite concerned, and chose to bark at my boss. He stirred and leaped up, hearing the frightening sound of gushing water. My master got on his hands and knees and turned the kitchen sink's shut-off valves; the water stopped flowing. He then opened the kitchen door to allow the water to run outside, but it had already made itself known in the hallway, dining room, and even soaked the living room carpet. Needless to say, my master seemed quite upset, but where was that darn, troublesome rat?

I found the rodent moving to a different location in the house in each of four days, but it was always moving to a new place behind furniture and inside various cabinets where I couldn't get at it. I watched my master place a large rattrap sporting a nice dab of peanut butter and also a plastic container with this "rat poison" he called it, high off the floor where I couldn't get at it. I didn't understand that—but we waited, and waited, and waited; there were no takers.

A few days later my master took me outside for our usual morning hunt—I got at least three every day—and into the yard we made haste after I grabbed the leash; he had taught me where to find it. Then, there, outside, I could smell it: I got a whiff of that wretched varmint under the master's transport and circled the vehicle trying to find the creature in the undercarriage, wheel wells, in the engine—transports seemed to be a favorite hangout for critters, especially cats—there, now there, it moved around so very quickly. I'm close; I can see its long slender tail! The grey rat ran from under the car. I chased the critter as it ran about in a horseshoe and serpentine-like path. It started to climb, I grabbed it, mouth on its torso, and clamped down. Got him. I got him! I released him and took a sniff. The master will be delighted. I picked up the critter and ran back into the house through an open sliding-glass door and hurried to find my boss. I growled a call of excitement and he came running.

"Dakota! No! Yeck! You got it, but take it back outside."

I dropped it in front of him, proud of my conquest.

"No, outside!"

Outside I ran, dropped it, and the master gave me a treat: a large bone-like thing that would take me awhile to nibble down.

I checked the house several days more, sniffing all previous places where I had smelled the rat, but no other rodents made themselves known. I'm always on duty and I'll get the job done [no matter what damage the result].

8. A SQUIRRELLY SITUATION

I dropped my front legs, then my hindquarters, so I could lie down on my chest and crossed my front legs in a calm repose. My mouth sagged open and my tongue dropped out over the lower teeth. I panted quietly. I was at rest, tranquil as an earthworm digging a tunnel through soggy mud. I sniffed the ground and found nothing of interest, but, unexpectedly, something fell from the sky and hit the ground. It wiggled and squeaked. I jumped to my feet like a scalded cat. The creature had feathers; I sniffed. I didn't care to eat things with shafts and barbs. I then heard something up in the tree: one of those creatures that flies, and it was squeaking loudly and constantly in some kind of a panic. I sniffed at the little feathered thing lying on the ground, and pushed it with my nose. It squeaked softly. Another flying creature in the tree cried out. I decided to back away; this feathered little critter was of no interest to me. The flying songbird in the tree quickly quieted down. I looked up and saw a wooden box hanging on a tree limb above me. I bellowed.

"What now, Dakota?" came my master's voice and then he came forward to see the feathered thing on the ground looking quite helpless. He picked up the young bird and held it in the palm of his hand. The two fully-grown flyers in the tree began frantically squawking again.

"Poor baby," said my boss looking up to see the tiny house above me and reaching up to put the chick back into a tiny round hole. At that, the mama and papa bird quieted down.

"See, Dakota, all creatures on this planet, great and small, are wonderful...well, except for rats."

I didn't understand what the master was saying so tilted my head trying to understand as he returned to the house. I looked up at the box with the hole in it.

Then, abruptly, I saw a squirrel galloping across the ground,

"All Creatures Great And Small?"

it's long, hairy, tan and white tail trailing behind—a good way for me to grab this critter. But much too quick was he and up a tree he scurried grasping the bark with his long claws. I jumped high, my hind legs coming several feet off the ground as I tried to reach him before he got away, but to no avail. I yelped strongly, calling for help, but the pack leader didn't show. I lay back down at the base of the tree and waited; it would have to come back down eventually. Oh, but no, there it goes, jumping to another tree! I barked sharply, ran, and jumped up the other tree trunk, and hey, I got a grip with my claws and up the tree I bound. The tree, luckily, did not stand straight up, but leaned at an angle and the squirrel was not far ahead of me. I moved slowly, carefully forward; the tree limb now as horizontal as the top of a street curb, but it became smaller and smaller as I inched along it carefully placing one foot in front of the other. The squirrel crawled ahead of me, but I stopped moving forward, the tree branch getting just too narrow. I stood still and looked down. I found myself in the air at least seven Great Danes high and so tried to turn around very, very carefully. I actually managed that, but the way forward turned steeply downward. I couldn't manage that. Going head first, I would surely flip and fall, so instead, I took a long leap to the grassy yard below. Breaking my legs a real possibility, but I was lucky on this day and no harm came to me. I would catch that critter some day. I barked up at the squirrel, saddened by my missed bonanza.

The next day I sighted another squirrel eating comfortably on the ground, but it saw me and ran toward a large oak tree. No hope for me now: the critter jumping onto the tree trunk and heading skyward. I reached for him and he moved around to the backside of the trunk, but when trying to continue upward, he found the tree was gone! Yes, apparently, it had been standing there for many years, but quite recently, was cut down by my master. Just four feet off the ground and the tree trunk stopped cold. The expression on that squirrel's face when it found no tree, priceless—a disparaging futility, time to say his prayers. Yes, squirrels have emotions too. So the squirrel moved to the left around the trunk and I followed. Then he went to the right.

So, round and round we went, the squirrel trying to calculate which way I would go next. Several minutes elapsed and I wasn't getting any closer to nabbing this varmint; he was just one move ahead of me—only two he could make, go left or go right, no way upward—but, finally, he made a wrong change of direction and ended up in my salivating jaws. End of story.

I had already caught two other brown squirrels and left them for my master. They were everywhere, but usually high in the trees. Their only predator the large-winged hawk. I knew this creature because I recently saw a squirrel drop out of the sky and land on the wooden deck out back. My master saw it to, quickly grabbed it by the tail, and rushed the motionless animal out to the street where he lay it down. Immediately, and I mean immediately, the hawk swooped down and picked it up—and was gone in an instant. I wondered if that hawk would thank my boss.

9. KNOCKED OUT COLD

My master took me on a walk and I came upon a scent notifying me a dog from another pack passed here earlier. I marked the spot myself to let it know I had also been here and this territory was not just his. As I finished taking a nice relieving leak onto a potted cactus plant in her front yard, several people exited their vehicle in a nearby parking lot. One of them, a lady human, came up to my master.

I tensed. A large female, taller and much wider than my master, pushed her face into his. I focused my gaze, pinned my ears back, and wagged my tail slowly, concernedly.

"Look what your dog done to my plant! She pissed all over it. It'll kill it. How could ya bring that...get that damn dog outta here!"

"I'm sorry I..."

"Get out of my face and don't let me see you and that pissin' dog here again."

"I'm sorry," my master repeated, "I don't have control of everything she..."

"You get that varmint outta here right now, you hear? If my cactus dies you're gonna hear from me."

"Yes, ma'am, I'm sure I will."

The lady human stomped away to her front door, but as my boss turned to lead me away, a young man came face-to-face with him and said, "Yous not gonna disrespect me nanna!" and then immediately, with a right fist to the master's face, knocked him to his knees. The mean man turned and walked way. I approached my master who now lay face down on the grass. I sniffed his face. He didn't move. I lay down beside him. He was quiet. A car passed by, and then another. I waited quietly with him, figured he needed some sleep.

After a time, my master started to move and slowly lifted himself up. He looked disoriented and confused, rubbed his face, and reached down to pick up his cap.

"Dakota, you okay?" he asked.

I looked up at him bewildered, my head twisting sideways in an effort to understand.

"Come on, let's go home."

I followed my master as he staggered home; he could barely walk. I pulled on the leash to help him find his way, but I kept turning back to look up at him; he appeared dazed and woozy. I couldn't even tell if he knew where he was, but I knew where our den was and took him there.

We arrived in our territory and entered my master's shelter where he immediately lay down on the living room couch. I lay down on the floor beside him and fell asleep...but with one eye open. I wasn't going to stray far from him.

The master seemed okay the next day when he took me for our morning walk, but we didn't go anywhere near that lady's house.

10. MESSING WITH A PIT BULL

I was taking a walk—a hunt—with my master when a big, muscular pit bull came running at us. He was going for me, trying to take me down and I was much smaller than this bruiser. My master kicked at it frantically, but it ignored him; the pit bull coming at me with its strong square jaw. My boss headed for the front door of a house in the territory we had never been to before. He opened the screen door and banged panic-stricken on the entrance door all the while trying to hold me back to keep me from fighting this killer. I had my teeth showing full tilt and I growled angrily, but to no avail. No one was apparently home, so he tried the doorknob and the door came open. My master pushed me into the house; I went easily, ready for flight instead of a fight. He closed the door behind me, I jumped on the couch, and looked out the front window. My master kicked at the hostile pit bull and he finally backed off. It was that tasty dog meal, me, that he wanted, not my master. He wanted these ribs, leg bones, and extremely fresh meat.

A next-door neighbor showed up with a rope, "I saw what happened, I called 9-1-1."

My master and the neighbor managed to get a loop around the vicious animal and then they tied him to a light pole in the front yard. He calmed down; his intended prey—me—was out of sight.

The owner of the house drove up in his transport and my master tried to explain what happened: "Sorry, I've got my dog in your house, this pit bull attacked my dog and tried to kill him. Your front door was unlocked. I'm sorry, I had to…"

"That's right, Mr. Snead, I saw it happen," announced the neighbor. "I called 9-1-1. The police are coming."

"I know this dog," my master said. "He is kept tied in the backyard of the house at the north end of the street. He's always tied to a tree on a very short chain not much more than five feet long."

"Look at his rib cage and skinny waist, the dog hasn't had anything to eat for a long, long time," added the neighbor.

"Makes sense," my master added, "I've never seen any person out there and no sign of a water or food bowl."

"I can't believe it," said Mr. Snead.

"There are lots of people in the neighborhood that don't give a tinker's damn about their dogs. I'm so saddened by the canines I have seen penned up or chained in their backyards in this neighborhood. No one comes out to play with them or take them for walks," declared my master.

"Why do they even have a dog?" asked Mr. Snead.

"Beats the hell outta me!"

Soon, I was reunited with my master and then we waited and

waited. Eventually, something my master called "Animal Control" showed up. It took four hours to take care of business, but an agent finally hauled off the pit bull and my master could continue the noon walk that was now our evening hunt.

[The owner of the pit bull got their neglected animal back several weeks later and tied it to a steel leash on a clothes line so that it met the city's requirement of a dog having to be on a leash no shorter that ten feet. But the dog, it turned out, still did not get fed or watered and one day in an effort to find food, it tried to jump the chain-link fence just beyond the end of the clothesline, but his front legs caught in the wire mesh and he died there all alone. He was dead for a week before anyone noticed!]

11. DOG PRISON

My master tied me to a tree in the front yard of a den across the street and went inside. While out of my sight, a female human with a curly, white-haired poodle came walking by. I barked, the poodle barked. I pulled hard and my leash came loose. The human with the poodle lowered her hand to push me back; I bit her on the arm. She screamed, grabbed her talking piece, and spoke into it. [The woman called 9-1-1 and soon two police cars, a fire engine, and an EMS ambulance showed up, all with flashing lights.] I could see humans in the neighborhood looking out their windows and doors. My master came out of the den and discovered the ruckus. What happened?

I was on one end of my master's leash and a human wearing blue was on the other.

"Dakota!" my master yelled out.

"This your dog?" asked the policeman.

"Yes sir, it is."

"She's bitten someone."

"Not seriously, I hope."

"EMS had to treat her."

"My dog?"

"No, a lady walking her dog."

"She has to be quarantined."

"The lady?"

"No, your dog! For ten days to verify she has no rabies."

"Does the bitten lady have to be quarantined to?"

"I don't know actually, I'll have to look that up," replied the officer, "but I know quarantining your dog is the law."

"Dakota had her rabies shot; you can call my vet."

"Sorry for the inconvenience."

"I can't believe this."

"That's the way it has to be," said the officer firmly. "If you can't contact your vet so they can quarantine him, you must surrender the dog to Animal Care Services right now."

My master entered the den and tried to get hold of the vet but...

"I can't get my vet; it's after hours."

"Then the impound truck will be here to pick her up."

I watched EMS personnel bandage the unhappy-lady's arm and observed the man in blue take her statement. It wasn't long before the impound trunk drove up. I didn't like this; I'd been in one before.

My master handed my leash to a funny-looking, young, white-jacketed man who then pulled something over my head to where I couldn't open my jaw. He lifted me into a small wire cage. I didn't try to fight back, but I had my tail between my legs and looked to my leader: he stood there concerned; I felt fearful. Would I ever see him again? I felt down and sickly.

"It'll be okay, Dakota," my master yelled out, "be good."

In the dog prison were rows and rows of steel cells preventing me from properly meeting any of the other inmates, but I could at least talk with them.

"What are you in for?" I asked a large brown-and-white Saint Bernard. He came over and looked me straight in the face, having taken a long careful sniff first.

"I don't know why I'm in here," he replied, "I'm just a quiet pampered pet, don't do much of anything. Had a good, loving Alpha. Fed me all I wanted."

"It shows," I said.

"Huh?"

"I bit a human," I added.

"No! How could you?"

"A lady tried to push me away from the puppy she was walking."

"That's all?"

"I guess I got too close," I replied.

"Well," said the Saint Bernard, "I think I might not have gotten the vaccination shots I'm supposed to have had: distemper, flu, rabies, ticks, heartworms, Lyme disease, parasites, allergies... you know, that sort of thing."

"No, I don't, but why is that Rottweiler over there tied with extra chains?"

"He tried to escape and bit every prison guard that came to feed him. He's real mean. In fact, he's escaped three times since I've been here."

"How did he escape?"

"Trickery. He feigned an illness once by lying on the concrete floor whimpering. They picked him up and took him to the vet and made a run from there. Another time he bit the hand that fed him, literally. Because of that attack, they moved him into solitary confinement and he escaped again, this time into the exercise yard. But he couldn't make it over the outside walls. They were too high—so don't get any ideas."

"I won't. So what happened to that Akita, over there?" I asked. "She's all chewed up, legs bandaged, one eye patched, and blood on her pretty brown, white, and black coat?"

"She got into a knock-down, drag-out fight with a dog bigger than herself."

"My, my, poor girl."

"My sentiments exactly."

I looked around the prison and saw one scared Dachshund cowered in the back corner of his cell. She was shaking and shivering. This steel-barred, piss-ridden cell had to be really scary for her.

"What's your name?" I asked.

The long-bodied, short-legged Dachshund stood up and replied, "My master calls me 'Stupid'."

"Well, hello, Stupid, nice to meet you. So why are you here?"

"I can't never do nothing right."

"Hello Stupid, nice to meet you."

"I don't believe that."

"He says I'm an ignorant dog and then hits me. He says that I don't know my 'ass from a hole in the ground.' That's what he says, but I do know something. My rear end smells a lot bettern' a hole in the ground. And I knows the canine alphabet, and I knows they is worms in them holes in the ground. Great for lickin' and nibblin' on."

"Is that right?"

Another dog, a white, black-spotted Great Dane was pacing her cell back and forth round and round, never stopping to even lap up a few swallows of water.

"And how about you, what did you do to get incarcerated in here?"

"I bit a mailman."

"Oh no!"

"He's always coming by; putting something in my master's mailbox."

"So, why should that bother you?"

"His noisy truck, it's hard on my ears."

"Oh."

I looked to the light-brown golden retriever on the other side of me who appeared happy and laid back, not a care in the world. She must have a really nice caring alpha. I looked at her eye-to-eye. That got her up from her restful repose—legs nicely crossed, mouth open, tongue out, panting easily—and she came over to me and peered through the steel bars.

"I lost my way home, been wandering for days. Don't have this 'microchip' thing in my neck so I'm here. I hope my master will find me. They put canines down here, send them to dog yonder."

"He will come, be patient. What's with that pit bull over there, he won't calm down?"

Down the central corridor was a light-brown, medium-sized, smooth-coated brute that kept growling and barking, wanting to kill anything that approached. He looked like the type of canine that attacked me, been chained up in his master's backyard all his life.

"I'm too afraid to ask," replied the Saint Bernard.

"How about the Pug over there in the corner, with the flattened, black-as-night muzzle?"

"He said he was part of a dog-only pack, no humans. Some of is little buddies are in here too. So very sad. His master sent him packing because he barked at squirrels all the time."

"Oh, squirrels, huh. Barked at them?" I thought long on that.

I lay in the prison for many long days, bored, and afraid. Would my master come to get me? Maybe he didn't like it that I bark at squirrels? To occupy my time in this trap, I gnawed on my right leg, tearing off all the hair down to the bare pink skin. You think they'd give me a bone or some such to chew on. What is this humdrum, mind-numbing place anyway? A human brought me food, but I didn't dare to eat it.

Finally, one morning, a human put a leash on me and led me out of the prison and into a big room—and my master was there! He was there! I was so happy I jumped up on him, tail wagging, mouth open, and tongue hanging out. He looked happy to see me.

"It wasn't the *Ritz*, was it Dakota?" he asked.

The *Ritz*? My master took me outside, opened the door to his car and I jumped smartly into it. I was so deliciously happy and hoped he would lower the window for some sorely needed fresh air with new tantalizing odors.

12. A BIG STINK

On this new day, I whiffed something very interesting, something new to me under my master's wooden deck. My nose twitched intently smelling the creature between the cracks. I crawled to the side and started wildly digging to get at this strange animal, but a big board stood in the way. I tried another side and dug there, deeper and deeper, until I could stick my head under the board. I dug some more and found I could crawl beneath. The odor became stronger so I continued to dig and crawl and crawl and found myself between two more boards but kept going until I found myself facing another large board. I dug and dug until I could work myself out and back into the light. No critter? Where? It was there, it had to be, I knew it, I could smell the blasted thing.

Then something came running out from under the deck and it waddled away. I ambled behind it; my eyes and nose focused on this thing. The critter raised its wide, black-and-white tail and its body swayed back and forth as it moved nonchalantly away from me. You're going to be easy, I thought, grabbing the hairy critter with ease and shaking it violently, but it squirted me! A very strong, unpleasant odor engulfed me. I shook and crushed the critter's body. The stench was by no means a lady's fragrance, but I didn't stop until it quit fighting. I then ran away across the yard and rolled around in my master's flower bed. I dug into it, tossed dirt skyward, and rolled, and rolled, and rolled, trying to get the horrible, untenable stench off me.

My master approached, his eyes wide, his fingers holding his nose.

"What have you done, Dakota?"

I backed away from him totally embarrassed, not wanting him to touch me. I tucked my tail up against my belly, retreated, and cowered every time he tried to approach. Finally, my master turned away and left me. I was embarrassed. I watched him approach my kill. I took down the critter for him, my pack leader.

"It's a nasty weasel! You, killed a dad-blasted skunk, Dakota! A nasty stinkin' skunk!"

The master retrieved a plastic bag—bigger than the one he took with me on our walks—took a shovel, and lifted the critter into it. He tied the bag tightly and put it in a big brown trashcan.

"Dakota, I could never have imagined a skunk in this neighborhood, but you found it. At this rate, there won't be any rodents or wild animals left in our neighborhood."

I stayed away from my boss through many sunrises and sunsets and the awful odor of my own body continued to hinder my sense of smell. How could I ever find another creature for my Alpha? They could smell me coming. I rolled in the dirt and rolled some more; I was heartbroken. My master sprayed me with an awful, mind-numbing chemical and forced me into his bathtub several times over the next few weeks. He doused me with hydrogen peroxide, baking soda, tomato juice, vinegar, dish-washing soap, de-skunking shampoos of all types, and just about everything on the kitchen shelf, and yet it took about thirty-five sunrises for the smell to fully subside. Yes, I was embarrassed. But I'd probably do it again, got to take down the critters that come into our territory. [He did take down another skunk.]

13. THE GHASTLY BATHTUB

The master always tries to fool me in his effort to give me a bath. He knew I knew the word "bath" and I would go hide if I heard it. I had learned the name from many weeks of skunk baths. I even knew what it meant when he just said B-A-T-H to fool me, but I'm not ignorant, I'm high on the smarts chain...and good-looking too. I could even surmise his intent by his vocal tone and the special interest he showed in me. If he offered me a treat, or tried to coax me out of my place under the nice hard-to-reach-me furniture piece, I knew something was up, and I knew what that something was. I could see in his eyes his real intent no matter what he said to me.

"Come on out, Dakota. I've got this great meaty bone for you, chicken and beef. And then we're going to take a trip in the car to the pet store, the PET store!"

Oh boy, I thought, the wonderful smell of many kinds of food, being able to rub my body on the fresh-bone treats to disguise myself, and best of all, the meeting of other canines that might be hanging out there.

"I know you like the pet store, Dakota: all those mice and hamsters and gerbils and the cute guinea pigs, and even the swimming critters you like looking at in the fish tanks, and even a few cats for you to wish for!"

I perked up at that word 'cats' and then realized it was a trick!

"Come on. It'll be over soon. You'll love this new toy I've got for you. It floats in the water; it's got beef treats in it, yum, yum."

At that, I came out from hiding.

He did fool me from time to time, but as soon as I knew I had no choice, I'd go ahead and voluntarily walk to the bathroom and climb into the tub where it always rained on me and this soapy, yucky stuff would be thrown all over me. The master would scrub me down all over, my legs, back, belly, and even tail. I don't even like water *and* this "soap" stuff on my face, but the rest was not so bad once I got accustomed to it. He poured the soap over me and scrubbed and washed, and then did it over and over again. Finally, my master allowed me to step out of the tub and shake myself off. I liked that part; I did this when returning from a swim, but in his room it was particularly fun watching him also get his own wash-down every time I rapidly shook my torso. He covered me with a towel to dry me off, but I shook away, ran to my bed, rolled in it, and then jumped on his bed and rolled in the sheets and blankets, and rolled yet some more. I couldn't seem to get dry. But I'm smiling, mouth wide open, tongue out, I feel so good, and refreshingly cool. Where's another one of those "skunks?" I'm ready.

14. A PRICKLY AFFAIR

One day in the dark of night, I dug under the fence and ran after this strange-looking creature. It waddled slowly back and forth and presented a hairy body. This should be easy, I thought, and approached carefully, my head held low. It stomped its feet, hissed at me, and shook it's expanding body. I had never seen such a critter but opened my muzzle wide and grabbed it. Something shot into my mouth and I let go. The critter ran, I followed it back into my master's yard, and it clawed its way quickly up a tree. I jumped after it, but the critter was out of reach so I dropped down and stepped backward, my tail wagging very slowly. I was befuddled, what kind of creature was this? I felt a lot of discomfort and stood embarrassingly silent.

I then heard the front door to our den open and my master came up to me. "Dakota, what's up? E-god, your snout! Your mouth, oh my heavens! Jesus!"

I backed away from him, sulking, my head low, ears flipping back and forth, my tail tucked under me. I was quite concerned; I didn't know what to think of my situation. And oh, man, it hurt!

"You've got long needles sticking out of your snout in all directions!" declared my master. "Cactus thorns? No. Pins and needles? No. A porcupine's...no, I don't think, oh yes, they are a porcupine's quills! Ahhhh! That must hurt. It pains me just to

"Ouch!"

look at you, Dakota. Oh man—oh dog—you poor dear!"

I heard the master talking, but didn't understand; I just knew these thorns hurt something awful. I couldn't move my mouth, I couldn't eat, I couldn't drink…"

"Come here, Dakota, it's late at night, but just a few hours to daybreak. We'll take you to a vet."

I watched my master close up his house and then he put me into his car. The look on my face obviously one of distress. I stuck my head out the side window to get some relief, my master driving to my doctor, a very long, painful, hour's drive away, so he said.

We waited and waited and waited in the master's transport—augh!—for the vet office to open. When it did, he took me in immediately. I didn't hold back. The doctor said I would require surgery! The quills had to be pulled. I was not smiling. Onto the operating table they lay me after being given some medicine to ease the pain, but the doctor said he didn't want to put me under completely. Why to hell not? Augh!

Bright lights glared over me, my mouth forced open with some kind of vice. The doctor, with two nurses holding me down, pulled the barbed quills out one by painful one. Finally, the torture ended and they placed me back on the floor dazed & confused and staggering helplessly. My master walked me out, but I knew I would not have any fun chasing cats and critters on this day.

Over the next two weeks my alpha drove me to the vet twice more and the doctor pulled still more quills from my muzzle: the quills kept pushing through my face from I don't know where. One quill just missed my right eye. Not fun. If I see that thorny critter again, I think I'll let it waddle on off undisturbed. It would be more fun to chew on a soft teddy bear, tear it open, and remove the cotton-ball stuffing and squawking squeaker.

15. CATS AND KIDS

Several kids came up to me and tried to touch me. I sniffed each one and then ignored them, well, until one of them asked me to sit, and so did cordially. He offered me a sweet treat in the palm of his hand. I took it. I would do anything for that kid now. I raised my paw to shake hands. He grabbed it. He then raised his hand and said "High Five" and I quickly pawed his hand. He jumped with excitement, so I lay down and did a rollover. All the kids were thrilled. Kids weren't so bad after all. At least not ones carrying big sticks. I walked on with my master.

Cats were another matter; I couldn't make peace with them. My job: to catch and kill them for my master. He didn't seem to like it though and insisted I walk past any cat sitting nearby. I did, but what a missed opportunity. They were aliens, we all knew that, here to take over the planet. Maybe my master cogitated a better plan. Maybe he kept stored and ready some big cat traps, or hanging cat toys that when grabbed would put a very bad taste in their mouth—or a few porcupine quills, ha!

"Dakota, you should show friendship and love to all creatures, well except for cockroaches," said my master. What? Cats are great prey, and so much fun in the chase.

I knew that a good way for a human to make peace with a reticent dog is to give him a few treats. Maybe I could give cats treats? Nah, I'd eat them myself, the cats I mean.

But my master knew best, he took care of me, food and shelter, a nice soft bed beside his, and he didn't mind my joining him in *his* bed. So when I heard my name, I always came running.

My master began to take me everywhere. Oh, so much fun! He took me to lumber yards, hardware stores, auto repair shops, some clothing stores, and wow, the pet stores. I met many people and dog-critters like myself, the world not so scary after all. Thunderstorms didn't even bother me, though that made a good excuse for jumping into bed with my Alpha.

16. AT THE END OF THE DAY

It was suppertime: my master filled my bowl with dry dog food and added some fresh food from his own bowl. I gobbled down the chow and licked the bowl clean.

The master turned out the lights and I jumped into bed with him. I looked into the bedroom's vanity mirror after a hard day and I was still pretty.

"Down girl," commanded my master.

I turned onto my back and he rubbed my belly. I loved that.

And then I got up to lick him on the face, my way of telling him I loved him.

"Goodnight, Dakota," he said and turned over to go to sleep.

I moved to the bottom of the bed next to his feet and curled up. But then I began to scratch the back of my neck. Something was biting me—an ant, a tick, what?

THE END
Thanks for listening, Dakota, July 2019

Dakota signed off after I read this manuscript to him and he gave me permission to publish his story. He said he would be happy to provide many more adventures for me to translate.
—Don Kirk

"Permission Granted"

"I Have Eyes For You."

3. The Lab And The Cat

By Don Kirk

Every dog has a personality of its own. They each have their favorite place to be massaged, their own likes and dislikes, and what they find pleasure in—like chasing varmints—and what they fear, like thunderstorms, water sprinklers, or a viciously attacking big-eyed Chihuahua. To leave a dog alone in a backyard is to imprison him, but he can find things to do even then.

A Labrador Retriever lay quietly in the grass,
Nothing much having come to pass.
But then the sweet scent of prey
From something not too far away.

There bound a furry feline,
Bigger than a possum, a favorite of this canine.
'Round and 'round they went,
Until the cat's energy was entirely spent.

Up an oak tree the critter bound,
Scurrying upward with nary a sound.
The Labrador bound after it not as a lark,
And jumped with forelegs on the bark.

The dog's hind legs three feet in the air,
And there in her face, a scared cat did stare.
The Retriever had now only to wait;
In her jaws was soon to be the cat's fate.

The Labrador And The Cat, Friends For Life

The agile feline couldn't jump to another tree,
Not an agile tree squirrel was she.
The Lab lay down waiting for sign,
Eyes fixed on the feline.

Just a matter of time the Lab knew,
And the cat would be bubbling fresh stew.
Hours past lying steadfast; the cat now feeling free
Attempted a jump to another tree.

Her paws reached out for a limb,
But found only a tiny leaf stem.
Down to earth the cat fell,
Her life now soon to be in hell.

The Labrador grabbed and shook the cat wildly,
Knocking it so unconsciously.
She then released it and there the cat lay,
But the Lab chose to walk away.

The cat clamored to her feet,
And sauntered off with a happy heartbeat,
But she returned to visit her new friend,
A Labrador and a cat, friends for life.

THE END

Baby Girl, a Kooikerhondje

4. Buddy and Baby Girl

By Don Kirk

During the winter of 2017-2018, America was experiencing the most serious influenza outbreak in over one-hundred years; the dispensed vaccine only ten-percent effective. Schools were being closed, adults not shaking hands, and they took extra time washing. Some even wore blue face masks. The year's flu vaccine was not working, and on this day, Mary Margaret sat at the bedside of her young daughter 'Angel' with pneumonia that followed from her initial flu symptoms. A saline bag hung from a metal stand; the hypodermic needle from a drip tube penetrating her vein. The bag hung there to hydrate a cute little girl and dilute the antiviral medications and painkillers. Lying quietly in the *Christian Mercy Hospital*, she was fighting a serious illness.

"My dearest Angel, everything's going to turn out just fine. You'll be getting out of here soon," declared her mother. Little Angel's tired, drooping eyelids stood barely open, giving her a tranquil appearance belying the disease assailing her frail body. Reaching out and putting her hand in her mother's palm, her eyes fluttered ever so slightly. "You're going to feel better soon; we'll get you home," assured Mary, closing her hand around Angel's. The four-year old had just celebrated her birthday, radiant and cheerful without a care in the world. She normally manifested flowing light-brown hair and a bright pink skin, but now her flesh looked pale as a ghost's; her hair horribly disheveled. Angel's blue eyes closed slowly and her head tilted away from her mother.

Angel was all Mary Margaret had left. Mary's husband, Albert, died in a violent car crash on the way home from work less than a year earlier and now Angel was critical. A couple of months earlier, Angel and Mary had been given flu shots. Around the country, over thirty children had already died and Angel might become just another hapless statistic.

A knock came at the heavy pine hall door of the semiprivate room and an attending physician entered the room. "Mrs. Wayne, I think you should go home now; you can do nothing more for your daughter right now."

"Doctor, okay."

Mary Margaret returned home late, and while climbing into bed, she received a call from a dear friend living a few houses down the street. Jeanette Werner also had a young child, a five-year-old boy named Jacob, who died about six-months earlier from a bicycle accident. He peddled around a parked car blocking the sidewalk and rode directly into the path of an oncoming automobile—so Jeanette well understood Mary's sorrow. Little Angel often played with Jacob; they were good friends.

"How is your daughter doing?" asked Jeanette.

"Her condition is serious," replied Mary," but I think she'll make it."

"Don't you worry, God will take care of her."

The next morning, quite early, Mary Margaret returned to the hospital and arriving in her daughter's room she confronted a bustle of frightening activity with much beeping and blinking. Stopped from entering, Mary was asked to leave the room.

"That's my baby girl in there!"

"We're giving her some new antibiotics and we'll be taking an X-ray of her lungs. Her respiratory tract infection is somewhat worse, Mrs. Margaret. Nurse Nancy will take you to the waiting room, keep you informed. Your daughter is in good hands." The long-on-the-tooth nurse led Mary to the waiting room and handed her a *Field & Stream*, the only magazine available.

But, less than a half-hour later, the Doctor and several white-jacketed nurses frantically worked to restore Angel's falling heart rate: electrodes quickly connected to a defibrillator, the machine charged, nurses stepping back, a lurching shock delivered. The cardiac monitor waveforms fell to horizontal. No one breathed a word, all frozen in place for a long, heart-wrenching moment; seconds feeling like minutes.

Angel's doctor, wearing a stethoscope around his neck—as all doctor's seem to do while in a hospital—removed his latex gloves and stepped in front of Mary approaching the hospital room.

"I'm sorry, Mrs. Wayne. We could do no more for her; she passed away from sepsis. Gone to heaven peacefully. Sorry for your loss."

At that news, Mary went weak at the knees; two nurses grabbed her under the arms and sat her carefully into a chair.

"My baby! My poor baby! How could this have happened?" Wet, emotional tears gushed from Mary's blood-shot eyes and yellow mucous dripped from her swollen nose. A nurse handed her some tissue and sat beside her. "I'm so sorry."

"This can't be! I loose my husband and now my little Angel."

Several months passed quietly and Mary Margaret found herself quite alone except for her neighbor, Jeanette Werner, who stopped by frequently to console her on her loss, help her clean out Angel's room, and donate some of the little girl's toys to worthy causes.

Mary's little Angel, utterly adorable and pretty as a peach, was always smiling. Not a little girl one could forget: joyously happy in the morning, throughout the day, and at bedtime, though at times she could use some uplifting.

Neighbor Jeanette had adopted a cute male, grey in color, scruffy looking, low-slung terrier she named 'Buddy' to replace her lost son. And so Mary Margaret, hoping to fill the emptiness in her own life, rescued a dog from the city pound, a dog to be put down soon if not taken in. She chose a female, medium-sized Kooikerhondje—a name almost unpronounceable—standing little more than a foot high. It was a small, spaniel-type dog of Dutch ancestry, basically black and white with reddish-orange patches, long hair, floppy ears, and a white, plumed tail that often danced merrily about—the little critter as cute as a bug in a rug.

"What am I going to name you? Missy, Maggie, or maybe Molly? Lucy maybe, no, uh…oh, how about 'Trixie'?" The pretty Spaniel shook her head with a clear sign of rejection. "No? Okay, how about 'Baby Girl'?" The dog tilted her head quizzically.

Baby Girl: "That's *French Vanilla***?"**

"You're my girl, you're going to be 'Baby Girl.'"

The Kooiker lay down on the carpeted floor and covered her face with her paws. It seemed as if she didn't care for the handle.

The next day, Mary Margaret's 'Baby Girl' lay quietly on the floor, her endearing blue eyes looking up at Angel's former baby carriage as her new owner sat in the living room watching a Saturday morning dog-training show featuring a Siberian husky.

"The husky is such an angel," she noted.

When Mary said the word 'angel,' her new dog sat up, started panting, tongue fluttering wildly, and placed her paws on Mary's knees.

"Baby Girl! Oh, you're so excited! What's with the sudden enthusiasm?" asked Mary Margaret. "Do you like this dog show?" Baby Girl jumped up on the couch where her new companion sat and quickly climbed into her arms. Mary embraced the little dog. "You're so wonderful and gentle. Somehow, you remind me of my Angel."

Baby Girl suddenly looked up and stared intently at her.

"Angel was my daughter. She died of the common flu a few months back," said Mary shedding a few tears. Baby Girl tilted her head left and then to the right trying to understand. "She's gone now, but I've got you." Baby Girl made a soft, mournful groan drawing Mary's attention.

"Baby, what's wrong, dear?"

The Kooiker let out whimpers of concern.

"Do you need to go outside you sweet thing?"

Baby Girl put her head down in Mary Margaret's lap, but her eyes stood high in their sockets soulfully looking up at Mary.

"No? Well then, let's watch a little television." Mary grabbed the remote and turned up the volume; it now seemed as if her thoughts of Angel had gone elsewhere...or she was trying to force them out of her mind.

A few minutes later, Mary retrieved a bucket of ice cream from the fridge, grabbed a spoon, and returned to the living room. Baby Girl approached and sat in front of her on the soft carpet.

"It's ice cream. You can smell it can't you?"

The dog twitched her nose and focused intently at the treat.

"This is *French Vanilla*, dear. It was Angel's favorite ice cream."

Baby Girl opened her mouth wide, her long pink tongue ready for a taste.

"I tried not to give Angel too much, but you know, well, she would stare at me just like you. Here, have some." Mary Margaret took a spoonful of the ice cream and lowered it to Baby Girl who displayed a disarming grin, stood up, and licked excitedly at the spoon.

The next afternoon, Mary's neighbor, Jeanette, was talking with her on the phone: "I've got your Kooker-Doodle at my house."

"Oh my, how did she...?"

"She dug under your fence and then under mine. I couldn't believe it; the two dogs met and instantly got along. They played with each other famously. I have never seen two unfamiliar dogs get along so well, so quickly. They didn't even approach slowly and circle. Nor did they check each other's rear ends."

"Buddy and Baby Girl instant friends?"

"Instantly, like long-lost brother and sister."

"Really? Okay, I'm coming to get her. She needs to learn not to run off…at least not without my permission."

"Bring her leash."

Mary Margaret led Baby Girl home, and after a little scolding, they sat in the living room facing each other, the newest member of the household staring fixedly at her new "Mom."

Mary continued with the reprimand and a pointed index finger. "You've been bad, girl. Don't you dare leave the yard without me, you hear? I promise I'll take you on more walks."

Baby Girl shrunk down submissively and flipped over to expose her underbelly.

"That's okay Girl, I forgive you."

The endearing Kooiker quickly sat back up.

"My daughter had pretty brown eyes just like yours, declared Mary Margaret mournfully. "You're so sweet, Baby Girl, but I'm sorry, you can never replace my Angel."

The spaniel jumped into Mary's lap and brought her muzzle forward attempting to sweetly lick Mary's face. This was too much for Mary; she pushed Baby Girl away. The rejected dog, clearly confused, dropped to the floor, and put her head between her legs. Mary's memories of her lost Angel came careening back to her.

One evening a few days later, cuddled-up beside Mary, the cute little Kooikerhondje raised her head and again tried to lick her owner's face. Mary pushed her,"Get away, get down!"

Baby Girl jumped to the floor, turned around, and sat in front of Mary. She lifted her paw and placed it in Mary's hand.

"I don't want your paw. The last thing my daughter did in the hospital was put her hand in my palm."

Baby Girl quickly dropped her paw, slid her rear end back a few feet, and stared stone-faced into her master's eyes.

"Girl, you're trying to tell me something? I know you're trying to…"

The dog whimpered and inched slowly back toward Mary Margaret.

"Angel used to…"

Baby Girl interrupted with a short grumble, an attention seeking whine, and cautiously raised her paw again.

"What do you want Girl? I don't have the time for this. You'll get your walk this evening when *I'm* ready."

The spaniel jumped up, putting her legs in Mary's lap.

"Get down, Girl. Get down, now!"

Baby Girl backed down, ran off, and soon returned with a children's hard-covered book in her mouth. She carefully placed it in Mary's lap who picked it up and read the title: "My Daughter Is Home." Baby Girl barked.

"What is it, Girl?"

Mary Margaret opened the book and read, "This is the story of my youngest daughter who I lost for a time. Who I cared about dearly, who came back to me, who…"

The sweet dog, with eyes focused, raised her paw once again to Mary.

Mary reached down to receive it, "Why Baby Girl! Dearest daughter!" rejoiced Mary carefully closing her hand around the dog's little paw. "It's you! You're my baby! You're my Angel!"

Baby Girl barked.

"You've come back to me! Heaven for you must be here on Earth with me."

Baby Girl barked.

"I'm so sorry for calling you by the wrong name. Your name's 'Angel,' *my* 'Little Angel'! I'll send you to dog training, get you the best grooming, teeth brushed regularly, and much much more. I bet I can even teach you to read—though it sounds as if you've already read this book. And you're going to get all the *French Vanilla* ice cream you want; that's a promise."

Angel broke into a wide, open-mouthed grin, panting joyously, and barked with unbridled excitement.

Mary Margaret heard noises in the yard out front. All elation inside came to a screeching halt and Angel bolted to the front door. Intense, repetitive scratching sounded on the door. The terrier barked again, louder this time. Mary slowly opened the door, and between her legs, dashed Jeanette's dog 'Buddy.' The two dogs jumped in excitement, wrestling together as if they hadn't seen each other in a long time even though they had met at Jeanette's house just days earlier.

Jeanette Werner followed Buddy in, "He so dearly wanted to come over."

"I can see that," replied Mary, "They can play together all they want. They act like long lost friends."

"Maybe they are."

"Yes, maybe they are. Jeanette, you need to listen carefully. I think you should call your dog 'Jacob'."

"Jacob! Why should I call him my son's name?"

"Because that terrier *is* your son!"

Buddy barked.

"My son?"

"Did Jacob like *French Vanilla* ice cream?"

THE END

5. Lead Detective

By Don Kirk

THE OPENING

Jumping on the kitchen trashcan of a modest second-story apartment was an eager little beagle. The tall trashcan fell over easily and the dog began to rummage through it hoping to feast on human cuisine. With the treats out of the trashcan, he sniffed, pulled, and tugged, on those tough plastic bags and containers to access the goodies (just like humans have to do). That bomb proof plastic was a real pain in the jaws. This small, male hound dog suddenly stopped chomping and turned his head toward the front window of this apartment in Dallas, Texas. He barked, expressing concern for the noise outside the front door and ran lickety-split toward it. He heard a key in the lock and the door slowly creaked open. Upon seeing the person at the door, the beagle stopped bellowing and jumped for joy: his master was returning home from work. The alpha male had today's mail in his hand including a large brown envelope.

"Hey Beer Gut, I'm home."

The canine, with a sagging oversized belly, jumped up trying to greet his also overweight master who bent down so he could lovingly lick the bosses face. Beer Gut's tail wagged wildly and his face had an appealing, soulful expression that anyone could love. In his sixties, with balding head, the Alpha male was Edward Eddy, a long since retired army sergeant, now working as a security guard at a bank just a few blocks away. His face was clean-shaven, but he wore a rather heavy black but greying moustache.

"Here boy, I brought you a treat."

Beer Gut sat down in front of Eddy who pulled forth from his jacket a tough, but tasty, rawhide bone. The attentive dog sniffed

Beer Gut, a Curious Beagle

it and carefully took it, making sure not to bite his master's fingers. He then bounced joyfully over to a green leather couch and jumped up on it. The rawhide bone was indeed a pleasurable treat for the beagle.

This hound, just a tad over a foot tall, weighing in at about twenty pounds, would clearly qualify as a cute dog—except for his gut. He sported a three-toned hair color in brown, black, and white. His back was black. His head, ears, and upper legs were brown, and white finished off his chest, snout, and lower legs. A strip of white ran up between his enticing light-brown eyes. Large, deep brown, floppy ears covered his ear canals; he didn't have to worry about spiders crawling into them. This beagle stood low to the ground because of his rather short legs and had a short easy-to-care-for coat even though it shed enough in a year to build Vietnamese Quonset huts for a whole tribe.

The Sergeant removed his blue uniform jacket and his duty belt that held a radio, flashlight, handcuffs, and a .22 caliber revolver. He placed the belt on a coat rack by the front door. Pinned to the jacket, a sparkling silver-colored Security Guard badge and a black name tag with white letters reading 'EDDY.' Beer Gut paid no attention to his master; the bone his whole world just now. Sergeant Eddy made a beeline to the kitchen and retrieved a cold bottle of *Pabst Blue Ribbon* and popped the top. He took a long refreshing swig.

"Alright, Beer Gut, ready for a walk?"

The spry beagle dropped his rawhide bone, jumped from the couch, and ran to the door. Sarge grabbed the leash from the coat rack beside the front door and snapped it to his collar.

"Oh wait, what is that I smell?" asked Eddy.

The hound yapped.

"So, I see. You turned over the trash can again, bad boy. It smells worse than you do."

Eddy returned to the kitchen, proceeded to pick up the scattered garbage, and then took a wet sponge and wiped up the mess on the kitchen floor.

"Back in a minute, Beer Gut, *then* we can go for a walk, I'm taking these scraps to the Dumpster to keep you out of them."

Sergeant Eddy left the apartment, closing the door behind him.

Eddy's dog lay down on the carpeted floor and lowered his head in waiting. No more delicious food scraps today. But he waited and waited and waited some more for his boss to return. Becoming quite restless, Beer Gut jumped back on the couch and peered through the fully open venetian blinds. The troubled dog could see it getting dark outside and his master not yet in sight. More somber time passed. And still more quiet nothingness. Beer Gut fell slowly asleep but slept very lightly, waiting patiently for his master. The slightest noise outside would perk him up, eyelids opening halfway, his ears moving backward and he would run to the window. No one there.

THE ALLEY

Morning sunlight cut through the venetian blinds. Beer Gut jumped up, searched all the rooms, and went for a thirst quencher in his water bowl. It was empty. All at once, reflected on the living room wall, an eerie piercing alarm and flashing red lights. The beagle heard voices approaching, jumped for the front door, and sniffed at the door frame.

A key slid into the door lock. Beer Gut was thrilled. He howled. The door creaked open slowly. A man, wearing a suit with an oversized coat, and narrow, black, boring tie, held a Glock 19 out in front of him and scanned the room with it. The canine creature, now standing eagle-eyed, yelped a loud, irritatingly squeaky bay.

"It's okay, dog."

Beer Gut roared again, took a few steps backward, and sat down as the armed man and two others entered the living room. The unnoticed hound moved past the three men, left the apartment, and bounded down the stairs. He was headed out to look for his master with nose high in the air and on occasion placing his twitching black nose close to the ground. He followed a familiar scent into the nearby alley and passed right by the odorous Dempster Dumpster. Other men stood around, but Beer Gut did not find his master. He passed through one of the men's legs.

"Hey dog, stop!"

The anxious beagle approached a man lying on his back on the cold asphalt pavement in a large pool of bright-red blood. He bayed into the air and squealed. A bloody body lay inertly there: the dog's master, Sergeant Eddy, with dried blood on his contorted face, neck, and on his newly pressed white shirt.

A kneeling CSI technician spoke, "Knife to the throat. Bled out quickly."

"How long?"

"Ten to twelve hours."

"No, I mean, how long was the knife?"

"About an inch."

"Got to the juggler easily then?"

"Yes. And his pockets were rummaged through."

"Billfold?"

"On the ground, papers scattered. He had an ID card showing him to be a security guard for the First National on 21st street."

Beer Gut let out an audible, moved to his master's lifeless head, and licked his pale face. He sniffed at his master's clothing and the ground around him. One of the investigators tried to pull the dog away, but he gripped Eddy's clothing with his claws and refused to move.

"Come here dog! Get me some help somebody; call the pound! Give us some room to gather evidence; everybody move to hell back. We've clearly got a crime scene here," yelled one of the investigators.

The assigned homicide detective, Ethan Shirley, leaned down in front of the cute beagle, "Hey boy, it's okay now, let me take you back upstairs." Turning to the dog-harassing CSI, Shirley demanded, "Let the dog loose." The CSI did so, reluctantly.

The recently arrived detective turned, walked to the stairs, and headed up. Running well ahead of Shirley, Beer Gut bounded up the stairs to reach the apartment. In the apartment, other men were gathering possible clues to what happened, and who did the dirty deed.

Sergeant Eddy's dog made his way from room to room looking for his master, a sad sight to witness.

One of the crime scene investigators removed the security belt hanging on the coat rack and approached Detective Shirley: "The knife on the belt is in its sheath and the gun has not been fired. Nothing appears to be out of place, but the kitchen floor recently cleaned up. We're taking samples."

Beer Gut made his way over to the green leather couch and demonstrated exceptional interest: he sniffed at the space between the couch frame and a cushion. The detective noticed the dog's focused attention on the couch.

"Just food crumbs," declared a CSI.

"I'm not so sure," replied Ethan Shirley as he moved over to the couch, lifted up the cushion, and peered underneath. Nothing. He then raised the next one, and there, a large manila envelope. "Brimley! Here."

The CSI, with his latex gloves, came over, lifted up the envelope, and opened it. It was full of $1,000 bills! The hound jumped up on Brimley trying to reach the envelope.

"Good boy, you know something—*don't* you?" inquired Shirley.

Beer Gut let out an audible groan.

"Brimley, take good care of this dog, I'm going to the bank."

Detective Shirley turned and headed out the door, but the hound quickly bounded after him before the door could close. Beer Gut passed him on the stairs and hit the sidewalk well ahead of the detective.

"I guess you're on your own, dog. The city is all yours."

The detective's new partner, Samantha Simms, returning from the crime scene in the alley, opened the passenger-side front door of their black *Ford Crown Victoria*. Beer Gut ran up, jumped in, climbed onto the center console, and jumped to the rear seat. Detective Shirley opened the rear door.

"Dog gone it, dog! Get out, come on, please, pretty please."

The canine moved away to the street side of the car's interior.

"Here dog, you can't come with us, I'm sorry."

The dejected mutt lay down and whimpered.

"Okay, okay, you can stay, but you must behave…and don't you piss in my car! It's a government vehicle, no tellin' what it would cost the taxpayer for a cleaning," barked Ethan Shirley.

Beer Gut stood up and wagged his white-pointed tail.

"You sure about this Ethan?" asked Samantha Simms.

"I'm not sure of anything, but I like beagles."

"More than me?

"More than you. You're not a beagle," replied Ethan Shirley as he got into the driver's seat. "And more importantly, he could be a witness to the crime."

The car drove off.

THE FIRST NATIONAL BANK

Detective's Shirley and Simms rolled up in front of the First National Bank and piled out of their unmarked police car.

Beer Gut jumped for the open door, but Ethan closed the car door just in time. "Boy, you stay here; we'll be right back." The dog, scratching at the window, watched the two detectives walk away into the bank. Beer Gut waited impatiently, but not for long; in the *Crown Victoria* he found a door latch to be easy to pull with his paw, and out the door he was in short order. He ran toward the bank. The detectives were already inside the bank, when out came a customer, and this sneaky beer gut took the opportunity to scamper quickly inside. He waddled into the lobby and began smelling along the floor, walking around and around, sniffing under double-pedestal desks, and rubbing against a lady's panty-hose-covered legs. The customers, beginning to enjoy the show, cheered the dog on. Disruption of bank business had begun. Behind the teller windows, Beer Gut walked merrily along sniffing the leg of every bank clerk.

"Where's Sergeant Eddy?" shouted one of the tellers, "He needs to get that dog out of here!"

At that call for help, Detective Shirley and Simms came out of the bank president's office. A Mr. Jonathan R. Ehrlich, also came to the door holding a large 16-ounce coffee mug. He leaned calmly against the door frame and crossed one leg over the other.

"Mr. Ehrlich, we've got a dog running loose!" asserted a desk clerk.

"I see," Elhrich replied, seemingly quite unconcerned.

Detective Shirley came forward to get the dog, "Here dog, come here."

Samantha Simms interrupted the disarray, pulling her cell phone away from her face, and yelling, "Shirley, CSI found a vet record. The dog's name is 'Beer Gut'."

"The dog's a military vet?" questioned Ethan, "What rank?"

"No, you...you...dummkopf! A *veterinarian's* record! And the dog, in case you're interested, has had his shots."

"All vermouth?"

"You're hopeless."

"Here Beer Gut, come here," called out Ethan.

The cute little dog critter—no more than a few years old—looked up and focused on detective Shirley.

"Beer Gut! Here."

The independently thinking hound dog came forward, though he was a breed of dog that felt he could choose who he wanted to pay attention to. A beagle would rarely come back when called, and yet here sat Beer Gut in front of Shirley. A bank clerk brought a length of rope and handed it to Detective Simms, who then passed it on to Shirley. Shirley tied the rope onto Beer Gut's collar causing the dog to jump up exhilarated.

"He thinks we're going for a walk," declared Simms.

"I see that," said Detective Shirley as he turned back to Mr. Ehrlich, "Thank you for your time, Mr. Sanborn."

The bank president gazed at him strangely, then replied, "It's Mr. Jonathan *Ehrlich*."

"Stand corrected."

The detectives and their harnessed dog left through the wide, glass, front door with all the bank tellers and customers still looking on.

Once all three were back in the police car, Samantha spoke, "He's not in there."

"Who?" asked Ethan.

"Our crime suspect. Didn't you see that?"

"See what?"

"The beagle was looking for him."

"Hum."

Detective Shirley put their police cruiser in gear and drove off.

"Oh, and you called the president 'Sanborn'," uttered Samantha softly.

"That's all I could remember after watching him guzzle all that coffee," replied Ethan. "How many cups did he chug while we were in his office?"

"Three, four maybe?"

Beer Gut climbed onto the center console and looked out the front window.

Shirley continued, "Beer Gut didn't have a chance to meet the bank president. When does Ehrlich get off work?"

THE BANK PRESIDENT

That afternoon the detectives parked outside the bank waiting for Jonathan Ehrlich to leave as Beer Gut munched on a luscious treat Detective Shirley had given him: *Gummy Bears*.

"The boss didn't seem too concerned when we told him Sergeant Eddy had died," pointed out Detective Simms.

"No, and he didn't miss his security guard…"

"Ethan Shirley, you really need to change your last name," declared Samantha, "Did you see that smirk on Ehrlich's face, that irritatingly smug expression that just about everyone you introduce yourself to exhibits?"

"That can be a good thing. When I interview someone, it helps keep a suspect distracted when answering my questions."

The bank president finally came out of the glass-paned front door and locked it up himself. No security guard on this day.

The two detectives looked at each other and then exited their vehicle. Detective Simms intentionally left her door slightly ajar.

"Mr. Ehrlich, can we speak to you again?"

"Uh sure. We can go inside."

"That won't be necessary, just one question."

"Fine."

"Where were you last evening between four and seven P.M.?"

"Let's see, four o'clock, five, seven…yeah, I was still here at the bank, finishing up my paperwork until about eight."

"Anyone we can call to verify…"

Unexpectedly, Beer Gut left the car and sprang forward to smell the president's legs. Ehrlich took a step rearward, but Beer Gut leaped up trying to smell his hands.

"This your dog? Get…get him off me!"

"Off Beer Gut, come here dog."

"Beer Gut? Isn't that Sergeant Eddy's dog?"

Samantha tried to grab the canine critter, but he jumped excitedly and turned a few 360-degree circles.

"Dog pound?"

"It's okay, Mr. Ehrlich, the dog's just a little over enthusiastic," reported Ethan, "Simms, get that blasted dog in the car." Ethan returned his attention to the president, "We apologize, so heart-felt, we were headed to the dog pound."

"Sooner than later," added Ehrlich.

The sweet little pooch raised his right front leg, bent it at the knee, and appeared to stand at attention facing Ehrlich, apparently disturbed with what he was looking at.

"It's okay, boy," said Samantha grabbing Beer Gut's collar and leading him to their vehicle.

"We're so sorry, sir. The dog had jumped into our car at the crime scene and…"

"I'll have none of this," demanded Elrlich, "Are you through with me now?"

"Oh, yeah sure…at least for now."

"Keep that dog away from me."

"Yes sir. I'll see to it."

Detective Shirley turned to walk off, but Ehrlich grabbed his shoulder, "That dog was enthusiastic about what?" he asked.

"What did you have for dinner?" asked Shirley.

"A *McDonald's* double-meat burger."

"Well there, who could resist that fresh-grilled aroma!" raved Detective Simms. "Thank you for your time."

Ethan walked around the car and got in on the driver's side.

"Did you see that, Simms?"

"Yeah."

"Beer Gut has picked up Ehrlich's scent somewhere."

"We need to get a subpoena to go through his house. Maybe find Eddy's blood on his shoes."

"Don't have sufficient cause."

"Then let's go back to the crime scene."

A RETURN TO THE CRIME SCENE

Beer Gut, nose to the ground, sniffed carefully the alley next to Sergeant Eddy's apartment.

"CSI searched every inch, even 'rummaged' through the Dumpster," said Detective Simms.

"Yeah, but they don't have a nose like Beer Gut's."

"Thank God for that; in their profession that would be…"

Behind them, Beer Gut let out a shrieking audible; the two detectives ran toward the-not-so-cute-now canine. He was scratching at a crack between the Dumpster's concrete slab and the apartment's brick wall.

"He's got something: a tender juicy rat, or a greasy cream-of-possum?"

"More likely a greasy fried-chicken bone."

Ethan pulled his flashlight from his belt and dropped to his knees. He scanned the opening, trying his level best to see into the crack.

"I see…I think I…oh here…find me something to stick into this crevice, something I might use to pull out what I see."

Beer Gut scratched at the crack some more as Simms made her way to the far side of the Dumpster and opened the access door.

Out fell a stinking mess of garbage and dirty, moldy clothes on wire hangers. Samantha grabbed a hanger and took it to Ethan.

"Hold Beer Gut back," ordered Detective Shirley.

Ethan bent the hanger to lengthen it, stuck it in, and pushed and poked and pulled on it. Soon, up came a silver-colored utility knife with the blade extended.

"It's got blood on it; don't touch the handle," insisted Simms as she pulled on a pair of latex gloves.

Beer Gut smelled the knife and roared excitedly, in fact, with feverish madness.

"Looks like it could penetrate as much as an inch," declared Ethan.

"That's got to be the murder weapon," added Samantha, also breathlessly thrilled, "but who's going to get that trash put back into the dumpster?"

"And who's gonna take this knife to forensics?"

"You want me to do that too?"

"And while you're at it, Beer Gut needs a bath."

"No way, he's *your* soul mate," replied Samantha.

Ethan looked the now-homeless dog directly in the eyes, "*You* need a bath, boy."

The hound twisted his head sideways and then tried to pull away, and when he couldn't, he whined and turned over exposing his belly.

"I don't think he likes baths," said Samantha.

"What dog does?"

A MOTIVE

"I think Ehrlich is our man," declared Samantha, "Maybe he didn't do it, but the guilt shows in his lifeless olive-green eyes."

"You noticed that too?"

"That enamoring olive-green color."

"No, the hollow, vacant look!"

"Oh yeah, that too."

"He's guilty," said Samantha, "I'm sure of it."

"Hey, Beer Gut, do you know how to find a motive?" asked Ethan.

The dog barked softly, his mouth open, panting, even though he quietly lay in the back seat of the police car. Shirley had given the dog an extra blanket in case he got cold waiting for them, but right now he lay curled up on top of the comforter.

"The brown envelope Beer Gut found hidden under Eddy's couch cushion has to be the key," noted Samantha.

"And CSI said the kitchen floor had been recently cleaned up. Lets go back and take another look."

"I'm not getting on my hands and knees," declared Samantha.

"Wouldn't ask you to…"

The pooch whined and climbed up on the center console between the front seats.

"What are you trying to tell me, Beer Gut?" asked Ethan. "You know who, *don't you?*" Turning to Samantha, "We're going back to the apartment."

THE KEY

The three detectives returned to the deceased person's apartment, with orange tape still crisscrossed over the locked door and a cop standing guard. Detective Shirley pulled down the tape and unlocked the door. Beer Gut followed Shirley and Simms inside.

"Here, come in the kitchen, Beer Gut. Beer Gut! Here," Ethan called out asking this beagle—he seemed to have acquired—to help him solve this case. Ethan knew the hound would know the smell of his master and would prove real useful in finding clues. "Beer Gut, come here; take a whiff of this floor." The hound eventually came in, and not one to follow orders, he seemed to want to lead the charge. He glanced around, sniffed the air, sniffed the floor but appeared unconcerned. He went to the refrigerator and tried, unsuccessfully, to open it by pushing his snout through the rubber seal. Samantha saw this and came over to help with the door.

"What's he up to now? Does he drink beer?" asked Ethan.

"Not likely."

"He acquired that handle somehow."

"One doesn't have to drink beer to exhibit an ugly gut."

The very focused hound dog rummaged through the beer cans and plastic food containers, his nose sharply engaged.

"I hope he didn't do this at Sergeant Eddy's," said Samantha, "He wouldn't make a very good pet. This dog is his own boss."

The determined canine grabbed a thirty-two-ounce tin can and pulled it out and onto the floor. It had a yellow plastic lid on it so the can had obviously been opened before.

"Did the forensics go through this fridge," asked Ethan.

"I don't know, not likely, this wasn't the crime scene per se."

"Grab your gloves."

"I wonder if the department ever recycles our gloves…sent to China maybe."

"Repackaged…"

"And sent back here!"

Samantha tried to take the can from the unrelenting hound who was moving about the room trying to keep it away from her.

"It's probably just dog food, that's what the label reads: '*Alpo: Prime Cuts With Beef.*' Ooom good," declared Samantha.

Ethan tried to corner Beer Gut, but the dog dropped the *Alpo,* ran into the bedroom, and crawled into a clothes closet.

Ethan pushed the hanging clothes aside to see what the hound was after and that's when he saw a false door of paneling covering the sheetrock. "Simms, get me a flathead screwdriver."

While Beer Gut nibbled on the side of the couch in the living room, apparently bored now, Ethan and Samantha opened the wall and found a steel safe between the wall studs about thirty-inches high, fourteen-inches wide, and having a hinged door on the front…but it was locked.

"Damn!"

"We're gonna need a locksmith."

"Or find the keys."

Abruptly, the hound howled from the other room.

"What does he want now?" asked Samantha.

"Where is that dog food can?"

"I put it back in the refrigerator. Thought you could give it to Beer Gut later."

"Why me," asked Ethan getting up, going to the kitchen, taking out the food can, and wrestling irritatingly to pop off the snap-on plastic lid. He looked inside:

"Damn, Beer Gut! You're a jewel! Damn!"

"What is it?" insisted Samantha.

"It's a key and I bet it's for the safe!" cheered Ethan as he returned to the closet. "This safe is what the intruder tried to find. He probably accosted Sergeant Eddy by the dumpster, and when he refused to talk, cut his throat and let him bleed out."

The two detectives tried to lift the safe out of its hiding place but couldn't, much too heavy, so they tried the key in the lock where it stood. And it opened!

"Simms, still got your gloves on? Tell me what's inside."

Samantha began to lift vanilla envelopes from the safe and opened one:

"Money! There are many more thousand-dollar bills! Stacks of them! There could be hundred's of thousands of dollars here."

THE KILLER

Detective Ethan Shirley sat at home with Beer Gut lying quietly beside him on the couch. Ethan spoke to his new canine partner: "Maybe the bank president didn't do the killing, but he hired someone to get the cash back, and when that didn't work out, that someone in an evil rage killed Eddy."

The hairy critter looked at him quizzically.

"How are we going to find him, you ask?"

Beer Gut tilted his head.

"Unfortunately, the forensics on the utility knife aren't back yet. If *you* had done the lab work, Beer Gut, it would have saved us a lot of time."

The canine, trying to comprehend what his new partner had said, deliberately fixed his eyes and noggin on him.

Ethan continued, "Beer Gut; you're going to be our lead detective; I'm demoting myself. I'm giving you corporal stripes."

The beagle whooped.

At that Ethan's cell phone rang.

"Yes?"

"The lab results are in," announced Samantha.

"And?"

"The knife blade is positive for Sergeant Eddy's blood, but the fingerprints on the handle, well, they're not Ehrlich's!"

"Damn, just what I was afraid of, bring the car around."

Beer Gut hollered for attention.

"Yeah boy, you're coming with me. Maybe when we're done we'll stop in at a *McDonalds*. A double-meat burger just for you, but if, and only if, you find your master's butcher."

Beer Gut bellowed again.

The two detectives returned to the *First National Bank* with Beer Gut in toe—on a leash this time—and as they climbed the steps to the front door, a tall, slender man wearing blue-stripped overalls, a tape measure on his belt, and a pencil in his chest pocket, came through the glass doors. The beagle sniffed the man's leg as he passed and then turned and pulled against Detective Simms.

"Hey boy, we're headed this way."

Beer Gut raised his lips, snout curling up, a low growl emanating.

"What's wrong, boy?" asked Ethan.

The hound nudged his new partner's hand.

They both watched the construction worker walk away down the street. Samantha and Eddy's dog stayed outside on the steps as Ethan went into the bank.

Inside, Detective Shirley hurried up to the counter, showed his badge and asked, "Who was that man in the overalls?"

"Ask that teller down there, she waited on him."

Returning to his two detectives outside, Ethan announced, "We've a suspect. That carpenter was Scott Reed, lives on Probandt. I think that when Beer Gut confronted Reed he recognized the smell of his master's killer, the odor he surely picked up from Sergeant Eddy's dead body. What do you say we pay Mr. Reed a visit?"

At 125 South Probandt, just outside of downtown, stood a small rundown wood frame house with weathered white peeling paint and rotting fascia boards. The detectives stopped a few houses away and exited their vehicle. Ethan took extra pains to tie Beer Gut to his headrest and lock the doors, leaving him held captive.

Scott Reed, still in overalls, opened his front door, but the screen door stood between them.

"Can I help you?"

"Scott Reed?"

"Yes."

"Samantha Simms and Ethan Shirley. We saw you at the First National Bank."

"Oh yeah, you two with that ugly, nosey mutt that almost tripped me!"

"So sorry, he's a good dog, well, he does chew on the furniture, inherited him from my deceased wife. You need a dog?"

"No, hell no!"

"May we come in?"

"No. I can see you just fine."

"I just wanted to ask you if you know Sanborn, personally?"

"Sanborn, ha, hah! Uh, no, don't know the man. The guy runs a good bank though."

"I bet he makes a lot of money."

"I wouldn't know."

"Probably millions, wouldn't you want a piece of that?"

"I'm doing just fine."

"Well, this is kind of a survey," continued Ethan as he pulled out his pocket notebook and opened it. "So you do like the bank services?"

"Fine, just fine. Interest rate on my checking account not too good though, point zero three percent. Hey, what's this all about?"

"We were hired by Mr. Ehrlich to do a survey and we heard you had done some work on an addition to his house."

"Where did you get that, it ain't so. Never met the man…"

"Okay, okay, thank you for your help with our survey. There'll be a little extra money in your checking account next month."

"What to hell? Get out of my house! And I hope your dog gets run over real quick like. Oh, and you should get a new last name. Shirley, ha, ha."

Reed abruptly closed the door, the two detectives jumped into their vehicle, and Ethan drove off without delay.

Once on the road, Ethan spoke first, "I like him for it."

"For what exactly?" asked Samantha.

"Tried to get the money, couldn't find it. Edward Eddy wouldn't talk so Scott Reed did indeed do the deed, a most inconsiderate murderer; left Eddy for the rats."

"Why do you think it's him?"

"Well, first of all, he laughed when I called Ehrlich 'Sanborn' even though he said he didn't know the man, and secondly, his blood sugar was going way up, face flushed and stood uneasy on his feet. It had to be him that did Eddy in."

"We don't have enough eviden…"

"And thirdly, the murder weapon was a utility knife. Every carpenter has one of those."

"So he's the killer…"

Detective Shirley pointed his right finger skyward, "And fourthly, our wonderful, sweet little Beer Gut hasn't been wrong yet. The bank president must have been skimming money 'off the top' as it were, somehow turning it into cash and getting his Security Guard to hide the cash with an offer of some real good deal…like letting him continue to work for a nice paycheck…and a little more on the side."

"He's not living like he received a sweet little stipend. Beer Gut wasn't getting the best of dog foods. I looked."

"Yeah right, and Reed," Detective Shirley continued, "was hired to get the cash back when Sergeant Eddy either refused to continue to do 'his job,' or just wouldn't give Mr. Ehrlich's skimmed cash back to him."

"Let's go back to Reed's pad."

"I wouldn't give that apartment such a nice cushy name."

The detectives turned their vehicle around.

Shirley and Simms knocked on Scott Reed's door. This time the hound stood alongside, his nose twitching with focused curiosity.

The door opened. Ethan pulled his police badge and displayed it. "Dallas Police Department. We'd like to speak to you again."

Ethan pulled open the screen door.

Reed slammed the inner door shut.

Shirley took a step back to kick in the door but noticed their Beer Gut no longer with them, and Samantha, she had already left to go around to the back of the apartment to catch Reed if he chose to run. Ethan then heard growling and barking inside. Beer Gut must have snuck between Reed's legs when Ethan opened the screen door.

Ethan Shirley kicked in the door with his gun drawn, and entered the room. No Scott Reed in sight, nor was there a Beer Gut. Ethan looked around and headed up the stairs to the second floor. He heard another yelp and serious growl, and followed the sound to a bedroom on the street side. Reed was climbing out the window, the beagle attempting to follow, but the canine stopped short, his front paws on the sill. Beer Gut, seeing he could go no further, turned around quickly, and ran back down the stairs— clearly a persevering, bull-headed dogged dog. The bad trait of stubbornness this breed owned, was, in this case, quite useful.

Scott Reed landed on the sidewalk, knees bent, legs twisted, and fell to the ground, but he managed to get up and limp painfully down the street. Beer Gut bounded out of the front door and ran after the suspected murderer. He yelped wildly, something he could do quite well. Reed turned back to look at him and saw the unwavering hound gaining on him. The panicked man stumbled down the sidewalk, ran into a parked bicycle, grabbed an occupied baby carriage, and pushed it in front of his pursuer. He then inadvertently slogged through the freshly poured concrete of a sidewalk repair as two men in overalls, holding a wheelbarrow and trowels, launched a series of swear words. The baby carriage and the mother were also sliding straight for the wet concrete. The unnerving screams didn't stop Beer Gut from leaving his own paw prints in the sidewalk. The dog was not slowing down! He seemed to love going after a hot scent, going after appetizing prey. Scott Reed tried to escape by crossing the street but passing cars, and other vehicles hitting their brakes in an effort to avoid him, caused some near crashes that slowed Reed's progress. The little twenty-pound dog creature, not hindered, totally oblivious of the danger, made big strides toward his goal: to capture the murderer of his master. Detective Shirley and Detective Simms jumped into their police cruiser and switched on their flashing lights and blaring siren. Racing down the street, they found the traffic suddenly and erratically breaking to a halt. Scott Reed ran into an alley and the short-legged Beer Gut was losing ground, but the carpenter came up against a red, rusting, wrought iron fence...and spray painting was not what he needed to do. The fence was six-feet tall with pointed barbs on top. Reed saw he could go no further and turned around only to see the canine approach with a mean, evil-looking expression: his lips pulled way back, the sharpest of canines showing. But instead of immediately attacking the murderer, he stopped abruptly and roared violently.

Ethan and Samantha came running up the alley, guns drawn. Scott Reed stepped right, and then stepped left, but finding no options—the dog wasn't backing off—he pulled from his breast pocket a carpenter's folding rule and tried to stave off the dog. Beer Gut grabbed the wooden stick that had feet and inch marks on it and bit it in two. Six feet became three feet, now to go for eighteen inches. That display warning enough for Reed to reluctantly put up his tired, paint-stained hands. Ethan came up to him, spun him around, and cuffed him. Ethan didn't try to tone down the delightful countenance on his out-of-breath mug. The hound sat down and watched, apparently also pleased.

THE CLOSING

Beer Gut lay curled up seemingly content with his new master. Ethan Shirley let him lick on his ice cream cone. Dogs will hang with any humanoid who shares his ice cream.

Ethan's cell phone vibrated. The sweet, normally chilled-out beagle looked up anxious, his ears rising.

"It's okay, Bear Gut," said the detective as he pulled his cell from his belt pouch, "Yes?"

"The fingerprints on the utility knife's handle are indeed Scott Reed's. He already has a criminal record. And Mr. Ehrlick's records have been subpoenaed. Case closed."

Ethan flipped his cell phone closed and then looked down at the sweet, brown, black, and white trimmed beagle, "You did good, kinder. I think I'm going to keep you."

Beer Gut licked the new top dog's face and turned over to reveal his bulbous stomach for petting.

"Oh, did I get you that double-meat burger?"

The excited canine jumped back up.

"I guess not. Do *you* have any objection to my last name?"

The hairy creature tilted his head in puzzlement, or was he laughing deep down inside?

THE END

Case closed, time for a little rest.

Duke, a Great Dane

6. Special Victims

By Don Kirk

"Come on, let us loose. We'll be good."

A strong bark emanated from a very big dog.

"Come on now give us the key."

A giant-sized male Great Dane weighing well over a hundred and twenty pounds—and standing almost three feet tall at the shoulders—jumped up in apparent joyfulness. Standing on his hind legs, he would be as tall, maybe even taller, than a human. With a massive head—narrow and flat on top—and triangular ears flopped over, this short-haired 'gentle giant' dominated the environment, well, except for two other huge canines approaching: a cute female long-haired dark-grey Scottish Deerhound and a smaller—but still hefty at around 110 pounds—two-foot-tall mammoth creature known as a Bordeaux. This breed, well known to be fearless and protective of home and family, would make a great guard dog. These three dogs manifested great power, not canines anyone would want to challenge individually or together. They'd make great defensive football players and still be sweet as strawberry wine to their masters.

Three, large, dilapidated doghouses, each next to a different Arizona Ash tree, stood in a fenced-in backyard. The fence was not the usual three-foot chain link, but instead, a six-foot tall wood cedar slat making it hard for a passersby to see into the yard.

A middle-aged man with scruffy hair, beard, and badly soiled workman's overalls was chained to one of the ash trees. Tied to the other two trees, where they could not reach each other, were his wife and a teenage daughter. The watchful and dignified Bordeaux sat there quietly, apparently waiting for an attempted escape by the humans.

The long-legged grey-and-white-coated Great Dane with smears

Scrappy, a Scottish Deerhound

of black spots, tore into what looked like a sack of dry dog food sitting on the back porch, but sadly, it turned out to be an organic potting mix; nothing edible there. Apparently the dog couldn't read.

The female grey and white one-hundred-pound Scottish Deerhound, with her dirty and matted three-inch long hair and black ears folded back in repose, began to dig a hole under the cedar fence. She knew she would eventually have to find food elsewhere since her former master, now tied to an oak tree, could no longer fill her food bowl. She didn't know it would take an awfully big hole to get under the fence.

"Scrappy, come here girl, let us loose," called out the Master, "We'll take you on a walk. I know we haven't done that in years but we will from now on, we promise, come on now, please."

The Deerhound turned to look at their former Master Jailer, and let out a mean yap, quite unusual for this gentle and polite pooch.

"How about you Duke? Come over here and chew through this rope…oh wait, I see, I used a short chain to keep you guys from escaping. I'm sorry to discover that it works for us humans too.

You'll get yours, Dog, a Vietnamese glue factory."

The Great Dane called 'Duke' let out one yelp.

"You know that I had to keep you apart so you wouldn't fight… or reproduce."

At that Duke went over to Scrappy and jumped on her back and began thrusting her hips forward.

"Stop that!" yelled out Mrs. Nobody, "Not in front of my daughter."

"Doorstop, here Boy, come to me, you're strong, break this chain," said the teen, "I promise I won't hit you with a broomstick anymore."

This third dog, the Bordeaux, was dubbed 'Doorstop' because he could easily block the garage door of a speeding eighteen-wheeler. The enormous head and muscular body of this short, stocky mongrel with dark-red hair would bring anyone up short causing them to give wide berth. Doorstop wore a wide, black, dog collar, but it had no vaccination tags attached. His loose coat, lots of hanging wrinkles, and folds on his snout, made him look like he spent a tumultuous evening in a clothes dryer. His thick upper lips hung over his lower jaw hiding the fangs that could easily do anyone in. He looked like a dog no one would dare to mess with and was probably his own boss.

"They do need to go for walks, dear," said Mrs. Nobody.

"What they need is a good beating with my studded waist belt, replied the Master Jailer.

"Last week I brought a hen into the backyard," said Mrs. Nobody, "to give them some exercise, but I didn't think they'd take it down that fast."

"But they did give us a nice 'turkey' for thanksgiving dinner," added the chained uncaring teen.

"It was indeed good, darling dear. Thank you."

Scrappy clawed at the screen door, tore through it, and went to the nearby double-door refrigerator. She scratched at it, pawed at it, stuck her nose under the bottom of the door, and pulled and chewed and managed to open it. Food! This could keep the dogs fed for days, though admittedly, these were awfully big critters.

Did the Master Jailer have these dogs for security? If so, why were they tied to trees not allowing them to contact each other? Maybe they fought among themselves? But, if so, they weren't doing it now; just playing and exploring each other, and expressing pleasure about their newfound freedom: running and jumping about the yard, digging holes, and chasing squirrels.

Scrappy returned to the backyard with a sizeable aluminum dog bowl in her mouth. The large and lanky Duke came bounding up, took the bowl without resistance from Scrappy, and then carried it to the water faucet by the house, laid it underneath, and pulled open the levered valve with his canines. Out came nice fresh water. Scrappy took a thirst-quenching drink and so did a drooling Doorstop. Duke then lapped up a good portion, grabbed the water bowl, took it over to his former master, and laid it carefully in the dirt—no grass; hadn't been for a long time. The three gargantuan dogs tied to the trees destroyed all semblance of plant life long ago, but the ash trees loosing their leaves in the fall, left a leafy mattress to lie on.

The male human, once claiming to be the top dog by torturing his pack, dropped to his knees and bent down to lick up some of the water, but he didn't have the tongue of a dog's—which curls up like a soup spoon to retrieve food and water—and so he took his two hands and lifted the water bowl to his mouth. Doorstop came up, and with his dominating head, knocked it out of the human's hand, spilling the life-sustaining water.

"Damn! You son of a…"

Doorstop bayed.

The Great Dane followed suit.

"Duke, I promise, I won't tie you up again. I might even take you hunting and a swim in the lake, or maybe you'd just like to explore those stinking moldy sewers…"

Duke let out a wail and then a loud ear-splitting bellow.

Scrappy returned from the house with a big plastic container full of cooked spaghetti and meatballs he found in the refrigerator. It was time to eat, at least for the canines. The humans had

Doorstop, a Bordeaux

apparently not been chained up very long, but they looked to be dispirited, their ribs already beginning to show, and their faces lacked any color, but at least this could be considered one way to loose weight.

The approaching night was going to be quite cold: the temperature dropping appreciably and the north wind picking up. The mother human spoke up, "Hey Scrappy, maybe you could at least get blankets from the master's bed and drag them out here to put in the doghouses."

"Yeah," agreed her daughter, "and could you bring me my mascara and toenail polish?"

Mom took a sideways look at that. Scrappy also tilted her head trying to understand the little human that never came out to play, or even visit, with them.

Evening was drawing close, the sun slipping away toward the horizon. The three monstrous dogs made their way back through the screen door and sniffed and peed their way throughout the house, having never had a chance to explore it before. They found three bedrooms, a living room, and a garage full of boxes to rummage through. Back in the kitchen, the refrigerator, with open door, ran continuously. The dogs scattered the food packaging about the house after licking up every morsel of food, and they lapped up their liquid nourishment from the bathroom toilet. They stuck their noses into every closet, found a few teddy bears to chew on, pulled them apart, and scattered the synthetic fiber filler about the house. These dogs were big, and to see them roughhousing together, you could almost feel the house shaking...and just see the fine furniture being torn apart, glassware thrown about, carpet mangled. That's just what the chained-up humans were probably thinking just now...and they'd be right.

For his nightcap, Duke—clearly the alpha dog—chose the queen bed in the master bedroom, and even though it was barely big enough for him, the acres of sheets and blankets made for fine bedding. Scrappy climbed into the living room's leather arm chair and curled up. One could probably expect some claw scratches, maybe even shredded leather, on the fine expensive lounge chair. Doorstop chose the entry hallway and circled around to end up lying against the front door. He was always on the job.

The next morning, the three enormous dogs returned to the backyard where they saw the humans curled up in the doghouses, cold and shivering. The handsome Great Dane barked and lowered his front end by bending his forepaws. Did he want to play? The humans crawled out of their holes and shook their sleepy heads. The former head honcho—spoke first, "Duke, come here boy, have I got a deal for you."

The Great Dane picked up a teddy bear and brought it to the master.

"Why, thank you! I'll get you a T-bone steak, I promise."

The former jailer took a step backward. Duke dropped the teddy bear and raised his lips slightly, his snout wrinkling up. The other two dogs came forward. Doorstop looked stressed, made obvious by the tense partially open mouth, intense focused eyes, and ears pushed backward. He was clearly not happy with his former master and had no plans to play with him unless he wanted to play tackle football. That, I'm sure he thought, would be so much fun.

The teen spoke, "Scrappy, let me loose and I'll take you for a walk."

The long-haired Scottish Deerhound, a distant look, stared unhappily at the teen and barked. The young girl looked down to see the yard muddy with puddles of water in the lower areas. The humans stood up to find their knees and feet covered with mud.

Master Jailer shouted out, "Duke, you square-headed yo-yo, you left the hose faucet on!"

The Great Dane, and the other two loving mutts, howled. Duke and Scrappy turned away and made for the fence. Doorstop, with his deep broad chest and brawny legs, waded to the master's dog house and quite easily pushed it over. After this display of disrespect, the three dogs then pushed through a couple of loose wood slats on the clapboard fence and out they strolled happily to parts unknown. Free at last.

THE END

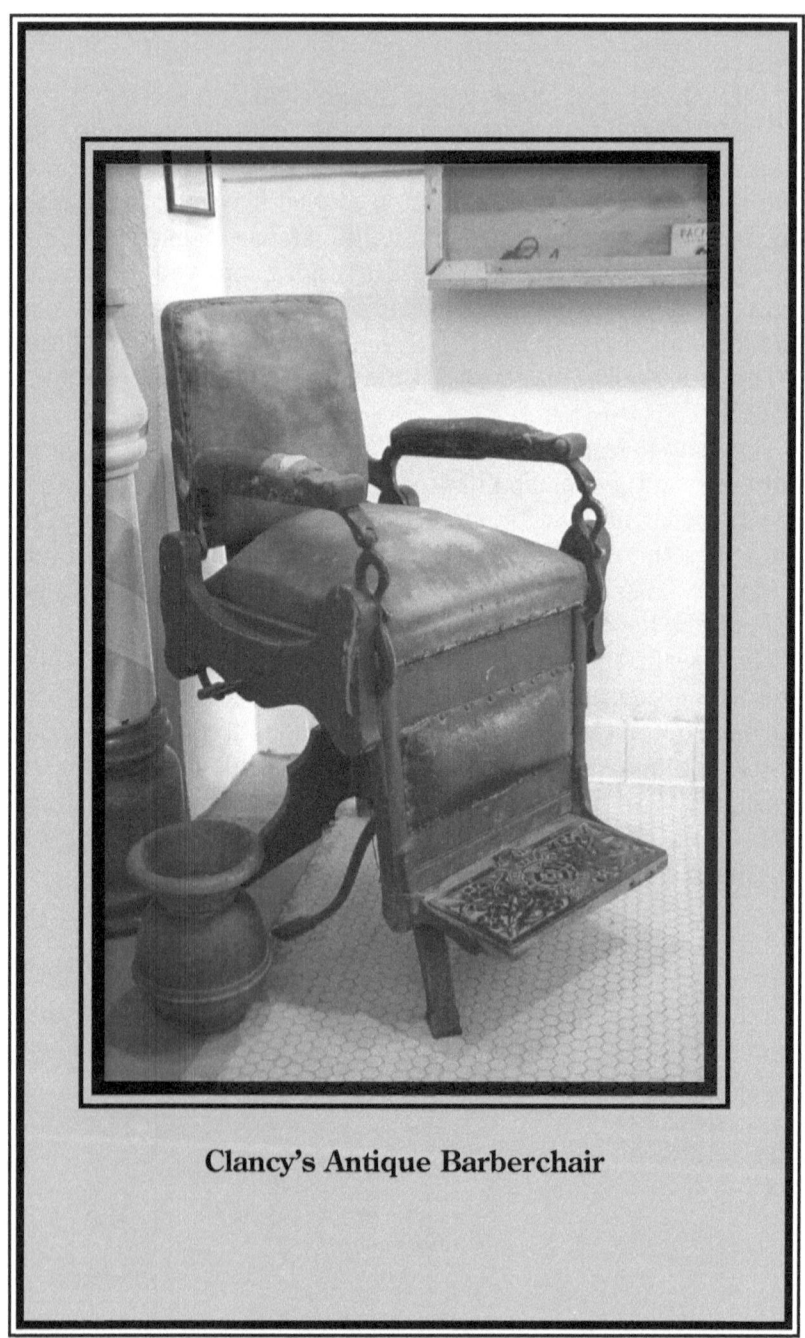

Clancy's Antique Barberchair

7. Clancy's Barbershop

By Don Kirk

The bell rang. It clanged and rattled over the door as I entered *Clancy's Barbershop*.

"Welcome, come on in," said the proprietor as he grabbed a towel and pointed to one of the three barber chairs in the long narrow room. "Shave? Haircut?"

"Haircut will do for today."

"How much to cut, two inches, six inches?"

"Just a little over the ears, please."

The barber cranked the big, green-leather steel barber chair up to a comfortable height and threw a black-striped white sheet over me as I lay my head back to relax. I closed my eyes. There was something peaceful about getting a haircut or shave. But, as it turned out, that wasn't going to happen on this day. A loud, deep, gurgling snort got my attention and I abruptly leaned forward causing my hair to be yanked from the barber's hands.

The barber called out to the back of the room, "Dog! Wake up! I can't get my work done with your snoring…"

I heard clacking footfalls on the linoleum tile floor and an eye opener stopped in front of me and sat down: a drooling seventy-pound or better overweight-looking monster with large pink tongue dangling, a huge square head, and flop-down ears. It carried focused brown eyes, alert as a lion in spring and could scare off a tyrannosaurus, but then again, those eyes looked so sweet and endearing, something loving coming from deep within.

"That dog's been living in here all his life, since puppyhood," announced the barber. He likes it quiet and tranquil. Loves the air conditioning. Sweet as a…"

"Does he bite?"

"Oh hell no. He's not the smartest kid on the block, but he's one-hundred percent laid back and lovable."

"What, that thing? No!"

"He's a boxer, an alert and watchful guard dog, but the neighborhood kids come in here for a haircut and a chance to climb all over him. I get a lot of repeat customers because of that dog."

"Coulda fooled me."

"Sit back, you can hug him when I'm done."

"I'll pass."

Sporting a brown and white breast, white paws, and black around the eye sockets, it might be the creature from the Black Lagoon. Oh, and a tongue so big it could wash a car in just a few strokes. This dog sported rather short hair and a stub for a tail. How could one know if the critter was happy or upset? No tail wagging to reveal his intentions, and he couldn't raise his hackles if he wanted to. His drooping lips and upturned jaw made him look like a powerfully-jawed monkfish, and white foaming slobber oozed from each side of his mouth. The 1950's horror-movie monster I was looking at just sat there staring up at me. How was I to get out of my chair?

The dog's disquieting attention on me was unnerving. I gripped the arms of the barber chair tightly so I'd be ready to practice kick-boxing if necessary.

"Does he know any tricks? Will he do what you say? "

"No and no," replied the barber.

My eyes widened.

The black-striped sheet on me was covered with my white-streaked black hair, 'greying' they called it. The barber whisked my shoulders and pulled the chair cloth from me and shook. He handed me a mirror.

"Looks fine," I said.

"Seven ninety-five."

I carefully stood up, but stepped sideways from the barber chair so as to not disturb the mammoth dog. This creature could have come from another planet. I was sure his slobbering, sagging

Creature From The Black Lagoon?

mouth could easily take a gargantuan bite out of me. I covered my neck with my hands to make me feel a mite safer knowing full well my hands would be no hindrance to those canines.

Once I had touched the floor and taken a few steps backward, the "big dawg" took a flying leap onto my chair, landing comfortably on the black-leather cushion of the antique solid steel barber chair.

"That's his chair," said the barber, "that's why he kept staring at you."

"I-I-I seeee," I replied, handing the barber a ten-spot, "cute dog, but if that's his chair, why did you seat me there?"

"It's the most comfortable."

"Uhh huh, okay."

As I turned to leave, a hooded man pushed violently through the glass door, pointed a small pistol at me, and insisted I "step back." I froze in my tracks, fear rising in me, rising all the way to my eyeballs. "Step back!" I stepped back...slowly. He then shifted his handgun to the barber, "Give me the money in your cash box. Now! Or you'll be whisker infested shaving cream."

"Okay, okay," the barber agreed, raising his hands head high, fingers spread, and turning to the small cash register sitting behind him on the hair-tonic counter. He slowly lowered his hands to open the register. The boxer, still sitting comfortably in his favorite chair, raised his head and growled. The robber turned around, his breathing coming to standstill, sweat dripping from his forehead, and the hair on his forearms reaching to the ceiling. The canine clearly had the robber's undivided attention.

"What ta..."

The dog stood up and leaped onto the gun-toting criminal.

"Ahhh, get him off me," screamed the robber as his pistol slid across the floor. It was a Russian Makarov, nice compact size, great for robberies. The criminal tried to wrestle himself out from under the leviathan, but with no luck, he reached out for one of the chairs used for waiting lined along the mirrored wall opposite the barber chairs. He got hold of a chair leg, pulled, lifted it up using the other hand, and hit the overpowering mutt with the chair, but it bounced harmlessly off the dog, went flying, backrest over casters, and hit the mirror. The looking glass shattered into hundreds of sharp pieces. The canine went for one of the robber's ankles and pulled. The thief flapped his arms and wildly tried to kick with his other foot.

"Aaaahhh, leave me, let go," he screamed.

The canine released the leg but climbed onto the chest of the robber and went for his terror-stricken face, covering it with his wrinkled, salivating muzzle.

A muffled "help" emanated from the bandit.

The "I'll-show-you" dog then let out a big, walloping fart! The robber's eyes bulged as he pulled back from the dog's gripping mouth, and that's when the thief's nose puckered up and he mumbled something like, "Ahhh, get back! I've reached my fighting limit. That stench is way too much for me to...*¡Ay, caramba!*" That's when I could see the man's nostrils close up in self defense.

The barber called out, "Here, boy, come here," as he placed a large bowl of food on the floor. The sweet canine turned and took quickly to a more satisfying pursuit when the profusely-sweating robber jumped up and stumbled drunkenly out the door.

I slowly got up and brushed myself off and said, "So this is what happens when there's a boxer in a barber shop."

"I've got insurance. More importantly, I've still got my cash and my sweet baby. He's my security guard."

"Nice dog."

"A real jewel. His breed bred to take down bulls."

"And humans, I see."

"No one tries to leave here without paying me."

I see that, well, thank you uh, for the haircut..."

The canine looked up and came toward me. I took a step back and reached for the front door.

"He likes you. It's okay, you can pet him."

"You're kidding, right?"

"Go ahead."

I leaned forward and carefully stretched out to touch him on the shoulder. The critter tried to lick my face with his huge wet tongue. I reared back. The delightful "sweet" hound shuffled

"I'll show you."

away into a corner and lay down.

"He's going to take his afternoon nap," stated the barber matter-of-factly.

"I see. He looks calm as a cucumber; probably never had an elevated heart rate…but mine's pounding like an irate executive banging on his desk, fast and hard."

The barber brushed off a chair, "Sit down; take a deep breath."

I started to pick up the robber's gun when…"

"Don't touch it, fingerprints."

I backed off and sat down, "I know your profession is considered an art form requiring skill, training, a steady hand, and a sharp eye, but I had no idea your profession also knew something about forensics and also sported a handy tool that is sweet and kind…a courageous, ready to protect, boxer."

"Beneficial in this part of town."

"That gloomy mug of his, I guess, doesn't reflect his inner feelings."

"You a psychiatrist?"

"Oh, no, no, I just…"

Unexpectedly, the dog grunted and the loud snoring began again.

"He's got to get his rest; been up a whole hour today."

"Ooh-kay."

As I headed for the door I heard a deafening police siren growing louder and louder followed by screeching tires. Red lights flashed through the windows onto the remaining mirrored wall. The glass entrance door swung open; in came a uniformed police officer with the barbershop thief.

"This man been in here? Said he was attacked by a vicious dog."

"That's correct. This, not so gentle, gentleman tried to rob the place. There's his gun."

"I just tried to protect myself," screamed the thief as he displayed the canine's teeth marks on his arm and ankle.

"He tried to take my cash money."

"Are you Clancy?" asked the cop.

"Oh no, that's him sleeping in the corner. He's the pack leader."

The sleepy-eyed boxer got slowly up, stretched his front legs and then his back legs. When the cop saw his size, he took one step back, maybe two, "That's the dog that stopped this armed man?"

"That's him, Clancy. This is his place."

"I'll testify to that," I added.

THE END

Aussie, an Australian Shepherd

8. Aaron And His Dog Aussie

By Don Kirk

"Hey, Girl, it'll be fine. We'll hit the road soon," promised Aaron in a rough, harsh voice.

A cute six-year-old Australian Shepherd sat beside the wire-framed twin bed of her master, Aaron Wells who carefully, lovingly caressed the dog on her head and shoulders. Aaron was recovering from a surgical procedure to remove part of his breastbone and the cartilage around it. A cancerous tumor had been found and successfully removed, Aaron's full recovery expected.

Aaron had hoped, on his impending retirement from an oil refinery in Bay City—a small Texas town near Houston—to visit all the national parks in America, like the Grand Canyon, Yellowstone National Park, Glacier, Bandelier, and even the Carlsbad Caverns. He talked to his dog Aussie about the magnificent trips the two of them would soon make. He told her he would even find a way to get her into Carlsbad.

"You'll love to see—and smell—the American West and we might even check out the eastern U.S. The Everglades, you'll love that. All kinds of things to see: natural wonders and man-made monuments to American ingenuity."

On Aaron's bedside table lay two large dog-eared guidebooks describing America's national parks and pinned all over his living room wall hung highway maps of the western states. Apparently, Aaron was ready to explore some age-old attractions: outside the front door stood a large, off-white, four-door pickup truck with an enclosed bed outfitted with a mattress, ice chest, chest-of-drawers, and a spare tire. Aaron and his Girl would spend their nights in this pickup.

"Aussie, I'll be taking you for walks again soon."

The Shepherd nudged Aaron's left hand with her nose, put her front paws on his bed, and leaned in to lick her master's face.

"Okay, Girl, down."

Aussie sat back down but continued to stare at Aaron. The Shepherd stood at about eighteen inches tall and always appeared to be grinning—her mouth hanging wide in a relaxed and confident manner. Her tongue dangled loosely conveying complete trust in the pack leader. She had a long, four-colored coat that included white, brown, black, and some grey hair. The breast and paws were white and the white coloring ran from her nose up her muzzle between her light-brown eyeballs. The rest of her face (cheeks, around the eyes, her big shaggy ears) displaced a patchwork of all the colors overlapping and blending together, the resultant ash-grey and brown coloring resembling a smoldering fire. An awesome coat to say the least.

Aaron Wells had been loosing weight for some time, with unremitting chest pains, and he exhibited a shortness of breath while on his welding and engine maintenance job, an occupation requiring him to climb around and through tall rigs at the refinery. He lived alone—except for this sweet and caring Shepherd—in a small cedar log cabin with just one living space, a small kitchen, and a barely-functioning bathroom.

Several months later, after his initial surgery, Aaron still felt tired, weak, and listless. And so he returned to his doctor and, with further testing, was informed that the cancer had spread to one of his kidneys.

"Don't worry," said the doctor, "you can do just fine with one kidney."

Aaron went through the agony and anguish of getting the kidney removed, and it seemed to be working, CT scans negative, in fact, he felt good.

The next week Aaron was up and running with new spark plugs and a full tank of gas as it were, and taking Aussie for walks again, though not as long as she was used to. Aussie had a forested area nearby where she could run free and explore. She was born to herd cattle, but rounding up *anything* on four legs delighted her. Adolescent deer, rabbits, possum, and even raccoons ran crazily about looking for places to take cover. Wild geese, a few mallard ducks feeding in a marshy creek bed, and a couple of meandering skunks fought to stay clear of this determined stock tender. Aussie even tried to catch a snake, got a facial bite, redness, bleeding and he came begging for help.

"Hurt didn't it? And the fun trip to the Vet. I hope you learned your lesson: snakes, they ain't to be messed with, hear me?"

Aussie twisted her head sideways apparently not comprehending what her master had said, but lay down on the floor and turned over to reveal her pink stomach.

"That's right Girl, I'm the boss. You will always follow my lead or get a butt whippin'!"

Aussie got back up slowly, approached Aaron, and put her right paw on his knee.

"Yeah, I forgive you, but next time, you ask me first if it's okay to round up some wild critter. You should understand, these woods are also their home."

One evening Aaron began to feel pressure at the center of his chest, an uncomfortable squeezing that would come and go, and he felt giddy. He closed his arms around his chest, squeezing tighter and tighter, hoping to make his heart stop throbbing unmercifully. With little relief, he lay down on his bed.

"Aussie, I…I've got a bad headache. I can't feel my left arm, it's…it's numb."

Aussie put her paw lovingly on Aaron's chest, Aaron's face beginning to sweat. The strange discomfort concerned Aaron, but he couldn't quite get himself out of bed. Aussie whined and appeared anxious, a confused expression on her face. The dog's uneasiness made even more apparent by her moving about restlessly, sitting for only a moment at a time. Finally, she turned away from the struggling Aaron, and went to the log-paneled front door, bolted through a rubber-flapped 'doggie door,' and took off running down the gravel driveway to the street. She darted across a two-lane highway forcing cars to swerve erratically and drivers to slam on the brakes to avoid hitting her. The Australian Shepherd dashed to an old, white clapboard farmhouse and bounded up a few concrete steps onto the front porch. She then scratched at the screen door and barked.

A middle-aged lady came to the door. "Why, Aussie, hello! Where's Aaron?"

Aussie barked and whined, spun in a circle, and jumped up on Mary Martha Wayne, Aaron's nearest neighbor and a long-time friend.

"Aussie dear! What's wrong?"

Aussie turned, jumped over the concrete steps in a single bound, and ran back down the driveway toward the highway until she saw that the neighbor lady wasn't coming and so stopped,

Aussie: "Boss? You okay, Boss?"

turned back, and barked again.

"What's wrong, Girl, what's wrong?"

Aussie did another 360-degree spin.

"Okay dear, I get it, you want me to come with you."

Aussie barked.

Martha Wayne went back into the house, returned with flat-soled leather shoes and sat on a wooden bench swing to put them on. Aussie barked impatiently.

"I'm coming, dear, I'm coming."

Finally, Mary Martha headed out after Aussie who led her back across the street and to Aaron's cabin.

The winded Shepherd pushed through the rubber flap in the front door. Mary opened the door to find Aaron lying in his bed shaking and taking deep labored breaths. Aussie jumped up on her master's chest and bounced rhythmically up and down.

"Aussie, get down!" demanded Martha as she grabbed the house phone and called 9-1-1.

Several days later Aaron came out of an induced coma and smiled when he saw Aussie sitting there on the floor watching him. A doctor wearing a white lab coat ambled into the room: "Mr. Wells, you should be able to go home in a few days. We will have home services set up for you, meals, meds, and nursing visits."

Aaron tried to move his mouth but found that he could not speak.

"Yes, Mr. Wells, you can't talk at this time. You had a mild heart attack. You'll be fine. A nurse will explain what happened and what you will have to do. You can go home in a few days. That dog of yours has been waiting for days for you to open your eyes; the outpatient wing you're now in allowed Aussie to visit. Fact is, once she was allowed in, she refused to leave. So yes, we've been feeding her, she's a good girl."

Aaron turned his attention to Aussie and reached out to her. The pretty Australian Shepherd stood on her hind legs and placed her front paws ever so softly on Aaron. Aaron tried to crack a smile, but he found it hard to do. Aussie let out a mild bark of excitement and relaxed her mouth, panting with a not-so-sublime happiness.

Three days later, Aaron was able to go home. He felt good and was doing well. Aaron and Aussie played with each other and went for short walks through the woods. The oil worker again seemed hopeful for the travel he had envisioned. He picked up one of his national park books and began to read out loud to Aussie: "Glenwood Canyon is thought by many to be the most beautiful of all of Colorado's canyons. The magnificent Colorado River sliced through this rocky landscape, slowly but surely, for thousands of years to leave behind an awesome place for hiking, biking, and river rafting."

The Shepherd sat there with undivided loving attention.

Aaron didn't yet have to go back to work; he had plenty of unused vacation time. Finally, he decided to go on a week-long trip to Colorado, to visit a few of the national parks. Aussie was of course with him, and she loved it. New places, new smells, and new critters to round up, though hopefully she would not try to herd the black bear commonly found in these woods.

Even though Aaron and Aussie had been on their little trip for less than a week, Aaron returned to Texas because he was again feeling quite weak, experiencing a shortness of breath, and showing some signs of mental confusion. He informed his employer that he wouldn't be coming back to work any time soon.

Returning to the hospital, and after several blood draws and MRI scans, the doc informed Aaron that the cancer had metastasized to his other kidney. His only choice now was to get his remaining kidney removed and be put on dialysis three days a week…for the rest of his life, and no longer would he be able to take Aussie for long walks.

So Aaron went home, turned on the television set, lay down with a sorrowful gloominess—even though in a well-lit room—and teared up. The Shepherd wasted no time jumping up on the bed and curling up next to her master. Both of them went quietly to sleep.

After just a few days of watching television and pondering his fate, Aaron decided he would not—absolutely no way—go on dialysis; his dream of seeing America was over anyway. Aussie cuddled up beside Aaron on his narrow bed and stared into his soul mate's eyes.

"Look girl," said Aaron, "You and me, we're both working breeds. We both have lots of energy—well, I had once. You like hunting, rounding up livestock, search and rescue, even playing Frisbee, and I like to fix things, do electrical work, plumbing, engine maintenance; ain't nothin' I won't try and you neither."

Aussie twisted her head sideways.

"Girl, I know you don't like laying around watching television so get your butt out of here and go find something to do. I ain't gonna be around here much longer."

Aussie would not leave; she stayed right there with Aaron.

When any help came, Aaron usually ran them off. He began to eat and drink less—much less—and began to loose weight. His beloved pooch stayed with him every minute, well, except for trips out the doggie door for a potty break. Aaron had no family to visit him, much less to stay and help. Martha Wayne, from across the street, and a few other oil-field co-workers, brought him meals, but, after just over a month, Aaron died quietly on his steel-frame bed. Aussie stayed with him, sitting quietly watching, waiting, and hoping his master's eyes would once again open.

But they never did.

Two days later, Martha discovered Aaron's emaciated body.

It was taken unceremoniously away, but the Australian Shepherd refused to leave the small cabin, lying quietly on the carpet at the side of his master's bed. She stayed there for almost a week longing for Aaron's return. During that time, the cabin was eerily quiet except for a few squawking sparrows and grazing deer... those enticing creature sounds that Aussie now chose to ignore.

THE END

Postscript: The Australian Shepherd lived two more years, dying from lymphoma, a skin cancer common to this breed.

The *Natchez's* **Paddlewheel**

9. Dog Heroes
By Don Kirk

Like rifle blasts at a quail hunt, four short blasts of a steam whistle blew wet, white mist skyward. An enormous 25-foot paddlewheel on the stern of the *Natchez* churned up river water and propelled the boat slowly forward. The passengers on this triple-decked sternwheeler, all standing against the rails, looked thrilled by the new experience they were about to undertake. The boat was leaving the New Orleans *French Quarter* to take the passengers for a stimulating ride over river water instead of hot asphalt. At 11:00 a.m. on a breezy blue-sky day with cumulous clouds billowing wondrously overhead, the boat moved slowly away from the dock and out into the awesome Mississippi River. The passengers, leaving on a two-hour tour along the river, would enjoy waterfront views of the Big Easy. An onboard, live Jazz band filled the air with a few Dixieland favorites like Louie Armstrong's *Muskrat Ramble* and *Tin Roof Blues*. Metallic blasts from a trumpet, fluid notes from a clarinet, twanging banjo strings, a brassy trombone, and the low timbre of a string bass, could be heard over squawking birds and the port's huge container ships blasting their ever present horns.

On the white tablecloth of a four-person dining table sat steaming plates of Cajun food in front of a delighted mother and her two young daughters. A small dog sat quietly on the floor beside them. Mother had been looking forward to ingesting some gumbo, shrimp, crawfish, white rice, and maybe some mushroom boudin balls.

"Mommy, what is this?"

"You'll love this seafood, ladies. I'm sorry, they didn't have any fried alligator at the buffet table."

"Mommy, no!"

"On your plate is some wonderful Cajun gumbo," declared the mother. "It has sausage, hot pepper sauce, onions, celery, a pinch of garlic, some beef bouillon salted to taste, and two fingers of..."

"But Mamma, can this be eatin'?" asked the three-year-old brunette Sherry, her normally warm, flushed face now scrunched-up like wet roofing felt.

"Certainly dear, no fried muskrat, at least I don't think so."

"Mamma, stop," protested Charlotte, her five-year-old daughter. "I don't think they'd have musk...you're kidding aren't you?" asked the yellow-haired beauty in a flowery pink dress as she held her spoon high in the air, not yet willing to grease it up.

Mr. Moustache, a Schnauzer

But, the fourth family member, their handsome, grey-haired male Schnauzer, with arched eyebrows, a prickly moustache, and white goatee, gave his full attention to the steaming dish.

"It's too rich for you darling," declared the mother to the family's affectionate companion wearing an orange service-dog harness with the name '*Mr. Moustache*' printed on both sides.

Daughter Charlotte took a cautious bite from her gumbo, "Oh, it's not so bad Sherry, and I know how hungry you are."

Sherry poked curiously at the dish of food and dared to sample it. "Not bad but do they have ice cream, mamma? *Cinnamon Peach* maybe?"

"Don't know, dear, you eat your gumbo, then we'll see."

The two girls poked and prodded their New Orleans cuisine, ingesting only a few bites, and then moved from the table to look at the passing boats. Mrs. Boone continued to enjoy the hot Cajun food.

Inside and out on the bow of the Boiler Deck of this historic Sternwheeler stood dozens of dining tables. The passengers could unwind, forgetting life's daily grind for two hours as they took in the passing Mississippi shoreline and savored the bountiful onboard cuisine.

On the deck, near the Boone family, ambled a middle-aged lady with greying hair, walking stick, and female service dog strolling dutifully at her side, though the pooch was trying so sweetly with a slight pull on her leash to cajole her master toward the railing so she could see the seagulls and the heaving, swirling, white water. The gentlewoman called out to the lady sitting at the dining table, "I see you've also got a service dog."

"Yes, this is Mr. Moustache, a most affectionate companion. He hangs with us so he can watch over me and the girls."

"I can see the reason for your dog's name; he sports a sizable white moustache, and overwhelming beard for that matter. My black Labrador Retriever answers to 'Huckleberry.' I named her after Doc Holliday's statement in the movie *Tombstone* when he said 'I'm your Huckleberry.'"

"What does that mean?"

"It means, my Huckleberry here, this lovable critter, is just the right dog to help me. She does a stand-up job of watching over my limping carcass."

"It's a darling name, I must say."

"They call me Carol Clarkson."

"Nice to meet you."

"Huckleberry's been trained to be obedient, and follows my every command. She loves to play in the water, except when succumbing to a bath. My baby doesn't think that's fun; I know not why."

"Maybe it's the soap."

"Maybe I should change brands."

"I like the black-as-night look of your Labrador," added Mrs. Boone. "You don't trip over him at night, do you?"

"No, she knows where to hang out. Your Mr. Moustache is a German Schnauzer?"

"Yes, his breed is athletic, agile and learns quickly. He always wants to please. He keeps me and the girls in line and can call for help by barking and pressing this button on my medical alert beeper. He loves to cuddle in my lap when I watch TV. Your Labrador looks much too big to climb into yours."

"Believe me she has tried. Huckleberry makes a great pet too. She has a friendly disposition. She stands upright and proud and helps me stay on my feet. You see, I've had a knee replacement."

"If you keep making an effort to walk it'll get easier, just watch out for those chewing-gum wads."

"That's funny, but a gum wad could actually do me in," replied Carol Clarkson as she took a seat at one of the tables nearby. The black Lab then lay quietly down at her feet.

Nearby, little Sherry Boone, playing about unnoticed, decided to feed the seagulls with a piece of bread. She climbed up on the shorter, three-foot-high loading gate of the four-foot railing, reached out to the squawking gull flying alongside to give it a piece of bread, and her body fell forward. She lost her other hand's grip on the railing, and her feet came up off the railing. Sherry tumbled overboard—arms flailing, searching for something to get hold off—and fell fifteen feet into the river's undulating waves below. The impact was hard, but Sherry was still conscious. Her older

Huckleberry, a Labrador Retriever

sister Charlotte witnessed this horrifying mishap and screamed. Everyone on the bow of the boat looked up startled. Mrs. Boone stood up, coming unglued, screaming with unbridled terror. The little Mr. Moustache got to his feet from under the table and ran to the railing where he squeezed under the bottom rail and dived into the churning river below. A waiter grabbed a life buoy and threw it over the railing and yelled, "Man overboard!" Three rings of the pilothouse roof bell signaled the crew to action and the steamboat's paddlewheel came to a quick halt. One of the waiters pointed to the girl overboard so rescuers could pinpoint her location.

The determined Schnauzer paddled up to the freaked-out, flailing girl, grabbed her by the white collar on her pink dress, and began pulling her toward the sternwheeler, but he couldn't quite manage the task and his bearded head bobbed below the surface of the murky water much too often.

Clarkson's Labrador saw the calamity, stood up, and leaped over the guardrail, hitting the water with an enormous splash.

"Huckleberry, my Huckleberry!" screamed Carol as she stumbled toward the railing.

The Lab paddled rapidly toward Sherry and the Schnauzer. People on all the decks moved to the port side of the ship, prompting a warning announcement over the loud speakers: "This is the Captain speaking. Please step back from the railing; keep the area clear so the rescuers can work. Please stay back."

With the powerful waves splashing savagely over her, the bewildered and choking Sherry Boone found it hard to take a breath without also taking in gulps of river water. She was inhaling water and suffocating. Sherry did finally capture some air and tried to make sense of her desperate situation. She spread her arms and legs in an effort to stay afloat, hoping not to sink to the muddy depths of the Mississippi.

Two crewmen on the Main Deck (the deck that lay just above water level) lifted a small self-inflating lifeboat over the side. Two other men with orange life vests dove into the river as the lifeboat filled with compressed air and opened up.

Huckleberry grabbed the floundering girl and pulled her toward the lifeboat. Mr. Moustache let go of Sherry and paddled wildly trying to save his own life.

Mrs. Boone yelled out, "Swim Sherry, swim! We love you."

The two crewmen paddled to Huckleberry, Mr. Moustache, and the barely afloat Sherry. One crewman grabbed and lifted the sopping-wet little girl and lifted her into the lifeboat. The other crewman hoisted the exhausted Schnauzer into the boat, his tangled mass of hair looking as if he had just taken a wild ride in a washing machine. Huckleberry calmly, confidently, paddled alongside the lifeboat as the passengers on the steamer cheered. One passenger, not letting the excitement mitigate his hunger, took a big bite out of his fried shrimp.

In the lifeboat, a concerned Schnauzer nudged his fellow pack member.

Sherry opened her eyes, saw Mr. Moustache staring squarely at her, and asked, "Do you think mamma will give us peach ice cream?"

The men in the boat looked at each other, immensely delighted.

The Captain of the *Natchez* let out one prolonged blast of the steam whistle.

A few seagulls landed on the railing of the Boiler Deck eyeing the abandoned plates of food. The Dixieland jazz band strummed up another Louis Armstrong tune: *"The colors of the rainbow so pretty in the sky and also on the faces of people going by. I see friends shaking hands saying how do you do. They're really saying I love you. And I think to myself what a wonderful world."*...What a wonderful world.

THE END

Slugger, a Boxer

10. The Adventures Of Shag And Slugger

By Don Kirk

THE ESCAPE

"Come on let's get out of here."

Slugger had been digging for some time under the chain-link fence and now was the time to act, time to make a run for it.

"Come on, Shag, let's go," insisted Slugger.

Shag slowly got up from her bed: a hole next to the house with nice soft comforting dirt. She liked to dig—the yard was full of holes—but this was her favorite trench for sleeping; she had even removed the rocks. Very little carpet grass was left in the yard—once a nice wholesome green landscape—but the running around of Slugger and the digging of Shag had cleared the land of all vegetation. They each had a doghouse to sleep in, a bowl of water to drink, and food trays filled to the brim every evening, though they surmised the nutrients came from the humanoid who frequently yelled obscenities at them through an open window... and they knew not why.

"Let's go," repeated the mischievous Slugger, an imposing, male, two-foot-tall-at-the-shoulders, black-faced Boxer weighing in at sixty pounds or better, sporting a short, reddish-brown coat with white coloring on his chest, paws, and forelegs. Slugger crawled through the hard-earned hole under the fence. The sun was rising; a new day had begun. The shaggy, fifteen-inches tall, soft-coated, golden-brown female Wheaten Terrier known as "Shag,"—her wavy hair so long it covered her eyes and face— followed the short-muzzled Slugger through the freshly-dug depression. These two unlikely-paired dogs ran off down the alley, jumping with joy, making a high bouncy run for freedom.

THE TRASHED ALLEY

The two thrilled canines came upon a pile of abandoned furniture, putrid mattresses, rotting lumber, moldy food scraps, and all manner of landscape-altering rubbish. Slugger, and the much smaller Shag with her scruffy, matted-hair, searched wildly through the mildewing odds-and-ends, rapidly sniffing throughout the awesome pile of trash.

"Ah, this is amazing," blurted out Shag, "so many new odors... but hey wait, I smell cat!"

"A cat! Wow, it's mine."

"No, it's mine!"

The two dogs scurried posthaste through the pile trying to be the first to find a treasure: a cat slow on its feet. After climbing around the exterior of the awesome pile, they began to push into the refuse and found broken metal shelves, cardboard boxes full of odds and ends, and ooh, wow, some tasty leftovers from either a *McDonald's, Wendy's, Dairy Queen, Taco Bell,* or *Long John Silver's,* or all of them! Um good!

"Hamburger, fish, pizza, enchiladas, this is the place, my man," declared Slugger in a deep guttural voice...but then, in a flash, a scrawny grey-and-white cat came running out of the pile. Both dogs looked up and were off-to-the-races in wild leaps and bounds as the feline critter sprang down the alley at break-neck speed. Slugger was in the lead, but Shag stayed close behind and let out a deep squeaking bark. And, amazingly, they gained ground; the trailing cat's tail just inches in front of Slugger's muzzle. He tried to snatch a bite, but the feline was just out of reach. And it found a tree trunk to scamper up. Slugger jumped up on the rough bark, hind legs several feet off the ground as the front claws tried to get a grip. Shag came up, circled the tree, smelled the ground, and began to track the cat's trail backward: twisting and turning, changing directions, nose to the ground, nothing, but then she looked back up into the tree, and there, the cat was sitting, unmoving, on a branch just ten feet above them. The little

Wheaten Terrier leaped up the tree trunk trying to get a foothold, but Slugger snapped at him with raised lips.

"He's mine. I got here first. I got dibs," pronounced the Boxer.

Both dogs finally sat down facing the trunk, stared upward, and waited and waited and waited. The petrified cat sat there on the same branch without daring to make a move. It had no place to go because it couldn't jump from a tree limp to another tree's limbs like squirrels could do so successfully with there seeming ability to spread wings and fly.

About two hours passed slowly before the two watchful dogs lost interest and moved on. So down the alley they continued onward, their noses sniffing out new adventures.

THE PARAKEETS

The two dogs soon found themselves on a blacktop road lined with old, wood-framed houses built off the ground on piers. This looked exciting, had potential. Great place to find opossum, raccoon, and even skunk, but instead of going under, Slugger and Shag leaped up a stairway onto a wooden porch. Hanging above the porch floor was a birdcage housing a couple of cheerfully tweeting blue- and yellow-feathered parakeets.

Shag, the tiny Terrier, hopped on the porch swing and reached for the cage in an effort to pull in the scent of these strange-looking creatures. Reaching as high as she could, Shag pawed at the bottom of the cage causing it to swing back and forth; the frightened, feathered creatures chirped confoundedly.

"Here, let me help," insisted Slugger—taller and much longer-legged—as he pushed on the cage and grabbed it with both paws. With his strong, thick muscles, he tried to lift himself up onto the cage, but when he did, it suddenly came crashing down, hitting Shag. One of Shag's hind legs got pinned between the slats of the porch swing as the birdcage door came open and the two pretty parakeets flew out to their not-necessarily-desired freedom. Shag's foot was twisted into a scary, painful position, her body hanging over the edge of the swing putting dangerous stresses on her leg.

"Mophead, you okay?"

"Don't call me that, Slugger, dang it! No fair! Just because you say I look like a kitchen mop without a handle…"

"You okay, Mophead?"

"I'm fine, I'm fine. Don't call me Mophead!"

"I'm the much bigger canine and that's who decides what you're called."

"I won't mention that the neighbors call you 'Dummkopf.'"

"I'm 'Top Dog.' I'm in charge," voiced Slugger as he turned and approached the screen door of the house and scratched at it. He let out one weak bark, waited, and followed with two quick, deep-throated, yaps. Nothing. No sounds from inside the house. The Boxer began to whimper and started to scratch at the door again when it suddenly creaked open. A young, blond-headed lady pushed the door wide and Slugger sat down quietly facing her.

"Why doggies, who are you?" asked the woman.

"I'm Slugger and this here is Mophead, she needs help."

The woman's eyes widened, very wide indeed, her pink eye sockets showing.

"Did I hear you speak?"

"She needs help."

"Who?"

"Mophead! There. Her foot's caught."

The lady looked over and saw her birdcage lying on the porch floor.

"My God, what have you done?"

"Sorry ma'am, but…"

The lady came out, picked up the cage, and held it up to her face.

"Josephine? Jennifer? They're gone. My babies, they're gone!"

"Sorry ma'am, we didn't mean to…"

"Get out of here now."

"Mophead needs help." Shag then whined and whimpered.

The lady turned to see the shaggy little dog and saw her predicament so she lay the cage down and carefully lifted Shag free.

"Thank you, oh, thank you," said Slugger in a joyful, slobbering tone with his docked tail trying to wag.

Shag / a.k.a. Mophead, a Wheaten Terrier

Shag then spoke in a high-pitched dog talk: "Thank you ma'am, I surly do appreciate it. Sorry about those flying things. If we encounter them we'll bring them back to you."

"I'm sure."

At that Shag and Slugger leaped down the stairs and onto the sidewalk where they continued their hunt for thrills…and maybe two 'on-the-fly' parakeets.

THE HAWK

Noses to the terra firma, Shag and Slugger checked out every inch of the sidewalk. Abruptly, they both came to an unscheduled stop, startled at something falling from the sky into the thorny pyracantha bush next to them. They reached carefully in with their snouts and together pulled out a brown tree squirrel. But the critter wasn't moving. They each sniffed it carefully. Was it dead? There was no movement, a squirrell's black eyes sitting wide open. Shag looked up into the sky, and there, on a telephone line, sat some kind of big bird with long tail and curved beak.

Dressed in a couple of shades of brown, a few white feathers and a red-feathered tail, and it had unwavering eyeballs. It might be a hawk that dropped its prey. Shag grabbed the squirrel—the Boxer showing no real interest in it since it wasn't trying to escape—and dragged it into the street. Without a moment's notice, the broad-winged hawk swooped down and grabbed the squirrel. The sky-commander and its prey were gone in a flash.

So much for that. No alive-and-kicking four-legged critter to hunt down so the shaggy Wheaten Terrier and flat-nosed Boxer moved on down the street.

THE BUS STOP

Walking along the sidewalk, the good-sized Slugger—followed closely by the smallish Shag—approached a covered bus stop with three people: two woman, one holding a baby carriage with a little one inside, and a man. All sitting there waiting for the city transport. The dogs came up to the humanoids, searching all about the bus stop with their noses, savoring the aroma of the trashcan, and sniffing the feet—and other parts—of the waiting passengers. Luckily, on this day, happily reaching out to pet them, none of these people feared the dogs. Shag stood on her hind legs and looked into the baby carriage and reaching out to pet the long-haired Terrier, was a smiling, curious child. The dog had no problem with the baby's hand, leaned forward, and 'kissed' it with her tongue. It was a wonder how this dog could see anything through her unkempt hair. The baby, thrilled and joyous, smiling and laughing, her hands reached skyward. The male passenger dove into his front pocket and laboriously brought out something that might serve as a treat: chewing gum. When he did, both canines sat down and gave him their full attention. The man removed the paper wrappers and gave each dog the treat. He was reaching for another stick of chewing gum when a huge diesel-propelled city bus approached plastered with ads you could call legalized graffiti. Everyone waiting at the bus stop stood up. The bus's bi-fold door opened and the man showed a bus pass he'd removed from his shirt pocket, the others paid in cash. The doors closed and the city bus blasted away on up the street leaving a trail of black engine exhaust.

Slugger sniffed the bus-stop bench where the people had been sitting, obviously looking for mislaid treats. But instead, he found a man's black leather billfold. He smelled it, looked up the street, grabbed the billfold in his mouth, and without hesitation, ran at breakneck speed after the smoke-billowing bus. Slugger was gaining ground on the bus when it slowed down, coming to a squeaking, worn-out-brakes halt at the next bus stop. As the last passenger at this stop climbed the steps, Slugger leaped up and passed the boarding man before the door could be closed. Shag also caught up to the bus, but halted outside the now closed bi-fold door. The fixated Boxer passed the driver at his stern objection, "No dogs allowed unless you're a licensed service dog." But Slugger stomped down the aisle to, guess what, the man that had given him a treat. Slugger held the billfold up to him as if he wanted to play keep-away, but instead, released it softly into the man's hand. So thrilled, smiling ear to ear, the man pulled out the rest of his chewing-gum pack and gave it to Slugger.

Slugger replied with an audible, "Thank you."

The man's eyebrows jumped skyward, "Uh, no, thank...*you, nice dog.*"

"Dog, come here?" yelled the driver, putting his bus in park, undoing his seat belt, and stumbling erratically toward the rear. He'd obviously not been on his feet in hours. Slugger came forward, passed beneath the overweight man, and found the exit door to be closed.

"That beautiful dog brought me my wallet," announced the delighted man.

The bus passengers clapped and cheered as the driver worked his way back to the front and opened the bi-fold door. Slugger quickly exited the bus. Shag was sitting there quietly. The Boxer offered the long-haired pooch some of the chewing gum.

Mission accomplished, Slugger and Shag headed on down the street.

THE STEEL TRAP

Shag sniffed at a long, narrow, wire structure. An aluminum bowl at one end seemed to have something tasty in it, but how to grab it through these metal bars? Shag moved around to one end where she found it open. She knelt down and crawled in. There, the treat! She pushed closer to the bowl and without warning—after stepping on a raised section of the floor—there was a big metallic BANG. Shag tried to push her way back out, but no, she found the way out blocked. A closed and locked door! The concerned Terrier barked in fear. No response. Then, here came Slugger. He approached the cage, sniffed, and looked at Shag directly in the eyes. Shag whimpered. The mystified Boxer circled the trap looking for a way in.

"Mophead, what have you done now?"

"I don't know."

Slugger tried to stick his snout under the metal panel that had slid down a track like a garage door. He stuck his nose underneath and tried to lift it, but it didn't budge.

"Well here, Mophead, push the spring above you with your paw."

Shag reached up with her right leg, stuck it through the bars on top, and pushed and pushed and pushed. The spring moved backward and the door slid upward on tracks. Slugger lifted until the door locked in the up position allowing Shag to back out of the cage.

"I'm staying away from bowls with food," she said matter-of-factly.

THE WILD PACK

Slugger came upon a pile of something nasty, took a long, thoughtful whiff of it, and quickly turned over and rolled in it. Shag came over to check it out; she too rolled over on her back, legs high in the air, and rubbed her hairy coat in it.

"A great disguise. No one will mess with us," declared Slugger.

Up the street came three mongrel mutts, curious as cats, or more likely concerned about the two unfamiliar dogs in *their* territory. They approached cautiously, tails straight back, ears forward, eyes wide. Slugger and Shag stood close to each other, also at an anxious attention. The three dogs circled the unknown Boxer and Wheaten Terrier, checking them out carefully, trying to sniff their rear ends, but Slugger and Shag jumped back and forth to keep the curious dogs from getting behind them. None of the dogs switched to a dominate-aggressive stance with tails and hackles raised, lips curled, and nose wrinkled. No, it turned out to be a peaceful meeting, and the five of them ran off together to explore the neighborhood.

The canines entered the back alley of a restaurant and captured lots of captivating odors around the dumpsters. They found wooden crates, cardboard boxes, and fast-food paper bags— some, they hoped, containing wholesome treats. It was, oh boy, to be an early dinnertime! Slugger stood up to look into a tall, rusted metal trashcan. The lid, off center, fell off when Slugger peered in, and a big black cat with long hair jumped out in abject terror and ran for its dear life. The five dogs were on it. The tom ran out into the street and down a covered sidewalk lined with commercial businesses; the new pack of dogs following in hot pursuit. They avoided the hastened people on the sidewalk, but the human packages went flying…and unexpectedly, a glass door opened in front of them. The frightened cat scampered inside. A bewildered patron held the door open and the dogs raced into the entrance of a *Shipley Do-nuts* shop. Customers sitting at tables with red-checkered tablecloths caught their treats in mid-bite. The black-coated alien, known on this earth as a 'cat,' scampered about the place, the dogs slipping and sliding everywhere. Total chaos! The cat jumped up on the counter with displays of pink-and-blue-sprinkled donuts and scattered them wildly. A patron's iced drink went flying. It was beginning to look like a North Texas tornado had been, well, was still twisting at high velocity. Now on the display counters, a couple of the dogs were licking at the Lemonade, *Coke*, and sweet treats, and thinking this a whole lot tastier than what they found in the nearby alley.

THAT EVENING

The end of the day was approaching, the orange sun falling below the horizon, just a few people still up and about, and the boisterous canines were still cruising on Main Street. The drooling, self-assured Boxer and the dirty, debris-covered Terrier saw an open car door and each leaped in, finding nice comfortable cloth seats, and chose to lie down for a soothing snooze. Slugger began to snore so loudly that he could probably be heard for an entire city block. But soon, a man climbed into the open driver-side door and Slugger sprang up, letting out a threatening wail. The male human turned, his eyes wide as a pair of barn doors, and saw the monster in his face. He jumped back out of the car, quickly slamming the door shut. Slugger sat back down in hopes of a peaceful resolution and Shag, still in the back seat, opened her mouth in peaceful repose. The driver peeked back in and spoke, "It's okay; I won't hurt you."

"I won't hurt you either," responded Slugger.

The driver jumped back again in total disbelief and denial. Did he just hear a dog speak? Did he hear them utter English? No, this couldn't be. "Please, get out of my car," he insisted, the two pair of beady-eyed canine peepers glowing brightly from the just turned on streetlights; a scene right out of a horror movie.

"Yes, certainly, offered Slugger. "Could you open the door for us and we'll be gone as fast as a Cheshire cat."

At that response, the driver fell back onto his rear end. Slugger put his head through the open driver-door window and looked down at him. The driver, with arms behind him to support himself, leaned back and looked up, "you *can* talk!"

"On occasion."

"I see that."

"We just wanted to take a little nap, found your…"

"Door open, my mistake."

"Open the door and we'll be gone. I might can jump out the window," said Slugger, "but my partner, she's smaller, well, it could be a hard landing for her."

The driver got back up and brushed himself off, "You dogs hungry?"

"Are we!"

"Then come with me, I'm going to *Church's Fried Chicken*."

"You're on."

Slugger backed up into the passenger seat as the man jumped into the driver's seat of his car and drove off.

Soon, the vehicle driver with the two dogs edged up to the ordering screen.

"Okay doggies, what do you slobbering canines want?"

"We have a choice?" asked Slugger.

"Just pick a photo."

"A photo?"

"There, on the lighted menu."

"Menu? Can you maybe let us smell each of our options?" asked Slugger.

"Uh, well, how about I order for you."

"We're not particular."

"Good."

The driver placed an order and drove to the pickup window. The dogs could now smell the treats; there noses twitching left and right. The nice man paid, picked up his order, and drove into the parking lot and, guess what, parked. Slugger and Shag watched as the young gentleman ate and handed them some samples of his fried chicken, especially that delicious, greasy skin.

"I don't think I should give you the splintering chicken bones so I'll…"

Without warning, a loud BANG: the fast-food restaurant door swung open hitting the outside wall and a hooded man rushed out with a large brown paper bag in hand. Slugger, without hesitation, jumped over the driver, out the car window, and ran after the gentleman. The driver ducked down and Shag, well, she just waited for more chicken.

Slugger quickly caught up to the running dude, jumped on him, and, with his size and weight, easily knocked him to the ground. The dude kicked at the Boxer trying to push him away, but Slugger grabbed his leg and bit hard with those glistening sharp canines of his. The man let go of the paper bag and out came some bundles of cash and Slugger grabbed for the bag of money. Shag barked and scratched at the window wanting to get in on the action. The driver pulled out his cell phone as the apparent thief struggled to his feet and reached for the bag of money, but Slugger scrunched up his snout and showed the thief his big, sharp, clean white canines. Shag howled. The robber backed off in fear and ran for dear life.

"Great boy!" cheered the driver as he let Shag out of the car. A restaurant employee came outside and picked up the paper bag and loose cash. "I saw him through the window, some dog you got there."

"He's his own boss."

Slugger ran down the street and Shag followed.

The driver called after them, "You guys are welcome to ride anytime!"

THAT NIGHT

Slugger and Shag ambled back over territory they crossed over that day. Their heads hanging listlessly, bodies ready to collapse, Shag heard something alongside the walkway. She stopped. Slugger stopped. There, in the bushes, a blue-feathered parakeet! Shag approached and sniffed at it: the parakeet didn't move, but it tweeted. Shag reached for it and carefully took it into her mouth. The tired, lost parakeet didn't protest. Shag, carefully, with her soft mouth, strolled on down the walk with the little bird. Soon, she found herself at the old wood-framed house and up the front steps she bound. She looked around; where could she leave the bird?

Shag saw the birdcage sitting on the porch swing, the door still open, and stuck her snout into the opening releasing the parakeet. It chirped, twiddled, and twisted it's head left and right, and then uttered these words in a shrill voice: "Thank you, thank you, thank you, cheep, cheep, cheep."

"You're welcome," replied Shag and nodded his head.

At that, the young lady came out of her house and both hands went to her astonished mouth, "What? Why it's Josephine, my… my Josephine…where is Jen…"

Shag turned away to see Slugger approaching with a yellow-feathered parakeet softly gripped in *his* mouth.

"Oh my! Jennifer!"

Slugger carried the strange bird to the lady and she carefully took it from him.

"Why thank you. You dogs are wonderful. You, you're Slugger, and you, you're Shag, I remember."

"Oh, no ma'am, her name is Mophead," corrected Slugger.

"Mophead, well I'll be a…"

"My name's not 'Mophead,'" protested Shag.

"Yes you are."

"No, I'm not."

That night, in the late evening, not much before midnight, the Wheaten Terrier and the Boxer arrived back home, crawled under the fence, and found fresh water and bowls of food waiting for them. This had been one adventurous day. Maybe tomorrow there would be some more fun in the offing.

THE END

Josephine and Jennifer, Home Again

Blue, a Siberian Husky

11. A Boy And His Dog
By Don Kirk

"**H**ey Blue, good morning," said Billy sweetly to a fetching black-and-white four-year-old Siberian Husky lying snuggled up to him in his twin bed. Billy's bedclothes lay all over the floor in a tiny, ship's-quarters-like bedroom. The boy and his dog "Blue," sitting face-to-face, stared into little Billy's eyes waiting for signs of life. When the boy opened his sand-filled eyes, Blue licked his face with a loving coat of slobber.

"Ahhh, Blue, I'm going to have to wash my face."

Billy slid out of bed, Blue stood up, shook herself, and jumped off in a big billowing bounce of excitement. Billy reached under the bed, opened a drawer, and pulled out a T-shirt with a picture of Jack Sparrow and the words, "Nobody move! I dropped me brain!" Billy was six years old with blond hair and pearly-white skin. And the walls of his little wood-paneled room were covered with *Pirates of the Caribbean* movie posters and pirate collectables of all sorts. And threw a small window, a view of a snow-capped mountain far off in the distance; this was Colorado Springs, Colorado.

The always cheerful husky—face and legs bright white, black hair mixed with white in a two-layered coat, and light-blue, piercing eyes—sat at Billy's feet waiting for the next move. Blue, a female, twenty inches at the shoulders, weighing in at thirty-five pounds, displayed a nice narrow waist like more Homo sapiens should strive for. The young boy grabbed his orange tennis shoes with yellow laces and ran down a flight of narrow stairs to the first floor. Blue leaped past him, hitting the kitchen floor before Billy could, and immediately probed her doggie bowl: nothing appetizing so Blue looked up at Billy and stared into his eyes looking for that generous heart and soul. And sure enough, Billy poured Blue a cup of dry dog food, added a touch of fresh human sustenance, grabbed his blue *Sky Sox* baseball cap, and ran out the kitchen door. Blue said to herself "forget the grub" and ran out after Billy before he could close the door.

Billy pulled a worn out, faded-red *Radio Flyer* wagon with wood-slat sides out of the garage as Blue watched. He worked rather laboriously to strap an also red service-dog vest onto her, trying his best to adjust the size to fit Blue comfortably. Billy's father had brought the vest home, having found it in a thrift store. "Might come in handy some day," he thought.

"Blue, go get your leash, go get it, girl."

Blue ran off and soon returned with a deep red, dog leash.

"Good girl! We got a match."

Billy took the leash, hooked it to the top of the harness, and attached it to the front of the wagon handle. He tied it with two half hitches, a type of knot he learned from his father, a sailor of sailboats in competitions. "The double half hitch wouldn't come loose in a million years," declared Billy who hooked the other end of the leash to Blue who was noticeably curious about what was transpiring and wanted to join in the fun. She began to express the declaration "Oh boy, we're going for a walk!" with lively, bouncy body movements. Finally, Billy managed to attach the leash and jump into the little wagon, not exactly made for hauling people, built more for potted plants and teddy bears.

Blue pulled on the red wagon but she did so in every direction trying to figure out what the contraption attached to her was all about. Billy yelled, "Mush!" Blue pulled, but instead of moving forward, she turned in circles and bounced and kicked up her heels. Not surprisingly, the wagon turned over and Billy rolled out of the wagon. Just then a mud-covered red Jeep Wrangler entered the driveway and Billy's father jumped out.

"Son, you alright? What are you doing?"

"Did everyone see that because I will not be doing it again," insisted Billy.

"Jack Sparrow in the *Pirates*?"

"Yeah, Dad, I'm fine. I want to teach Blue how to pull a sled."

"Well, that's fine son, but that wagon turns over too easily. You need a real sled, it's much wider."

"There's no snow, Dad, this is summertime."

"I know, son. Here, come in the house, we'll figure something out."

Billy's dad detached Blue from the wagon, "Hey, a double half-hitch! Very good, son."

"Thanks, Dad."

Back in the house, Billy jumped on the back of Blue causing her to turn back and grab him by the arm. Billy made her go for his other arm, and Blue bit, but it was a very light, soft bite. Just playing, she gave a slow, playful wag of her tail. Billy jumped on her again and Blue tried to shake him off. She was having fun and so was Billy. It would probably be called roughhousing, but they both loved it. Billy didn't have a brother to play with and his mother left them for parts unknown. Just he, his dad, and their pretty, wolf-like dog, Blue, together in Colorado.

"All right boys and girls, its time for breakfast."

Blue was first to the table.

"You know, Dad, she follows me wherever I go. She follows me into whatever room I'm in and lies at my feet and even blocks the front door so I can't escape without her knowing it..."

' "And she comes to you when you put your shoes on," said Dad.

"She don't even need the shoe cue; I quietly put my socks on in another room at the other end of the house and she comes a runnin'...even when I'm upstairs!"

"Yes son, now eat your bacon and eggs."

At that, Blue did a yodeling howl as if trying to sing.

"Don't feed her at the table, son."

"No sir."

That evening Billy—his dog Blue lying in bed beside him—was reading a pirate novel out loud: *Treasure Island* by Robert Lewis Stevenson. The Siberian husky, with her soul-searching eyes, peered intently at him as if actually understanding the words.

"Just before him, Tom lay motionless up on the sword, 'I'm poor Ben Gunn, I am. Marooned three years agone, and lived on goats since then.'"

Blue tilted her head quizzically one-way and then the other.

"Well, it was written a long time ago, Blue. Here, girl, you'll get it: 'I can't have these colors, Mr. Hands, and, by your leave, I'll strike them!'"

Blue rolled over onto her submissive, belly-up position and Billy raised his arm and pointed to the ceiling, "Take a cutlass, him that dares, and I'll see the color of his inside, crutch and all, before that pipe's empty!"

The husky jumped up and off the bed and bound down the stairs, passing Dad on his way up. Dad entered Billy's room and announced, "Time for bed, son."

Little Billy peered out of his bedroom window, "Dad, the moon, it's got a cut out of it."

"Not a cut, that's the shadow of the Earth, son."

"Looks like something has taken a bite out of the moon."

"It won't be long now," said Dad. "It's soon to be a full moon with no bite at all. Just a few more days."

At that, Blue began to howl from downstairs.

"Her breed is not a very distant descendant of the wolf," added Dad.

"I know. She doesn't bark, but she sure can howl at the moon."

A week later, on a nice warm Saturday morning, the three of them were headed west into the mountains looking for a little leftover snow from last winter. Sitting in the *Jeep Wrangler*, Blue hung her head out the rear window trying to snare some riveting scents with her focused nostrils. The Jeep left a paved highway onto a dirt road that wound around the edge of a hillside and entered a forested mountain range. Arriving at the base of Pike's Peak, Blue, the first out of the jeep, ran into the slender, towering, white aspens with their black scuff marks all over their trunks and light green foliage fluttering high in the tree canopies.

"He'll come back won't he, son?"

"Yeah Dad, but he loves to hunt."

"I know that, but will he come…"

"He knows where the Jeep is—and I can whistle for him."

"Show me."

Billy puckered his lips and out came a weak, garbled whistle. But, right quick, here came Blue bounding out of the woods at full tilt.

"See, Dad."

"Well I'll be a son-of-a…well son, let's go for a walk. Grab your backpack. Got water?"

"Yeah, Dad."

Dad and Billy followed a trail through the woods as Blue ran among the Aspens, her nose twitching wildly. For her, this was heaven on Earth.

"Dad, look, I see some snow up ahead!"

At that, a heavy rustling in the woods and Dad and Billy could see some bushes moving ever so slightly, and there, not too distant, standing on all four legs, was a big black bear! It opened its mouth and appeared hungry.

"My, God, back son!"

The bear kept walking forward slowly, then stopped, and stood up on its hind legs.

"Run son, run!"

Billy did just that as his father's face turned ashen. That black bear meant harm; he was sure of it. In fact, Dad thought he could hear the creature's rumbling stomach pangs. He could also hear his son running down the leaf-covered forest-floor path, but he kept his eyes fixed on the bear. What move was he—or the bear—going to make next?

Out of the blue came Blue, and with front legs and hind legs extended, head down low, he yelped frantically at the black bear but didn't approach the gigantic creature, a smart move. The bear dropped back down on all fours, turned away, and sauntered off.

Blood flowed back into Dad's face, his hands, and all other parts of his bleached-white body.

Blue turned away and ran down the path after Billy. Dad followed but soon pulled up short, not knowing where they had gone, and

"What do I hear?"

no longer seeing—or hearing—any sign of his son or the husky.

Billy climbed quickly and radically up a precarious pile of boulders and turned to see if the bear was following, but no sign of anything moving except for a few wandering possum, gophers, jackrabbits, chipmunks, a few athletic squirrels, and curious fawns scampering about. All great targets for the independent-thinking

Blue; she might never again return to Billy. Then unexpectedly, after another long-reaching step upward, Billy slipped and fell backward from the rock. Falling downward, he bounced off several rocks on the way down. Eventually he hit the tundra and his red backpack followed him shortly thereafter. Billy grabbed his twisted ankle, and said a word he shouldn't. The aspen trees trembled.

The rustling Aspen leaves from a light breeze was all Billy could hear. No animal or bird sounds, and no Dad calling out for him.

Then, out of the blue, there she was: Blue! Billy's face brightened as his loving dog came up to him with tail wagging and body twisting and turning like an earthworm saddled with a sticky cocklebur. He licked Billy's hope-filled face.

"Blue, so glad to see you. I'm hurt, I need you."

Blue yipped and howled like a wolf, calling out for help. No reply from Billy's father. Billy tried to get up, but his ankle was twisted like a New York pretzel; he dropped back down. It smarted something fierce.

"Blue, I have an idea," said Billy as he rolled onto his backpack, "Here girl."

Blue reached forward and grabbed the shoulder strap with his mouth and pulled, but the backpack didn't move very far—only a few inches. The lame boy zipped open his pack, pulled out a dog leash, and snapped it to Blue using a rolling hitch knot—*three* half hitches—to tie the other end to one of the backpack's shoulder straps.

"Mush, girl, mush."

Blue had an inquiring look, "Huh, what?"

"Pull girl, pull."

Blue understood that word and tugged and pulled and pulled some more with Billy holding on tightly. Blue clearly comfortable pulling. The backpack moved a few inches, and then a few feet. Luckily, they were working their way down hill—making the move much easier—but there was still no sign of Dad. Had the bear caught him and devoured his carcass for a splendid afternoon meal?

After some distance tugging, Blue stopped and Billy pulled out a bottle of water to quench his, and Blue's, thirst. Getting dark, and a full moon already high in the sky, the boy and dog found a pile of boulders to shield them from the wind. Blue howled at that moon, a real mystery as to why. The mountain air was also turning quite cool, no mystery there. But on hearing rustling in the woods, Blue's long, pointed ears, standing-tall, turned left and then right, each in different directions at once. The aspens trembled and quaked. This was getting downright scary. The blond-headed Billy and the black-and-white Blue had never spent a cold, outdoor night at a 6,700-foot elevation.

Blue circled the area, marked it, grabbed a few twigs with her snout, and carefully piled them up. She then went to Billy and scratched at his backpack.

"What do you want, girl, you hungry?"

Billy dug into his backpack and came up with a bundle of matches. "Wow! I get it, Blue! You want me to make a fire."

Blue threw a soft, yodeling howl.

"I need lots of dry leaves and twigs. Go get some, girl."

The full moon gave them plenty of shadow-filled light as Blue collected leaves and small limbs.

"Now where be me knife, Blue?"

Blue went to the backpack and pushed on it with his muzzle. Billy pulled his bone-handled *Pirates Of The Caribbean* knife from its sheath, took a match, and struck the blade. The match head flamed up. Billy put the match to the leaves, but they didn't catch fire. He tried several more times and was running low on matches. Billy then found a school notebook in his bag scribbled with new assignments for school, but using it here was more important. The ruled pages with hand-written notes did the trick; there was white smoke and a few teeny-weeny orange flames…that grew, and grew. They had a fire! But it would take a whole lot of timber to keep it going for a whole night's warmth. Blue seemed to know that and started scratching at the dirt next to the large boulders, and she dug, and dug some more, shooting dirt rearward. She was digging herself a trench under the rocks for a warm, cozy night. Once finished, she lay down in it, then looked back at Billy, walked over to him, and with his help, pulled him over to the hole, and rolled him into it. The exhausted husky lay down next to Billy, snuggled up close to him, and once again lovingly licked Billy's face. It seemed like she was trying to say, "Good night, sweet dreams."

During the long night, Blue coughed a few times and licked at Billy's injured ankle, and there was a lot of rustling brush that kept Blue's nose twitching and her eyes, with fully dilated pupils, on constant watch.

"It's okay, Blue, we're going to make it; bears don't like dogs, at least I don't think so."

Blue gave out a mysterious moan and squeal. What she was trying to say was anybody's guess. She jumped up and looked into the sky. Without a hint of forewarning, there was a distant thunderclap and a flash of blazingly bright light! Blue spun on her hind legs and appeared agitated. The thunder was getting louder, the wind picking up, and the frightened aspen leaves began to speak. Billy and Blue felt they were 'up a tree,' to be tormented by unwelcome weather.

"Come here, Blue, it's just lightning," asserted Billy.

Blue came and lay down beside Billy as the six-year-old boy grabbed the backpack and pulled out a yellow slicker. He carefully threw it over the both of them and they cuddled up tight. It wasn't clear who was comforting whom.

"'All hands to the boats!' a Captain Jack Sparrow quote," said Billy to Blue, "but if there aren't any boats, what then?"

Blued whimpered.

Some very wet rain fell, but it was light and didn't last.

After a few hours, the sun began to peek through the grey mist and cheery aspen leaves and the stratocumulus clouds went all rippling orange and then brilliantly red…and then faded away into a deep blue wonderment. Blue stood up, yawned and stretched, first the front legs and then the hind legs.

"We made it, Blue," said Billy, his breath condensing into tiny

"I'm sure glad you came with me, Blue."

water droplets, "This was either brilliance or insanity!"

Blue roared.

"It's amazing how often those two traits coincide," continued Billy, quoting another line from a *Pirates of the Caribbean* movie. "I'm sure glad you came with me."

Blue bellowed.

"It was an adventure all right, but we're going to have to get going. I hope Dad is okay," announced Billy, "Help me up, girl."

And that's just what that Siberian husky did, pulling at Billy's shirt, but then she began to howl and howl some more, quite not like her, except under last night's full moon.

"Stop it Blue, you'll get the bears looking for us."

Blue kept howling.

All of a sudden, Billy heard something, or someone, calling out: "Billy, where are you? Billy…Billy!"

At that familiar voice, Blue ran off down the hill.

Back home, Billy sat in his bedroom with a cast on his leg, "My *Jack Sparrow Pirate Cane* is going to come in handy."

Blue whimpered with joy, her tail curled up over her backside exposing the white on the underside of her tail.

"Sorry, I can't take you for a walk."

Blue jumped on the bed next to Billy.

"We had a swashbuckling adventure, didn't we mate?"

Blue tilted her head up and howled. Young Billy grabbed his latest pirate paperback, opened it, and began to read,

"Not all treasure is silver and gold, mate."

THE END

Neighborly, a Dachshund

12. Dog Gone It!
By Don Kirk

"**I**'m not ever holding you again; my good neighbor can go to Hades next time. I have enough trouble with my wife Maybelline. Want this, want that, want attention, and want what's in my bank account. Your name 'Neighborly,' how can that be? You're as friendly as a Golden Retriever after two glasses of wine, not even! You're always, in a meanly manner, barking at me across the chain-link fence."

The little, short-legged, red-haired Dachshund looked up at me all quizzical like. He was a good looking, sweet, boot-scraper-looking hound dog no more than twenty-five pounds but two-dogs long and his long snout could reach into the next state.

I was asked to keep him for the weekend while my neighbor flew to Las Vegas to make a few bucks.

"Okay, dog, what do you want for lunch? A chocolate candy bar? Oh, that's right, chocolate is poisonous to dogs…so all the better. Maybe if I pepper your dog food with cayenne? Oh, don't look at me that way, twisting your head sideways and raising your ears high. Hot pepper would be a great addition, help you loose weight by eating less."

Neighborly snapped back at me.

"Somebody must have used a block & tackle pulley; you couldn't hardly fit in a stretch limousine. Maybe that broomstick you ate is still in there. Okay, lets take you for a walk sos you can relieve yourself somewheres else 'sides my yard."

Neighborly looked up at me with his big black eyeballs focused intently on me. I attached the six-foot leash and off we went. I had taken my neighbor to the airport and he left Neighborly with me for just the weekend; that's all it was to be. And now, on a walk with

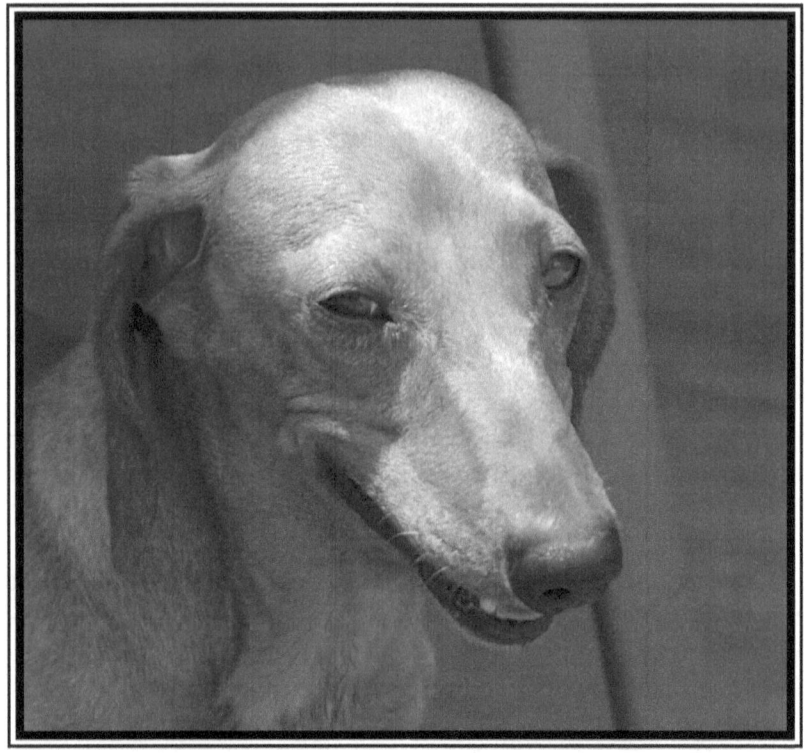

"I won't pardon you and that's that."

the wiener dog pulling to beat the band, he unexpectedly came to a halt to sniff in someone's flower garden. He then started to dig.

"Get out of there, dog. This ain't your property."

Neighborly backed off and then pulled himself into the street—and was barely missed by a passing car.

"My neighbor will kill me if you get hurt," I screamed. "Get back to the house and behave. This weekend I'm the boss, you stubborn-as-a-mule weenie dog!"

Neighborly came to a halt, pulled on his leash, and refused to budge.

"Damn, dog, the next time we go for a walk it's only going to be you a-doin' the walkin'. You kin git your exercise just as well if I hang you on your leash out my car window and let you run with

only your hind legs a-touchin' the pavement."
Neighborly barked and showed his canines.

Eventually I led the unheeding, smooth-haired, badger dog back to my house, but he wasted no time digging my yard up looking for small prey.

"There ain't no prairie dogs or cats 'round cheer. Get! Enough already! I'm a gonna replace your powdered flea medicine with talcum powder a-hoping you'll scratch yourself to death."

Neighborly backed out of the hole, raised his leg, and peed on my leg...and I was wearing shorts.

"Damn! You're a-stayin' out cheer all weekend a-far from me."

But then Neighborly kept barking at every stranger that passed on the sidewalk, at every passing car, at every airplane, and he was especially loud screaming murder at the delivery trucks.

"Alright, Neighborly, you're a-comin' in the house with me. I want you to settle down. Weeze got a whole weekend to go; this here is only Friday."

Neighborly followed me through the kitchen doorway and began to sniff about the house...and mark the new territory: every corner of every blasted room!

"You're gonna get something other than water in your water bowl. If you don't behave you're gonna get carbonated water made with laughing gas."

Neighborly sat back on his hind legs and tried to crack a grin on his resentful face. I thought he was saying to me, "You want me to laugh myself to death, don't you?" And so I replied, "You got that right, Neighborly boy." At that, he immediately stood up, turned around, and farted in my face!

Hours went by. I cleaned up the urine mess. The little dog seemed awfully quiet. He wasn't making a sound, well, he wasn't near me, no longer at my feet, while I read a book about dogs: how to get rid of them. I got up to look for him and found a pillow on my bed all torn apart with acres of feathers strewn about. Then I noticed the blanket—my mother's hand-sewn quilt all balled up with the rambunctious Dachshund wrapped up in it. This was the last straw!

"I'm cutting off your tail so I kin use it as a quill pen to give to my wife since she so loves dogs. It was her idea for me to take you for the weekend knowing full well she'd be at work most of the time. Wait'll she sees what you've done. Maybe she'll ask for a dog-paw stamp made from one of your feet."

Neighborly continued to tunnel under the blanket seemingly unconcerned.

"I know you heard what I said, just my deep angry voice should have given you the message; now get down off my bed, dog!"

Neighborly quickly jumped down.

"What's this? You left dirt and dog hair a-plenty all over my nice clean sheets, but I know exactly how to stop that from happening again. I'm going to bath you in a gallon of Elmer's white glue— that should stop your shedding right quick."

Neighborly turned back as he was leaving the room and he whimpered, putting his body belly down and head to the floor between his legs, his eyes sitting high in their almond-shaped sockets.

"Don't give me them eyes; I won't pardon you and that's that."

Neighborly made another innocent whining sound as if to beg for forgiveness and quickly turned over on his back.

"Alright, enough, my wife will be home soon. You can entertain her with your shenanigans. I don't know what she's a-goin' to have for dinner, but you'd make one hell of a good two-foot-long sausage in my barbecue pit! Might even have enough for the neighbors."

Neighborly's eyes dropped and his mouth closed, concerned.

A bit later, the Dachshund was lying quietly in the living room at the foot of my recliner when I got up and accidently stepped on a front paw; a painful yelp came forth.

"Oops, Neighborly, I'm so sorry, I didn't mean to step on you. I hope you'll forgive me."

Neighborly jumped up and backed off, keeping some distance from me.

"Sorry, Boy, it's okay, I won't hurt..."

The strange, as-long-as-a-yardstick, creature sat down and rolled over on his back to expose his stomach. I kneeled down to pet him. "Okay, it's okay, what do you want for dinner? To appease you for my ill will toward you, I thought I'd give you a micro-waved cat for dinner. No, just kidding. Maybe you would prefer a gopher or groundhog? I've decided I won't make you walk over a carpet of cockleburs and then wipe your feet with alcohol. I promise, I won't. That would be too much work for me anyway."

Neighborly turned back over, jumped up, and tried to kiss my face. Okay, enough, I don't know if you've had your shots. Maybe you just want me to throw up so you can get some of the meal I last ate. Neighborly let out a soft bark, a loving bark, if there is such a thing. He then heard a sound outside, barked wildly, and ran to the kitchen door. I opened the door and out Neighborly ran. He hurried around to the backside of the carport and moments later came to me with a white-faced, pink-nosed opossum in his jaw. I really didn't want to see our neighborhood opossums killed; they were good at taking down some insects, snails, and slugs, but he didn't know that, just wanted to please me. He laid the critter down in front of me and turned and ran into the front yard. A car drove up. It was my wife.

"Ahh, Maybelline, maybe the rest of our weekend won't be so thrilling."

"Why here, Dear, I bought a tennis ball for Neighborly; he'll love to chase it."

"Good thing we don't have a cat around to have fun with."

"Honey, why is the yard all dug up?"

THE END

Mr. Tucker, a Pug

13. A Courtroom Case
By Don Kirk

"This is a trial by judge. We don't have a jury so get on with it gentlemen."

The lawyer for the defense stood up, "Did the Pattersons file a report? File an insurance claim? Do they have any security cameras? Motion sensor lights? Security service? Alarm monitoring?"

"No, Your Honor, none of those things," replied prosecution attorney Larry Lafferty, "but the owners found the back window shattered."

The defendant's attorney, Walter Schultz, continued, "The Pattersons may have destroyed key evidence by entering the house to make the phone call to the police. And did they touch anything?"

"I don't know, Your Honor," replied Mr. Lafferty.

"Then you don't have a case," said the judge as he picked up his gavel.

"Wait, Your Honor, the owners, Mr. and Mrs. Patterson feel violated, have had sleepless nights, boarded up all their back windows, afraid when they're at home, afraid when they're gone… they've even gone out looking for a gun to purchase."

"Okay, Mr. Lafferty, you may present your case. You've every right to do that."

"Thank you, Your Honor. I'd like to question the accused."

"Mr. Schultz, the defendant please, sir," requested Judge John Parker of the Bedlam County District Court.

The man on trial, David Dudley, stood up from the defendant's table, walked over, and entered the witness box.

"Please stand."

Mr. Dudley stood. The court clerk held out a bible and Dudley placed his hand on it. "Do you solemnly swear that you will tell the truth, the whole truth, and nothing but the truth?"

"Uh, yes, sure, reckon so."

Dudley took a seat.

The prosecution attorney rose from behind the plaintiff's table and stood at the podium where he could face the accused to ask him a few questions.

"You, sir, say you were never in this house at 316 Golden Place?"

"I was not."

"Then how do you explain the muddy footprints and broken rear window…"

"Weren't me. I took nothing from that there house."

"Didn't say you did. Burglary doesn't require a theft, just unauthorized breaking and entering. Did you *enter* the Patterson home?"

"No sir, 'course not, I would not, no way…"

"That's all, he's yours, Mr. Schultz, said Larry Lafferty."

The attorney for the defense got up to question his client.

"Have you ever been in the Patterson home?"

"Why, hell no, not never."

"That's all, Mr. Dudley, you can step down," said Schultz.

The accused returned to the defense table.

"Is that all Mr. Schultz?" asked Judge Parker.

"Yes sir, Judge."

Walter Schultz returned to the defense table, sat down, and glanced at Dudley with a slight upward turn of his mouth. He felt confident in a not guilty verdict.

"Mr. Lafferty, is there any evidence you wish to present before I rule in this case?"

Mr. Lafferty quickly stood up, "Your Honor, we have an expert witness who can testify as to whom was in the house. He has a special ability and peculiar knowledge acquired from practical experience."

"Is this the Mr. Tucker Patterson listed on the docket?"

"Yes, Your Honor."

"Bring him in."

The double doors at the back of the courtroom opened and a man with a leash brought in a small dog: a Pug that stood less than a foot tall and weighed in at about sixteen pounds. He wore a light-brown coat and presented an all-black wrinkled up, short-muzzled face with huge, bulging, brown eyes. The few spectators in the gallery turned around to look.

"What's this?" asked the judge of the court clerk.

"This is the prosecution's witness, Your Honor."

The Defense attorney stood up abruptly again, "This is unprecedented, Your Honor!"

"Sit down Mr. Schultz," declared the Judge. "Lets see what they have to say."

The handler and Pug came through the bi-fold doors of the low wall that separates the court from the spectator's seating. The handler motioned with his hands and said "up" and the dog jumped up on the seat in the testimony box, turned around, and sat quietly in a seated position.

"Your kidding right?" questioned the Judge.

"No, Your Honor, we're serious, this witness will show that David Dudley was at the Patterson household."

"Witness?"

"Yes, Your Honor."

"Then proceed. This better be good."

The court clerk spoke to the dog, " state your name for the record."

Everyone in the gallery looked at each other quite flabbergasted. The handler looked to the dog and repeated the request, "Mr. Tucker, state your name." The Pug looked directly at the handler, stood on all fours, and released two quick, soft barks. Everyone's eyes protruded, looking a lot like the Pugs own bulging eyeballs.

"I'll try to interpret his barks," said the Handler. "His name is Mr. Tucker and he's owned by Mr. and Mrs. Patterson of the house in question."

The court clerk came forward and held the bible in front of the compact-bodied toy dog with his black, floppy ears and the always concerned-looking flat-as-a-pancake face. Mr. Tucker Patterson immediately put his right paw on the bible. Everyone in the courtroom was fixed on Mr. Tucker…simply awestruck.

"Do you solemnly swear to tell the truth and nothing but…"

Mr. Schultz jumped up in protest, "This is ridiculous!"

"Your Honor," interceded Lafferty, "if you let Mr. Tucker move about the room he will use his very sensitive nose—a thousand times stronger than a human's—to sniff out the person in the courtroom who was in the Patterson house illegally."

"Your Honor, this is laughable."

"What do you say we let the dog speak for himself," declared Lafferty. The handler raised a hand palm down, "Mr. Tucker, find him."

Tucker jumped down from the witness chair and moved about the courtroom going from person to person, first sniffing at their feet and then sniffing up a leg. The Pug moved under the table of both the prosecution and defense—even checked out the bailiff—but when he got to David Dudley, he unexpectedly barked and took a fearful step back. Dudley pushed his chair back and stood up alarmed. The people sitting in the gallery raised their eyebrows and a low murmur could be heard in the courtroom.

"Here, boy, come here," called out the handler.

Walter Schultz stood up, "Your Honor, this means nothing. This dog, he looks, well, he clearly can understand hand signals. How do you know the handler didn't direct the Pug to bark at the accused?"

The prosecution attorney, Lafferty jumped to his feet, "Your honor, he did no such thing!"

"Maybe Mr. Dudley got a food snack from the vending machine in the hallway."

Lafferty turned to the gallery: "Anyone else here get a snack from the vending machine?"

Several people raised their hand including the bailiff.

"So why did Tucker bark only at the accused?" asked Mr. Lafferty.

There's no response from anyone in the courtroom.

"I rest my case."

"This proves nothing," declared Mr. Schultz. "The prosecution has no modicum of proof. Your Honor, sidebar?

"Mr. Tucker, state your name."

"Approach." The judge motioned with both hands like a dog owner would do to get his canine to come.

Both Lafferty and Schultz approached and talked softly with the Judge.

"Mr. Schultz, you may bring me Mr. Dudley's shoes."

Walter Schultz had the defendant slide his chair back and remove his shoes. He then took the shoes to the bench.

"Your Honor, look, there is cheese in the treads of the sole of one of his tennis shoes. What dog would ignore that?"

"He's got a point, Mr. Lafferty," said Judge Parker, "Step back."

Schultz returned to his table and handed the shoes back to his client.

"But, Your Honor," protested the prosecutor.

"The curiously sniffing dog doesn't prove anything," answered the judge. "Is this all you have? Any other witnesses? Does your dog have any more to say?"

The gallery snickered.

"No, Your Honor, no more witnesses, but I have Defense Exhibits A through E." Mr. Lafferty turned to the assistant at the plaintiff's table and she produced some photos and a plaster cast of a dog's mouth. Mr. Lafferty took it from her. "May I approach?"

Judge Parker motioned him forward.

"Your Honor, this is a casting of Tucker's jowls, both upper and lower teeth, and this is a photo of bite marks found on the defendant's right lower arm when he was picked up by the police. The spacing of the canines and fangs are a close match. We'd like to enter these in evidence."

"So ordered."

"As you can see, the teeth markings on David Dudley's forearm are close to that of Tucker's bite pattern."

"Close? Not sufficient proof. Any other evidence, Mr. Lafferty?"

"Yes sir, Exhibits C, D, and E. First, we have a golf club. Mr. Dudley tried to fend off the Pug with this three-iron he found in the entryway of the Patterson residence. The intruder kindly left his fingerprints on the club. We also have a photo of Mr. Tucker's bruise from the impact on his withers. And finally, Exhibit 'E', a piece of his pant leg torn off by Tucker."

"Why, it seems, Mr. Lafferty, you have plenty of evidence to convict David Dudley. Anything further you have to say, Mr. Schultz?"

"Your Honor, this evidence is not admissible. The cast is far from conclusive, the fingerprint is only a two-point match, and the piece of cloth supposedly from his pant leg can be demonstrated as having come from any pair of jeans of the same brand. The Patterson family didn't find anything missing that could be traced to my client."

"Is this true counselor?"

"Yes, Your Honor."

"Do you have any other evidence, Mr. Lafferty?"

"No sir."

"Then the defendant is free to go and court is adjourned."

Dudley jumped in joy, hugged Walter Schultz, shook his hand forcefully, and spoke breathlessly, "Thank you, thank you, thank you!"

But as the dog handler led Mr. Tucker past the Defense table, the Pug pulled to the end of his leash and attacked David Dudley, grabbing his leg. Dudley screamed, "Get that damn dog off me! He ain't a-bitin' me agin."

The prosecution and the judge heard that perspicuous statement. There was a moment of silence among all those in the courtroom.

The dog handler called out, "Tucker, stop, come here!" Mr. Tucker released Dudley's leg and returned to the handler.

"So, Dudley, you've seen this dog before?" asked the judge.

"Hell no, no sir, not me, I meant…I…to say I…"

"Cuff him bailiff," commanded the judge.

"That dumb-ass dog's gonna die!" screamed Dudley.

"Turn around," demanded the bailiff.

Dudley turned but kept on ranting, "I'm gonna kill that little rat."

"Tucker doesn't much like rats either," replied Larry Lafferty.

THE END

Yorkie, a Yorkshire Terrier

14. Scene Three, Take One

By Don Kirk

"Everyone on their marks?"

One actor stepped a foot to the left; another looked down at a red camera tape "T" mark on the floor where he was to place his feet.

"Ready? Roll sound."

"Sound."

"Roll camera."

"Camera."

"Scene One, Take One." The First AC held his camera slate in front of the actors and snapped the clapper shut.

"Action!" called out the director.

The actors, Mrs. Marple and Professor Flynn, began their scripted performance. But all eyes, including the crew, were on Yorkie, a Yorkshire terrier sitting on a high chair at a kitchen island covered with food servings, two dinner plates, napkins, and a cereal bowl. The cute terrier placed her paws on the counter top and stared at a bowl of tandalizing dog food.

"Umm, this is great!" said Professor Flynn as he took a bite of his chicken salad sandwich.

"Yorkie, it's okay, you can eat now," said Mrs. Marple to the terrier.

The pretty, long-haired, grey and white terrier with a golden-brown snout, let out a soft bark and took a bite of her food. She scarfed down a few morsels.

"How was that?" asked Mrs. Marple of the dog. "You like it?"

Yorkie let out another bark, this louder and more thrilling.

Off camera stood the dog trainer, Johnny Dumont using hand signals to direct Yorkie as to what to do next.

As the camera rolled, the thirty-second commercial continued:

"Yorkie, go get me your *Cougar's*," ordered the professor.

Yorkie jumped off her high stool and the camera followed as she hurried to the corner of the kitchen, opened a pantry door with her nose, and drug out the dog food packet. She pulled it over to the professor who then picked it up to show it to the camera.

"Yorkie loves *Cougar's Chicken and Rice*. The finest natural ingredients enhanced with vitamins and minerals. He'll do most anything for a fully satisfying meal."

The Yorkshire terrier barked in agreement.

"Okay, cut! Good," asserted the director. "We got the wide shot. Now move in for a medium of the professor selling the product and then a closeup of Yorkie eating her plate of *Cougar's*."

The crew began a frantic move for the next set up: dollying the camera into the medium shot, resetting some lights, scrims, colored gels, and flags, while the makeup lady did some touch up work on Professor Flynn. Those not in the shot stepped back out of the scene for a coffee break. The canine handler called Yorkie off the set and gave her a drink, some treats, and a light brushing.

"Good girl, you did great, but we're not done yet, much more to do before you get a raise," said Johnny Dumont. "You're talking-dog parts are yet to come." Johnny gave Yorkie the hand signal to lie down and stay. She did so smartly. The trainer made his way through the commotion to the director, Simon James, a beefy man of short stature but manifesting a big commanding presence.

"Great job, no serious delays yet," said Simon, happily. "Your dog's doing great."

"I want to ask you about the talking-dog shot," said Johnny.

"It'll be our next setup. The off-screen actors can retire. The dog's eye direction: to look left, right, up, or down. Are you clear on which way the dog is to look on each scripted line?" asked the director.

"Yes sir."

"As you know, I'm counting on Yorkie to actually mouth her

lines. We're not going to do any of that computer graphics stuff; it has always looked fake to me and our audience knows its computer enhanced. This will blow the ad agency away."

"I'm sure; might even get Yorkie some more gigs."

"It will for sure."

Yorkie returned to the set and jumped up on her bar chair at the canine handler's command.

"Everyone ready? I'll ask the actor's questions. We've already got speaking close-ups in the can," declared Director James. "Close on Yorkie. No sound here. Roll camera." James looked squarely at the dog's soft brown eyes. "Little Miss Yorkie, what do you think about *Cougar's*?"

"Uum, good," replied Yorkie, barely moving her jowls.

"Cut, that's a take. He moved his lips just right. Love it. Roll camera. "Little Miss, is *Cougar's* nutritious?" Johnny gave the Yorkie a hand signal.

"*Cougar's* is very nutritious. I love the barley and oatmeal."

"Cut. Splendid mouth movements! The dog is doing great. I even think she smiles a bit. Love it."

"Johnny, have him looking at the professor," commanded Simon James. The handler, still having the dog's full attention, pointed to the left. "Roll camera. Little Miss, is *Cougar's* good for you?"

"Why certainly. Strong bones and teeth." Yorkie grinned showing her front teeth and canines and continued, "Healthy garden vegetables, whole peas, potatoes, carrots and more."

"Cut. Fantastic! Amazing, he's mouthing the words quite perfectly. Now lets…"

"Sir, Mr. James," called out the sound mixer. "Shouldn't we record the dog's dialogue?"

"Huh?"

"Yorkie is actually speaking out loud."

"Huh, what…I…wait, I did hear dialogue…I…I just thought it was Continuity speaking."

"No sir, Darlene didn't say a word."

The director looked to Darlene, the script girl sitting in a chair near the director's red canvas folding chair. She shook her head.

"No?"

"No sir."

"This can't be! Dog's can't talk!"

"Tell Yorkie that," said the professor.

Simon James looked back to the Yorkshire Terrier who was still sitting quietly at the kitchen counter, facing her plate of dog food.

"I don't…roll sound!"

The sound mixer turned a knob to 'Record' and as the director repeated his questions, Yorkie repeated her verbal responses.

"Cut! This is amazing." All the film crew's eyes were fixed on the cute little dog with an uncanny ability. They all knew a dog has the intelligence of a two to three-year-old human child and thus could probably speak if they only had a voice box…

"Makeup! I need some eye shadow," demanded Yorkie.

At that, everyone's eyelids retreated. Makeup hurried into the room and looked squarely at the director.

"Do what he asks," insisted Simon. "The set isn't mine anymore."

Makeup looked at the director dumbfounded, "You want me… he can…"

"Humor him," replied the director. "Yes, he can talk, or he thinks he can."

Makeup moved over to the terrier still sitting on the high stool at the kitchen counter island. "Let me take a look," she said to the sweet, adorable, fifteen-pound dog who appeared alert, curious, and had quickly figured out how to get what she wanted.

"And my canines, are they sparkling clean?" asked Yorkie as she raised her lips.

"Yes, dear, they're bright as stars on a clear night."

As Makeup toyed with Yorkie, the director pulled the handler aside, "Stardoms gone to her head. She's got two more lines to do, Johnny. Bring this 'star' into line."

"Yes sir," replied Johnny, firmly.

Johnny called to the dog, "Yorkie, come here." The terrier jumped off of her stool and ran to the handler. "Girl, we need a heart to heart. Get over there."

Director James called after them, "You've got five minutes."

"I want a comb out of my gorgeous hair."

Johnny Dumont sat down with the terrier, Johnny in a metal folding chair and Yorkie sitting in one facing her handler.

"Girl, I've got a great treat for you when you finish this spot."

Yorkie opened her mouth, her pink tongue hanging out. Then she began to speak:

"I want a comb out of my gorgeous hair before I go back on, and I want a pink ribbon on my forehead."

"Ah, we can't do the ribbon, Yorkie, we've already shot most of the commercial. We can't start over and you wouldn't want that. I've got this great treat."

"Show me."

"What?"

"The treat."

"Girl, I've been with you a long time; you know you can trust me."

"Trust yeah, but you know I'll only learn what I want to learn. You won't get any more gigs if I don't learn what you want to teach me for our next commercial…"

"There won't be a next commercial if you don't finish this one. Make this director happy, please."

"Okay, okay, and I get the comb out?"

"After this setup; you look fine now. Go back in there and make me proud."

Yorkie jumped down and ran onto the set and jumped up on her assigned chair.

"Scene Two, Take One, lights, camera, action."

Camera and sound rolled, the lighting was already burning brightly.

"Is this the best dog food you've ever had?"

"That depends."

"What? Cut!"

"Johnny, doesn't she know her lines?"

"Well, sir she wasn't taught dialogue, just mouth movements."

"What ta hell, you say? The dog did so good with her first two lines."

"Maybe it's because she was on the set when you shot Professor Flynn's reaction shots to the dogs lines read by Continuity. The terrier learned them."

"To hell you say!"

"Only thing I can figure."

"Then I'll get Mrs. Marple to repeat her reactions as Darlene reads the last two dog lines. Okay?"

"Okay."

Sound."

"Rolling."

"Such delicious deboned chicken," reads Darlene out loud. Everyone looked at the terrier; she didn't make a move.

Yorkie," said Johnny Dumont, "repeat that line."

The Yorkshire terrier jumped up on top of the counter, spilling food, and spoke defiantly, "Why should I, it's a stupid line."

"So now you're a writer!" screamed the director.

"I'm not gettin' paid enough."

"This is blasphemy," retorted the director, "you signed a contract."

"No, that's Johnny's doing; you won't see my paw print on it."

"Enough of this nonsense!"

"I quit," blasted Yorkie.

Johnny approached the dog. "You can't quit now."

"Watch me."

"You've just got two more lines and an eating close-up. We'll put something really tasty in your bowl. Ice cream, maybe."

"Ice cream!"

"Yeah, your favorite: vanilla."

"Okay, okay, help me back onto the stool."

As the handler grabbed Yorkie, the set dresser approached the counter and returned mangled and disarranged china to its former place using the Polaroid she had taken of the original setting. The terrier then spoke directly to Simon James, "Mr. Director, how about if I say 'Chicken without bones, what every dog should have 'cause bones is not good for 'em.'"

"Okay, fine. Take Two. Roll sound. Roll camera."

"Rolling."

"No wait. Cut," screamed the director. "You're a holier than thou low-life rat killer! I can get a replacement faster'n a rat to a rat hole. If you want to stay, you have to follow the script approved by the agency or we all don't get paid, including you. No ice cream ever, and you'll never work again in this town. Mark my word!"

"Fair enough."

"Scene Three, Take One, Roll sound, roll camera. Why do you like *Cougar's* so much?"

"'Cause the ad agency said I did."

"Cut! Print. That's good you spunky little canine critter. We counted on your feisty independent streak. We've recorded everything you did and said on *and* off the set, and we'll cut it into a fine original commercial. You can retire to your dressing room now and get that comb out you so dearly wanted."

THE END

Charlie Chuckwagon, a Redbone Coonhound

15. Charlie Chuckwagon

By Don Kirk

"Wagons Ho," called out the wagonmaster after blowing his horn to move out. He joyfully swung his tall, wide-brimmed wool hat high in the air like some kind of cattle driver—well, he was that, and much more. A wagon pulled forward and then another, each moving forward in a single, regimented line; a line that wouldn't stay that way once the choking dust and meandering herd of cattle caused them to spread out and travel abreast. The cowhands moved the livestock forward—those animals needed for man to settle in California and Oregon Territory. Thirty-five loaded-for-bear, canvassed farm wagons were heading west with this train along the now well-established Oregon Trail. Scores of families we're hoping to make a new life on fertile lands, hoping to be free of the choking, polluted air and the rising land costs in the East.

The wagon train, currently running along the Sweetwater River valley, had an ample supply of good grass and fresh water for the settlers and their animals. The train, already moving through the valley for about ten days, needed another ten—hopefully less—to get to the Rockies and cross over the South Pass. None of the pioneers planned to settle in Colorado. The trail's easy grades here allowed the wagon train to move anywhere from ten to twenty miles per day. The train, about halfway through their five-month trip, would end up being two thousand miles or more from the East; a trip starting way back in Independence, Missouri. The settlers had already abandoned most of their furniture and heavy goods along the trail; the 2,000 pounds stuffed in each of their prairie schooners turned out to be way too much for their oxen and the rough trail. They used the slow moving oxen instead of mules so they could keep up on foot and could lead the oxen instead of riding atop the wagon holding reins and cracking a whip.

On this splendid, cool, but sunny, day, I seen a mongrel a-sittin' atop the wagonmaster's saddle. 'Twas none other than Charlie Chuckwagon a-sittin' there observin' the wagonmaster's movements on the ground whilst also looking for raccoons and such on the open prairie beyond. I reckoned him to be the chuckwagon cook's dog, but only because he hung close to the cook's wagon. This Redbone Coonhound had long trekked and tracked and trapped his favorite vermin whilst tagging along with the Independence wagon train. He stood a strong, strappin' two-foot tall, with a purdy, mahogany-red coat, large dangling ears, and a large black nose that could find anything. This sweet, loyal dog was the love of this here wagon train's pioneers. Charlie's sort, having come from Scotland, was partial to hunting.

"Fact is; he's a mighty handsome dog. A hunk of a critter," said the wagonmaster, Buck Waite.

"But them floppy ears 'o his is so long they could reach his nose," another settler pointed out.

"And big 'nough, if necessary, to use for wagon-brake shoes."

"Get off now! You ain't a messing with our hound."

"And that there bark o' hissin could down an elk."

Charlie Chuckwagon yelped sharply at that, and we took a quick step backward.

"That there coondog always has a begging-for-attention look on his insistent face, a-seemin' to want sometin' even if he wern't actually a-askin' for anythin'," added Cookie Hambone, the cowboy's chuckwagon cook who sported a grey beard and beautiful, furry, raccoon hat. Maybe hound-dog Charlie had rounded up the headcover for him.

"Git down, Charlie."

Charlie jumped off the horse.

"You hafta to look into them grippin', hazel eyes, to see clean through them pupils, to figure his real meanin'," continued Buck.

"He's got an independent streak," added Cookie. "He ain't

a-gonna listen to ya iffen he's picked up a scent, but he's loyal to a fault. I'd stick up for him 'cause I know he'd keep an eye on my backside."

The settlers began to circle their wagons to protect themselves from the prairie winds, bad weather (they might get little notice), and to corral the animals to stop them from a-runnin' away. The young'uns started collectin' buffalo chips for the evenin' campfire. This was an early stop for dinner and hopefully a quiet, starlit night on these plains 'cause the next mornin' the wagons would ford the Sweetwater River and that would most likely take all day.

Cookie Hambone dropped the back of his chuck box to make a table for preparing a meal for the men herding the cattle on the wagon train. The wagon box was built with drawers and shelves for his cooking utensils, pots and pans, and perishable foods like beans, coffee, salted-meats, and sourdough biscuits. This evening Cookie would make son-of-a-gun stew, a favorite of the cowhands since it was made from the brains and internal parts of a freshly kilt calf: tasty innards like the kidneys, liver, and heart. Cookie would add tomatoes, onions, chilies, and potatoes to taste. Hound dog Charlie stayed close to the chuckwagon, lying next to Cookie hoping to get a sample of the cook's creations. Once the wagons were settled in place, a campfire was built, and the oxen and horses ranged for their evening meal. The cowboys had dismounted their horses, removed bridles and saddles, and retrieved their sleeping gear from the chuckwagon, all because this was an early encampment, and it looked like this might be an evening of music and storytelling. You knew Cookie was ready to shindig because he pulled out a bottle of coffin varnish and popped the cork.

"We's gonna have a hog-killin' time tonight," he said.

The always buddy-buddy Charlie Chuckwagon made his way around the campfire a-gatherin' with each and every settler who'd spend time petting or playing with this most reliable coonhound. Charlie, indeed, served as a good watchdog, and with a nose picking up scents miles away, brought in edible vermin from

Charlie Was Always Pulling Guard Duty

time to time, including rabbits, squirrels, raccoons, and even the pestering badgers. The wagons navigated all kinds of terrain from stinking swamps to rough, rock-strewn ground, and Charlie lent his paw—and his bark—to warn of hazardous holes. He also helped, from time to time, to round up stray cows.

Charlie's original wagon family died of cholera a few weeks back and he just naturally began to hang around with the ol' sourdough who possessed many a tasty vittle. The hunters used the red coonhound's particular loud bay so they could track him as he led the men to their quarry. With the hound, the hunters brought in wild game for a plumb-good evenin' of eats. The dog even danced around the campfire on special occasions.

Time for a hoedown. Time for a break from the wearisome humdrum of the long trail. The fire burned brightly and the night not too all-fired cold so a few musically inclined settlers with a harmonica, banjo, concertina, and sweet little fiddle began to pick the *Virginia Reel*. A little laddie even tried to make some music with a comb and tissue paper. The rhythm kept with good 'ol down-home clapping. That's all it took for a few menfolk to ask the ladies for their hand at square dancing. The thousand miles traveled so far to Oregon was a hard row to hoe so this reprieve provided some sorely needed solace.

The dance was on. A couple of men swung their partners high into the air. Others downed a swig of their hooch.

A young Benjamin Sawyer came up to Charlie and grabbed his front legs, asking him to dance…and, be damned, he did! Charlie, on his hind legs, followed along with Ben's gyrations while trying to keep clear of his partner's boots.

"Swing your partner round and round, let's all do the do-si-do…"

No, Charlie didn't know what this hoedown was all about, but he seemed to enjoy it anyways, and the settlers could only hope he didn't decide to sing along using that searing bark a-hisin's. Charlie looked about, and the crowd clapped and cheered, loving the dog's contribution to the festivities.

A mustang wandered onto the 'dance floor' and Charlie quickly left his dancing partner, walked proudly, head high, over to the confused horse, and grabbed its reins. He pulled the horse toward Buck Waite.

"Hey Charlie, great job. You's a-workin' for your food ain't ya?"

Charlie let out a yelp.

"Cookie'll get ya some vittles."

Charlie Chuckwagon voiced a joyful woof.

"You just love the sound of your voice, don't ya Charlie?"

On cue, here came another yap from him.

But before Buck could take Charlie to the chuckwagon, a loud gun blast drowned out the crickets. Straight away, the coonhound jumped up and ran toward the source of the sound. He crossed between two wagons and found a cowboy a-standing there with a smoking shotgun.

"Go get it, dog!" called out the hand.

Charlie ran off into the darkness, and faster than you can say Jack Robinson, he came back with a large grey, black-tailed jackrabbit in his snout. Charlie had no problem a-making a decision.

"Okey-doke, Charlie, yous got us a couple 'o good meals. You makes a great gun dog."

Charlie dropped the rabbit in front of the cowhand, the hare's huge pink ears half the length of his body.

"Do you like ears, Charlie?"

Charlie sat down and let out a soft, sweet bark.

"These hoppin' legs maybe?"

Charlie jumped up on the cowboy in anticipation.

"You's got us over six pounds of fresh meat. Cookie will like this 'un! With a little of his Apple Jack, taters, and red beans, it'll make a fine spread."

"Rabbits is the best chuck, mighty good eatin', better'n river rats," said another.

"Apple Jack ain't bad neither, a couple swigs of the firewater…"

Charlie's head suddenly rose up, he looked about, stood up quickly, and hollered. Several of the settlers took notice and followed Charlie to the wagon train perimeter where they seen two men a-riding in. The settlers pulled their pistols.

"Halt, who goes there?" shouted one.

The men rode out of the shadows into the light of the campfire and pulled up on their horse's reins. "Easy, gentlemen, we're from Medicine Bow south a-here. We's a-hopin' to tag along fur a spell."

"I reckon you kin iffen you've got your own grub and bedding. And yous won't do nothin' yo' mamma wouldn't want you to do. As you kin see, Charlie here makes a great guard dog."

The next day with the train back on the trail—but a-havin' a right slow start—Charlie seen a critter coming out of a burrow just yonder on the prairie and lit out after it. When the critter noticed Charlie, it picked up its pace, but Charlie caught up to the galloping critter, grabbed him by the neck, and shook him violently, trying his best to shake the life out of him. The critter was squirmin' and wigglin' to beat Banagher! Finally, Charlie lay the critter down; most of its livin' plumb taken out of it. It was wriggling only slightly. Charlie sniffed at it carefully, wrapped his large mouth around the body of the critter, and trotted back to the chuckwagon. He sashayed up to Cookie Hambone and dropped to the ground a grey critter with broad black stripes on each side of its snout and a white stripe across the top of its head and along its back.

"Boy, whatcha got there? Ahh, a badger! Won't be a-pestering anyone anymore. It'll make a good casserole or crispy badger scratchings. We'll have this short-legged piebald for dinner, Mr. Charlie. You're a-keeping me stocked."

Soon the settler boy, Benjamin, began to show up at the chuckwagon a-takin' a likin' to Charlie after the fandango. He seemed to like the mongrel and the mongrel seemed to like him. Ben wore a black vest, coat, and a wide-brimmed black hat with a white hatband and stood a might short for his nine years of age. That made him not a whole lot taller than Charlie Chuckwagon.

"Am I keeping you stocked?"

"Okay, boy, go get it," commanded Ben Sawyer as he threw a stick yonder and Charlie bound after it. The hairy, red mongrel seemed to love goin' after things and a-bringin' 'em back. Charlie dropped the stick in front of Benjamin and the mongrel's tail went to waggin'.

"Lookie here, Charlie, I wantcha to git usun a treat from Cookie."

Charlie knew who "Cookie" was and ran off to find him, and find him he did.

"Watcha want, critter?" asked the cook.

Charlie let out a soft wail.

"Uh, hah! I know yous wants a cookie. Here's one for you and one for Benjamin. But ya gotta take hisins to him first, understand?"

Charlie, now in a sitting position and panting with anticipation, stared up at Cookie.

"I don't think you get my meanin'. What say you go fetch Benjamin and bring him back here. Go get Ben. Charlie, go!"

At that, the beefy canine jumped up and headed out.

And soon Charlie came back a-leading Ben! Yes, plumb true, Charlie was a-pullin' on Ben's suspenders. For the effort, they each got a tasty sourdough cookie made by the cook.

That evening, Charlie Chuckwagon let out an alerting howl at somethin' out beyond the wagons, but when no one came to his calling, he turned back and ran to Benjamin. Ben Sawyer looked to Charlie as he sat down in front of him begging for attention.

"What is it, boy?"

The coondog jumped up on Ben, then turned to run away, but when Ben didn't follow, he stopped again and looked back.

"Okay, okay, I'm a-comin', Charlie Boy."

At that, Ben ran after the fired up dog and soon came upon somethin' four-legged and furry. Ben pulled one 'o them newfangled slingshots from his pants pocket, one he was given back East. He picked up a stone and took aim, pulling back hard on the pocket and stretching the vulcanized rubber bands back as far as he could manage.

Charlie barked.

The creature looked up and growled deeply. It was a white-faced, rat-tailed, pink-nosed opossum the size of a young pig, a critter Benjamin seen many a time back home in Tennessee.

"Dinner," Ben called out as he fired the rock, but it missed it's mark and Charlie ran after the prey. The opossum ran willy-nilly, but Charlie kept up.

Straight off, the opossum dropped down, rolled over, and became stock-still, it's legs extending stiffly into the air. Charlie came up close to sniff the creature, but a foul smell caused him to back off. He turned away and showed no more interest in the "dead" critter, but Ben came up and grabbed it. He knew the creature was only playing dead. He looked into it's big, black eyes, repeated "Dinner," and dropped the opossum into a burlap sack.

One evening of late, after all the chores were completed and the children and animals bed down, it was time for a little…

"All right gentlemen," said Cookie Hambone, as he, from the top of the deck, threw out one card face down to each player. "Highest card wins."

Each of five players, sitting around a makeshift table made of a folded canvas tarp, threw a two-bit Spanish real into the pot. "Winner takes all. Turn 'em over gentleman."

All the players turned over their one card.

"Ah, see there, I'm the blessed one tonight," said Jonathan Cody, one of the settlers, as he raked in his meager winnings.

Charlie Chuckwagon lay on the grass next to Cookie, his beady eyes riveted to the goings-on.

"What say we play five-card stud?" suggested the sourdough.

"I'm in," replied each of the players.

Cookie shuffled the deck of cards and gave each player five cards, but the first card was placed face down, the rest dealt face up. Each of the players sneaked a peek at his hole card and placed a bet, or chose not to if he felt his hand had no chance of winning.

"I'm out."

"Me too."

The remaining players threw in two bits.

"All ready? Who's got the highest hand?"

The men turned over their hole card.

"Two pair."

"Ah, hah! Three-of-a-kind!" declared Heath as he reached out to rake in his winnings.

Cookie handed the cards to the player to his left, Jim Cody, so he could deal the next hand. At that, Charlie Chuckwagon sat up with newly focused attention on the players. Cody dealt out the five cards to each participant. They all looked at their hole card. Charlie let out a soft moan. Cookie looked down at Charlie and took a peek at his own hole card.

"I'm in," Cookie said and threw in his bet.

"Everyone in?" asked Cody.

One last player threw in his two bits.

"Show me your cards," announced Cody.

They all turned over their hole cards and all the players but one displayed a disappointed expression: "I've a straight!" announced Cookie as he jumped up and quickly raked in his winnings.

Jim Cody passed the deck to the next player who dealt out the cards. The players who thought they might have a winning hand threw in a few bits—if they had any left; the others bet with ammo or a tuft of tobacco. Cookie stayed in and showed Charlie his hole card, "Wish me luck, boy." Charlie stood up, circled as if looking for the right position to take a nap but dropped to the ground with his eyes focused on Cody.

"Show me your cards," said Heath.

Everyone threw in their worthless cards, except Cookie who raked in his winnings.

"Ahh, damn! Not you again!" declared Cody.

The cards were dealt out once more. The hole cards got a quick glance and one man backed out quickly.

Charlie looked at him, and all the players attempted to hide their emotions, but this sly dog could tell which players thought they had a winning hand. If any player tried to hide his hopeful look and reveal no true sorrow, the hound would look at the ground, appearing quite disinterested. But Cookie recognized the dog's cue.

"I'm out too," declared Cookie, "No money in the kitty for me."

The hole card was turned over. Cody took the winnings.

This sneaky game playing went on for several more hands with Cookie raking in more than his fair share. He soon called it a night and pocketed his winnings. Cookie held his hand up in an Indian "Howgh" and Charlie raised his paw to his open palm and seemed to say with wide eyes, "I did good, huh!" At that, Cookie left quickly with his faithful dog Charlie.

A remaining player asked, "Anyone for checkers?"

Back at the chuckwagon, Cookie gave Charlie, his consummate confederate, a very special reward, his favorite treat: peanut butter.

As the wagon train trudged across the Sweetwater River—one of several river crossings it would have to make—each team of oxen tugged with the water a-reaching to their bellies, and the settlers forded on foot, including the womenfolk and children. Fortunately, the river's rapids were manageable. The wagon drivers, now riding on their seats, were spurring on their teams with a whip and the most penetrating of yells:

"Hah! Get up! Come on dad-blame it, move it! Git yoself outta this hang-fire water." The whip cracked between the whistles and the piercing hollerin' of the driver.

Some women held their young 'uns in their arms, whilst other children walked alongside the wagons with the adults. Benjamin Sawyer and his sister Savannah held tight to their mother's hands, but straight away, Ben fell into a hole in the river bottom and lost his grip on his mamma. Ben's head dropped below the surface but quickly resurfaced. Mamma couldn't reach her son as he began to float down river, his wide-brimmed hat floating away from him. Mamma, with Savannah in one hand, shouted after Benjamin, wailing in abject terror. Another settler tried to jump for him, but Ben was already out of range. A second settler waded toward him, but that relatively calm river did have a sprightly current on this particular day. Cookie saw the mishap and called out to Charlie Chuckwagon riding atop the chuckbox.

"Charlie, Charlie, down river, there's Benjamin, go boy!"

Charlie looked up and sniffed, saw the "critter" thrashing in

Charlie's Chuckwagon

the water, dove in, and paddled toward the fearful youngster. The hound made better time than the two menfolk wading after him 'cause the dog was a-paddlin' down stream and the men were a-tryin' on foot to navigate the rough, rocky, river bottom. Charlie soon reached the boy, grabbed his vest, and tried pulling him back toward the wagons. That didn't work, but he had successfully stopped Ben's forward progress. The two settlers closed the gap and finally caught up to the floundering Benjamin. They grabbed him out of the water and trudged back. His mother and sister Savannah cheered, "Yah for the coondog!"

The struggling oxen, slowly, but successfully, pulled the prairie wagon out of the water and Ben reunited with his mother. Ben's first words after taking a deep breath and expelling a glut of river water was, "Where's Charlie? Charlieee..."

Benjamin turned to see the coonhound sauntering onto shore behind him with his black hat gripped securely in his snout.

The next mornin' Charlie Chuckwagon managed to get a thorn in his front left paw and raised it up to Benjamin so he could remove it. Ben took a good look and grabbed his pocketknife. Charlie snapped at that so Ben put the blade away and tried by hand to pull the one-and-one-half inch thorn from Charlie's tender paw. You could see the dog's unease with surgery—or the thorn's piercing pain—on the coonhound's face and a-seemin' to say, "I know this is gonna smart, I don't want you to touch me." Charlie let out a holler and it was all over. Ben kneeled down and hugged Charlie. The grateful Charlie lovingly licked Ben's face. The boy, with his two hands, girdled Charlie's face and they gazed at each other eye to eye with clearly some kinda connection. "Good boy," Ben said, "I love you." One could be certain they was now beholden to each other.

The next day, in early mornin', long a-fore daybreak, the Sawyers came a-runnin' to Cookie. They said Benjamin was nowhere to be had. Cookie first thought he might be a-huntin' in the nearby thicket, but it was gettin' late and the wagons needed to be on the move; the oxen were harnessed, wagons loaded, the livestock rounded up.

"We can't hold up the whole train," declared Wagonmaster Waite.

"But you cain't leave muh boy behind!"

"You kin stay behin' with him."

"Hold on a dad-burned minute," asserted Cookie, "Charlie kin find him!"

Cookie found Charlie calmly lying next to the chuckwagon and put a neckerchief of Ben's in front of the coonhound's nose. Charlie now appeared to be concerned, his eyes wide and watchful.

"Charlie, where's Benjamin? Sniff him out, boy. Go find him, ya hear?"

At that, the Redbone Coonhound got up, lazily stretched his

front legs, then his back legs. He did a high jump, spun around, and let out a deafening bark heard across the entire train, if not for miles yonder. Then, holding his tail high, he put his snout out ahead of him and moved it back and forth a-tryin' to pick up the scent. He put his long ears tight to his head and focused all his attention on the hunt. Charlie was a cold-nosed dog a-meanin' he found it easy to follow even an old trail. But Ben's trail wasn't old, he was at the camp the night before, in fact, the Sawyers had put him to bed, so this hunt should be easy for the hound. Charlie ran off in the direction the wagon train had come the previous evening. Two menfolk jumped horseback and spurred their mounts to follow Charlie Chuckwagon who's powerful, undulating muscles, and hell-bent-for-leather sprint, made it a chore for the horses to keep up.

Soon the coonhound slowed down to a walk, having lost the fresh scent. And the two cowboys slowed their mount to a walk.

"Maybe Benjamin got shot last night by one o' our settlers a-shootin' into the dark at them strange sounds."

"And there's buffalo out there! Benjamin coulda got hisself mixed up with a pair 'o them sharp horns."

"A half-a-ton or more of meanness," added the other.

"They's prairie-grass eaters, but that don't stop 'em from leapin' after a figured threat…like Benjamin who seems a curious sort."

"Maybe he kin take one down with that slingshot o' hisin."

"You havin' a laugh?"

"We could sure use that meat and buffalo hide."

"True enough."

The two men followed close behind, Charlie changing directions frequently. The coonhound ran into a stand of cottonwoods, but the low-hanging limbs required the men to dismount and lead their horses in, and eventually they had to leave their mounts behind in the thicket. The hound moved forward quickly now, his ears twitching. He carefully tilted and rotated his ears to locate a sound he seemed to be very interested in, then abruptly, he let out a loud, piercing bark. A few dozen strides later, the men heard a voice calling out, "Charlie! Charlie!" It was Ben's voice. The two

settlers followed Charlie toward his voice and there: Ben a-sittin'
up against a tree, his pant leg torn and fresh blood dripping from
his right limb, but Charlie was all-fire excited about his find,
jumping in unrestrained joy.

"Benjamin! You okay, son?" asked one of the men.

"Mr. Collins, Mr. Jenkins, praise the All Mighty! Glad ta see ya!
A bison got me. I think my legs broken."

"Well, lets get you up and outta here."

The wagon train had already moved out by the time the two
men and Charlie brought Benjamin back to the campsite, but they
continued on and soon caught up to the settlers. Cookie found
Ben's right leg to have some deep cuts, but nothing was broken.

"What was you a-doin' outside camp?" demanded Cookie.

"Last evenin', I heared somethin', took me a lantern. It was a
badger, thought I could play with him. I chased him around, he
chased me around. A fun little critter, but I stepped into one of his
burrows and down I went and then seen this big animal a-comin'
at me. I ran. I dropped my lantern, it broke, and it got so very
dark. I ran to the nearby woods a-hopin' it'd quit a-chasin' me and
I crawled a-deeper in to get safe. Yeah, I reckon it were a buffalo."

"You're lucky you wasn't trampled."

Charlie let out a wail.

"Quiet boy," said Benjamin, "he's out there a-wantin' in."

Cookie bandaged the boy and sent him to the Sawyer's wagon.
Charlie followed after, not a-wantin' to leave the boy out of his
sight. At the wagon, Ben was cuddling, and talking quietly to his
savior, Charlie, who looked at Ben with dreamy brown eyes and a
beggin'-like face. What did Charlie want, Ben wondered? To stay
close to Ben? Show concern as any dog would.

That afternoon, Charlie came upon a rattler moving into a coiled
defensive striking posture with its tail a-rattlin' and a long, thin,
black-as-night, forked tongue flailing wildly out of its triangular
head, a warning to predators to leave him be or else. The hound
wisely took a step back, but—with his head lowered—tried to
get a whiff of the strange creature he had never come across

afore. This light brown, three-foot-long snake with dark-brown splotches and round eyes on each side of its head focused on the hound. The rattler kept her needle-like fangs in her head but was doubtless ready to strike, so Charlie moved to circle behind the venomous snake. The large Prairie Rattlesnake simply twisted its head around, its beady eyes fixed squarely on Charlie.

"Charlie! Get back!"

Charlie looked to Benjamin.

"He'll kill ya! Get back."

It was clear Charlie didn't get the message so Ben pulled his slingshot from his back pocket, picked up a rock, and took aim.

"Back Charlie! Back!"

Ben took a shot. It missed its target. The scaly-tail of the snake rattled louder. Ben grabbed another rock and shot again. This time, it hit its mark: right in the kisser. The rattler retreated under a boulder.

Charlie moved forward to take a sniff under the rock.

"No Charlie, come back. Charlie, NO!"

Charlie looked around then came to Ben.

"You might near coulda' got yoself kilt!"

In reply, the hound dog sat down and whined a confusing communication of gobbledygook, "arf, yup, au au, ruff, eeff…"

Ben replied, "You is a-talkin' jibber-jabbber, Charlie Chuckwagon. Don't ya understand what I'm a-saying to ya, coondog? Don't you be a-fussin' with that rattler, ya hear? I don't wanna loose ya."

Charlie and Ben walked quietly side-by-side back to the wagon except when the dog wanted Ben to play. Charlie bounced around on all fours, two legs at a time, high off the prairie grass.

"Stop it boy, we's got many-a-mile to go afore we reach Oregon."

Late one evening, Benjamin saw the two men that joined the train many days earlier, but they were climbing out of the Sawyer wagon with saddlebags—apparently filled with his parents personal valuables, maybe some silverware and jewelry. They also had two other horses in tow loaded with rifles and large burlap bags weighing down the horses. Maybe the bags were filled with pickled pork, dried buffalo meat, and twist tobacco from back east. Wonder if they also took a corn-cob pipe?

"Stop, what is you doin'?" asked Ben.

The two men ignored Ben, saying, "Go away, boy, we's don't need your help."

"Straight off, the voice of Savannah, Ben's sister, spoke from inside the wagon, "Help, Help, bad men!"

As Ben rushed forward, one of the bad men grabbed him by his long hair and the other kicked him off his feet. One man took the lariat from his horse's saddle and tied Ben's hands and torso to the wagon wheel.

"Ben! Is that you?"

"Savannah!"

The men jumped on their horses, turned them, but, out of the blue, Charlie Chuckwagon showed up and growled at the horses causing them to raise both of their front legs in an effort to stamp down the intruder. The two riders fought to control their mounts. Charlie bit one of the horse's legs. The coonhound a tiger when he's after something, not his usual sweet, loving self. He had no trouble taking on large animals, what these men were regrettably finding out. Charlie let out a harsh, deep-throated bark in an effort to bring help. One man pulled his six-shooter, but Charlie jumped high and grabbed the man around the wrist. He let go of his gun, but Charlie's sixty pounds pulled the man from his horse and grabbed the outlaw's neck. That drew fresh, bright blood. The other man, wanting no more of this, rode off. Charlie ran after the galloping horse, his own air-piercing speed allowing him to keep up. The rider drew his shooting iron and turned back to shoot at Charlie, but the bullets only hit the rocky ground, sparks a-flying. The outlaw's horse was clearly concerned about the ensuing coonhound and so changed directions, veering back and forth; the thief loosing his wide-brimmed hat to the wind. Charlie ignored it. The badman threw one of his heavy saddlebags at Charlie, but that didn't stop the coonhound. His determination and lean muscular body would allow him to stay with the thief for as long as it took.

Back at the wagon encampment, several cowmen showed up

to free Benjamin and Savannah and then they got horseback to track the outlaws. Benjamin insisted on going with them so he was picked up to ride behind one of the cowhands.

With the last outlaw a-makin' a run for it, Charlie caught up and grabbed a stirrup. His canines took hold and wouldn't let go. The bad man pulled his boot from the stirrup and kicked at the hound. Charlie was being dragged now, having lost his footing.

Coming up the rear, two men on horseback...along with Benjamin. One pulled his pistol and started taking shots. But it was getting dark, only a three-quarter moon showing the way. Benjamin called out to the hound, "Let him go, Charlie, let him go! Come here, Boy!"

Sure enough, Charlie released his grip on the stirrup and hit the ground hard. He turned to stagger back. Ben jumped from the horse and ran up to this loyal dog, cradled Charlie, and the elated dog licked the young Ben's face most excitedly. In fact, his slobbering pink tongue licked Ben *all over* his face. And Ben did a fair amount of kissing in return.

"You ready for some water, Charlie Chuckwagon? Or maybe you'd take a likin' to a little Apple Jack?"

That evening, Cookie noticed Charlie curled up on Ben's sleeping bag and both of them out cold, out like a lantern light without kerosene. Apparently they had a busy week.

The next day, on the road again, the wagon train was headed up into a mountain pass and the going was a-gettin' rough. Up ahead a steep grade so the settlers unloaded some gear from each wagon and gathered several men behind each wagon to push like the devil to manage it over the rise. Even the older young 'uns were a-helpin' to push. On this day, Charlie walked with Ben, his new partner, as the boy helped the older men to push. The driver hollered at the oxen and whipped them as the Conestoga hit some large rocks. The wagon bounced left and then right, twisting and turning with all manner of hanging goods swinging back and forth inside. But then, unexpectedly, the wagon came to a dead stop and wouldn't move any farther forward. The oxen had apparently reached their weight-pulling limit over loose rocks. Some of the settlers called out for more help but when doing so they released some pressure on the wagon; the wagon began to roll backward, but, in a flash, Charlie Chuckwagon jumped up on Benjamin and knocked him clear of one of the large rear wheels of the wagon. Ben fell sideways and off his feet, hitting the ground hard, but the five-foot wagon wheel with iron band rolled over Charlie...and killed him.

Tall, bright-white cumulous clouds in front of a deep-blue sky now had an underbelly of dark gloomy grey. It was not clear what they intended to do on this day.

THE END

AFTERWORD

Charlie Chuckwagon was interred on the plains and a monument of rocks with a wooden cross was placed to memorialize his contribution to this wagon train's trip west. The first outlaw died of a neck wound—bled to death—and the second thief was shot while riding off and was found dead by a pioneer who had continued the chase. The personal belongs and weapons the two badmen had stolen were brought back to the train.

Sergeant Adolph, a German Shepherd

16. Der Deutsche Polizist

By Don Kirk

HEIDELBERG, GERMANY 1974

"So gentleman," announced the Station Sergeant, "these dogs have completed their training at the Police Academy and they're ready to take on their new duties. Officer Schultz, I know you don't like dogs, but you and four other officers in our unit have been chosen for this experiment."

At that, a *Wachtmeister* walked a handsome German Shepherd into the squad room. He was wearing a heavy charcoal black and cream coat—the black patch on his back looked like a horse's saddle—and he had a mixed black face and black ears that stood tall and erect, but with his mesmerizing light-brown eyes, he looked so disarming.

"Schultz, this is Adolph, he's going to be your partner."

Officer Schultz stood up, "Sarge, you can't do this, you know how much I dislike dogs…"

"That's one of the reasons you were chosen for this endeavor."

"And the other?"

"I can't tell you at this time; after all, this is meant to test a hypothesis."

All of the officers turned to look at each other, "Hypothesis?"

"This German Shepherd will travel with you in your Beetle, sitting in the right seat and…"

"Sarge…"

"…you will have to roll down the window for him, but, after that, he's going to lead you to areas where crimes may have occurred. He can sniff out trapped victims, inform you of a certain sound, find drugs, and track down a missing person if we have clothing from them. Officer Schultz, meet Adolph."

"I thought these dogs just herded sheep."

"If you know any..."

"My wife. She flocks with her friends to the jewelry and clothing stores almost every day."

All the officers in the room howled.

"Maybe we should assign Adolph to your wife," interjected the Station Sergeant.

The officers laughed again.

"At least I could find out what stores she goes to."

"I thought that credit card bill you get each month tells you that."

The men cracked up.

"Adolph, meet Officer Schultz. Adolph can go with him now."

Schultz hesitantly took his leash. Adolph tilted his head sideways with unease; Schultz did much the same.

"What you need, Schultz, is a Chihuahua," added one officer. "I don't think you can handle a German Shepherd."

"Maybe not a two-kilogram Chihuahua either!" said another.

"Up yours, Finn," asserted Schultz.

The officers snickered.

The Station Sergeant took back the room, "Enough gentleman. Adolph has had training in several skills. Officer Schultz, you need only know the commands and then he's yours. Oh, and you need to know he outranks you corporal: this is *Sergeant* Adolph."

"Sergeant! He outranks me?"

"Yes, to get the respect he deserves, he's not just a dog, he's a police officer that must not be abused by his partner."

"Oh, no sir, I wouldn't...he'll get the best cheese, *Rauchkuäse.*"

FIRST TRIP IN A VW

"*Komm schon, Hund,* come on dog," demanded Schultz, "*Fido Heir.*" Sergeant Adolph got up from his sitting position and walked at the Officer's side as he left the room. They exited the building and approached Schultz's 1969 Volkswagen Beetle labeled POLIZEI in white on doors painted bright green. The hood and engine door was also green, but the roof and fenders were painted white, and a single purple rotating light was affixed to the roof near the front windshield. Affixed to the vehicle's front side panel was a large horn, and on the front bumper two potentially loud, attention getting sirens. Officer Schultz opened the passenger door for Adolph.

"*Reinkommen*, get in, dog."

Adolph kindly obliged, and Schultz closed the door behind him, but, as Schultz walked around to the other side of the car, the German Shepherd moved over to the driver's side and put his large front paws on the steering wheel. Schultz opened his door.

"Damn! Get over dog, get over, *I'm* doing the driving."

Adolph moved without objection and sat in the right seat looking out the front window as Schultz climbed in.

"*Braver Hund!* Good. Now look dog, Sergeant, with that long black muzzle of yours, you can open and adjust the vent window to your liking." Schultz demonstrated how, though he didn't use his own nose.

Adolph weighed in at thirty-six kilos and stood 60 centimeters at the shoulders, more than enough to fill that Volkswagen seat. He had no trouble seeing out the window and his size could probably take down even the largest of criminals.

"I don't know what the Station Sergeant wants me to do with you, *Sergeant* Adolph, or you to do with me. He made clear you've got lots of skills, but listen, I don't need a Shepherd, *verstehen?* He said something about you being a companion, a protector, and a friend. Give me a break! I've got my Beetle; that's my companion."

When Officer Schultz pulled over to a curb, a pedestrian on the sidewalk stopped outside the VW when he saw the cop's partner and had to ask, "Is that your new police partner or handsome boyfriend?"

"Step back, *zurucktreten!* My new partner just loves to take healthy bites out of strangers."

The pedestrian stepped back quickly. Officer Schultz drove off smartly.

Adolph grinned.

ON THE ROAD

Still sitting quietly in the right seat, Adolph stared intently at Schultz.

"Don't look so uneasy dog, I'm your new partner and you're going to have to get used to it." Adolph twisted his head sideways, not quite comprehending.

"Look dog, do you want me to get you some cotton-filled teddy bears to corral? It's the closest thing to sheep I've got. That'd make you happy wouldn't it? I guess the bosses think you'll help me round up the bad guys...or maybe find toys for the officer's quarters."

Schultz pulled up to a street-side parking space and turned off the engine. He waved aside dog hair floating about his face.

"Get out Adolph, look at this mess! My Beetle is dad-blasted full of dog hair! No wonder you're known as the 'German Shedder.' I know you have a double coat of hair so you can survive through our winter months, but now...now you have to let it all fall out in *my* beetle just because it's spring? Why didn't you do it in the squad room?"

SCHLOSS HEIDELBERG

The CB radio suddenly blared out, "*Der Aufruf Sechs-Vier-Drei.* Schloss Heidelberg. *Kind fehlt.* Missing child. *Verstehen?*"

Schultz picked up the mike, "See, *Verstehen.* Copy." He then looked to Adolph still sitting in the right front seat, "Okay, dog, we've got a job for you."

Schultz made a U-turn on the narrow cobblestone street with its three, and four-story houses packed, shoulder to shoulder, on each side.

"Have you been to the castle ruins before, Mister Dog?" asked Schultz.

Adolph whined.

"What the devil does that mean?"

Adolph whined again.

"The brass don't expect me to learn *your* language do they?"

Adolph lifted his left front leg and put it on Schultz's right arm.

"No way will I learn dog speak. I don't know why they partnered you with me?"

Schultz drove over a stone bridge that crossed the Rhine River and then went through a round-arched stone gate where several other *Polizist* Beetles were parked. The beautiful castle ruins stood on a hill that overlooked the historic city of Heidelberg.

"Schultz, bring the Shepherd!"

Adolph quickly exited the VW and Schultz took his leash. He walked quietly alongside the police officer through the main gate even without being asked to heel. An officer approached, "Officer Schultz, show your dog this baseball cap."

"What? He's not a sports fan—that I'm sure of."

"Have him sniff it. We've a lost three-year-old girl in the castle. The police and his parents have been looking for over an hour."

"And you think I can help?"

"Well not you, that dog of yours, hopefully."

"He's *not* my dog!"

"Your partner then."

"Okay, okay." Schultz took the hat and held it to Adolph's nose. He sniffed it carefully. "Adolph, go find the owner, please, so I can go to lunch."

Adolph looked up at Schultz.

"Go find her. Go. The job's all yours. This is an experiment."

Adolph followed the stone driveway and began to move his head back and forth, nose to the pavement. Officer Schultz held firmly to the six-foot leash.

"Am I supposed to let the dog run loose?" Schultz asked the other officer.

"Unless you want to run lickety-split after him you better hold on tight."

"Great! *Mein Hund*, Adolph."

Off they went with several more Polizist following close behind. There were many stone steps to climb and many rooms to course through. The German Shepherd led—pulled—Schultz through the coach house, stables, and a garage where the water wagon was kept.

"*Verdammt!*" screamed Schultz. "This castle is huge, this will take all day."

Adolph led Schultz up the narrow winding stairs to the king's quarters.

"Come on, Adolph, find anything? Anything!"

The shepherd sniffed all the corners of the empty stone room.

"This was the prince's residence over 700 years ago," said Schultz to his new partner. "A renaissance castle built in the 1200's! Yeah, 1200 A.D., Adolph! Can you imagine that long ago and it's still here?"

Adolph looked up at him bewildered—what to blazes was he talking about?

"A lightning strike destroyed the upper half of the castle in 1537," continued Schultz, "and then, after being enlarged in 1650, it was damaged by several wars, fire, a lightning strike in 1764 and...my, where could that boy be? All I see is stone and more stone."

The German Shepherd continued his obsessed search, pulling on Schultz for every painful, back-wrenching inch and then found another very narrow winding stair leading further upward. Eventually, they came to a tower with a high-angle view of Heidelberg—an awesome sight. Adolph raised his forelegs up and set his paws on the stone sill. Apparently he too wanted to see the breath-taking view of a historic city with a magnificent river running right through the middle of it. Boats and barges floated merrily along the Rhine River moving goods and goggling tourists. But, without warning, Adolph jumped down, turned around, and pulled Schultz hard enough to nearly pull him off his feet, but, with a long bracing step forward, he managed to stop his fall.

"What's with you? Where you headed boy?"

Adolph barked and pulled Schultz precariously down the winding steps. Just one missed step and Schultz's forehead would likely hit the rock-hard stone squarely—and then a few more flips would break and twist an arm and a leg, but no, he made it down intact. Even at the risk of endangering Schultz, Adolph would not slow and several additional officers tried there level-best to keep up. The obsessed German Shepherd led the men to the tower gate, down through the old town, and to a riverside marina. He went up to a boat where a smartly dressed gentleman in red & white-checkered jeans was accepting tickets from a line of tourists with 35mm cameras hung about their necks. He pulled ahead of them with Officer Schultz in toe.

"What in the devil are you trying to do, Adolph? We're looking for a little girl, not scantily-clad tourists...or are you after one of those onboard dinners? Weren't you fed before being saddled with me? Or do you know something about the grub on these tourist vessels? *Wienerschnitzel* on your last job maybe?"

Several more police officers followed Adolph aboard and everyone became quite alarmed. Could there be a bomb-carrying terrorist on board, or worse, contaminated ice scream?

Adolph sniffed his way quickly down the starboard and portside seats until he abruptly came to a stop next to an overly dressed gentleman with a young female child sitting beside him at the gunwale. The little girl, stiff as an ironing board, stared fixedly down at the floor, a frown on her face.

As the *polizei* approached the gentleman, he stood up, looked around in sheer panic, made a move toward the outside, and dove over the gunwale into the river. An officer approached Schultz, "We believe the gentleman was the ex-husband. We'll pull him in, not let him drown. This cruiser was about to leave the dock; you'll get an award for finding this kidnapped kid."

"Really?"

"How did you track the girl down here?"

"You'll have to ask my partner; he figured it out."

"He did, did he?"

"Absolutely. I think I'll keep him," said Schultz, "he's got a nose for detective work."

The German Shepherd, in a seated position—long pink tongue hanging out—looked up to Schultz with the whites of his eyes showing and Schultz responded to him with a *"danke schön."*

A BANK HEIST

Bankraub! Bankraub! Officer Schultz placed upon a CB call about a bank robbery. Within minutes Schultz and his new dog partner arrived at the bank just as an overweight man wearing an overcoat came running out of the front door with a large canvas sack. Schultz jumped out of his Volkswagen and ran toward the robber, but the bandit turned and pointed a 9mm Beretta at the uninvited guest.

"Okay, that's alright; don't need to fly off the handle," cautioned Schultz.

"Put your hands up, hands up, high!" demanded the robber.

Schultz did as the robber insisted and replied, "With that command you could be a cop."

"Halt den Mund!"

"Shut up, I will, yes sir."

Back inside the *Polizist* Volkswagen, the German Shepherd was calmly watching the goings on, but suddenly, he took a flying leap through the driver's side window and ran around behind the robber and approached.

"Drop your gun, Officer…slowly," demanded the robber. "Take that Walther out of its holster."

"Okay, okay, no problem, no problem…"

"Slow—ly."

Schultz dropped his PPK on the sidewalk.

"There now, you can walk away," asserted Schultz, "take your stash and go."

As the robber turned to run away, Adolph ran up to him and leapt for his gun-carrying hand, his tooth-filled muzzle wrapping itself around the man's arm. The thief jerked in abject fear, but Adolph wouldn't let go. The man dropped his gun and that's when Schultz picked up his Walther and targeted the robber, aiming carefully at the head, his left hand bracing the right.

"You want to see this German Shepherd take you down. He likes juggler juice for his meat sauce…a wonderful dressing for those crisp, uncured, flesh–enshrouded bones of yours. He'll gnaw on them for hours."

"He Likes Juggler Juice For His Meat Sauce."

The robber looked at the German Shepherd hard. Adolph stared back hard.

"Get down on the ground, now!" demanded Schultz.

"Ruuurrr," Adolph added his own threat to let the robber know they *both* meant business. The Shepherd stayed focused on the robber as two more cop beetles showed up. In no time, the robber was handcuffed and put in a VW; a cop carefully directing his head so it wouldn't be hit—to hard—on entering.

WHO MEANS BUSINESS?

Officer Schultz and Adolph sat in their VW cruising the back streets of Heidelberg when an anxious man, carrying a brown paper sack, ran from a *McDonald's* and started down the cobblestone street until he came to an abrupt stop and turned back to see Officer Schultz and his dog sidekick jumping from a police vehicle. The frightened man pulled a small pistol from his breast pocket. Schultz realized they were facing the criminal who robbed the hamburger stand and now meant business; he wasn't going to be stopped by a cop walking his dog. Adolph growled. Sometimes a snarl with bared teeth was enough to get a crook to surrender, drop his weapon, and not run or fight, but, apparently, that would not to be this time.

"My dog means business," declared Schultz.

"This gun is loaded with thirty-eights that'll make the pooch back off. He doesn't scare me."

"Well, he should. He won't reason with you, you'll get no deal from him."

Adolph growled as if he understood everything his partner was saying.

"Me, on the other hand, *can* reason with you. I don't want to see your blood all over the sidewalk; city maintenance workers have enough to do. Adolph, here, on the other hand, loves to use his canines for tearing into fresh meat."

The thief showed the whites of his eyes and were fixed on the dog, not on Officer Schultz. His weapon fell slightly.

"He's harmless when he's in my command," added Schultz. "Just drop your weapon. If you try to turn and run, one of your legs will be clamped in his powerful jaws—and he won't let go until more police arrive. That's a promise. So drop it!"

The thief didn't move, frozen in Siberian tundra.

"If you try to run, well, he's fast! Faster than I. Drop it, hands up. Now!"

Adolph growled again as if on command.

The crook dropped the pistol and quickly put up his hands. Schultz handcuffed him easily because Adolph's eyes stayed fixed on the thief. The officer was forced to admit: Adolph a great partner, making a collar a rarity before now.

So that began an engaging relationship for these new partners; their hunts and apprehensions likely to make the nightly news after every successful arrest. They would live together and love it—on TV.

Officer Schultz reached down to pet his new partner, "Jesus Adolph, I'm going to have to get me a vacuum cleaner."

THE HOCKENHEIMRING

Officer Schultz and Sergeant Adolph sat outside a *McDonald's* sharing a free hamburger when a voice from police headquarters blared over the vehicle intercom: "Officer Schultz, Officer Schultz, we need Adolph A.S.A.P. He has some training in bomb detection. There's a Formula One Grand Prix race at the Hockenheimring tomorrow. Word of possible terrorist attack."

Schultz picked up his radio mike, "Bomb detection? You mean this patrol dog is good at that too?"

"He loves to hunt, so whatever we ask of him, narcotics, currency, electronics, gunpowder...explosives detection just took him three weeks to get pretty darn good at it. You're the one that didn't get any bomb training so Adolph will tell you what to do."

"I'm sure. Is the bomb in one of the race cars?"

"We don't know that yet. We're going to have to check the vehicle pits, restrooms, announcing booths, and acres of grandstands. We need every police dog we can muster. Our K9's can cover the ground quite rapidly using a nose that has 40 times as many scent-receptors as humans—200 million to our measly 5 million."

"We obviously don't have much time. I guess the intention is to blow it during the race tomorrow..."

"Get going."

"I don't know how to direct this dog."

"Get going."

Officer Schultz motioned Adolph to get back into their VW; he jumped in, and off they dashed—Hochenheimring only about 25 kilometers from Heidelberg.

Adolph and Schultz arrived at the ring only minutes later and into the front entrance they barged. Immediately assigned an area to search, they hurried off, walkie-talkie in hand in case they found something suspicious. The two cops were a team. Adolph seemed to trust Schultz and Schultz seemed to trust Adolph. They checked out several restrooms and then Schultz let him sniff some gunpowder. He took Adolph off his leash so he could move faster and not be constrained by his handler.

"Go find a bomb, Adolph, go."

And off he ran, nose high.

"How was Adolph going to alert him of a bomb?" Schultz wondered. "German spiel?"

Adolph moved swiftly, scanning the ground rapidly with his long black snout, but soon he abruptly came to a stop and looked back at the lagging-behind Schultz.

"I'm coming, Adolph, I'm coming. Boy, you look happy and motivated, and you outrank me, so I'll follow your lead, Sergeant. Move out." Off they both bound along rows of bleachers and down walkways looking into trackside trees and every cubbyhole they could find. Other K9s could be seen around the course also energetically at work.

Adolph stopped, looked back at Schultz, and barked.

"What are you trying to tell me now?"

Adolph repeated his commanding bark, "Ruff, ruff."

"You found something?"

Adolph stood still, frozen in place, pointing with his nose. There was a large canvas backpack lying under one of the bleachers. Schultz approached the backpack, but then Adolph turned, blocked his advance, and actually pushed Schultz backward.

Schultz got the message, hit the call button on his walkie-talkie, and, in less than a minute, several officers showed up.

"Good boy, good boy." Schultz pulled Adolph aside, reached his leash, and caressed him so very gratefully on the face, chin, thighs, and belly. The German Shepherd's tongue hung out so far it almost touched the pavement.

"Let's go find some water, you and me."

Adolph barked.

"I think this is the bond the Station Sergeant was talking about, Adolph; if I can trust you with my life, then you, I'm sure, expect me to keep you safe from harm. I won't let you jump out of the police wagon without stopping first...yeah, you better not.

Adolph barked.

"Dogs really can be man's best friend, want an ice scream treat?"

Adolph whined and begged, jumping with joy.

In no time, the grounds were cleared and the bomb squad successfully disarmed a dynamite bundle with a clock timer. Two more packages were found on the course. Disaster averted. After their water break, the new Schultz-Adolph team returned to the station in Heidelberg.

"The experiment was successful," declared the Station Sergeant. "How well you could relate to an unfamiliar K9 without much training of your own. Do you still dislike dogs?"

"Uh, no, not at all, not this one anyway."

"You two clicked real fast. It's a fact that a dog can tell if you're having a good day. If you're feeling good, he feels good, and vice versa. If you're feeling bad, he's feeling bad. He will learn to read you and you have to learn to read him: his small movements, his behavior, and even how he looks at you. You did well so far… thanks to Adolph. He'll get a medal."

"Adolph will?"

The Station Sergeant bent down, "Good job, Sergeant Adolph."

"He was indeed a brave soul," said Schultz. "You wouldn't find me sticking my nose into someone else's business."

"I hope not."

"Can we get back to patrolling now?"

"This canine experiment seems to be a success. You'll be taking the dog home from now on; he' going to be your new buddy 24-hours a day. Hope he likes your bed."

"Say what?"

THE END

Little Sheba, a Yorkshire Terrier

17. Two Talking Toys
By Don Kirk

Perro Grande trotted as stately as you please into the open front gate of Ms. Petersen's front yard. For a change, he didn't have to move dirt and crawl under the chain link fence to get inside. Ms. Petersen was a young, pretty, thin-as-a-rail hairdresser working at *Shana's Salon* and she acquired her adorable dog, Little Sheba, from her house-cleaning mother. Petersen had gotten the canine and a four-poster bed from an aging film star that had to move into a nursing home. But now, Ms. Petersen lay sound asleep in her new majestic bed at the back of the saloon, unaware that Little Sheba was running around outside.

The cute little head turner came running to the front gate.

"About time you got here," declared Sheba. "Come on let's go. My master's asleep inside."

"If she leaves the gate open, well that's just tough," replied Perro Grande.

Sure enough, the gate had been left open. Little Sheba was much too short to reach the latch above and so this was going to be a treat. It's true that she loved her new human soul mate, but, energetic and clever, Sheba wanted to go places. Sleeping all the time not her thing.

Sheba, a Yorkshire terrier, weighing in at just seven pounds, and Perro Grande, a tiny long-haired black and white Chihuahua, were gone in a flash, trotting with heads high down the neighborhood sidewalks as if in a Hollywood parade.

"This is Heaven," declared Grande.

"I thought Heaven had nothing but dogs…and maybe a few cats to chase."

"I hate to disappoint you Sheba, but Heaven hain't got much to be the queen of, and they won't let you chase *el gatos*, cat critters."

"Don't want to, I adore those furry felines."

"Was ya raised with 'em, Dearie?" asked Perro Grande.

"Affirmative. They were more sizeable than myself so I didn't dare meddle in their affairs."

Sheba looked as if she was dressed for a stage performance. A figure of flowing brown and grey hair dangled straight down on either side of her body and hung all the way to the floor. You couldn't see her body at all, just a small head with tiny V-shaped ears that stood tall and erect. The cranium also had long hair, dark eyes, and a round, black nose, but the rest of her looked like a stage curtain just waiting for Johnny Carson to show his face. Sheba tilted the scale at about seven pounds and most of that probably hair. And she stood at little more than half a foot. With a crown on her head, she'd look like the Queen of Sheba, so that look would likely explain her given name.

Little Sheba walked side-by-side with Perro Grande, both their heads facing forward and high as if they owned the territory even though the Yorkshire Terrier had rarely experienced it before: a leashed walk once in a while was about it.

Sheba sniffed, squatted down beside a flowery bush, and Perro Grande raised a hind leg to make his claim to this route.

Standing at just seven inches tall and weighing in at less than six pounds, Perro could fit easily into a ladies purse. His chest and paws were white, the legs and nose tan, and the rest of his stately stature covered with short black hair. His cute little round head sported upturned ears, a short snout, and focused, bulging black eyeballs.

The two toy breeds walked on and continued to converse.

"Can a cat be trained?" asked the Chihuahua.

"Not as easy as a human. My roommate Miss Fussy—she goes by Ms. Petersen—was easy to train. I can get what I want with just a grin and fetching eyes."

"Your eyes are that, and I see she keeps you well groomed."

"The hair is a little too long sometimes; I step on it," pointed out Little Sheba.

Perro Grande, a Chihuahua

"In *me casa*, I also rule the roost. Even *el jefe's* lounge chair is mine. If he tries to sit in it when I want to lounge, I let him have it with a low-pitched bark and growl, but he knows even when I just show my tiny teeth that I mean business. But even that's rarely necessary; he understands me with my fixed stare of warning and jumps out of my chair promptly. He even leaves me his television remote. *Comprende?*"

"I do. You're good with those little paws of yours. me, I know what Miss Fussy's thinking before she does."

"I kin pick up a lot of what *jefe* is a-sayin'. I know when to come and when to vamoose. "He even thinks I can't spell and now says 'You ready for a B—A—T—H?' Thinks I don't know what he's up to. I'm under the china cabinet before he kin get to the letter 'T'."

"I don't like taking a bath either, but it helps keep my silky coat clean and comfy."

"I can't say that about me or my den," said Perro. "I chew up toys and furniture and keep my *jefe* off balance. *Me casa* is a dog's breakfast: a confusing, untidy mess. I call my master, 'Bedraggled.'"

"Not so in my place of residence; Miss Fussy cleans house hourly."

Perro and Sheba scurried on down the sidewalk of this relatively nice suburban neighborhood.

"Where did your master find you, Mr. Grande?

"In a big steel cage. I reckon I was put there 'cause I bit someone."

"They didn't put you down?"

"Does it look like it? I was three days from *muerte*, and this here elderly gentleman in wrinkled suit and loose tie came in and fancied me for some reason. I played *muy simpático* as nice as I could."

"And…"

"He took me home."

"Wow! Every dog has his day."

"I reckon so; he was, he is, a pushover."

"That accent of yours?"

"I'm from *Méjico*. My grand pappy was the Aztec King of Brazil."

"Is that right?"

"We're good at predicting the future," voiced Perro.

"I see."

"In spades."

"Then maybe you can tell me where I can find rodents?"

"In trash dumps."

"I mean, I can't locate the rats anymore," said Sheba. "And they scurry about faster than lizards."

"If you could stop letting Miss Fussy use that nasal spray on you, you could sniff a lot better. After a time, your nostrils anticipate the spray so they go ahead and close up every day. Stop taking it and that there will clear those sinuses; you'll again be able to detect those vital scents and find them long-tailed vermin easier."

"Marvelous, Perro Grande. Where did you assimilate that knowledge?"

"My pappy, Poquito, was from Argentina, he learned me."

The two laid-back, easy-going toys turned into an alley.

"What is that up ahead? A fellow mouser, maybe a cat?" inquired Sheba. "What in the Devil is it? It's moving, looks quite large, I'm out of here!"

"Wait! Hold on," replied the self-assured Chihuahua. "I seen one on a family trip to West Texas; that there is an armadillo!"

"A what?"

"It's got a shield-like covering so don't even think a grabbin' it with your canines; it won't do no good and could require a trip to the tooth doctor."

"I'll go for the neck."

"No good there either, stay back, the neck's well protected too. The good thing is they eats them fire ants that sometimes gets on our bellies and bites us like real good."

"I saw an armadillo at the neighbor's house," said Sheba.

"No, I seen that critter too, that was just a cat wearing a baseball cap."

"Oh."

"How about those animals with the long thorns?" asked Little Sheba.

"Porcupines. Stay away from those critters; they's nothing to be sniffed at. Stay away if you don't want a mouth full of quills. They may look like cats, but they don't run like 'em. I had an uncle who was on the operatin' table from morin' to lunch…and them quills hurt him more than being dragged behind a human's car with a caught-in-the-bumper leash."

"Ouch! Oh my!"

Sheba and Perro walked on, checking out all the new smells.

"It's so wonderful here, lots of new scents," voiced Sheba as she sniffed a sewer drain. "Maybe this earth is heaven, and we're…"

"This ain't heaven," declared Perro, "I don't see 'nough cats to chase after."

"Maybe they have their own Heaven somewhere's else," supposed Little Sheba.

"That would be unfortunate for us," added Perro. "What does it take for a sweet dog like myself to go to Cat Heaven?"

"Maybe if you're nice to cats here on Earth for a change...and don't bark so much."

"In a dog's eye, ain't gonna happen."

The two dogs sauntered back onto a street surrounded with rows and rows of nice human residences.

All of a sudden, Perro Grande pulled up, "I smell trouble a-comin' just around the bend. I just know it." He put one paw to his forehead and said, "*Cerebro.*"

Off in the distance, sure enough, was a large creature that came into view.

"There, look! Hope you have your false teeth in."

"I don't have false teeth. These are the originals," insisted Little

"It's so wonderful here, lots of new scents."

Sheba as she raised her lips to show them. They glinted and showed no tarter.

"Pretty, very pretty. They're white as an aggravated baby after one of my sneering growls. I see you do have Miss Fussy at your beck and call."

A brawny, big-boned powerhouse, a Rottweiler, weighing in at over one hundred pounds and standing well over two feet tall at the withers, was approaching the toy dogs. He stood tall and was midnight black with tan feet. His snout was also tan, but the mouth was closed, having been alerted to the possible approaching threat...or thrilling quarry. Of German ancestry, the Rottweiler was raised to herd sheep and not chase small fries, but they would be so easy—and so much fun—to take down.

The little Chihuahua stopped and began to bark wildly. Sheba remained calm.

"Easy does it, Grande," said Sheba, "we don't know his intentions."

"He's bigger than us, what else do you need to know?"

"I thought you were good at predicting the future."

"One slight snap of the neck...that's our future."

"I know he's bigger than we are," announced the terrier, "but you have that threatening bite that'll fend off anyone...even through a chain-link fence."

"Okay, just stay behind me...and don't run."

The Rottweiler approached cautiously.

"Stand your ground, Perro. Use your dog smarts."

The big black canine came to a stop and his nose twitched.

"It's okay," assured Perro Grande to the Rottweiler, "I hope you've already had a good meal. If this is your territory, we're just passing through, don't mean to claim it."

"How can I be sure?" asked the Rottweiler.

"My word's good."

Little Sheba nodded in agreement.

The Rottweiler looked to the cute long haired dog, "And you are, *Fräulein?*"

"Little Sheba."

"Nice hairdo. You get frequent baths too, I assume."

"Don't say that word," interrupted Perro Grande.

"Why?"

"It can cause her to...do you like squirrels?" asked Perro.

"For dinner maybe, but they're awfully fast."

"Armadillos?"

A what?"

"Never mind. Care for rawhide bones?"

"I would love them but my master," added the Rottweiler, "is a little slow on the uptake. I'm having a hard time getting him to understand what I want. I don't think you can teach an old dog new tricks."

"You speakin' of yourself or him?"

"Him. I'm still a young dynamo, he's the one getting up in years. The tail is wagging the dog."

"You have to use positive reinforcement to train him."

"What do you mean by 'positive re-in...re-in-force...'?"

"You just have to make him think you love him like no other. Give him praise with a lick to the face and a loving jump into his lap."

"I'm afraid I'm too strapping for that."

"Don't know until you've tried."

"I'll pass."

"You should run to the door when he comes home. Sit in front of him and smile."

"What if I was to bring him a billfold he'd lost in the backyard. I did that once and he gave me a big ol' juicy collarbone."

"That works."

"But there's no more billfolds out there. Maybe I can eat my dung to keep the yard clean."

Sheba raised her eyebrows at that, "*I'll* pass on that."

Out of the blue, the Chihuahua's eyes widened, "I...I sense trouble, we're about to...something's coming..."

The Rottweiler looked up just then to see a huge red-tailed hawk with massive wings swoop down, targeting either Perro Grande or Little Sheba. The Rottweiler jumped on his hind legs and reached skyward. The toys stepped back as the four-legged monolith grabbed the predatory hawk in its mouth. The hawk's wings flapped violently.

The two toys were fearful, mesmerized, frozen in their tracks. The Rottweiler shook the life out of the hawk and lay it calmly down. Life went out of the bird's big beady eyes.

Perro, still tense, afraid to take a breath, finally moved and spoke, "What do you say we all go to the ice cream store; I know how to get in the back door…a torn screen door."

"But going with you two little ones could give a dog a bad name."

"We won't bark a word."

"Any bratwurst or schnitzel?" asked the Rotweiller.

"No."

"Okay then…chocolate mousse."

"No, I don't eat chocolate; it's harmful to dogs."

"I'll have vanilla with fried chicken caramel on top," declared Sheba.

"In a cone…"

"Hot diggity dog!"

The three of them ran off lickety-split for good eating in an ice cream parlor!

The three canines soon arrived at the ice scream store, panting, but excited, and raced around to an alley where stood a back door to the parlor. A torn screen door, sure enough, much too small for the Rottweiler, but Perro…

"I'm going in," announced Mr. Grande, "you two stay here."

The Rottweiler turned to the Yorkshire, "So how long have you been in the neighborhood?"

"I don't get out much on my own," replied Sheba. "Perro takes me out from time to time."

"Under the fence?"

"Open gate."

"Good, I wouldn't want to see you doin' any diggin' and crawlin' with that there gorgeous coat of yourn."

"I've got a little lady, Miss Fussy, who knows hair. She takes good care of me, lets me sleep with her and takes me everywhere."

"My master is a midget not much taller than myself," replied the Rottweiler. "I don't sleep with him and I'm careful not to pull him down when he takes me for walks."

"You've got the longest legs…"

"Nice eyes you have," said the Rottweiler as he circled little Sheba trying to get a look under her shaggy skirt and hoping she'd find a table to jump up on. After the Rottweiler's survey Little Sheba did her own circling.

"What's your name?" she finally asked.

"My midget master, R2-D2, calls me 'Let Me Lean On You'. You can call me what you like."

"Handsome."

"I love you."

Sheba's brown eyes glowed and her wavy hair swirled as she looked up at this imposing brute.

"My den is just down the street," said Sheba, "What's your favorite food?"

"Rawhide anytime, and I prefer duck over chicken. And those milk bones humans give us as a reward...are you kidding me? Where's the beef?"

"My lady, Miss Fussy, loves beef...and she gives me a share."

"This is going to be a hot day, better to just lay around, get a little shut eye...and maybe more...a good dog day afternoon," said the Rottweiler, "and I want you to know I don't have a quiet place to stay."

Abruptly, the screen door squeaked.

"Enough already, this'll be a shaggy dog story," declared Perro as he crawled through the screen door with a mouth full of dripping ice scream cones. He lay the treats down on the pavement. "Here, these are for you. I'm dog tired, I'm going home. Bone appétit."

"Can I see you again, Little Sheba?"

"I'm going with Perro."

THE END

Chief, a Dalmation

18. Firehouse No. 9

By Don Kirk

THE FIREHOUSE

The two-story, pink-brick firehouse with a small belfry projecting high above the roof was identifiable many miles away and the single truck bay with its closed, bright orange, multi-light, bi-fold doors was quite visible on Main Street. Large, black, antique cast-iron hinges tied the tall door panels together. It was probably a 1920's or earlier fire station, but this was the late summer of 1988 and the station was still in use. The bunkroom lay on a second floor and had a brass pole used by the fireman to descend to the ground floor when called to action. Helmets, smoke masks, bunker gear, and a few portable fire extinguishers hung on the perimeter walls. The head fireman lived at the firehouse full time and two other firemen pulled 24-hour-on, 48-hour-off shifts.

A shiny-red 1960's fire engine sat quietly in the vehicle bay: a *Seagrave* pumper with ladders, 500-gallon water tank, pump, rubber extension hoses, nozzles, and sitting on top: black hoses on reels. With an enclosed cab and fire extinguishers strapped to the side and rear running boards, the fire engine had, on each side of its curved hood, gold lettering that read: "Willieville F.D."

On this day, one of the firemen was bent over polishing the engine to keep it waxed and shiny to serve as a status symbol for the community.

Even though designated "Firehouse No. 9," this was the only fire station in the little town of Willieville and had one, past-its-prime fire truck, two on-duty firemen, and one dog that had actually been trained to hunt for trapped people. This male Dalmatian, known by all in the community as "Chief," was the life of the firehouse and responsible for keeping the firemen awake and alert, but, fortunately, there was rarely a major fire to be extinguished or a person to be rescued, in this very small community of just 1200 residents. A much bigger city once, but a major interstate highway passed it by. Only weekend tourists ventured in, and then probably by accident. Willieville hadn't had a structural or even a brush fire, in over four months. The fire engine was old, but it did have the basic equipment to fight the smaller fires. For bigger disasters, trucks from other nearby communities would be called in.

When Anson Sheridan, highest ranking of the two on-duty firemen—a large, heavy built, black-haired, six-foot-four tree trunk of a man—stood next to the short and skinny, blond-haired, five-foot-four David "Sonny" Day, he would wonder where the little man was. One might imagine them as direct descendants of Ollie and Stan, the *Laurel and Hardy* comedians or maybe the magicians *Penn and Teller*, also a short and tall team. No, these firemen were just straight men on perpetual duty in a lone firehouse. Sonny would often liven up the place with his always-positive attitude and off-the-cuff humor—that's why he was given the handle "Sonny" as opposed to "Cloudy."

And then, standing at their feet, and always close by, the long-legged, fifty-pound "Chief" who stood a few inches less than two feet tall to the backside. He wore a short-haired, white coat with dense black spots and had thin ears set high, close to the head, and tapered toward the tips, always ready for action.

Chief, a muscular dog capable of running for miles without fatigue, could put to shame any male athlete and demonstrated excellent endurance and stamina when on call. In fact, he needed lots of exercise to keep him happy and fit, and the boys, Sonny and Sheridan, gave him that. Climbing the winding stairs to the bunks was good exercise along with running with the crew on vigorous jogs—they all needed the exercise to stay fit for any actual fire fighting, though a rarity in this quiet little town.

A CARD TRICK

One day, Anson and Sonny, sitting at their green, felt-covered poker table, were playing a little stud poker when Anson called the polka-dotted Dalmatian over. Sonny held the bigger stack of poker chips.

"Chief, come here," said Anson as he tapped on an empty chair, "Hop on up."

Chief followed the order without hesitation, leaped into the chair, and put his paws on the table. Anson took the deck of cards in his hand, shuffled them, and fanned them out in his two hands.

"Okay, Chief, pick a card, any card."

Chief quickly grabbed a card with his snout, pulled it out, and dropped it on the table.

"Great, Boy, now let's see what card you've chosen."

Anson picked up the card, turned it over, and showed it to his partner Sonny, "He pulled a *Five of Spades*."

Anson lay the card back on the table face down. He then took two more randomly selected cards from the pack and laid them beside the chosen card but placed them several inches apart. Chief—and Sonny—carefully watched the proceeding. Chief was born with one blue eye and one brown eye, an unusual set of eyeballs that captured everyone's attention and made onlookers curious as to what he was actually thinking in that little brain of his. Anson placed the deck aside and rearranged the order of the three cards several times as Chief kept his eyes focused on the three cards.

"Okay, Chief, it's your turn. Which card is the one you just picked?"

Chief quickly put his paw on one of the playing cards. Anson promptly turned it over. It was, indeed, the *Five of Spades*!

"Alright, how did he do that?" demanded Sonny.

"You'll have to ask Chief, he fooled me too."

"Yeah, right, he doesn't speak English, at least I don't think so. Show me those cards."

Anson handed Sonny the three cards laid out on the table and Sonny looked at them carefully, examining both sides of the cards. "Chief, tell me, how did you do it?"

Chief let out a loving whimper.

"No, Sonny, I didn't force the card on him," declared Anson as he handed his partner the deck of cards. "Here, *you* can fan the cards and let Chief pick one."

"Sounds like a deal, no pun intended."

Sonny fanned them out and Chief picked one of the cards with his mouth and laid it on the table. Sonny then added two more cards to the table and reordered them as was done before. A quick ponder and Chief again aced the chosen card.

"How in the hell?"

"Just a little Dog Magic."

A COMMERCIAL

That afternoon, a green-suited man with an ugly, red-striped tie over a yellow shirt walked into the fire station.

"I'm the director, Michelle Abernathy."

"Michelle?"

"I know, my Scottish mother wanted a girl."

"Oh sorry, and she didn't get a gay…"

"No, hell no. As you must have heard, your city council has approved our use of the firehouse for a commercial."

"Yes."

"You've got pretty much what we need," added Abernathy, "a beautiful old fire house, brass pole, and the wonderful Dalmatian we've heard so much about, but, we will need to replace your newer fire engine with an older one to match your historic station. We have rounded up a 1920's *Howard-Cooper* vintage fire truck with wooden ladders on each side, a hose reel on top, and long black hard lines on one side. The engine's hood will have printed on it in gold lettering: "City of Pratt Falls.""

"What? Is this going to be one of those Saturday-night TV gags or a serious commercial?" asked Anson Sheridan.

"A commercial. But humor is a good way to hold an audience. We will also need to add a brick fireplace—just a temporary thing I assure you, to fit the needs of our script. Over it will be a Christmas wreath, colored lights, and some very special drink tumblers on the mantle."

"This for Christmas release?"

"Yes, to sell Christmas Cheer: a brandy and rum cocktail by our client *Noweiser*. We'll provide you with a few bottles for this Christmas and to last you into the New Year."

"Eggnog will do just fine," declared Anson.

"Here's the script for you to ponder. It's a sixty-second commercial for their traditional *Tom & Jerry* brandy and rum punch. We have a few shots with your dog in them."

"And maybe a few shots of spiked eggnog for me and the crew," added Sonny.

"If you wish."

DAY OF THE SHOOT

Anson, looking down at his favorite dog, "Today's the day, Chief. The film crew hired by the *Mercenary Productions* ad agency is coming to shoot that *Noweiser* commercial and you've got a part in it!"

The art department had erected a tall Christmas tree and built a convincing mock-up of a brick-facade fireplace decorated with a Christmas wreath and colored lights. In the firebox were fake logs neatly stacked on a steel grate and a Hollywood special effects rig behind it to create bright yellow-orange "fake" flames. Not sure about this contraption, Anson brought out a couple of fire extinguishers and set them nearby.

"We're not using real fire," said one technician.

"I'll believe it when I *don't* see it," replied Anson.

A LITTLE DALMATION HISTORY

"You've got an amazing dog there," said Director Abernathy, a script rolled up in his hand. "I know he'll be great for this spot, Mr. Arson."

"That's 'Anson'."

"Oh, so sorry, I apologize," said Abernathy, both of his hands held up as if preparing to fend off a hit. He then added, "The dog's residuals should greatly help pay for his room and board."

"*If* the commercial is a hit."

"Your dog's going to make it so. He's perfect for the firehouse setting."

"The Dalmatian," said Anson, "was originally a coach dog that ran along with the horse-drawn wagons. He had no problem keeping up with them and he would run off any attacking dogs that could panic the horses. And his breed got along great with horses, not typical of most dogs. Later, when the bigger horse-drawn fire engines came along, the Dalmatian would run out ahead, barking at bystanders to clear the street so the horses could gallop down the street and through intersections without stopping."

"Mr. Sheridan, does he run alongside *your* fire engine?" asked Michelle as he looked at the *Seagrave*.

"No, we've got a siren now to clear traffic so Chief rides with us inside the cab. In fact, he's the one that tells us where to go. He's got a masterful nose for tracking down smoke and fire."

"Why do you call him 'Chief'?"

"Because *he's* the one in charge."

"Is that right?"

"We actually found him in a dog pound several years ago. He had been passed between several owners who couldn't deal with his deafness."

"He's deaf?"

"No, not completely. Loss of hearing in one ear and the other is on the way."

"How do you…"

"Sign language. His eyesight is good, odor perception great. I promise you, he'll be easy to work with. He's highly obedient."

"I hope so, the add agency is betting on him."

"Chief knows all the basic commands like sit, stay, down, and come here, all by sign," declared Anson, "and he can do a few magic tricks."

"You're telling me he's a magician?"

"You bet. Here Chief, come here. Anson motioned him over. I've got three of your toys and I'll put one under each of these three tin cups—a green frog, a red tennis ball, and a small, blue teddy bear."

Anson moved the three cups back and forth as Chief watched closely.

"Alright Chief, where's the frog?" Anson passed his palm over the cups.

Chief placed his nose close to each of the three cups and then

"Alright Chief, where's the frog?"

quickly took his paw and pushed over one of the cups. Sure enough, there was the frog!

The film crew clapped. Chief bowed his head!

"Chief, which one has the tennis ball?"

In short order, the talented Dalmatian turned over the tumbler with the ball.

The film crew cheered.

"What about the teddy bear? Chief, where's the teddy bear?"

The Dalmatian picked up the last cup with his mouth...but nothing was under it! The teddy bear had disappeared. All eyes widened.

Chief lowered his body and reached under the table with his snout...and up came the bear!

The crew was awe-struck to say the least—mouths hanging open.

"Alright, men, enough, we've got work to do," announced Director Abernathy. "Mr. Sheridan, can you get your dog upstairs?"

"I'm on it."

The Fresnel lights and practicals were switched on.

"We're ready," called down an actor on the bunk floor.

"Roll sound."

The soundman, sitting in a chair nearby, turned on his *Nagra* tape recorder. Tape began to roll.

Up on the second floor, a good-looking actor dressed as a fireman climbed onto the brass pole, wrapped his legs around it, gripping tightly with gloved hands, and then Anson placed Chief on the actor's shoulder.

"Roll Camera."

"Rolling."

"Action," and the fireman slid smoothly down the pole.

"Cut, great! That's a take. Great job, Chief! Next setup."

"Chief, go get the director a drink," called out Sonny using a hand signal with right hand sliding over his left palm. The Dalmatian dashed to the refrigerator in the firehouse kitchen and grabbed a length of rope tied to the door handle. The door came open and Chief grabbed a bottled drink sitting at the bottom of the fridge. He brought it to Abernathy.

"Why thank you, Chief. I could use an assistant like you."

Chief, let out an eager yelp, took a step back, and rolled over on his back.

"But he'll want something in return," said Sonny.

Abernathy bent down to rub his belly.

"So cute. You got something to wash off my hands?"

"Oh, don't worry, he plays in the water when we test our hoses."

A DOG TEACHING AN ACTOR

The actor "Bud," now in front of the camera for a close-up, was having trouble expressing himself; unable to say his lines in a humorous, audience-gripping, way.

"Put some levity into it!" called out Director Abernathy.

Chief came up to him and put his paws on the actor's knees and then jumped up toward his face trying to lick it.

The director yelled out: "Get that dog down. We've got a scene to shoot here."

The actor spoke to Chief, "It's okay boy, your breath is better than Michelle's, him and that ladies mouth wash..."

"Get that critter out of here..."

The actor laughed.

"That's it, that's it, I want to see that smile, roll camera, go with your lines."

Chief got down and backed out of the shot.

The actor "read" his lines with levity and it was a take.

A TOP HAT TRICK

Several scenes later Director Abernathy asked, "Show me another magic trick your dog can do."

"Certainly. Just a minute, I'll be right back." Chief followed Anson upstairs, and a minute later they returned.

"Okay, Mr. Director, watch this."

Anson showed Abernathy an empty black-felt top hat and placed it on the poker table open-end-down. He told Chief to pick up the hat. Chief grabbed it by the rim, wrestling with it a bit but managed to get it turned open-end-up on the table. He then reached into the hat with his snout and pulled out a fluffy white toy rabbit. Chief looked at Anson.

"Yeah. Chief, you can have it; it's your new toy."

Chief leaped from the chair and ran off.

"That's down right amazing!" declared Abernathy. "Where did that rabbit come from? Maybe Chief can get a Hollywood gig."

"We'd be bored to death without this very special mascot at our fire station."

"We'll have to use this dog for more *Noweiser* commercials," said the director as he turned to the man representing the ad agency.

"Depends on how this goes," replied the stern-faced all-business agent.

Chief did a handstand with hind legs extended high in the air, began walking forward, and then did a forward flip.

"This canine needs to be in a circus."

"Another commercial."

"Maybe."

A REAL FIRE CALL

Out of the blue, a clanging alarm went off in the firehouse.

Sonny came running up to Anson.

"We've a call. 26 Grayson Street. House fire, two story." Looking to the director, "Chief will have to come with us."

Their 1960's *Seagrave* had been parked outside, ready and waiting. The men needed only to gear up. Donned were yellow fire suits and rubber boots. They grabbed their helmets and face masks and out the door they went with Chief close behind. Chief jumped into the cab, sat on the center console—"riding shotgun" as it were—and Anson was the last to climb in. They started the engine and off they blared.

When they arrived, flames were coming out of a small side window and black smoke emanated from under the eaves of a two-story house. They pulled up to the curb and began to unroll their fire hoses, but, unexpectedly, a young lady in a nightgown came running out the front door screaming, "My baby, my baby, help me! Dear God! She's upstairs. Help!"

At that, the brave and beautiful black-spotted Dalmatian ran into the open door. Smoke billowed high, the house interior still relatively clear, air breathable a foot or so above the floor. Chief plod from room to room and sniffed his way to a baby stroller, but no baby was there. He continued his search. Living room, dining room, kitchen, oh there, a stairwell, but it led into dense smoke. Up the stairs he bound anyway, through dark, noxious air, but his nose took him to a baby crib. He pushed his snout between the rails and searched through the bedding with his nose. Nothing. Chief moved to a human's bed and stood on his hind legs to sniff it. He heard a baby crying, but with only one good ear, he couldn't quite tell the sound's source, but his nose could. He jumped up on the bed and walked to the opposite end. There, Chief grabbed with his canines the sleepwear of a baby and dragged it to the edge of the bed where he released it and jumped to the floor. He carefully lifted the baby to the floor. Chief barked, once, twice, three times, waited a moment, and repeated the call he'd been trained to yelp in this situation, but there was no sign of Anson or Sonny. Chief picked up the crying little human, carried it to the stairs, and started down.

Anson, in full fire-fighting gear, entered the house only to find choking white smoke completely engulfing the interior, his vision down to almost zero.

Sonny Day tried to hold the lady from going back in while also trying to spray the water from the onboard water tank.

Inside, Anson went looking for the stairwell but wasn't finding it; the stair was at the back of this old two-story wood-framed house. In fact, it was back behind the kitchen where fire engulfed the room: the kitchen stove was on fire. Chief barked. Anson hurried toward the yelp and found Chief at the bottom of the stairs with the baby. He took the baby and left the house amidst smoke and flames.

Sonny sprayed water into the open windows of the upper story as another truck showed itself, siren blaring, and set out to help. The crew twisted a hose onto a fire hydrant some distance down the street.

Anson handed the baby to her mother as Chief trotted over to them and looked up with concerned eyes.

"This Dalmatian found the baby and brought her downstairs," pointed out Anson.

"My baby, she okay?"

"We need to look her over. An ambulance is on the way."

"Chief, back to the truck."

BACK AT THE STATION

Hours later back at the station—truck and gear yet to be restored—the firemen took to the shower and had something to eat. This was a big event for them, bigger than the commercial. If preparation for the next fire call interfered with the shoot, then that would be *Mercenary Productions* problem. Chief also had to get cleaned up. While the showering moved forward the soundman took a break, but Director Abernathy figured he could get a few pickup shots: close-ups that didn't require sound.

Meanwhile, Sonny got the Dalmatian in the shower with him, gave him a good scrubbing, and Anson dried him off. The director got a few MOS—*Mit Out Sound*—shots meaning no synchronous audio required.

CHIEF GETS AN ACTING PART

"While we were out and about, I see you've been shooting," said Anson Sheridan, still drying himself off.

"We didn't miss you, but Chief there, that's another matter," said Director Abernathy. "I sure want to use him for another shot. Could you get him to pick up something and carry it?"

"Probably. Show me what you got."

"I need him to carry a packaged Christmas present into the scene, place it in the lap of a lady sitting in this arm chair, and then I want him to sit."

"I can give him most commands with hand signals so the soundman can record the scene."

"That's great! Let's try a rehearsal."

Abernathy set up the shot and with just a few "rehearsals" Chief got the hang of it.

"Roll sound."

"Rolling."

"Roll camera. Action."

Anson gave a hand signal, Chief brought the Christmas present to the lady, laid it in her lap, and then sat down in front of her.

"Where's Bud, darling?" asked the lady actor.

A male actor, "Bud" Henderson, came over and kneeled in front of the lady as if begging her for something. The lady shook her head "No." The man quickly stood up, and as he took a step back, his foot caught under an electrical cable providing power to some of the film-set lights. He fell backward and his outstretched arm reached for the tree causing it to fall and the both of them hit the floor. Sparks flew and all the lights went out. The actor's body shook violently.

"He's been electrocuted!"

Sonny ran for the medical kit and Anson went to cut the power at the main distribution panel. The gaffers also took to disconnecting cables and pulling the tree aside. Chief approached the man on the floor and licked his face. The actor's hand was shaking a bit and he was having difficulty breathing, but he tried to speak:

"I, I, my...where am...where am I?"

Jim, the Best Boy electrician, came over and kneeled down, "He's got a little redness on the hand! Stay away; don't touch him. He'll be okay, not enough volts, just 110."

Bud started to move, "I...I, I'm okay. Help me up."

"Power's off," yelled the Gaffer.

Jim helped him up as Chief tried to find out what had happened to the actor.

"His hand is red and charred, but he's okay," announced Jim.

Sonny showed up with his medical kit.

"Are you okay, Bud? Muscle pain, tremors, head humming?"

"No," Bud replied. "Probably just more wholesome, good-eatin' brain damage, so no loss there."

"Alright good, stand up, I think you're okay."

"I forgot my lines."

"You didn't have any."

"Oh."

Sonny smeared a topical antibiotic ointment on Bud's hand and dressed it. "You'll be fine. No trip to emergency will be necessary."

"That's good, my ex-wife works there; she'd make sure I needed surgery."

"Maybe you do need the scalpel," interjected the director, "you've always been about a half a bubble off, but that's another matter."

"I'm alright, *Michelle*. You could use a name change."

Chief barked approvingly at that.

"Get that tree back up, we've a commercial to finish! And Chief, don't pee on it."

Chief barked again.

The director and crew managed to right the Christmas tree and finish shooting the scene. It took a lot of work to shoot a commercial, but Chief seemed to enjoy every minute of this one.

ANOTHER MAGIC TRICK

"Okay good that's a take. Lunch."

The crew went for the craft service table in the kitchen to get their meal and find a seat. One of the crewmen had to ask, "can we see Chief do another card trick?"

"I suppose, once he finishes his bowl of food. He has to eat too you know."

Chief scarfed down his lunch and Anson called him over, "Sit boy."

The crew gathered around.

Anson shuffled a deck of cards in and out of his left hand and fanned out the cards. Chief picked a card from the deck, not a problem for him, he'd done it many times before. The Dalmatian apparently liked doing card tricks. Anson showed the film crew the selected card—a *Seven of Diamonds*—then put it back in the deck and returned it to the box. Anson took a handkerchief from his pocket, unfolded it, and laid it over the box of playing cards.

"First Chief, I want you to find the box of playing cards. Chief... find the box."

Chief dragged the handkerchief from the table and picked up the box of cards in his mouth.

"Now find *your* card, Chief," commanded Anson, pointing with an index finger.

Chief worked to open the box, picked it up, and shook it causing the cards to drop onto the table.

"Which one is yours?" asked Anson. "Which one?"

Chief pawed at the cards and tried to pick up one of them with his mouth. He finally succeeded and mouthed the card to

Anson who took it and held it up to the audience. It was a *Seven of Diamonds*!

"Alright, how in the hell does he do it?" asked Sonny. "You're forcing him the card aren't you?"

"I am not. Chief sees with his nose, he can 'see' what you can't. The trick is—and you promise not to tell anyone—when chief grabs a card he is leaving saliva on the card that he can then smell when looking for the chosen card. It's that simple."

"What about the toys under the cups?"

"I previously taught him to identify these toys by name. He associates a toy's name with its odor. That's all there is too it, just a little training."

"Amazing!"

"Enough of this lollygagging," called out Abernathy, "We have one more shot to get in the can. Our snow special effect should be ready now. A dolly shot on the street."

The crew dropped their paper plates and plastic forks in the trash and hurried off to get ready for the next set up. One of them pushed the camera dolly out into the street—twenty feet of Dolly track had already been laid.

A fake snow made of recycled paper called *SnowCel*, had been sprayed along the ground outside the fire station to make it look like a wintry snow-covered scene. Camera and lights were placed, turned on, and the camera assistant measured his focus distances. The dolly grip stood ready to pull back to a wider shot. Sound was rolling.

"Action!"

A fireman actor rushed out the front door, opened the bay doors, and out came the vintage Howard Cooper fire engine with it's horn tooting. The fireman, in all of his period fire-fighting gear, jumped onto the back of the engine. Riding with the driver in the front seat was Chief, sitting high, ears flapping.

"Quite a critter you got there!"

"You know it."

"Cut. That's a print. It's a wrap."

THE END

A Playful Russell Terrier

19. Get Me An Old Bulldog
By Don Kirk

I'm old and tired and looking for a little peace and quiet,
Fussing about with pointless exercise, I just don't buy it.
I just want to devour blueberry pancakes with *Karo* syrup,
But, instead, I've a Russell Terrier who is spry as a pup.

He wants to leap and play and walk and jump,
And spring and frolic 'round an old tree stump.
He wants to race and chase me about the yard,
And play with my next door neighbor's St. Bernard.

No. Get me an old bulldog that sleeps and lies about all day,
Who snores contented and needs no leash for him to stay.

At morning's first light, my Russell licks my face,
And seeks a long, loving, locking embrace.
He hankers to go a-huntin' afore the rabbits have gone to far,
And he's not a-wantin' me to sit quietly a-playin' my guitar.

No. Get me an old bulldog that sleeps and lies about all day,
Who snores contented and needs no leash for him to stay.

Every mornin' he yelps for food in his breakfast bowl,
And with a slurp of fresh water, he's ready to rock-and-roll.
He jumps and bounds and brings me a toy with which to play,
And that's afore I kin shave and down my oatmeal for the day.

No. Get me an old bulldog that sleeps and lies about all day,
Who snores contented and needs no leash for him to stay.

You want *me* to get it?

My Russell Terrier insists I throw him a ball to retrieve,
But when I toss it to far, he wants *me* to get it; that you can believe!
My Russell chases cats with boundless energy and enthusiasm,
And he runs and jumps on me to deliver painful muscle spasms.

No. Get me an old bulldog that sleeps and lies about all day,
Who snores contented and needs no leash for him to stay.

I don't need a running buddy, just one happy to sleep and snore,
And, when the need arises, can find his way out the back door.
I don't need a dog that loves to fetch balls and find silly toys.
I just need a tame and tidy dog that nips at his feet and enjoys.

No. Get me an old bulldog that sleeps and lies about all day,
Who snores contented and needs no leash for him to stay.

I just want a slow moving, always tired, cute couch potato,
Who can open the fridge to make his own *Sloppy Joe*.
I just want a canine critter that chills out in Bermuda shorts,
Not a Russell Terrier that wants to play canine sports.

No. Get me an old bulldog that sleeps and lies about all day,
Who snores contented and needs no leash for him to stay.

THE END

A cute couch potato?

Larry, a Shih-Poo

20. Moe, Larry, & Curley
By Don Kirk

Running down the alley of a small neighborhood in West Hollywood were three small dogs each weighing around eighteen pounds and standing no taller than a foot. Short-legged, but agile, no rat would have a fighting chance. They had been given the names of three famous comedians known as *The Three Stooges:* Moe, Larry, and Curley. Many residents in the neighborhood knew these dogs because they escaped, on occasion, from Jimmy Peters' small mansion where he kept and trained the dogs for occasional performances at *The Beverly Hills Palladium*. Today, they ran loose, ready to have a little freedom fun.

THE ALLEY

Larry stopped at a trash dump behind the *Silly Fool* restaurant where he found something of interest: an odoriferous box of fried chicken. But Moe came up to him and smacked him on the side of his face with his right paw.

"Whoa! Whoa! Why did you do that?" asked Larry.

"It hasn't been inspected by me you nitwit!" declared Moe. "Could get ya sick as a dog with a retching stomach."

Larry dropped the meat-filled tin foil. Moe took a whiff, then looked back at Larry, "I'll hafta taste it first."

Larry was a curly-haired shag carpet with a cuddly, teddy-bear look. He was two shades of grey, the drooping ears the darker of the two, and carried a golden-brown snout. His dark-as-night eyes appeared to always be on alert and a narrow pink tongue hung out between two sparkling-white canines. He was an oddly-named, long-haired crossbreed called a Shih-Poo!

"This ain't fair," declared Larry.

"What ain't fair?"

"You're always gettin' the first bite."

At that Moe pawed him again, "You're cute and all that, but I run this pack."

Moe, a queer-looking *Boston Terrier,* was compactly built with short legs and a square-shaped head. His pointed ears stood tall but sometimes drooped down halfway, looking as if the ear installation was not quite finished. He had a short muzzle that looked as if it had been flattened by a steamroller. Moe's large, round eyes were set wide apart, very close to sitting on the sides of his face. His coat, a strange pattern of black and white almost as if it had been all black until he fell into a pan of white house paint. Such a catastrophe would have resulted in this strange pattern of white wrapped around the left side of his body, down one leg, on all his paws, and weirdly enough, left an off-center white streak on his head between his prominent eyeballs. He also had a fair amount of "white paint" on his snout. What wasn't "painted" white was left black, definitely a "fall-in-a-paint-bucket" appearance or maybe he was wearing his evening tuxedo. That appearance couldn't be said for Larry: no formal wear for him, just that dirty shag carpet look. Easy for a human to accidentally step on.

Curley joined the conversation by striking his own forehead with one of his large paws and then with the other. "We must share food scraps, Moe."

"We must do what? I'm the leader here; I eat what I want first!"

Standing about a foot tall, Curley, an overweight *Pug*—another strange name for a breed—had a compact body, a yellowish-brown coat, well-developed muscles, and a black, flat-muzzle on a round head with deep, dark wrinkles on the forehead that looked like a bad concrete pour. His black upper lips covered his mouth and his bulging eyeballs looked as if they were about to fall out. This all gave him a concerned look with a comical tone.

Without warning, a furry, calico cat darted from behind the Dumpster, and this changed the conversation into a howling, yapping primal pursuit by the bumbling and stumbling Moe, Larry, and Curley. They didn't care about the attractive feline's white, brown, and black patterned coat.

Moe, a Boston Terrier

THE PLAYGROUND

The sprinting cat ran into a children's playground and bolted onto a see-saw. Moe followed, so the cat ran to the top, but this move wasn't going to stop Moe's hot pursuit. The Boston Terrier carefully started his climb, but the cat crawled to the high end and jumped off. Moe continued on over the fulcrum causing the see-saw to drop down hard. Larry, having just stepped on the low end, was slung into the air taking a forward flip that landed him on top of Curly.

Curley hollered, "Get off me! I don't need a wig."

The shaggy-coated Larry climbed off of Curley and both dogs

Curley, a Pug

continued on after Moe and the cat that had just jumped onto the playground's stationary Merry-Go-Round. But the momentum from the last two dogs hopping onto the turntable caused it to start turning. Seeing its escape options dwindling, the cat climbed to the top of a narrow handrail.

The dogs each stood up on their hind legs trying to reach the Calico, but it was Larry that managed to pull himself up and on top of the handrail. He carefully inched along the rail approaching the cat. It was a sight to see: a feline tight-rope walking on a metal pipe and Larry pawing the railing in a balancing act. The Shih-Poo treaded so very carefully but stayed close behind. He reached out for the cat's extended tail but was not quite getting close... enough...to...

The cat immediately made a tall, long, aerial leap off the Merry-Go-Round and landed on some tree-house-like playground equipment. She scurried about the play structure and soon found herself trapped at the top with no escape options, no nearby tree to leap to, just open ground beyond. The stooges surrounded the tree house so the calico chose to slide on its four paws down a spiraling, slippery-as-hot-chocolate slide. Larry, now on the playground equipment having used the available metal stairs, reached the slide first, and without hesitation, slid down and spun out of control as the slide itself looped around and around. Moe followed him down. The overweight Curley, the serious-faced Pug—after first reconsidering this strange plastic shoot—took a spine-chilling leap.

Larry, sliding fast, and trying to stop himself with his front legs, went head over paws, hitting his noggin before flipping off the slide and onto the ground. Moe came next—trying his best to remain on his rear end—and managed successfully to come to an easy stop at the bottom of the slide. But then came Curley sliding wildly and crashing headlong into Moe. They both flipped onto the ground.

"Ahh, ouch!" howled Moe, "How could you? You shoulda gone first."

"Me? I couldn't! You was already ahead of me."

"Get goin', get that aggravatin' pain-in-the-neck cat!"

Up and going again, the three canines ran into some colorful round plastic pipes of different sizes protruding from a wall of the playground playset. The cat climbed through one of them first, then, Moe, then Larry, and finally Curley...no, the beefy Pug couldn't quite make it through; his big round, wrinkled head was caught tight as a cork in a wine bottle. He couldn't go forward and he couldn't back out so he yelled out, "Moe, I'm stuck! Come back!"

The cat was far ahead so Moe and Larry stopped their pursuit and returned to the playground.

"What did ya get yourself into?" asked Moe.

"A pipe," replied Curley.

"Yeah, I see that. You're in a pickle, you dumb bunny!"

"No, it's a plastic pipe."

Moe hit him with his paw.

"Get me outta here!" demanded Curley.

The sweet, innocent-looking, curly-haired Larry, the Shih-Poo—a cross between a Poodle and a Shih Tzu—went around to the back and grabbed Curley's short, curled-up-tail, by his teeth and pulled.

"Ahh, babba, babba, babba," wailed Curley along with a loud, squeaky whine emanating from his massive lips.

"Here, let me try," barked Moe.

Moe came up to Curley's face and licked it; something you would think sweet, kind, and loving unless you knew what he had just eaten…some fresh cat stuff.

"Ahh, how could you…" screamed Curley.

Moe then grabbed an ear and bit down on it.

"Ahh, whah, whah, whah," shrieked Curley as he pulled back hard and successfully eradicated himself from the pipe. He shook his head trying to gain his senses and then with a paw, wiped his face of all the slobber Moe had left behind.

"Come on," screamed Moe, "Let's get outta here; these playgrounds, they're just for kids."

THE SKATEBOARD

The three rambunctious dogs left the playground and made their way down a street enveloped with expensive, good-sized, Hollywood homes. A teenage boy on a skateboard was approaching, moving at a relatively high speed, but he stopped and stepped off the board when he saw the three cute little dogs approaching neck and neck. The young man reached down to pet the adorable, shaggy-rug, but Larry reeled back and barked. The boy took a step back and that's when Moe jumped onto the skateboard. The jump caused it to roll forward down a driveway and into the street, but that road ran downhill, the terrier gaining speed on his new transportation. Moe turned back to the canines, "Help! What's the matter with you? Come and get me!"

Curley sneered back, "Yuck, yuck, yuck. You know the old saying, 'easy come easy go'."

Larry stood up on his hind legs and pawed at Moe with a show of pleasure.

"Help! barked Moe, "Your heinie's mine."

The two pack members finally decided Moe needed help and ran after him. The teen, seeing his skateboard rolling away without him, also ran after it, but the skateboard was now approaching a busy cross street.

Seeing the danger, Larry and Curley ran down the street like bats darting out of a cavern and gaining ground just as a car turned onto their street. Moe, still on the skateboard, dropped onto his belly as the car approached and it drove right over him. Reappearing from the back of the vehicle, his floppy ears and hind legs drug roughly on the ground. His big, ballooning, fear-filled eyes looked as large as billiard balls. He was indeed behind a pair of eight balls, the cross street lying just ahead full of automobile traffic.

The Pug and Shih-Poo skirted the car and were now running alongside the skateboard. They each tried grabbing the little two-wheeled transport with their wide-open snouts but to no avail. Curley made a flying leap toward Moe...and hit him broadside. He fell sideways off the skateboard and it flipped and slid into the cross street causing vehicles to hit their brakes in an attempt to avoid the obstacle. But one driver jerked his steering wheel too fast, the car flipped over, hit a fire hydrant, and a powerful spout of water shot skyward!

The three dogs, finally safely together again, were awed by the spectacle.

"Alright, where have you two been?" asked the incensed Moe, "Dinner at *The Hungary Cat*? You took your good howdy-do time."

"We was looking for a trailer for your skateboard," replied Curley, "sos we could ride along. Yuck, yuck."

Moe raised his right paw and walloped Curley.

"Why did you do that?"

"Just for grins," replied Moe. "Come on, let's get outta here."

The boy watched the three dogs scurry off. He then turned back to the street calamity to see his mutilated skateboard. On this day, he would be walking home.

THE SWIMMING POOL

The three canines went through an open, freshly-painted black iron gate that led to a large well-groomed backyard and discovered a nice, big, refreshing swimming pool.

"Hey, you no-count mongrel types, we gots ourselves a way to cool off," shouted Moe as he ran to the pool and, without hesitation, jumped in. Curley, the overweight Pug, climbed onto the diving board and tried a few bounces with his four stubby legs. But that moved the board only slightly so he walked further forward, but then his front legs overstepped the end, and he did a nice headlong flip into the pool. Curley landed in the water just beside Moe, leaving a moon crater and a big, eye-washing splash.

"Why you..."

"Yuck, yuck, yuck," mouthed Curley.

Moe splashed him back with his paddling forelegs.

"Ahh, eeee, whop, whop," Curley replied. One couldn't tell whether he was enjoying the soaking—or not. It was like a bathtub bathing, but not quite: no foaming soapsuds with a tormenting human scrubbing you all over, head to tail, top to delicate bottom.

Larry walked up to the edge of the pool, lay down with his head over the edge, and carefully reached into the water to test it's temperature.

"Why you wuss, get in," scolded Moe.

The Shih-Poo carefully crawled in as if he didn't really want to get his grey hair dampened. The chlorine maybe?

"Is this really necessary?" queried Larry.

"You don't like going for a swim?"

"Not without some oatmeal and aloe vera shampoo," replied Larry.

"You're brain dead, you know that?"

"At least my coat will be silky smooth."

Moe jumped on his soggy, matted back.

"Giddy up, crossbreed. You think you're a poodle. We'll see if you're a boat and can float."

Larry's head fell below the surface immediately and Moe came free of him. Larry surfaced, "What's the big idea?"

"Just playing with ya."

"I'll play with you like me playing a grand piano with you trapped inside."

The three dogs circled some colorful, floating balls and tried to get a bite of them, but they were too big to get a healthy grip on so they pushed them around with their snouts. Then, totally unexpected, a businessman in a checkered suit and stripped tie showed up in the backyard and saw the three mutts swimming about.

"What, who are you?"

The dogs turned to see the perturbed human.

"Where you from?" he demanded. "Not from this neighborhood!"

Moe threw a couple of raised-lip, teeth-bared barks at the stranger.

"You've polluted my pool!"

At that, Moe crawled onto a sun-tanning float, raised a hind leg, and ceremoniously marked the pool.

"Why you no good..."

The human turned away angered and marched toward his house.

Unexpectedly, the calico the stooges had been chasing earlier, jumped from the top of a privacy fence into the yard and scampered toward the pool, apparently going for a cool quenching drink of water. But then it eyed the dogs. Curley, the first to pick up the furball's scent, swam toward the pool's coping. To escape, the cat climbed up a little basketball stanchion sitting poolside, and Curley, the muscular canine, climbed out of the water using some underwater steps. He reached for the feline standing tense and anxious on top of the backboard. Curley then tried to climb up on the hoop holder, but, when he jumped at the cat, he slipped and fell into the net. The feline jumped off the backboard into the grassy yard and was back over the fence in one spectacular leap.

"Now you've done it," yelled Moe, his wide eyes and floppy ears reaching to the clouds.

"I can't get out," yapped Curley, his heavy body and legs entangled in the netting.

"We'll get ya. Come on Larry."

Moe was able to climb out of the swimming pool, but Larry could not lift himself up so Moe grabbed Larry by a leg and pulled, and pulled, and dragged him out. The two dogs climbed onto the sand-filled base of the basketball hoop and reached for Curley using their teeth and paws to pull on the net, but pulling in both directions just pulled the net taught and Curley's legs slipped further through the netting.

"Cut the net above you," called out Moe.

At that Curley started chewing on the rope netting. He chewed and chewed and chewed some more. A few laces came undone. And then a few more.

Finally, the whole net, with Curley in it, fell into the water. He landed on the orange basketball floating in the water and rolled under it. Curley's head came to the surface.

"Two points!" called out Larry.

Larry climbed out of the pool and the three of them were headed out of the backyard just as the human returned—still in his suit—but now holding the tool of another sport: a baseball bat. He first swung at one of the plastic swimming-pool balls sitting pool-side and then attacked a lawn chair. The chair flew into the water and the three canines scattered looking for cover. Larry ran into an open tool shed, Curley crawled under a wooden sunning deck, and Moe eyed the water faucet at the house. He rushed over to it, pulled on the lever-type handle with his paw, and moved it. Immediately, a massive yard sprinkler system saturated the air and doused the overly dressed human.

"You wretched mutts are going to get it. I had court to go to!"

The cute, compassionate Larry exited the shed dragging a broom. Once outside, he picked up the stick in his mouth, carrying it horizontally. He moved toward the human hitting some of the scattered-about ball floats. One hit a chair, it popped, and air fizzed out sending the ball flying erratically.

"Why you filthy mongrels!"

Moe pushed a button on the power supply of a robotic pool cleaner and the tank treads began to turn. It rolled toward the pool. The human ran toward it but got his legs caught in the long curled up power cable and he tripped, falling into the pool and pulling the robot and cable with him. That gave the three stooges enough time to get the hell out of Dodge.

"Come back here!" the human yelled, spitting chlorinated water.

But out the gate the three canines skedaddled.

BACK HOME

"Moe! Hey Moe! Larry, Curley!" called out Jimmy Peters who was on his front porch waiting for his dogs to return when a new member of the neighborhood came over.

"Hello, My name's Carl Smith."

"Jim Peters."

"Are you calling for your dogs or your cats?"

"Dogs. Well behaved usually. I use them in a vaudeville act at *The Palladium*."

"I see."

"Yes, for real. Wearing dark glasses, bow ties, and bowler hats; they're a card."

"Really?"

Jimmy turned into his open front door and grabbed a couple of theatre tickets on his entryway console table.

"Here, two tickets to our Saturday show."

"Why, thank you."

Jimmy abruptly looked up, "Boys, you've come back!"

All three dogs ran up and sat at attention in a line in front of their leader.

Where, boys, have you been?"

The three stooges lowered their head and cowered.

"It's okay," said Jimmy, then turning to Smith, "I want to introduce you to Moe, Larry, and Curly."

"A return of *The Three Stooges*?"

"Maybe so; they may have been reincarnated.

"As dogs?"

"These critters are crazy funny like *The Three Stooges*. They can do slapstick. Pantomime. Let me show you. Moe, slap Larry..."

But before that could happen, the three dogs sniffed something, quickly turned their heads, and there, sitting across the street, was the calico cat. And off they ran.

"Well, you should know, those 'crazy-funny' dogs of yours just peed in my swimming pool and I want it drained and refilled..."

THE END

Momma, a Beagle

21. Dog Lessons
By Don Kirk

About a dozen cute-as-a-button tri-colored Beagle puppies and their happy-go-lucky mother sat in their Master's living room having some kind of verbal communication that was more than just barking and yips, in fact, the mother spoke some very human-like dialog:

"All right, April Shower, sit down with me. I know you got that name from a human who's seen you pee everywhere, but you'll get better at controlling it—then they might change your name."

"Controlling what, Momma?"

"Sit, April Shower! It's time I let you sweet loving things all know the way of the world and some important survival skills, but first, you must learn proper behavior around other dogs and around those human types: homo sapiens, the creatures that'll do things for you—not other canines—so listen up. If you need to take a break to slurp some water, let me know—and feel free to ask me questions."

"Ask questions? Ask questions about what, Momma?"

"You'll come up with some. With humans it's kind of like the rules of the game. If you play along, they'll likely let you do some of the things you want to do. So listen up, listen carefully, you must learn these signals, not just to communicate with other dogs you meet on the street and in the park, but you must let your Master know how you feel so you can get away with things."

"Get away with things?"

"Yes, like lying beside your Master in *his* bed or getting some of *his* grub. Maybe even some crunchy peanut butter or vanilla ice scream, or better yet, getting some of the broiled hindquarters of a cow they just devoured on their dining-room table."

"Real steak? Not *Purina's* dry dog food?"

"Yes, on occasion. Some of you will probably be taken from me real soon so you need to learn and remember what your momma says; it's no tellin' what kind of Master you may be saddled with. Just because you have an adorable face with big brown eyes doesn't mean you'll get what you want from humans and critters of your own kind."

THE PLAY POSITION

"All right, first, how do you tell a fellow canine you would like to rumble, just play-like, not serious. When you just want to play and not start a fight, it's actually easy, but I know if you get taken from me too soon you won't know these rules of play, so listen up."

"Rules of play? Why would there be rules?"

"As I said, to prevent fights you won't like serious confrontations. They can be very engaging but quite painful, trust me. Mongrels will go for your neck—straight for the jugular—then for your belly. At the very least, your nose will be scarred, and maybe something worse. This is how it is. To tell another pooch you want to tussle, lower your front legs to the ground and raise your rear end. If he wants to play with you, he'll do the same thing."

"I don't under…"

"If you want him to play with you take a teddy bear—or some such fluffy thing—to him and put it in his face. If he wants to play, he'll grab it and pull. But don't growl at him, and if he growls at you, that means he never learned the rules of the game. He thinks that every pull is life-and-death, a fight for food, a fight for survival, or a fight for position in the pack; skills you would need if you lived in the wild. But you'll have humans to take care of you, to feed you, and to provide shelter, unless you're, heaven forbid, left out in the cold to fend for yourself. In fact, that's the number one reason why you should suck up to a human."

"But Momma, what can we suck from a human? Warm milk?"

"No dear, I mean behave obsequiously."

"Huh?"

"I learned that from my first human pack leader, a lawyer."

"A lawyer?"

Some Of The Little Ones

"I prefer humans over other dogs because they, hopefully, feed and care for you; other canines won't do that. So remember, listen to the human critters first. Now, lets start with dealing with humans and their eccentricities."

"Okay, Momma. Can I get an ice cream cone before we start?"

"See there, you're talking to the wrong animal. You want a human."

"A lawyer?"

"Well yeah, if you know your legal terminology."

"My what?"

"Bail, burden of proof, cause of action, in my chambers, arraignment…"

THE STARE

"Let's examine the stare. When you first meet an unfamiliar canine, don't—do not—look him directly in the eyes, turn your head to the side. And if he tries to make eye contact, turn your head the other way. Direct eye contact with a mongrel you don't know is considered a threat that could, in fact, lead to a fight for your life. Staring is rude and he might think you're challenging him. Even humans feel uncomfortable with stares so be careful. Meeting an unknown dog is risky business, downright dangerous."

"Then what do we do?" asked one of the Beagle puppies.

"First, just remain calm. He will try to circle behind you to check your condition and to see if he has scented you in the neighborhood before."

"And if he has?"

"He won't feel you're such a threat."

"Can we become friends?"

"That's a good possibility, but remain diligent?"

"Dil-uh-gent? The lawyer again?"

"Sorry, it means you should be cautious, be as careful as a Chihuahua running loose on a football field at game time."

MARKING TERRITORY

"You've got two ways to let others in the neighborhood know that this land is yours to hunt. The easy way, of course, is to urinate on various bushes. If you happen on a scent from another dog, or even a cat, leave your mark so they know this land is not all theirs, and anything out there, the rats, gerbils, possum, and deer, are all up for grabs. It's whomever gets there first, fair game. And the higher you leave your mark, the bigger they will think you are. So hoist high."

"I don't think I could take down a deer."

"You'll be able to—just be patient—soon enough. You have a lot of growing up to do."

"Growing up?"

"Getting bigger! And maturing."

"Maturing?"

"Enough. You can also defecate to mark territory and you can also use your front and hind paws—scrapping them on the ground—to leave your scent. The more area you cover, the more territory you can feel free to roam."

"My territory?"

"Yes yours. So enough of that, let's talk about training humans."

"Training humans?"

"Absolutely. They don't always know it, but you're the boss."

PETTING YOUR HEAD

"Humans will try to tap or rub your head. I know how stressful that is, but you have to let them do it. They somehow think it's cool even though they wouldn't like it one bit if *their* human friends did it to them! You must put up with it."

"What can we do?"

"You can turn around and encourage them to scratch your rear, under your tail, I know that's where you like it."

BLABBERING HUMANS

"You'll find humans talking at you all the time; all kinds of miscellaneous banter, but you must listen to them best you can. They, for some reason, think you can speak their language, whether it be English, Spanish, Dutch, or whatever, but if you pay close attention to their facial expressions and hand movements you can eventually figure out what they want you to do...if anything."

"If anything?"

"They often don't have anything to say that you'd be interested in. Just pay close attention; look at their faces; watch those eyeballs."

"Are they edible?"

"Eyeballs? I wouldn't know. I doubt if they are very flavorful; might be nutritious though. But don't get any ideas, lick the face only. You can hope your human will learn your language, like the frequency and intensity of your barks, your smiles, tail wagging and your own facial expressions. If you can tell them what you want, you can get what you want. It's that easy.

TAIL WAGGING

"Okay youngins, let's work on your tail wagging. This is important; you say a lot to other dogs with your tail. Humans have no idea what information you can communicate with your tail. You have more than eight positions."

"What if we don't have a tail?"

"You, kiddo, have one, so don't worry your little self about it."

"But Momma, if another…"

"I'll get to that later. Now, if you feel friendly and want to meet, you should use only a slight wag: you're telling them 'hi.' A wider, broader wag and you're telling them you won't challenge or threaten them: 'I'm pleased to meet you and mean you no harm.' So hopefully they won't be afraid of you and will let you approach."

"What if he *does* intend to start a fight?"

"If the dog you're facing—and remember, don't look at him directly in the eye—is moving his tail with tiny, high-speed movements, he is quite concerned, fearful, and might choose to fight you if he doesn't decide to flee first."

"What do I do, Momma, if he attacks?"

"You run like a bat outta hell!"

"What? Hell? Bats can run?"

"No, Dear. And one more thing, the height of your wagging tail also means different things. If your tail is just hanging loose, it says to others that you are relaxed. If you bring your tail low, even curling it under to your belly, it means you are submitting to his desires, what he says goes. Or you can use the same low tail to admit that you are ashamed of something you've done."

"Like what, Momma?"

"Peeing on your human's living room carpet. Do I need to say more?"

"No Momma."

"So, do you now know all of the tail positions for interfacing with other dogs and humans?"

"Inter…facing?"

"Talking with."

"Well Momma, sometimes I find myself holding my tail high and…"

"You're probably doing it because you are excited. Food being poured into your bowl or you can see that your Master is about to take you on a walk."

"Yes Momma, that's it! And my hips start shaking back and forth with my tail…"

"When your hips get involved with your wagging, that's a real sign that you are so very happy. I hope that happens a lot for you. You just have to hope you'll get a good loving pack leader; so many will lock you up in their backyard and ignore you, deny your very existence. If that happens, feel free to try and escape."

BUTT SNIFFING
"Oh, and when you sniff a butt to check on another's diet or emotional state, don't panic if the dog—or human—spins around and confronts you, just back off a bit and show him you mean him no harm by turning away."

"And if he keeps trying to get at *my* rear end, or jumps on my back and thrusts, what do I do?"

"Prey!"

ROLLING IN IT
"And finally, if you run into any dog or cat poop, don't roll in it and don't eat it unless you feel you're not getting the nutrients you need. I know rolling in it will help to disguise yourself, but I must inform you, your human Master will not like it one bit and, heaven forbid, he might make you take a bath!"

"Ahh! Oh no! I rolled into a dead bird in the alley yesterday!"

"Your Master won't like that either. It's a great way to conceal your identity, but your Master will not like the odor and the possible diseases you might bring to the pack."

WORKING WITH YOUR HUMAN
"Okay kids, gather 'round, move in close, I have a few more things to say to you all and I hope our human is not listening in."

"Momma, we're hearing you, we've got our ears up."

"Okay, this is it. You must pay close attention to your human's facial expressions and movements."

"Facial expressions?"

"Look at his face. For example, if you see him raise one eyebrow higher than the other, he doesn't belief what you're trying to tell him, like your attempt to inform him that the urine on the kitchen floor wasn't yours. If both of his eyes are wide-open, that means he's interested in what you are doing, he's paying close attention, but if they are too wide-open you should feel concerned. You better retreat from what your doing and maybe even apologize. Lie down and show your belly for forgiveness. If your human stares you down and crosses his arms, you can be sure he's not happy with what you've done—maybe you've barked or marked his carpet. You must learn from this. Sometimes you can tell from his distorted face when you can get away with things and when you can't. Take heed, he could send you off to a kennel."

"A kennel?"

"Steel bars and junk food, quite unhealthy. And they won't let you play with your cell mates."

"Momma!"

"Back to your human. Some of them will want to teach you tricks. Crazy things like rolling over and doing a 'High Five.'"

"A High Five?"

Just play along. They'll give you a treat when you do something they want you to do, but don't do what they want too quickly, that way you'll get more of those tasty treats."

"Now, if you don't like what your human is doing to you—or with you—you need to let him know by dropping your tail, and your head, and turning away. That will appear to him as disapproval and will show concerned uneasiness. He will think you are feeling hurt and will try to make up for his unfair treatment. He will pet you, maybe even follow through with your initial request."

"But momma, I can't remember all this," interjected one of the other puppies.

"Don't worry, you'll get the hang of it. I don't know where you'll end up, but I hope you'll be with me a bit longer so you can acquire more good advice from your dear old mom. You should know that every human is different. Each has his own personality, character traits, behavioral limits, and self-control of his emotional responses to your behavior. I mean, don't even take a leak or defecate in his abode. No human likes that. Just go to the door and scratch on it, lightly, when you want to go outside. Hopefully, they'll install a 'doggie door' in their outside door.

"And again Little Ones, most humans will want to pat you on

the head. I know how irritating that is—you don't see humans patting each other's heads when *they* meet—but don't pull back and reject their advances; they mean you no harm. Just wait and see what the humans have to offer. They might actually scratch you on your rear end or rub your tender belly, and I know you'll like that."

"Mommy, will you lick my rear end?"

"Later dear, now listen up, humans will give you dog food in a bowl, but they usually eat their own food at a big table or while watching this thing they call a 'television set' in their 'living room'—at least that's what they call that room, a 'living' room. I don't know what the rest of the rooms are for, not for living I guess. Even though their food is not very nutritious, it taste's great because it usually has lots of grease and fat. So play on their sympathies—stare intently at them or paw their knee—and it's a good bet you'll get a taste. Yum, yum."

"What is this 'pawing,' Momma?"

"They call it 'begging.'" Works every time. If you see your human putting on his socks and shoes, jump up with excitement— jumping on your hind legs works with front paws a-begging—that way he gets it that you think he's about to take *you* for a walk. So even if he was not actually planning to take you with him, he will feel guilty and take you along anyway. It might be a ride in his means of transport so you can put your head out the window. Not as good as going hunting—a 'walk' they call it—but hey, it might actually be a trip to a park!"

"To park?"

"No, to go for a run, not to 'park;' those confusing human words again."

"And one final thing for you today. It's your job to keep your human in line. There are techniques you can use to help him behave and follow your lead. If he hasn't filled your bowl with food, lie down beside it and lick the bowl, and lick it some more— clean that bowl real pretty like—they will bring you something, guaranteed. If you want to go outside, you can bark—only softly though, more of a yip—but it works best if you go to the door and quietly lie down in front of it and wait. Make sure he sees you, of course. If he tries to leave the house without you, run to him, sit in front of him, raise one paw, and show him those sweet, endearing eyes of yours. Look your human directly in the eyes. If he can, I guarantee it, he'll take you with him. When he takes you for a walk on a leash and you want to follow a scent in a different direction, pull gently, but show enthusiasm at what you've found, jump with excitement, and he will likely follow you."

"What is a leash, Momma?"

"Well, dear, unfortunately, some cities require by law that you be tethered. You'll have to live with that, but, hopefully, your human will show you how to 'heel'; learn it well and he might walk you without that confounded leash."

"Without a leash?"

"Yes, dear. The point is, you can train your human to do your bidding. Don't worry, you'll get the hang of it and he'll pick up on your demands. Now Little Ones, you need to get back to your play. I need to get the Master's attention so we can all go outside and get out of this filthy bed of grimy human clothes, greasy rags, and dirty towels. Oh, and hey, if you hear a human say 'Bath' run for it, quickly! Find a place you can hide where he can't get to you. I use that cabinet over there in the corner; wood braces on the legs keep them from picking me up.

CATS

"What are those little fury things sneaking around?" asked one of the Little Ones.

"Those are cats. Don't worry yourself. They came here to this planet a very long time ago. A small force of them landed here thousands of years ago. These little hairy critters needed another place for their fast multiplying masses—they intended to take the planet over—but when they arrived they quickly discovered that the humanoids would actually feed them and care for them, so why eliminate them? Let them work for us, they figured. They could stay here, multiply. They figured they could take over the 'earth' anytime they chose. Instead, they could use humans to their best advantage, so they did, and the rest is history."

"Momma, were did us dogs come from?"

"Well, it's like this Little Ones, we started hanging around the campfires of these human types and they would feed us. It seemed as if they wanted us to help defend their campsite. They fed us regular like, so we stayed around these humanoids and they taught us to bark—ruff ruff—so we could warn them of interlopers. And now we keep barking to warn them at every noise or invader, and wouldn't you know it, they don't like us doing it anymore! Such is life."

"We can't stop?"

"No we can't. Just stay clear of getting hit."

SOME FINAL HEALTHY ADVICE

"Oh, and be sure to let them know how much you like ice cream," noted Momma.

"Ice cream?"

"Yeah, you scream for ice cream."

"Huh?"

"Well, for you, you whine and whimper. Just drop on the floor and look sad when you see them enjoying a tasty helping of ice cream. They'll give you some. And oh man, is it good!"

"How do we know it's ice cream?"

"You'll know."

"And girls and boys, there are certain things you must *not* eat. You'll be able to identify them with their odor, so don't eat anything until you know what it is."

"What can't we eat, Momma?"

"No grapes, onions, raisins, chocolate, avocados, macadamia nuts: they're a death sentence."

"Death what?"

"Not you to worry now, dear. Let them know you like asparagus, blueberries, sweet potatoes, pumpkin, even spinach..."

"How do we do that?"

"Put your paws in their laps and beg."

So now go play, find some human socks, teddy bears, or plastic containers to play with. You'll find crunchy, squeaky plastic toys and food treats in your human's trashcan."

THE END

Frida, a Maltese

22. Mario & Frida

By Don Kirk

Mario Weber had been in the United States for many years and worked most of those as a roofer in Las Cruces, New Mexico. When I first met him, he was living with his mother and a cute little dog named "Frida."

Mario had gotten too old to be a twelve-hour-a-day roofer and his mother was in the elder class of humans. They lived in my neighborhood several blocks away and I would stop in to speak with them from time to time. He was always glad to see me and so was the little "Frida," a female Maltese who stood on her hind legs in an effort to lick my face. I would, of course, lie down on the carpet so she could accomplish the task. But it was just a few months after I met them that Mario's mother died. Mario never talked about any family...or any friends he, or Frida, had in the neighborhood other than myself.

After his mother had passed, I stopped in to speak with Mario more frequently. Mario said he didn't know what to do now that his mother had left this earth—had left this house. It was just himself and Frida alone in an un-maintained home. Repairs were not being done, the washing machine was broken, the toilet leaked—I did fix that last problem for him, took just a few minutes and $7.95. He washed his clothes in the kitchen sink and hung them on the clothesline outside. And he talked to me about Germany, said he was born in Koblenz. Mario and his mother were immigrants from Deutschland, had been in the U.S. for over forty years. He told me he would like to move back to his homeland but didn't know how to do it. And he was concerned that he might not be able to take his beloved Frida with him.

I decided to gather some information on how he could make the move, but it turned out not to be so easy with Mario unable to give me any real facts; his mother had taken care of everything. Who was paying the bills? I didn't know. And in my attempt to research their family, I came up with zilch.

His little Maltese, "Frida," was sweet as acacia honey. The canine and Mario appeared to be best buddies, just the two of them, no dear old Mom. They were living alone in a residential house in a middle class neighborhood, and Mario hadn't had a job in years. I assumed his mother's Medicare had been paying the property taxes and utilities. And now that was all gone. Mario was too old to shovel shingles on a steep, hot, asphalt roof in one-hundred-degree desert heat.

The cutest of dogs, Frida, wore an all-white silky coat that would have grown to the floor if it had not been trimmed—but it had. The dog sported big, dark eyes and a black nose that looked more like a chocolate mousse sphere, ready to be eaten by anyone hungry for a tasty treat. Her long tail looped over her back and that looked like a coconut-frosted donut. She appeared to be a wholesome, delectable cat, an especially appetizing find for the bigger canines running loose in the neighborhood. And as for Mario, he was tall and lean and always wore torn, ragged, blue-denim jeans and a pink, long-sleeved long-john top. He even wore Vietnam-era combat boots, usually without laces.

Frida, as gentle as falling snowflakes in spring, hopped around in their large living room, always happy, always ready for play. Eagerly jumping skyward, her hind legs reaching several feet off the carpet. "Lively as a spunky kitten" would be an understatement. Even with her tiny seven pounds and ten-inch height, she found a way—climbing atop a bar stool—to get on the kitchen counter. Mario always made sure nothing, like his own dinner, was left out for Frida's exploration, though I never witnessed Mario eating anything himself. I had no idea what his diet was like since his mom had passed.

Sadly, Mario didn't take Frida for walks, kept her inside most of the time, in fact, Frida had her own cat-like litter box indoors.

Frida: Sweet as acacia honey.

Maybe Mario also had one before I fixed the toilet. When I was visiting, the little dog begged me to play, a visiting outsider clearly a joy to her...and surely a rarity.

On the occasion of one of my visits, I watched Mario cut the naturally-growing long hair of Frida with a pair of rusted scissors into something more manageable, clipping it to a length similar to a lion's, at least that's what Mario called it, a "Lion's Cut." Short and curly, it revealed a fetching dog for a not-so-handsome Mario because Mario's skin was blistered, scaly, and dark from a life of crawling around on roofs. I asked him if he had skin cancer, he said no, but he added that he was still young. Indeed, he *was* still in his fifties.

During another visit, Mario told me that Frida had been found just a year earlier running loose in the neighborhood, with apparently no home to return to, so Mario and his mother began to feed her, and in short order, Frida returned daily and stayed around for longer periods. It wasn't long before they invited her to move in with the generous and giving Weber family. They had even given me, a neighborhood stranger, a big bowl of spaghetti-like German ice cream. What human, or dog, could refuse that? The little *Fräulein* quickly accepted the name "Frida," given to her by Mario, meaning "peace" in German, and she seemed to give him just that.

When I was there, Mario always seemed to be cuddling or playing with Frida. They were rarely apart. But a worrisome "separation anxiety" shown apparent in the Maltese even when Mario stepped outside with me for just a few minutes. When Frida scratched crazily at the screen door, Mario rushed back inside, not the cute little Frida rushing *outside* to join Mario.

Frida was indeed the perfect companion for Mario and the residence seemed to be the doghouse for the both of them. I say "doghouse" concernedly because Mario was probably in a pickle, or one big vinegar-deprived cucumber. How, with no income, was he going to keep the house? Not be thrown into the street?

When I got up to leave, Frida showed her affection for Mario by jumping into his lap. Frida didn't walk me to the door. Mario told me he and Frida often slept together on the living room couch. He said they would be together always.

A few months passed, at least four, and I made the mistake of not checking by, not on a regular basis like I had been doing for some time. But one day, I finally stopped in to tell him what I had found out about his returning to Germany and discovered the house locked up tight as a drum. I walked over to the next-door neighbor and talked to him. He said he was trying to buy the Weber house. I said "What?" He gave me the sad news that Mario's dog Frida had died several months ago and that Mario was later found dead in his home, having been deceased, according to the coroner, for almost two months. "Two months! Dead and putrefied! What to Hell?" Apparent cause of death: starvation...and maybe, I think, a perpetual loneliness. This latter possibility appeared very real because a wooden cross lettered "Frida Weber" was found in the backyard. It was determined that Mario's dog was indeed buried there.

Where Mario Weber would be buried was anybody's guess. He obviously couldn't be buried in the backyard next to his beloved Frida; I'm sure that would have been his preference. Maybe he could be cremated and sent back to Germany, back to a family that had long forgotten about him? But if that was done he would want Frida to be sent home with him.

THE END

Always With Me, A Pitbull

23. Always With Me

By Don Kirk

My dog follows me wherever I go: in grass, asphalt, or snow.
He slumbers with me and goes for walks a-feelin' so free.
He chomps on my steak and guzzles beer for Heaven sake!
The only place he doesn't follow is to the bathroom hollow.

Always with me, always there, waiting with a wandering stare.
Waiting for the next command, to sit, stay, or stand.
"Are we going for a walk, or just having a nice talk?"
"Are we going for a tasty treat, or a new gal to meet?"

Always with me, always there, sleeping happily in my armchair.
Looking keenly into my eyes, waiting for me to advise:
"Are we off to meet a Labrador, or to visit a lively pet store?"
Playing with a doll, playing tug-of-war, or chasing a basketball?

Always ready to go and explore, to find out what's in store.
Like food scraps or a cat scent, either way, a great time spent.
A joyful roll in another's dung, so tasteful on a curious tongue.
If done without a fight, a bubble bath will make it right.

Always with me, always there, great times we do share.
When alone he's tearing toys to pieces, boredom it releases.
With me, he's happy and free to play a little Frisbee.
Sleeping next to me, to bed at eleven, he's in seventh Heaven.

Always with me, always there, waiting for a world to share,
Waiting for a world to share.

Gran Chico In A Cell Block

24. Gran Chico

By Don Kirk

Behind the Olivia Hanna residence, across the easement, lived a lady with four dogs: a young white Labrador, two small, shaggy creatures with matted hair, and an even smaller canine than the two little ones: a black five-pound Chihuahua. But it was clear, he was in charge. He would snap at them, even bite their neck if the elderly Miss Hanna showed the other dogs any attention by putting her hand next to the fence.

On just two occasions, Olivia took the neighbor's four dogs a few treats, but the tiny Chihuahua wanted more attention and decided to squeeze through the chain-link fence, cross the easement, and climb between the posts of the personnel gate of Olivia's property. He came to play with her Australian Cattle Dog: a 40-pound critter against five skimpy pounds, but they played together famously. They had all kinds of fun chasing each other around the yard, playing tug-of-war, and playing the popular game of "Keep Away." The guest dog even came into the doggie door of the Hanna home and had a taste of the resident dog's leftovers in his food bowl.

These pages relate the story of the lonely Chihuahua as told by Miss Hanna, a 68 year old, retired, elementary-school teacher who lived alone, except for her comforting companion, the Cattle Dog:

One evening—as it was easy for the Chihuahua to get in and out of my house through the doggie door—he jumped into bed with me. That was okay, I figured, because my female dog "Peanut Butter," a mid-sized Cattle Dog with a black and brown coat laced with grey, usually took his assigned place in the doggie bed on the floor. After a few weeks coming and going, the Chihuahua had spent so much time here that I gave him a name, "Gran Chico." The little thing was always lying by my bedroom door when I tried to go to the bathroom during the night. The dog's real name was a very long Spanish name only a person from South America could pronounce. My neighbor actually tried to tell me its name on one occasion, but the name "Gran Chico" meaning 'Big Boy" in Spanish would do just fine. His strong will made up for his little size. The shorthaired Chihuahua had a smooth, shiny coat that fit close to his body. He stood at most a foot high at the shoulders and was black all over except for a strip of white on his chest. He had black-as-midnight eyeballs, a short nose, rounded skull, and large pointed ears that could probably penetrate a low cloudbank.

Gran Chico a Chihuahua

The shorthaired-Chihuahua breed had been discovered in the 1850's in the Mexican state of 'Chihuahua" and that's how the breed got its name. Americans visiting Mexico brought the little dog home and the rest is history.

Gran Chico was one of four dogs at the neighbor's house, none of them getting any attention by their owners. His toe nails were quite long, clicking on the pavement of my driveway, obviously no neighborhood walks, no play time, and no visits to the vet—no collar or tingling vaccination tags on him—just a life in a small backyard. No wonder he kept coming back to visit me. Gran Chico quickly developed a passion for his "new mate" and thrived on the attention and affection he got from me. With myself, and my dog, he had new companions. The dogs played together well and didn't fight for the food in either dog bowl—I had set a second bowl out for Gran Chico. Chihuahuas normally attach themselves to a single person, but this new "companion" was amiable to me and my *big* dog, a dog at least seven times Chico's weight. The new name I had given the Chihuahua was easier for my dog to learn—three syllables instead of eight or ten—and it was something my dog, an English speaker, could understand.

A little daily fun with the visiting dog was fine from time to time, but Gran Chico returned everyday and began to be a nuisance. He ran around everywhere, jumping on me, climbing on my lap while working at my computer, getting underfoot, and licking my face by climbing on the furniture and onto the armchairs. The cute Chihuahua began to be a bit too much so I took Gran Chico back to the owner's yard and dropped him over the fence. I informed the seemingly unconcerned owner what Gran Chico had been doing: getting into my yard *and* my house—day *and* night—by squeezing through small gaps in her fence. At this supposedly surprising news, Gran Chico's owner made an extra effort to block the fence with rocks, bricks, and tree limbs. But that didn't stop Gran Chico, no, he just dug *under* the fence and through my back gate allowing my dog Peanut Butter to have fun with the little Chihuahua.

I spoke to the Chihuahua, "Gran Chico, I need to change your name to 'Trapdoor' or maybe 'Houdini.' No matter what I do, you're able to break free."

That night, Gran Chico showed up on my bed and I couldn't get the dog to stop climbing on my face; his large round eyes staring me down. I dropped him off the bed several times only to have him jump back up; that very tall mattress no obstacle for the little Chihuahua. He would burrow himself under a blanket but stick his head out and lick my face. If he would just lie down and go to sleep there would be plenty of room for the both of us. Peanut Butter would often jump on the bed at bedtime and sleep there for a while—even snore—until I turned over, a sufficient disruption to make her jump back to the floor. But now Gran Chico was taking Peanut's bed space. My Cattle Dog snapped at the Chihuahua. He didn't back off. This wasn't going to work. Even back in the living room, Peanut Butter would find Gran Chico lying in his favorite "bed" on the cushioned armchair. Gran Chico made no effort to get down. It was apparently commonplace for the tiny Chihuahua breed to boss around dogs much bigger than himself. The smallest dog would be the one in charge. That was the case at the neighbor's house with the other three dogs, all bigger than Gran Chico; the tiny black critter letting them know who was boss. A big fight on my bed would not be kosher so I got up, took the dog outside, and closed the doggie door with a plastic insert.

It was a rainy night and I had hoped the locked out Chihuahua would go back home, but he found a doggie bed in the open carport and settled down there for the night. And all night he stayed. The next morning, when I headed out the door to take my Peanut Butter for his morning walk, there stood Gran Chico with tail wagging enthusiastically, him happy as a lark. So off I went to explore the neighborhood so my dog could relieve himself and mark his territory. Gran Chico came with us but was not on a leash so he circled my canine when not choosing to trot ceremoniously beside us. His little legs moved three times as fast as Peanut's. This freedom of movement unfortunately allowed him to go into the residential street from time to time, right where he could get run over by a passing vehicle.

We three walked our half-mile together and returned safely to my residence. But this happy-go-lucky dog tagging along with us couldn't continue. On our next walk, I stopped with the two dogs at the front door of the residence that had housed the Chihuahua, but, sadly, no one there for me to scold—and Gran Chico didn't stay around, in fact, he probably didn't even recognize the front of the house, having never been out of his backyard. We continued on down the street, the three of us, when, without forewarning, out of a side yard, came two large, unleashed, red-fawn Akitas with worn-out collars. They came up to Peanut Butter and he sniffed at their noses. I was concerned this could lead to a debilitating dogfight I couldn't prevent, but, thankfully, the three dogs remained as tranquil as dormant dishwater. But then the gregarious Gran Chico came up from behind me and

Gran Chico loved Peanut Butter

approached the curious dogs. One of the two Akitas must have looked at the little Chihuahua as prey so snapped at him and tried to go for his throat. Gran Chico turned and ran for dear life; after him the other two unbridled dogs bound. I didn't have my spray can of *Mace Pepper Spray*, or a high-pitched horn, or even my electro-shock weapon, so an unstoppable dogfight might have ensued, but instead, the two dogs chasing Gran Chico ran off and disappeared around a corner. I decided to walk on with my dog—I could do nothing now—and continued on down the sidewalk in the opposite direction away from the three dogs. Any tiny dog is potential prey to hawks and curious canines, so Gran Chico could easily be taken down, chewed to bits, bones broken, and heart eaten for dinner by those huge, sharp-toothed Akitas. What was going to happen? Then, abruptly, Gran Chico came running back toward me from behind with the hunters still in hot pursuit. Peanut Butter turned around, jumped up, and pulled hard on the leash. I lost grip on her leash, she broke free—almost pulling me down—and ran back toward Gran Chico. She passed the fleeing little dog approaching me and attacked the charging Akitas.

A fight ensued, all going for each other's necks. Gran Chico even tried to join in. I ran toward them, caught up, and began kicking wildly at the attackers. Finally, the two Akita's backed off and ran away. Peanut Butter turned back to check on Gran Chico, sniffing his nose and rear end. The Chihuahua seemed fine, no blood flowing forth. He jumped up trying to show love for the Cattle Dog he had been hanging out with for the last few days. He licked her face in a sweet, warmhearted way.

I became even more concerned with the safety of this tiny Chihuahua creature so I again crossed my easement and placed him over the neighbor's back fence. I watched and waited. Sure enough, only moments later, Gran Chico found a way out, but this time I saw his escape route. He crawled between a second layer of fence that his owner had put up, moving horizontally a dozen feet or so, and then up and over some boards. Okay, so I tracked down some pieces of 1x6 lumber, more bricks and rocks, and again tried to block the little Chihuahua's means of escape. Back over the fence again, I dropped the sweet little Gran Chico and he immediately tried to sidestep the new hindrances. No luck... at least for now. He stopped for a moment and took a gander at me. I thing I saw tears running down from his sorrowful eyes. How regretful the situation: a dog needing some companionship, caring, and cuddling—something he was obviously not getting at home. Chico: a little dog with a big personality who obviously fell in love with anyone who paid attention to him. And he was loyal to a fault. Normally Chihuahuas are mistrustful of strangers and that's why they supposedly make good watchdogs. No, he liked me from the start.

Two days passed without Gran Chico making his presence known. Maybe the lonely dog was finally "caged." I decided to go out my back gate, cross the easement, and check on the little Chihuahua. I saw him lying in the neighbor's yard chewing on something, tearing it to pieces, the object's identity unidentifiable. Gran Chico was definitely bored, but when he saw me, he and the three other dogs came running to the chain-link fence and jumped on the fence in unrestrained excitement.

"Sorry, Gran Chico, I can't let you out. You're not mine."

In a flash, his owner came out of the back door, "*¡Basta!* Don't touch me dogs, they's security dogs. Keep away!"

"I'm on my property; this is an easement not an alley. I've got every right..."

"*Manténgase Alejado!*"

I didn't know what she said but stepped back, raised both hands in surrender, and returned to my house.

The next morning I woke up and found Gran Chico lying in bed beside me. So much for his prison abode. Gran Chico stood up, shook himself off, stretched his front legs, his back legs, and yawned. The joy of my awakening was clearly visible on the little dog's face.

"Okay, Gran Chico, this is not your bed," I said, "you can't stay with me. I've been asking friends if they would take you in, but no one seems to want a Chihuahua. It seems your breed bites first and asks questions later. You don't do that Gran Chico, do you?

You haven't bitten me. You're so darn sweet."

Gran Chico wagged his tail wildly.

By now Peanut Butter had also jumped into bed with me.

"Damn!" I said out loud. "Rescuing dogs is like adopting children."

Peanut Butter barked.

"Alright, alright, lets go for your morning walk."

With that statement, both canines were off the bed lickety-split and running for the kitchen door.

I took my dog for his morning walk with Gran Chico tagging along. I did not have a leash on Chico because he still had no collar. Gran Chico stayed close but was free to explore the surrounding yards. But soon, he crossed the street and a speeding, big black SUV veered, the vehicle body tilting precariously. The driver recovered, saving his vehicle *and* the dog from an early grave. Blood and guts is all I could think about. Enough already. This wonderful, loving little Chihuahua was creating nightmares for me.

So, once again, I tried to return Gran Chico to his owner by dropping him over the fence, and again I watched to see where the little critter would go to make his escape. After I waited in the easement for about ten minutes, I could see Gran Chico still had not found a means of escape so I returned to my property, locked my gate, and blocked all narrow openings with even more bricks and bric-a-brac lying about. It was just minutes later that the Chihuahua turned up again; I could only surmise he had crawled through the front personnel gate of his owner's property, ran down the street to a cross street and back up my street to find me. Running full out all the way I'm sure. He jumped on me all joyful and eager to play. Cute as he was, enough already! I picked him up and put him in my car. The inside of a vehicle was obviously new to him; he sniffed around and expressed some concern. He then climbed on me as I drove of, blocking my view and licking my face. I managed with some effort to take Gran Chico to a town a few miles away—about three miles—and dropped him off in a small park with a gazebo. I figured someone would take him in even if they ended up taking him to an animal shelter. Gran

Chico, enamored with the new real estate, made it possible for me to drive off without him noticing.

Two hours later, I found Gran Chico back in my yard having survived street traffic on several main roads. This is where this determined Chihuahua wanted to be, that was obvious. He wanted to be with me and Peanut Butter, no one else. What now? The poor, sweet, lonely, abandoned dog, what was to become of him? Peanut didn't mind having him around, she played with him, shared her food with him, and they got into trouble together.

Gran Chico and I sat face-to-face, well, not exactly: I sat and he stood on his hind legs with his front legs on my knees. I looked at those endearing eyes of Gran Chico's; his desire to be a part of this pack quite clear.

The next morning, a young boy and his sister looking for a little income asked if they could wash my car. Sure I said, and they went to work. Gran Chico showed up with my other interested dog, though she kept a few feet distant from the splashing water. I'm sure it felt too much like her monthly scrubbing in the bathtub.

"We have a Chihuahua like this one, but he's brown and white," one of the kids said. "We sure could use another one to play with ours."

That's when a light bulb went on; their dog might need a mate. "You guys need another dog?" I asked.

"Yes! We want him! What's his name?"

"I'm calling him 'Gran Chico,'—Big Boy—but he's not my dog; his owner doesn't seem to miss him. I'd love for you to have him, but he needs his shots, see, no vaccination tags."

"Doe he have worms?"

"I don't think so, but you *must* take him to a vet."

"We will, we will."

"Then he's yours, but you have to know how to make friends with him. Here are a few treats to get him to approach you; treats that'll make him your friend."

The two kids played with Gran Chico a few minutes then finished with my car. I gave them a collar and leash and they took

Gran Chico away. He resisted only slightly. He just needed a few more treats from them.

The night passed quickly. And another day and another night, but here came Gran Chico, jumping through the doggie door of my kitchen door! So I let him spend the night, no one came to get him, and the next morning, quite early, I took the two dogs for a walk, only this time I dropped off Gran Chico—over the fence of his new owner. The other dog there, a Chihuahua, welcomed him. I went on with my own critter to finish his morning walk. My house was two blocks away, but fifteen minutes later here came Gran Chico! He looked up at me all smiles, a few long black whiskers standing straight and sharp on each side of his muzzle. With those long, projecting hairs he could probably receive some local television stations, but he was obviously tuned to me.

I decided to take Gran Chico to the vet when I took Peanut Butter for a routine follow up. Dr. Debone was happy to look over the pocket-sized pooch: no obvious health problems and no microchip to identify the owner. He told me there was a rescue center I could take the dog to, another option for me if I didn't find anyone to take him. We three returned home.

The next day, little old me fell and injured by stomach, cutting a thin gash in the area of the intestine. I cleaned it up and went to bed. Feeling sorely, I decided to skip dinner. Gran Chico jumped on the bed and licked the wound for several minutes. I guessed him to be my new doctor. He lay on my stomach all curled up nice and sweet like. Somehow that felt good.

Since Gran Chico had showed up, my allergies seemed to have subsided. I wondered, did Gran Chico have some kind of magical powers. Either way, a great companion. Peanut Butter felt a little jealous...and conveyed it by snapping at the Chihuahua from time to time and pushing himself in between us.

Until now, I was always sniffling, sneezing, and blowing my nose, allergic to cats but thankfully not dogs. I knew I was allergic to a lot of airborne allergens but had stopped taking my allergy meds and nasal decongestants many months earlier after reading the side effects that seemed to apply to me: nosebleeds, runny nose, sores, headaches, a cough, sore throat, and wounds that would not heel, so I quit taking them. I had used the nasal spray for many years to fight congestion; I couldn't breathe; I used the stuff two or three times a day. Hell, I might have even been allergic to the nasal spray! And, wow, after having stopped taking it for a week or so, I could breath again. I could breath, my sinuses as clear as a newly installed sewer line...and they stayed that way! And, I could smell things like never before. A whole new sensory world opened up for me; I figured I was picking up scents more like a dog. Since taking in Gran Chico, my allergies seemed to have subsided. I was allergic to something ten months out of the year and wasn't now in one of those allergy-free months (June and July). Several weeks drifted by, no sniffling—didn't have a handkerchief in my hand all the time—and Gran Chico wasn't bringing in anything to aggravate my sinuses. Was Gran Chico's spittle I absorbed from his kissing me some kind of magic elixir?

Yes, the Chihuahua had moved in. I think he tried to take over as 'Head Honcho,' the alpha dog, so, over the next few days, I taught Gran Chico a couple of tricks in an effort to make it clear to him that *I* was the pack leader. With that high intelligence of his, he quickly learned to sit and shake hands. It looked more and more like he was going to be a new member of this household, another dog I didn't need. Imagine an old lady trying to take two dogs for a walk on separate leashes that would surely get intertwined

and wrapped around her—my—feet…leading to a nice tumble to hard concrete.

The next day, Gran Chico started scratching at the base of one of my bookshelves, tearing into it with his mouth; he wanted to get at something. I pulled him away and closed him out of the room. The day after that he was back in the room scratching and biting but at a different cabinet. To make a long story short, it was a rat that Gran Chico had found. I had forgotten that one of the reasons ship captains took on a Chihuahua was to route out disease carrying rodents from small places where larger dogs couldn't get to. I guess I wouldn't have to worry about rats if I kept this dutiful Chihuahua.

I had the two dogs in my four-door sedan—after taking them to a park to run free—and stopped at the neighborhood convenience store to pick up a quart of milk. I set the car windows less than half open so that the two critters couldn't bite any curious human on-lookers. As I closed the icebox, a hooded man came into the store, pulled a pistol and pointed it at the cashier. He told everyone else in the store to get down on the floor. I did so quite quickly, as painful as it was. My milk carton fell and split open, pouring milk over the floor and soaking my clothes.

"Open that register!"

The attendant did.

"Bag it, all of it!"

The attendant handed him the sack, much of it just change. The robber pulled on the front door handle and ran out.

Back outside, my tiny Gran Chico climbed out of the rear window of the car—a long risky jump—and ran toward the robber. He nipped at his ankle, the one soft spot he could reach, and that's when the robber turned and took two shots at Gran Chico…the second shot hit him! There was a high-pitched yelp and he fell and rolled over. The robber disappeared around the corner of the building. I ran outside and knelt down to look at Gran Chico.

"I've got to get him to the vet!" I yelled. "He's been shot!"

No one hurried to help so I picked Chico up and took him to my car. The attendant ran out of the store and said, "Wait. The cops are on their way."

"I can't wait, he has to get to the vet, NOW! To Dr. Debone."

"But he's carrying evidence, the bullet."

"I'll tell him to save it. I'm outta here. Hanna, Olivia Hanna is the name."

I lay Gran Chico on the front seat and off I went.

The Vet office was open.

"I've got an emergency. Need the Doc now."

"That's the lost Chihuahua?"

"Yeah. He's been shot. Police will be here."

"Shot? Police?"

"Ain't life grand."

Doctor Debone came in.

"Save the bullet," I ordered. "It's evidence."

With that, the doctor took him to a stainless steel table and assistants prepared him for surgery.

"You can wait outside."

I did, and waited, and waited. A detective came, took my statement and waited for the bullet.

Finally, just as in the movies, the doc came out of the surgery room pulling off his plastic gloves.

"He'll be fine; missed the vital organs. Have you found the owner?"

"She doesn't want him...so I gave him a name, 'Gran Chico.'"

"Okay, I won't ask."

A week later, a nearby neighbor's front porch had a batch of newly arrived kittens but no mother. Gran Chico and I took a short walk down the street to visit the neighbor and while there, I showed Chico the kittens—their mother nowhere to be found. Had the kittens been abandoned? Gran Chico sniffed at the little furry critters and then actually lay down beside them.

"What in the world?"

"I know he likes to cuddle with me, but kittens? He's affectionate, that's for sure, a lap dog, and this one likes to lick my face...and jump into bed with me, and put his head on *my* pillow. I know that's not good. He'll be bossing me around before long. These kittens, hum?"

"He'd probable defend the kittens from aggressors."

"I think if Gran Chico had been female he might have actually nursed them."

Two weeks later we tried to go for a walk early one morning, later than usual because of the near freezing weather. As usual, we went up one street and down another. I tried to put in a half-mile or more on each of our walks...these dogs would help me live a long life. On our walk, without warning, across the street, I noticed a lady coming out of her grey brick home. She saw me and spoke excitedly, "Hey, what you doing with my dog?"

"I'm taking him for a walk."

"*Olvidarte.* That's *my* dog."

"Here, take him," I said, "but I'm keeping the leash since you won't be needing it."

I took Gran Chico over to the lady and removed my leash. She grabbed Gran Chico and picked him up.

"He didn't have any dog tags," I pointed out, "so I hope you gave him his rabies and vaccination shots."

"He's already had his shots."

"Where's his tags?"

"I keep 'em in the house so they don't get lost."

"Yeah right."

With my Peanut Butter in toe I quietly walked on. Gran Chico fought to get free of the pigheaded lady and come with us.

"*Tu mio.*"

Peanut Butter reacted, turning back, pulling against me, but we moved on. Peanut looked back several more times.

The two of us finished our walk. Days went by. Weeks went by. There was a distinct emptiness in our house; even Peanut Butter missed the little black critter with those big, black protruding eyeballs. He would go to the easement and look for him in the neighbor's yard but didn't see him there. What had happened to Gran Chico? My Cattle Dog had no one to play with and I had no loving Chihuahua nuzzling me on my bedroom pillow.

To keep the Chihuahua caged, the neighbor lady built a six-foot cedar slat fence to make sure I didn't pet any of their dogs: a sweet white Labrador, a scruffy unkempt terrier, a mixed breed of some sort, and Gran Chico. Chico no longer had a way out; there would be no digging under the chain link fence or moving rocks and bricks to get through the personnel gate. It finally looked like their little black Chihuahua would stay put; they could let him run free in the backyard and not have to be tied up all day.

Well, it took a few weeks, but Gran Chico did indeed find a way out. Maybe he was tunneling under the cedar fence and then the chain link fence...no, he was carefully climbing like a cat over the chain link into an adjacent yard that had another dog to contend with, and then he climbed over their fence to get into the easement, and over my chain link fence to get into my yard. He must have been watching the free-roaming cats in the neighborhood. Chico managed three chain links to come to me! Yes, three. The insensitive cretin of a neighbor didn't know Chihuahuas were at the top of the dog intelligence list.

When Chico's imbecilic owner got off that day, she showed up in her car at my front gate to retrieve her escape artist. Her Chihuahua and my Peanut Butter came running to the front vehicle gate. The neighbor lady got out and yelled, "Quit stealing my dog! Everybody in the neighborhood is gonna know you steal dogs."

She seemed to be speaking to the dogs because I wasn't even out there, I was inside! But I came to the front of the house upon hearing the yelling and peered through the front window.

Peanut Butter jumped at the woman in an effort to bite her so she didn't dare try to open the vehicle gate to get Gran Chico. Finally, the cute little Chihuahua came close enough to the opening at the bottom of the gate so the neighbor lady could get hold of him and pull him through the opening between the gates.

"I better not see him here again!" she wailed.

She put her dog in the car and drove off.

A few days later I saw Gran Chico tied to a clothesline pole in the lady's backyard, and the rope was only about three feet long. A City Code Compliance law required a ten-foot minimum cable if you had to tie up your dog, no chain allowed because it's too heavy. Just a three-foot braided cotton rope and after two days Chico managed to chew it loose and again climbed over three fences to get to my house. The neighbor lady returned once-again after work to recover her dog. She didn't have anything to say this time, not even some entertaining derogatory remarks.

With a 3-1-1 call, I decided to report the lady to the city's Code Compliance department. Chico barked for help day and night... an animal abuse case for sure, tied to a short rope, ignored by the owner. I didn't even know if he was getting fed. Several weeks went by and the city mailed a letter of warning to her and officially "closed the case" having never taken a look at the situation. This detestable neighbor lady ignored the letter and did nothing. Another neighbor reported the abuse—fed up with the barking—so the city opened another case but did nothing except send a "Nuisance Letter."

What happened to the animal abuse case? A month and a half passed and Chico had not managed another escape; the neighbor lady had reinforced the three-foot cotton rope with braided clothesline wire. Poor Gran Chico continued to bark most of the time, begging so dearly for help. The neighbor did give Chico a tiny plastic "doghouse" to retreat to in freezing weather and when the rainstorms came, and Chico made use of it several times, with lightning, frightening thunder, and gushing water as company. Chico was never invited inside to cuddle with her owner, just left all alone, shivering in a plastic box. Dogs are social creatures; being locked up, confined in a tiny backyard, deprives them of their "humanity." I could only feel for little Chico and wonder what he was thinking and feeling. It hurt me deeply. Chico had the intelligence of a three-old child and feelings to match. Lock up a human child for several months—for his entire life. That can't be good for the child. For a dog?

One evening, Peanut Butter began to howl, trying to tell me something and exhibiting pain on her face in the form of troubled eyes. I think she was asking me to come outside with her, but it was late in the evening. I didn't want to go outside in the dark of night among the mosquitoes, and other flying critters that would get into my hair, so I nursed her through the night. Peanut woke me frequently, wanting me for what, I did not know. She had her bowel movement earlier in the day and no bothersome street traffic to keep her up. I lay there unable to sleep, sniffling and sneezing with a runny nose while he made frequent trips through his doggie door to the outside.

The next day, neither of us, sleepy-eyed and wanting to go on with our lives, heard Gran Chico yelping and begging for help as he had done for months. The neighbor's yard was actually quiet. Even the other three dogs were silent. Several days passed and no squealing or howling, then through the grapevine we got this news: in another attempt to escape over the fence, Gran Chico, still tied on that short rope, choked himself to death.

THE END

Postscript: A few weeks after Chico's death her owner started exhibiting signs of anxiety and confusion—more than usual—and became even more agitated by her three remaining dogs. She was upset by everything in her life—house furniture, taxes, spilt milk, and she even had a fear of water! Her family was concerned. The neighbor lady having strange thoughts—more than usual—and exhibiting aggressive behavior toward family and friends—more than usual. She was eventually hospitalized and numerous tests found her to have rabies. Yes, rabies! Apparently Gran Chico had finally gotten even with her owner, had gotten the last laugh.

The Gang Leader, a Bengal

25. Showdown

By Don Kirk

Sitting at the end of an old western town in Arizona sat a tall yellow and black German Shepherd with alerted ears, a red bandana around his neck, and a shiny sheriff's badge on his grey plaid vest. In the far distance, a grumbling noise came from the heavily overcast sky. Then a crackle and a flash of lightning, but the Marshal of *Bonedoggle* sat firm with wide-open brown-tinted eyes fixed at something down the street. In front of him, nine cats, yes, nine cats lined up side-by-side all facing him: a Bengal, a Persian, a Siberian, a Maine Coon, a Bobtail, a cute little Devon Rex, and three others. Nine cats all sitting motionless, their eyes in various colors all fixed on the Marshal and a bearded Irish Wolfhound that sat next to him: an immense muscular two-and-a-half-foot-tall canine with a charcoal grey, long-haired coat and wearing a white bandanna and white checkered waistcoat with deputy's badge. The sky glowed brightly, the wind picking up, a storm brewing. Gusts of wind stirred the fur of the cats, all of them afraid to be the first to make a move, all of them afraid of what might be in the offing. They didn't dare close their eyes even with flashes of lightning reflected off their eyeballs. Their orbs did move a bit as they looked to the sides for an escape route: through open windows, under boardwalks, up telegraph poles. Another burst of wind stirred up the dusty street, then out to the cat-clans right, a third canine wearing a large green bandanna around his neck came out of the shadows carrying a big stick in his mouth. He was a large Bullmastiff with a short reddish brown coat and a stubby pitch-black square muzzle. He weighed in at over one hundred pounds and wore a chain with paw cuffs around his neck as he sauntered up to the Marshal's left

Marshal Dylan, a German Shepherd

side and sat down next to him, shoulder to shoulder, his wrinkled forehead looking alert and ready for action. These three armed lawmen—with long, sharp, pointed canines—were ready to bring in the bandit cats. The Marshal's office had cages sized just for them—formerly chicken coops—and these cats weren't there to sing Elvis's *Jailhouse Rock*. No band was allowed in this cellblock.

You see, the cat gang had robbed a human's stage of some of the foodstuffs rumbling past the ghost town of *Bonedoggle*. They took the bacon, molasses, eggs, dried fruit pies, and numerous blocks of cheese, but they left behind the breads, potatoes, and canned vegetables. And apparently they didn't find any wholesome rats to round out their four-course dinner. The cats, with full bellies, were now ready to stand their ground: nine homeless alley cats against three law dogs—not the fastest breeds on their feet— figured at least some of their cat gang had a fighting chance. The Marshal moved his black snout slightly and twitched his nose. A strike of lightning hit the road at the far end of town with a crackle sound making one's hair stand on end. A lot of cat manes did.

One cat, the Devon Rex—big round eyes and long upright ears set low on the head—jumped and ran on her long legs— that was all it took for the law dogs to make a move and attack. The felines ran for their dear lives, each mouser on her own. There retractable claws, cute faces, and soft cuddly fur doing them no good in this frontier town. The muscular Marshal Dylan, a German Shepherd, ran after the yellow and black-stripped Bengal—the apparent leader of these hooligans—as it ran under the saloon doors hanging high off the wooden floor. Deputy Dawg, the Irish Wolfhound, ran after the Persian and Siberian who bound off together. The second deputy, Mr. Druthers, the normally laid back Bullmastiff, was off to the races down Main Street. He was given that name by a human that once lived here because he would just as soon sleep as run down possum and raccoons. So what did the freeloading tabbys think would happen when they robbed the stage in the last town when it was changing horses? That they would get away free and clear? They were now in *Bonedoggle*, a dog town of law and order with a Marshal that would never give up. It was no longer a ghost town: the remaining, abandoned canines had multiplied.

In the town's saloon—the *Dirty Dog*—the Bengal jumped atop the bar, and she wasn't looking for a drink. Marshal Dylan reached up, his front paws reaching only to the tall brass rail. The saloon keeper, a massive bulldog on a raised platform behind the bar, stepped back when the cat eyed him as a place to jump

Deputy Dawg, an Irish Wolfhound

to freedom. He wanted no part of this cat confrontation. Dylan gave out a high-pitched whimper and then a low-pitched growl, probably asking the Bengal cat to come in peaceably or suffer the consequences. She didn't buy it. But then she saw herself in the bar mirror: one lonely cat with green eyes, pretty as a Bengal tiger but, unfortunately, not nearly as big. She looked back down at the Marshal; was there a way out? She looked up at a chandelier hanging over a large round poker table, but it hung some distance away. Could she make the jump? The German Shepherd looked over at the chandelier; he could surmise what the outlaw cat was about to attempt, but the Bengal didn't wait for the marshal to jump on the table; she leaped aaaaaand made it! The chandelier swung, the burning kerosene lanterns jumped in their carriers, and one fell from its support and hit the floor, bursting into flames. The marshal screamed a continuous rapid barking and the other dog patrons headed for the door. The saloon doors swung wildly hitting a few of the largest canines in the face, but they all made it out safely. But the Bengal cat gang leader, where had she gone?

Deputy Dawg chased the Persian and Siberian cats to a

telegraph pole. One cat followed the other using her claws to grip the wooden pole. All they found at the top: a thin cable of twisted copper and iron, too narrow to be able to "walk the line." Down below, Deputy Dawg looked up, barked a few times, and then lay down calmly. He was not the fastest dog in the marshal's stead, his size slowed him down appreciably, but he knew there was no place for the two criminals to go in this small Arizona town with sharp, prickly desert cactus all about. Clearly, no place to jump, they would have to come *down* the telegraph pole into the deputy's grinning mouth.

The third canine, Mr. Druthers, the two-foot tall Bullmastiff, with droopy eyes and floppy ears, was able to keep up with the biggest bevy of sprinting cats by letting two stragglers peel off to safety…at least for now. The four remaining felines crawled under a boardwalk along main street. Mr. Druthers knelt down and clawed at the perimeter beam. The boardwalk was relatively high off the ground but way to low for his one-hundred pound self so he began to dig a trench, sniffing all the while for his fleeing prey. His tail stood upright, shaking slightly, a challenge in the offing. He was determined they not get away; his failure to bring in a desperado would not go well with Marshal Dylan. Mr. Druthers dug furiously into the dirt with his front legs, dirt flying. The huge hole he needed for his size might actually be deep enough to search for gold. Once the trench was dug big enough, he pulled himself in and disappeared. He found it deathly quiet underneath and found it laced with other "crawlies."

Back at the *Dirty Dog* saloon, smoke emanated from the door and billowed through cracks in the eaves. Inside, the Bengal cat leaped to an open cast iron wood stove, the only thing *not* in flames, and crawled inside. She pushed her way up the narrow stovepipe—a pipe small enough and tight enough against her back to give her paws some gripping power. She finally—gagging all the way—made it to the roof, to still more smoke-filled air. Her fur was covered in black suet, looking more like a junkyard dog's coat. She bounded down the roof and made a successful leap to the neighboring building's rooftop. There, she ran to the far side and scurried down a tree trunk. Once on the ground, she turned and saw the German Shepherd staring her in the face. The Marshal easily grabbed the Bengal around the neck but did so very carefully as if his own youngin and took her to his office. There, he put the gang leader in a jail cell—a cage. Outside, the town's dogs raced about grabbing containers of water from the water storage tank to throw on the saloon fire.

Mr. Druthers continued to crawl under the boardwalk after the four bandit cats. He had hoped there to be no other way out, but finding himself at the far end of the boardwalk, he discovered a wide opening leading back outside...into the inclement weather. Not a good day for the Bullmastiff. Rain had begun to fall. He climbed on out and found he was with Deputy Dawg at the base of the telegraph pole. The Wolfhound with the deputy's badge stood and looked upward. Mr. Druthers followed his look and saw two cat burglars with no second story windows to jump into. His eyes widened, his mouth opened, and his tongue fell out in

Mr. Druthers, a Bullmastiff

anticipation. That Persian, a pretty cat, he thought—a tiny, snow white, long-haired feline, with the sweetest face you'd ever want to see—looked down at him but obviously nervous as a cat on a hot tin roof. She knew she had no escape route, and now TWO law dogs! The long-haired black-and-white Siberian also looked down concerned. She then looked to the Persian and the normally glamorous and gentle cat looked back one eye wide open. They knew they shouldn't have scavenged the stagecoach of its perishables. Deputy Dawg barked. Mr. Druthers looked to the troubled Irish Wolfhound and twisted his head to the side. Deputy Dawg tilted his head left and then right, not comprehending, but then he got the message and nodded in agreement. The big Bullmastiff walked away casually and Deputy Dawg followed him into a nearby alley. Maybe there was another way to skin a cat. The two felines hung there on the pole for another hour or so, then decided it was safe, and turned around to claw their way back down the pole headfirst. Once down, they looked each way…then ran…right into the sharp canines of the two deputies who had waited in hiding for this easy take down. They each grabbed a cat behind the withers—a large loose harmless soft spot—and took them to the Marshal's office where they wanted to throw away the keys for all the trouble these marauding outlaws had given them. These cat creatures had even attacked and killed harmless birds! And Mr. Druthers was sneezing, apparently the smell of a cat made him sick; he may have actually been allergic to cats! Marshal Dylan thanked the deputies with a lick on their noses and a pot of boiled chicken with chunks of cheese, and, of all things: a dessert of peanut butter. Three cats corralled, six to go.

The front door swung open. The mayor of *Bonedoggle*, a pure white Chihuahua, no taller than a raccoon, though a lot more intelligent, came in. He approached the marshal and snapped at him, his claws secured in the wood plank flooring. Dylan took a step back and sat down. The mean mayor, Harvey Scrooge, tapped his right paw on the floor. He pawed six times, the number of outlaw cats still on the loose. They had taken, eaten, and stashed enough foodstuffs to keep the dog population happy for weeks. He appeared upset. He growled. The bitchy, loudmouthed

Chihuahua expected results to his liking, or else. Dylan bowed to him and called for his deputies. The three Marshals hurried out the door. Mr. Druthers again carried a long heavy stick in his mouth. Driving rain stirred up the normally dry dust and made for a nasty, difficult to breath, air. And they did NOT like going out in the rain, but they jumped to the mayor's beck and bark; after all, they worked for him. The law dogs couldn't do any useful sniffing and hunting for sign, the rain adversely affecting their scent, but they'd do their level best.

Deputy Dawg chased two cats to the town's watering hole—a single storage tank for the whole town—where the two cats jumped in, reckoning the deputy wouldn't follow...but he did. He paddled after them with his front paws and swam around and around in the tank. The cats tried to bid farewell to the law dog by jumping out of the tank, but the slick wet rim was much too high to climb over. It hadn't rained in four months; maybe this monsoon would fill the tank so they could float out.

This tank had once been used to water the town's mules and horses—*Bonedoggle* inhabited by human westerners before being wiped out by Indians, or Union Soldiers, or some such, and the dogs, left behind, found they had to fend for themselves. The dogs established a pack with the usual ranking by fighting for position, but they needed more. They had witnessed the human's pattern of assembly, organization, and social structure and so tried to imitate it, though it too had its flaws. There would be a marshal and a mayor and a good saloon dog to serve their favorite drinks.

Back in town, Mr. Druthers chased the Devon Rex toward the Dentist's office. The cat scampered through the open door, but as Mr. Druthers ran toward the door with the big stick still in his mouth, the horizontally held stick hit the opening bringing him to a sudden, jarring halt. He tried pushing through several times with no luck. Marshal Dylan approached and grabbed the stick from him; Mr. Druthers relinquished it easily; the German Shepherd leader of the pack—second only to the mayor. They both hurried into the office. The curly-haired Devon Rex climbed on the dentist's chair and reached for the dangling tooth-extracting pliers and a drill that looked like some innocent toy to play with. She pawed at them; the dental tools swung back and forth. Mr. Druthers came up to the base of the stand that held the drill and turned the wheel with his paw. The drill spun. The cat looked down to see she was surrounded by enormous, leering canines so she jumped to an armrest and then to the headrest. A brass spittoon hung to the left side of the chair, and laid out on a round leather-covered table was all manner of frightening tools: forceps, pliers, sharp probes, scissors, and a monstrous wooden-handled tooth extractor. A pile of teeth lay on yet another table: teeth that had been pulled from the dead so they could be reused. At least no canine teeth present. A bottle of whiskey stood on a wall shelf, probably used to numb the pain of a tooth extraction. Mr. Druthers grinned at the Devon Rex to show his nice array of sharp teeth and then grabbed the large extraction tool in this jaws. Mr. Druthers howled, surely wanting to get at the cat. The Devon Rex raised both front legs and pawed the air as if to beg for mercy. Marshal Dylan abruptly jumped on the cushioned seat and grabbed the cat by the front legs. She surrendered without a fight. Five cats to go.

Back at the end of town, the watering tank level was rising quickly, but as the two cats were now finally able to jump out, they found themselves facing Mr. Druthers and Marshal Dylan. They looked back up the side of the tank only to see Deputy Dawg's head over the top staring them down. With his canines, the Marshal removed the chain with handcuffs from Mr. Druthers' neck and applied the cuffs to two pairs of sweet little paws. The two alley cats linked together, no getting away now. Three cats to go. Mr. Druthers sneezed uncontrollably as he helped to bring the cats in, allergy or no allergy, his assigned task.

Main street was now flooded with rushing water.

The other three cats had run into the barn earlier, so that's where the three law dogs went. They slogged through the mud, trying to deny the rain they hated so much, but they had a job to do. They couldn't allow the remaining outlaws to leave town. In the barn, among the bales of hay were panic-stricken rats, a couple of raccoons, a disinterested donkey, and several colorful chickens with red comb, black tail feathers, and brown wings scurrying about quite concerned because the three cats were chasing around their baby chicks. The hens chased wildly after the cats trying to stop them; the rain and lightning had apparently run all these creatures inside. A fight was eminent. A tussle ensued. The cats clawed viciously, the hens biting with their pointed beaks. One of the cats went for the chicken's wattles and neck, another after a thigh or drumstick. The third cat said to hell with it and dashed out the rear barn doors.

Marshal Dylan and Deputy Dawg chased that cat out the back of the barn and watched her run into an outhouse. The cat climbed on the wooden toilet seat and turned to face the two law dogs. Feeling threatened and with no means of escape (unless she could jump over the two dogs or jump through the half-moon cutout on the sidewall) the cat hissed at the Irish Wolfhound and then, when he didn't back off, arched her back, tucked her tail, and swatted him with her paw. Deputy Dawg backed off, hesitating with his advances. The cat lowered her front paws, but her hind legs slipped...and into the pit latrine she fell. Marshal Dylan entered the outhouse and peered into the dark smelly hole but quickly turned away and left the privy. Deputy Dawg wondered what his boss was up to; it couldn't be the odor that ran him off. Moments later, the marshal returned with a braided manila rope he found on a horse-corral post. The determined German Shepherd and the shaggy Irish Wolfhound lowered the rope into the deep hole by first, one of them releasing the robe, and then the other. It wasn't long before the cat climbed up the rope and out of the pit. Deputy Dawg grabbed her by the neck and the Marshal cuffed her. He pulled the rope out of the hole and then chose to use the pit himself: he hopped up on the seat and took a crouching position. After straining and a little muscle tightening, he twitched his nose. Bounding off the seat, he reached into a wooden crate with his snout and pulled out a corncob. He licked it, didn't taste much like food so he left it.

Back in the barn, Mr. Druthers wondered what the donkey was reaching for up high on a deck above the hay bales and hidden among other bales. He laboriously climbed a ladder and crawled around the bundles of hay, and there…a grey, long-tailed possum enjoying a fine meal of bacon, molasses, cheese, and some kind of pie—the cat gang's stash of stagecoach food! Behind Mr. Druthers, crawling nearby, a snake! And much too close. The Bullmastiff jumped and turned. The snake raised its head and its black pointed tongue shot out to forewarn. Mr. Druthers moved his nose closer trying to identify the creature. The coiled snake sprung forward to take a bite out of the curios nose, but the Bullmastiff jumped back just fast enough to be spared a bad infection, a swollen nose and cheeks, and so much, oh, so much pain.

Returning to the barn, Marshal Dylan and Deputy Dawg saw that the determined Mr. Druthers had successfully rounded up the remaining two cats, but Druthers was sneezing uncontrollably and scratching at his paws and ears. His eyes were beat red; he had both cats in cuffs made of leather thongs, and he was probably thinking he would have to find another profession if more outlaw cats were to be in the offing. He was physically miserable around felines for sure, but the marshal shared his vittles well. It was time to celebrate with a trip to the saloon and a few shots of welcome whiskey, but first they must haul all three remaining cats to the Marshal's office.

They succeeded handsomely, the cats caged. The lawmen capturing all nine outlaws of this notorious feline gang. Marshal Dylan raised his paw to each of his deputies and they pawed him back. The law dogs each grinned and consumed a healthy helping of water from their bowls, but this wasn't enough, they wanted to "really" celebrate so left for the saloon. In the saloon, a floor of powdery grey ash, but the monsoon rains had actually put out the fire and the liquor bottles were found intact.

Hours later, when the three law dogs staggered back to the office grinning like Cheshire cats, they found the feline cages empty! Entirely empty! Apparently, cats do have nine lives, all nine of them.

THE END

Hulk, a Boxer

26. The Incredible Hulk
By Don Kirk

"In Your Face," that was the other name I had given "The Incredible Hulk," a male canine weighing it at seventy-five pounds with square head and docked tail—but not cropped ears—who loved to put his front paws in my lap and look at me face to face. He slobbered voraciously and wanted to lick my face. Yeah, I was hoping he wasn't carrying anything contagious. So very friendly, he was even quick to lick the faces of strangers *after* jumping up on them—and nearly knocking them down. In his curious light-brown eyes was the joy of life...and also a longing to play, explore, and maybe get into trouble.

I, Clifford Rains, had agreed to take the yellowish-brown and white-breasted creature, with white feet and a black *Zorro* mask around his eyes, from a neighbor across the alley when he said he had to leave the rental house he was living in and couldn't take his dog with him. I didn't ask why. I was glad to see it; the dog had spent his entire life—four long years from puppyhood—in the backyard of this man's house—summer and winter—with just a cardboard box to sleep in. And this breed has only a thin coat of hair, not much help in winter, and his short nose is unable to cool the hot air in our Texas summers. His "white socks" didn't help. Four years and no company, human or animal, not even a friendly squirrel. Frequently, I would cross the alley and pet the lonely canine over the chain link fence. He would jump up thrilled, front legs on the top rail so I could pet him and so he could reach my face...and lick it. It was sad to see him there all alone; the owner coming out the back door once a day for just a moment to fill a large bowl with dog food. The Boxer ate what he wanted when he wanted; the owner didn't care how much.

The Incredible Hulk, with his large muscular build, I soon found out, loved to cuddle—yeah really, a seventy-pound cuddle! He would jump on the couch next to me and into my lap if I let him. He loved to play like a little Chihuahua, jumping around, twisting and turning his body, doing somersaults, playing wildly with me—thrilled out of his mind to be free. A human watching this couldn't help but forget his own dejected or depressing life. This dog was a joy; I couldn't help but break a big smile, a facial expression I'm sure he could comprehend and respond to. Dogs are far more receptive to human needs than we realize, they pick up on our emotions and we, hopefully, will take time to read theirs.

The neighbor had seen me walking my two dogs and saw how I cared for them so he wanted me to have his Boxer...and I, yes, agreed to take the canine knowing full well I couldn't keep him. But I had to get him out of that backyard so he could have a life of his own. The Boxer dog is an indoor breed, believe it or not, and with my two dogs, I sure didn't have space for an incredibly strong-willed creature that loved to get in one's face. This energetic breed needs lots of activity, and my dogs keep me sufficiently busy, so I called friends trying to find someone that would take him. One adoptive family had three Boxers in the past, loved them, understood them, but they couldn't take mine at this time. Another had some acreage the dog could run on, but was concerned about his seventeen cats! The Incredible Hulk would have loved that. And the city's dog pound was not an option because they put down dogs not quickly adopted. Hulk deserved better. The ARS—Animal Rescue Society—was my preference, because they cared for their dogs, made sure they were healthy, and they had a park-like establishment for interested parties to view the dogs for adoption.

I had been taking my two dogs on at least three walks a day for two to three miles a day and now this guest also needed a goodly amount of exercise. Walking three dogs at once on three leashes wasn't going to work. I tried, but the leashes got entangled; Hulk would need a separate walk from now on. It was obvious in his ground-sniffing excitement that this world was new to him—a child making new discoveries. Oh, such a happy dog, four years on this planet and this world of ours completely new to him. He might as well have been kept in a prison cell. In a way, it was bigger than the typical cell, an exercise yard as it were, but with no reason to exercise, he just lay there and slept, hopefully dreaming of something to hunt or corral. Hulk behaved nicely with the people we passed on the sidewalk, surprisingly friendly for a dog imprisoned all his life. He seemed to have been socialized. Apparently the new world of things, sights, sounds, and people kept him thrilled and too busy to be afraid…at least he was polite to friendly people; who knows what an intruder would bring. What would he do to a mean, aggressive human being? Attack him and chew him to bits? No, not a sweet caring, loving creature like himself. The previous owner had actually kept him for that purpose, to be a guard dog. But the owner didn't understand: a dog won't make any effort to protect a master that doesn't care about him, who isn't the leader of the pack. This dog would run off if he found an opening in the fence…big enough!

I had possession of The Incredible Hulk just two days when, on one of our walks, a dog attacked us. A forty-pound white bulldog raced up from behind us and grabbed Hulk by the neck…and held tight. I kicked violently at the attacking canine, but he wasn't going to release his grip. I was wishing I had a stun gun, but no, all I could do was kick some more; the Boxer's life clearly in danger. Hulk obviously couldn't get his snout around the teeth-locked bulldog. This is the way a dog takes down his prey: there jaws clamped on the enemy's neck until they bleed to unconsciousness. Moments later, several young people showed up and grabbed the bulldog by the waist and hind legs, but they too couldn't get the vicious canine to let go. One of the older kids said he was a military dog trained to kill dogs. What? You're kidding me! I kept kicking. I had just been given this dog to care for and now this. I stupidly reached down with my right hand… and the bulldog quickly took a bite out of it, blood oozing forth. But in doing so, the dog released his neck hold on Hulk and the kids pulled him away. My blood splattered to the sidewalk.

"Help, get me a bandage," I called out.

"Okay," one gasped and then ran.

The others dragged their dog to a house down the street. I waited and waited, holding my wound, but no one came. I headed home with Hulk.

After dressing my lesion as best I could using my good hand, I called my dog's vet. "My Boxer needs attention now," I declared. For *my* injury, I could wait to go to a medical clinic—having a deep gash that probably needed stitches—but The Incredible Hulk also needed help; even an ear was torn. More importantly, did that attacking dog have rabies or some other disease? Hulk was under my care. I had my rabies shot some years ago, but did Hulk have his? I felt like a friend taking care of a neighbor's child; the kid more important than myself.

The next day I got an appointment for Hulk with my vet and he was found to have two puncture wounds on the neck, a gash in the right ear, and a few bloody spots on the coat. He was also found to have fleas just waiting to spread their kind around my yard. That's all I needed was for my two dogs to become their latest meal ticket. The doctor gave him a pill for fleas and prescribed an oral antibiotic to be given once a day for ten days.

The next day I drove to my doctor and he—well aware of the dangers of a dog bite—gave me a rabies shot, an antibacterial shot, and two antibiotic meds to take. I was too late for sutures. No, I hadn't taken the bite seriously.

It was clear, I couldn't keep this high-energy dog; he needed lots of exercise. He wanted to play all the time! A muscular dog that probably could climb Mount Everest. His powerful ancestors were bred to control cattle in slaughterhouses. Yes, he needed stuff to do; no couch potato was he.

I finally called the Animal Rescue Society for an appointment. Before The Incredible Hulk could be taken, he would be interviewed and a physical exam performed. Hulk jumped into the back of my car, a little concerned, having been in it only once before. The owner was nice enough to have given me his shot records—yeah, the Hulk had actually been to a doctor once a year and was given shots including rabies.

Three days later I showed up at the Animal Rescue Society with the Boxer and sat in the lobby doing some tricks with him; he was smart and picked up on commands quickly. I had started teaching him tricks so I could get him to stop jumping up on me every time he saw me. When I was sitting, he always wanted to jump into my lap. So "sit" was the first command to teach him and then "lay down" so that he would calm down and not be so all-fired exuberant. But to teach him that command I would have to get him to stand back up so we could do another "down." And to stop him from putting his front paws on my knees anytime anywhere— even in the car, I tried to teach him to do it on command using the palms of both hands to tap my knees. If he followed instructions, he would be rewarded with a small training treat.

A physician's assistant came through a side door and handed me a clipboard with a form to fill out and then she asked for the dog. I handed her the leash; I was not invited to go with my baby! Surprisingly, the Incredible Hulk didn't protest.

The form I filled out included questions about his canine characteristics, personality traits, and a space where I could elucidate: point out his charming personality. I turned the form into the receptionist…and waited, and waited. Finally, she called me up to the counter, "Credit card please, that will be fifty dollars."

After I paid the fee for them to take the dog and feed and house him until someone new adopted him, she said, "That's it, you're good to go."

"Good to, won't I, get to see him? I can tell you more about him.

"No, that's it, we've got him from here. We'll take good care of him, we will."

"Okay, okay, thanks." I turned and walked out the door to my car…with no dog trailing behind. I wouldn't even get to say goodbye, face to face, the Hulk licking me lovingly in the face. I wouldn't see him again; he wouldn't see me again. Tears dribbled down my cheeks. I hoped the next owner would appreciate him as much as I did. In my mind's eye, I could see his face looking at me quite concerned as he was taken from his new appreciative owner. I'll probably see him in my dreams for a long time to come. I cried.

THE END

Cinnamon, a Rhodesian Ridgeback

27. The Brain Switch

By Don Kirk

Professor Edward G. Longstreet and I, Kathy Singleton, were working in the lab at the University of Information Technology, Oxford Kansas developing neurological systems that would better allow us to communicate with mentally ill patients and do a better job establishing links to the complex circuitry of robots.

Professor Longstreet—teacher, doctor, cognitive psychologist—and I, hoped to succeed in a momentous experiment years in the making. I had been his assistant for three years working on computational and cognitive neurosciences focusing on the neural substrates of mental processes. We were studying how the brain processes information—the structure of the brain that makes its functioning possible—and agreed to a "megatechnic" challenge. The professor was now ready to put my brain in a *dog's* cranium and the dog's brain would be put into my body—only temporarily of course. *The Brain Switch* we would call it. Using the latest computer science technology—some of it garnered from the *Smartphone*—we would not have to rewire anything within the brain, just splice the brainstem using connectors not unlike the HDMI to DVI and the USB connectors used to connect computers. We had tried a non-physical transfer of brain functions using an aluminum box attached to our backs containing our electronic equipment, a transmitter, and a rechargeable battery, but decided it would not give us a complete and legitimate study of what a dog actually thinks and feels, just more subjective and observational conclusions—little more than we already knew.

The professor's neurosurgical experience with various disorders would allow access to the brain, spinal cord, and the extra-cranial cerebrovascular system.

Admittedly, this would be a first, and, frankly, quite risky, but I was up to it. I had no other place to go and was always fascinated by dog behaviorisms and thought processes.

The Professor wanted a dog with the largest brain cavity to hold my three-pound cerebrum. Dogs with the largest brain mass would be dogs like mastiffs with wide heads so we chose a Rhodesian Ridgeback for our test subject. At least one of them, the other was to be me, Kathy Singleton, his short, small-headed but committed and trustworthy assistant. We together had made this latest experiment possible. And, if successful, we would travel the world revealing our latest discovery. The professor also chose the Ridgeback because he was even tempered and didn't bark. Quiet and gentle, he would be easy to work with, but he stood a good two feet tall and quite strong with seventy plus pounds on those long skinny legs. Yes, the canine was also female, which simplified a lot of our connections, wiring, and language. Longstreet also chose me because I was willing...who else would potentially harm herself for such an experiment? But I loved dogs and I loved this fascinating work we were doing to better understand the wonderful canine relationships with man.

The Rhodesian Ridgeback, with her long dangling, folded over ears that would blow easily in a breeze, and a thin line of hairs growing in the opposite direction down her back, was not the smartest of dogs; the Border Collie had that distinction, but we couldn't have both, a large brain *and* the highest intelligence, go figure? And bigger dogs don't have to process as much food and water as the smaller ones so they won't be distracted by the available food and water, *and* they won't need to use the bathroom as often. We didn't need a tiny hard-to-corral canine eliminating all over the laboratory and have to give him litter box training.

Before we attempted the transfer, I spent a month with the dog so she would become familiar with me and feel save. I taught her a few tricks and numerous other words and she learned something about me by picking up my scent—maybe too much. I wanted him to know I was just an equal partner, and yet still follow my lead when necessary. How this would all play out with *The Brain Switch* was anybody's guess. Both the dog and I had been given the neurotransmitter *Dopamine* to help control each of our reward systems so we could actually enjoy this experiment and be congenial during the study.

A week later, upon returning to the laboratory, the Professor came up to me, "Well, Miss Singleton, we can't do *The Brain Switch* as planned, there simply isn't enough room in the dog's cranium even by reshaping the brain and increasing the number of folds, so I've got this new approach for us to try. Instead of unplugging a hard drive from one computer and plugging it into another computer, what we, in effect, were going to do—one brain physically moved into another cranium—we'll transfer only the thinking."

"But all that we've accomplished so far?"

"It'll be much saver than a complete brain switch. I can develop 'cables' that I've determined could transfer brain chemical neuron activity simply by plugging one brain into another and simultaneously transferring the brain data between the two using chemical messaging. All the functions: speaking, thinking, listening, and body regulating systems, can now be transmitted with my neurotransmitters."

Three months later, the professor's new approach to analyzing the canine brain stood ready and I lay in an NTC, *Neuron Transfer Chamber,* that had neurotransmission converters and chemical "cables" to the Main Frame Computer. And from there they went to an adjoining chamber holding Cinnamon, our Rhodesian Ridgeback. These containers had glass on the sides so the professor could watch the progress. They looked much like large fish tanks with air pumps and filters, but we lay on a soft pad and not gravel. A cable had been attached to my brain stem in a previous surgery and that lead would be plugged into a USB-like port. The central nervous system transfer was not unlike moving system files from one computer to another, but the data would be moved in both directions at the same time. We lay in enclosed "tanks" because an airborne anesthetic would be used to put us under. We wouldn't be aware of what was happening; partially active brains didn't function so well. We had already been lightly sedated, especially Cinnamon; she would not have wanted to be put in a glass box. We hoped that both mechanical and chemical stimuli would counter any baroreceptor reflex. Yes, we were tied up with other pieces of equipment and connection lines, not just the neuron transmitter.

"Are you ready Miss Singleton? I don't know what will happen exactly and I definitely don't know for sure if I can bring you back, theoretically yes, so are you ready?"

"I...um, I'm ready Professor, flip that switch."

The professor lowered an aluminum lid on top of each us to seal the tanks; that's when I felt this could be my coffin, my last experiment. I didn't want to think about it.

"Here goes, Miss Singleton."

I looked over at Cinnamon and she looked back at me, our anxious eyes focused on each other. A white mist engulfed us.

The professor flipped a few more switches and pushed a hoard of buttons with red and green LED status lights; the control panel looking much like what you would see in an old black & white sci-fi movie. But behind that panel were combobulated the latest integrated circuits and thousands of microchips: I started feeling quite strange, my vision becoming hazy and the room moving left, then right, and back again, the sounds in the room I was so familiar with becoming distant, fading, fading, fading far away...

...My vision began to return, but I couldn't see all the colors of the rainbow I was used to, just shades of yellows and blues. The rest of the colors I once knew, the greens and reds, were now shades of grey. I can imagine if my husband—I didn't have one yet—had a narrowed vision like this one, I hate to think what our house décor would look like: all yellows and blues.

Soon, I found myself actually inside Ridgeback's noggin—I couldn't believe it—and my sense of smell: I didn't think I could handle it...everything was so very intense! Professor, help. What can you do to mask some of these odoriferous room odors? Professor, can you hear me...oh dog poop! Maybe my...oh, that's right, I can't speak to the Professor; I have no vocal cords!

I sauntered over to him and lay down with front legs forward, head held high, and I looked up at him, begging. He bent down toward me, arching his back, but was not able to get on his knees, so he towered over me, his head in the proverbial clouds.

"Are you in there, Miss Singleton? Can you understand me? Do you want to go outside...to poop?" I could actually understand what he was saying but didn't know how to reply. I tried to say something, but just a series of weak, sickly yelps came forth.

"Miss Singleton, Kathy?"

I looked up at the Professor, my neck back as far as it would go, his face looking so small and featureless. The Professor reached down—hand and fingers growing oh so large—and touched the top of my head. I jumped up, backed off, and showed my teeth.

"Oh, so sorry, I forgot, you are now a dog in most of your brain functions."

The professor pulled out a chair and sat down in front of me. He pointed to the floor and said "sit." I stood tall on my four long legs so I understood...and sat smartly in front of him.

"Well, you're here with the living; I wish you could tell me what you're thinking and feeling."

I stood up, went over to Cinnamon's water bowl, took a drink, and found that I had this wonderfully large tongue that curled under itself and allowed me to lick up tablespoons full of water. I looked over at the food bowl, a bunch of identical, strong-odored brown chunks of something, yeck...no, I decided to pass.

"Miss Singleton?"

Ooh, I've got an itch on my behind, and, wow, uh, come on, get it, bite, my teeth can...I can't quite get hold of it; I can lick it, chew on it, or maybe pull it. Maybe I can reach it with my mouth and lick voraciously, or I can scratch it with a front or even a hind leg. This is so cool, but how am I to communicate with the Professor so we can quantify our research? Applied mathematics with differential equations using information theory and signal processing...or simply paw taps on the floor?

"Miss Singleton?"

I like this, I can curl up so very tightly to get warm or stretch out on my back on the lab's cool ceramic tile floor...this is awesome!

How about a nice soft, afghan-covered couch to curl up on...I know, there, in the Professor's office I can wrap myself up nice and tight. I can stick my nose in my rear to keep warm.

Miss Singleton—at least her body—lay quietly on a lab table, pillow behind her neck. Professor Longstreet walked over to her and removed an IV. She stirred a bit, suddenly jumped up, fear in her eyes, and tried to push herself with her arms and legs back away from the Professor.

Longstreet now tried to speak to the *new* 'Cinnamon,' the dog now in *my* body: "Cinnamon, it's okay, you're safe with me; do you remember me? How are you feeling?"

The human body twisted her head sideways one way and then the other. She apparently had no idea what the Professor had said to her; she was just a dog now, no college degrees, no hopes and dreams, but she should be able to recognize the words Kathy taught her.

"Cinnamon, do you want to go for a *walk*?"

At that, the dog in a human's body jumped up with excitement, hit the floor, and hurried to the exit door even though she was still barefoot and in a hospital gown.

"Wait girl, not just yet," screamed Longstreet. "Jesus, do I have to put a leash on you? I don't have a collar to fit that beautiful neck of yours with the Adam's apple. I didn't foresee that problem."

From my doggy bed, where I had curled up, I could see what was going on in the lab. I could not imagine what Miss Singleton was thinking now that she was—at least her brain was—a *canis lupus familiaris*. What does she think about this new body she's now saddled with? She sees that she's standing up on two "hind" legs and has these long flexible arms? And she tries to lick her left paw—er, palm. Oops, she's now trying to get on all fours—two hands, two feet—and that's not working out so well. She then dropped on her side and lied down—this slender, five-foot-four girl with long black hair—and then tried to curl up, knees to her chest, and...oh, and wait until she finds she can't lick her own rear end!

'How does she see the world now?' I thought, a dog in the former me. Will she be looking for the litter box? Dogs have a two-to-three-year-old brain so they are able to learn quite quickly. Cinnamon, in a human's body now, can hopefully figure out that she can utter new sounds—can speak—at least hopefully, and then we could learn so much more about a dog's mental processes. All of this data was being recorded, but the professor's observations will be more useful to our study. I, a humanized dog, will have to try to teach this woman a trick or two the way I would teach a dog... only I'm the dog in body and she's the dog in brain! There's a learning curve of course, just like a young child, but she'll pick up a few words. Cinnamon should be able to speak now that she has vocal cords. She will find herself making sounds other than her usual barks, whimpers, yips and yaps. Once she starts speaking, we can learn so much more about the descendants of wolves. The Professor will be so very elated.

Just like children, dogs are affected by their surroundings and the environment can and will affect them for the rest of their lives. This laboratory has affected me after years of "living" here, but how is this experience going to affect this Rhodesian Ridgeback that I'm now a part of? And her canine brain is exploring a *human* body in a way no other dog has, no longer with just the nose. Cinnamon will never be the same...and neither will I.

Soon, the professor will hit us both with a brain scan to try to better understand what is going on. The Magnetic Resonance Imaging and electroencephalography will allow him to "see" what is going on in our brain mass and the cerebral cortex where the planning and decision making is done. He will analyze what new experiences influence us most and "light up" the cerebrum.

Just then, I saw Kathy's body walk over to the litter box, bend down, and relieve herself without even raising the hospital gown! Kathy's body saw herself as a dog, but she was clearly a dog in mind only. I needed to get her in front of me and have a "talk" with her. "Cinnamon, here"...oh no, I can't call her, so I bark. The *homo sapien* body came over to me, all bedraggled and beginning to stink, walked around to my behind, kneeled down, and sniffed.

Cinnamon should be able to speak at least 200 words...if taught through repetition and a connection to an activity, or place, or food! She can maybe string together two to three word sentences like "Can we play?" We only had time to teach Cinnamon a few words—commands—before the transfer, so here goes, this is what I observed from inside my dog body: the professor called Kathy's flesh and bones over, "Cinnamon, come here." The body—though a little slow to respond—actually did. The professor pulled out a chair, "Cinnamon, sit." She did. "Give me a high-five?" She raised her right palm. This was wild, a human doing dog tricks! Longstreet handed her treats like he would with a dog…the same treats—a familiar smell—he'd given the Ridgeback before this transition. Dogs have at least a dozen different sounds to communicate with other dogs so if these utterances could be re-configured so that the vibrations would come out as recognizable human speech, then wonder of wonders.

This word learning continued for the next few weeks, taught by the Professor, and I would continue to explore my new silky doggy body, trying as best I could to understand what made it tick: like how dogs communicated and where the feelings, emotions, fears, and love came from. I saw substantial progress when the professor spoke to Kathy's body, "Cinnamon speak, come on girl." A deep, garbled sound came forth, starting to resemble the human voice, but Cinnamon had no idea what was happening. How would other dogs receive information that no longer resembled the language they all knew, a language developed over thousands of years. Cinnamon, in my human body, could speak a few English words when wanting something: "Food," "Squirrel," "Food," "Belly Rub," Food," "Toy."

Two more days hence and the Professor brought another dog on a leash into the lab. What to hell! It was another strong, muscular Rhodesian Ridgeback, very similar in size and coloring to my temporary dog body, with its smooth, short coat in red wheaten with a little white on the chest and toes.

"What is this all about?" I tried to ask, but it just came out as a yip and growl.

"Miss Singleton, I want you to meet Excalibur."

The uninvited Ridgeback came up to me, not looking me

directly in the eyes, and tried to sniff each side of my face. Then, he moved to one side and that's when I did a one-hundred-and-eighty-degree jump. He was obviously trying to reach my rear end. I wasn't going to let that happen, not yet anyway. Why was the professor bringing him here? *I'm* his dog, *I'm* his partner. I immediately tried to jump on the dog's back to show I outranked him, but he snapped at me. I backed off and barked at him; he backed off. I peed on a table leg; this is *my* territory, dog!

I then tried to sniff him, yes, he was a male, he seemed in good health and his odors told me he had been in the same dog recovery center as I. And he'd apparently been around other humans; I would know them if I ever ran into them.

His tail wagged faster and he started to circle me oh-so-very eagerly. It was clear he wanted to get to know me. I felt more relaxed now—he wasn't going to be trouble—he bowed down with front legs extended; he was ready to play. The new dog took off, running about the lab; I followed him. The Professor yelled out, " Excalibur, come back here, easy now! Cinnamon, eer, Kathy, come here!" Those commands didn't slow him, or I, down. Excalibur jumped up with his front legs onto a lab table looking for nourishment. I knew Ridgebacks absolutely loved food and would eat until they were sick. They would do anything for food. Maybe I could use that to advantage.

Excalibur then saw Kathy's body lying, curled up, on a carpet beside one of the lab tables. He strolled over and sniffed her head, ears, under the arms, and between the legs. Cinnamon was afraid to make a move; you could see the tension in her sweet, pearly-white face. She was quite concerned by this new dog on the premises. Excalibur then barked joyfully and got into the "I wanna play" position, front legs down, rear end held high. Cinnamon didn't move.

The Professor came over and broke up the game with a large rawhide-stuffed roll...for each of them: he gave one to Excalibur and then offered the other to Kathy's human body. She took it!

Another week sped by and Cinnamon—in my body—was enunciating her dog words, trying to speak "dog" to me, trying to tell Edward Longstreet *and* Excalibur what she wanted or was concerned about. If she heard a sound outside the front door, she jumped and said "Company," and if there was a knock, it was "Alert, Alert, Alert" not the usual dog's "ruff, ruff, ruff." And at mealtime she asked, "What's for dinner?" This was strange: a human talking like a dog, well, not like a dog, like a dog with vocal cords. What a whole new world it would be if dogs could speak… and it would be in different languages depending on who raised them, no different than raising a human youngster.

Finally, after five weeks, it was time to return to my human body; Professor Longstreet confident a restored conformation would work. He had gathered an amazing amount of data, witnessed something never before attempted. We could now study the brains of other animals. On this day, Longstreet helped me into the *Neuro Transmitting Chamber.* Cinnamon had already been placed in hers and cables connected to the Main Frame. The last of my neuroconnectors were attached.

Longstreet turned a few knobs and the idiot lights blinked. I could feel my thoughts dwindling and no longer was I aware of my environment. The whole world became just me and nothing else. I was turned completely inward into my own mind…then I heard strange sounds, screeching, squeaks, a harsh terrorizing hum. I felt hands on my body and I could see the laboratory coming into focus. The Professor had his hands on my back and he managed to lift me into a sitting position.

"Kathy, Miss Singleton, you're back with us." I looked at Edward's grey-bearded face and then looked over and saw Cinnamon in her tank lying down and shaking.

"Was it…was it…"

"You're here, aren't you?" asked the Professor. "We have reams of data to analyze and only you can tell us of your experience, your feelings as a dog!"

"Dog? Was I a what, a dog?"

On my successful return from the mysterious beyond, I was hospitalized with a minor neck injury from an unknown dog bite, some brain abnormalities of unknown origin, and mild trauma, but after four days I was able to return to the lab ready to continue our research. Our dog, Cinnamon seemed light-headed and staggered on her first attempt to walk. But, a week later, I was feeling tired, couldn't explain it, but the Professor kept me busy analyzing the data we had collected in our experiment. We discovered that dogs do have a sense of time and they can predict future events. They curl up, not just to keep warm but to protect vital organs.

"I could often tell what you were thinking, Professor—no direct interactions required—like the time you planned to take me outside, just *thinking* you might do it, and I got up and came to you with my leash—I just knew. I had a certain amount of what we humans call 'telepathy.' I also felt jealous, Professor, when you paid more attention to Excalibur, petting him, and talking to him, and I could actually smell how you felt about him. When you concerned yourself about a CT scan or Main Frame printout, I could pick up the scent of it. Oh, and Professor, you have cancer."

"What? To hell you say?"

"I do say. Better go see a doctor."

Longstreet made a visit to his doctor and, sure enough, an early stage of throat cancer was identified. He now had something new to deal with; I had something else: after another four weeks I reported to the Professor that I was pregnant. I told him I had missed my period and felt tired, sometimes nauseous, so I performed a home pregnancy test and it was positive.

"Positive! What ta...you're, you're not..."

"I am, and no, I haven't slept with any man, not even you. You know how dedicated I am to my work. This new reality makes no sense; I can't be pregnant!"

I was carrying a child, that was a fact, but with my breasts and belly growing, I continued to work, caring for my unborn child when, finally, I was able to get an ultrasound scan and found my baby to be a dog—to be Excaliber's son.

THE END

Fluffy, a Pomeranian

28. Fluffy

By Don Kirk

Fluffy, a small female toy dog, turned out to be a very comforting dog to the incarcerated "inmates" of an assisted living center. No one knew how the dog got her name, but it caught on. Maybe it was her foxy face and long, flowing hair, a coat that made her appear a lot larger than she was: she weighed in at only seven pounds.

Fluffy had been a full-time resident of *Caroline's Senior Care Center* for over a year where she successfully raised the spirits of many of the residents. Some had regular visitors—family members—but most often only had daily visits from the nurse and the busy, business-like assistants.

Fluffy, a tiny, long-haired, orange-and-white Pomeranian, would go from bed to bed so residents could adore her and pet the living daylights out of her tiny body. Even with her compact size, she could, and would, jump up on a bed and look happily in a resident's eyes to reveal the sweetest of dog smiles, a tiny pink tongue hanging out. A cheerful expression would appear on the cheerless resident and out would come a vein-riddled hand to stroke her. Fluffy stayed with a patient as long as she received the attention she so loved, but when one elderly person stopped petting her, she would leap to the other resident in the room. And when that person stopped stroking her, she'd jump off the bed and go down the hall to the next room, or stop to visit residents sitting in the hallway in wheelchairs, their heads hanging low. They would look up slowly, and joyfully pet her. Sometimes Fluffy lay quietly sleeping in the lap of a wheelchair patient. And when moving about, she never tired of her commitment to raise spirits. One could easily track down the shaggy dog because soft, loving talk could be heard coming from any resident she had recently been with. Fluffy needed very little overseeing and thus was free to roam the nursing home; so well trained and socialized that she had no problem with strangers and rarely barked, not typical of a Pomeranian. She was so gentle and charming that even visitors had fun with her.

Without a doubt, the gentle-as-a-feather-stroke companion dog was warmly therapeutic to the lives of the isolated residents. She would not take food from the bedside tables, would welcome new guests and visitors to the establishment, and would ignore sudden noises and follow the hand signals of patients and staff. Commands like "stop," "wait," "lay down," "move back," and "come here" she followed without hesitation. She was a joy to the world, well, at least to the residents of this nursing home. Fluffy could not have been any nicer of a house mate and she even knew where her own "toilet" was.

An outdoor patio garden at the assisted living center gave Fluffy a place to run and play. One day a wheelchair-bound male resident enjoying the sunny outdoors suddenly gasped for air and grabbed at his chest. He reached out to Fluffy as if to ask for help and the dog actually showed concern. She barked, and barked again, then went to the electronic patio door and jumped at it, and jumped again higher until her front paw hit the installed-low push button. The door opened. Fluffy ran inside and barked some more. A nurse and nurse's aid came running.

"What's wrong, girl? What's wrong, dear? You know not to bark around here? Naughty, naughty."

Fluffy turned away and scratched at the now-closed glass door. The nurse looked into the patio garden and immediately saw the problem, ran out, checked the man's airway and pulse, loosened his clothing, and called for help on her mobile phone. Could it be cardiac arrest? The nurse turned up the wheelchair foot plates, pulled him from the chair so that he lay flat on the ceramic tiles, and began to give him chest compressions. Fluffy came up and licked the resident's face.

After a trip to the hospital, the resident recovered fully and returned to the Home. The entire resident population cheered at the man's return. Even Fluffy greeted him at the front door and jumped into his lap.

On another occasion, one of the elderly patients pulled out her tiny plastic IV-tube from a hanging bottle of liquid meds. Obviously distressed, she maybe wanted attention and that certainly was one way to get it. Maybe she didn't like the television program? It was an episode of the *Wheel of Fortune*. She tried to sit up, grabbed the raised bed rails—the only physical restraints—reached for a cable of some sort, and started to moan loudly. At that, Fluffy walked into the room, saw the distraught resident, quickly turned around, and ran out into the hall. Moments later Fluffy returned with a nurse in toe. This incident, and the past one, made it clear the Pomeranian had become more than just a companion to the house residents: she had become a very helpful staff member. Even the certified nursing assistants enjoyed having her around. Her presence reduced stress and actually lowered the blood pressure of everyone there.

Then things changed. Fluffy showed signs of an illness; this time her own. She lay around in the back corner of a resident's room and even hid out in a broom closet. She stopped eating and was loosing weight, now down to five pounds! And she was having urinary accidents. Her smiling face and vivacious personality no longer apparent. Fluffy had become a very important part of the lives of the long-time residents and employees, having given unbounded love to all. She had warmed the hearts of all, and now this. It was time for a trip to the vet.

The staff made an appointment with the local veterinarian and Fluffy calmly and peacefully walked with the vet's assistant into a back room. Before long, Dr. Nelson came into the waiting room with a solemn face.

"What's wrong?" asked Teri Messer, one of two nursing home employees that brought Fluffy to the vet.

"Fluffy seems quite healthy except that one of the kidneys

is failing. The second kidney is also deteriorating. Stage-3 kidney disease. A simple serum blood test showed a low GFR—Glomerular Filtration Rate. She's going to need a kidney transplant."

"In a dog?" asked Johna Housman who worked in the admitting office.

Yes, it's fairly common in canines, but it would cost quite a bit and we'd have to wait for a donor."

"A donor?"

"It would cost between $10,000 and $20,000 for the donor surgery and an additional $3,000 to $5,000 for medications and regular vet checks throughout her life. But an even higher hurdle has to be jumped: the donors have to be related."

"Related?"

"The dog's own immune system is likely to reject the donor kidney if it's not from a consanguineous dog."

"Con-sang-guineous?"

"Blood relations. It's not compulsory in cats. Cat donors and recipients don't have to be related."

"We don't have cats."

"Do you know the whereabouts of any of Fluffy's siblings?"

"Well, not off hand, but we can try to track them down...but then, who would give up their dog?"

"A dog can live just fine with one kidney."

"This scares me."

"It's possible to put a canine on dialysis treatments just like a human," added the doctor, "two to three times a week. A veterinary teaching hospital would have to do the work. We do have one in..."

"I don't think so," interrupted Johna.

"Then we have some supplements and medications to temporarily restore Fluffy's energy levels and improve her appetite to gain weight. She'd be able to come home with you."

"Now *that* would be great!" added Teri. "We have a lot of residents who would love to see Fluffy come back, and she helps greatly to make our residents tranquil and quiet."

"Can a human donate a kidney to a dog?" asked Johna. "We so love this dog. All of us."

"A human kidney in a dog? Workable in theory," replied the doctor, "but I don't know. And even if she was to get an organ transplant she wouldn't last more than two years."

"There are many residents who won't be around much longer," added Teri.

Fluffy was brought into the waiting room and tried, but failed, to jump into Johna's lap, so Johna bent over and Fluffy joyfully licked her face.

Here was Fluffy, her *own* life in jeopardy, and the residents of *Caroline's Senior Care Center* wanted to do something, two years was two years. They would have to find out where the dog had come from. Did a resident's family member give her to the Home? Where could they find Fluffy's parents? Did the Pomeranian have a registered name recorded at a kennel with an ownership history?

Johna, Teri, and several other assistants at the Home went to work. Teri contacted the *American Kennel Club* to see if Fluffy was a registered pet, no help there. Johna looked in *Caroline's* records and *did* come up with her previous owner, a Mrs. Martha Madison who had left the dog with her husband in the senior care center. The Home kept the dog when Mr. Madison died, the Pomeranian having been such a sociable, loving animal to all the residents. But it turned out Martha had rescued the dog from a local animal shelter and that dog pound found her as a stray roaming the streets alone and hungry. Such a pretty dog with no home! And no breeder with records on her, so also a dead end.

The search for Fluffy's parents was getting nowhere so Johna and Teri tried using *Facebook*, *YouTube*, *Instagram*, and other online pet groups. They called a couple of other local veterinarians, displayed a Wanted Poster with Fluffy's picture in several pet stores, and used word-of-mouth in the surrounding neighborhoods to track down any Pomeranians. It was hoped Fluffy might actually identify a littermate by smell. A scent can stick with a dog for a long time, but how long? Months, or even years, to recall a brother or sister might actually be possible. And Fluffy was only about three years old. They tracked down a few local people who owned a Pomeranian—not an everyday dog—and took Fluffy to a few of the willing firstly informed of the purpose of their hunt: a kidney transplant. If she sniffed the neighbor's dog and immediately felt comfortable with it, that would be a good sign she had been around that particular dog before, but after seven cordial visits to various dogs, no such luck.

It was a Friday evening when Johna and Teri knocked on the door of yet another person identified as having a Pomeranian.

"Come in, thank you for your call. I just love my dog so. This is Einstein."

Smart, huh?"

"Exceptionally so; I'm just his keeper, Miss McGillicuddy. He tells *me* what to do."

Fluffy led the way into the house and sniffed this latest find more intently than any of the others introduced to her. She acted especially interested in this canine, and it in turn showed undivided interested in her presence, and behaved unusually calm and collected. Both of their tails wagged exuberantly.

"Your dog, Einstein," cried out Teri, "has to be a sibling of Fluffy, look at that!" They must have been together for some time before being separated. A dog that is adopted when first born won't have any memory of their parents or siblings."

"Look at that instant bonding," declared McGillicuddy, "They are already wanting to play with each other."

"They must be littermates. Will you do it?"

"Do what?"

"Let us take a kidney from Einstein, or better yet, do you know any of his parents?'

"I don't know his parents, but you're welcome to try and track them down."

"We've tried from our end, no luck, maybe your dog's history…"

"You're welcome to it."

"It's obvious dogs recognize the humans they've met before, just the faces even without the smell, so it follows they can recognize the faces and smells of other dogs."

Einstein, a Pomeranian

"That's an awesome thought."

"They always jump with excitement when meeting an old acquaintance. Just a simple DNA swab from the cheek would prove or disapprove this connection. Can we let them play in your backyard, see how they interact back there?"

"From what I've seen, they're brother and sister!"

"We could return, visit your home as longtime friends, and you could visit us at the Home."

"Okay. If you're not able to track down Fluffy's parents, I know my baby can do without a kidney if it will help Fluffy and your residents."

Several more weeks went by and Fluffy's parents were not found. She continued to be given temporary medications to keep her going, but she was slowing down, looking most pekid. The Home began raising money for the canine kidney transplant. Visiting families were welcome to contribute—and did, quite familiar with Fluffy and the joy she brought to the residents. Money poured in.

Fluffy was brought to the vet and put under. The surgery would take a while, it would be a long wait, and reading old cooking and sports magazines didn't help pass the time. How would her immune system deal with the new alien kidney? It was, indeed, a sibling's kidney, so a successful outcome was good.

Almost three hours later both dogs came out of surgery, wide-awake, well not quite, the anesthesia not yet completely worn off. They were carried on blankets and put in the hands of Johna and Miss McGillicuddy.

The doctor showed himself, "Well, the surgery was successful and Fluffy now has three kidneys," announced the doctor.

"Three kidneys?"

"No need to remove the old ones; it's easier to leave them. We used the artery from the nearest leg to feed the new kidney. And Einstein is also doing just fine. He won't miss his. The cross-match was negative, meaning no antibodies to react with the donor kidney. All looks good, *but* kidney rejection could still happen in the next few days."

Johna and Teri took Fluffy home and dedicated a wheelchair to her. They kept her medicated and made follow-up trips to the doctor. All the staff and residents had received her love so they wanted to return the favor, wanted to return the joy they had gotten from her presence, and so did. Fluffy did a lot of smiling; the back of her mouth turning up, who could resist that?

There was no kidney rejection.

After a few weeks, it became obvious that Fluffy was spending an inordinate amount of time with nurse's aid Teri Messer. The rejuvenated Pomeranian would follow her around from room to room and when she sat down for a break or a bite of lunch, Fluffy would jump in her lap and want to cuddle. She would also reach up and lick behind Teri's ear. Teri didn't think anything of it and unconsciously scratched it herself, rubbing it red and raw.

"Fluffy, why are you following me around all the time? I've got work to do and you've got many guests to visit."

Fluffy gave a sharp bark and looked into Teri's eyes. She then twitched your nose.

"Okay girl, you're right, I'm not feeling quite up to snuff."

The next day Teri had a nurse take a look at the sore behind her ear.

"I don't know, it doesn't look good, a small lesion, you've been scratching it?"

"On occasion, but Fluffy's been licking it quite a lot."

"I'm getting you an appointment with the doctor."

Two days later the doctor ran some diagnostic tests posthaste and determined that Teri had a malignant melanoma—yes, skin cancer!

A Stage-I tumor was removed surgically from Teri because it looked like a local issue; the cancer had not spread to lymph nodes or body organs. Fluffy had identified it just in time and she, surprisingly, never had any training to sniff out cancer. This is when Teri decided to get Fluffy into a cancer identification course. A dog trained to pickup the disease with their nose can detect many kinds of cancers. They can detect lung cancer from a person's breath, colorectal cancer from watery stool, bladder cancer from urine and of course skin cancer. Fluffy would, and did, become an even bigger asset to *Caroline's Senior Care Center*. New elderly residents were begging to get in. A wonderful place to live thankful to Fluffy.

THE END

AFTERWARD

When a dog looks into your eyes and you look back into his, there is an instant connection, a bond with shared emotions and feelings, and it's no different than a small human child's desire to relate. They use those puppy-dog eyes to get what they want, those raised inner eyebrows, "smiling" mouths, and a strategic, magical pull on your heart strings. And dogs learn to trust you—if you're trustworthy—and they'll go to the ends of the earth to protect you. And they don't try to sleep in your bed to get rolled on, or lie in the doorway to get stepped on, they just want to go wherever you go, after all, you are their pack leader, and not just a source of food and water, you're family. Just rub their head and say "good boy" and they'll appreciate it.

— Don Kirk

PHOTO CREDITS
(Story No.—Page No.—Canine Breed—Source)

Page 0 (Footprint) Don Kirk/Sweetwater Stagelines
Page 0 (Golden Retriever) Don Kirk/Sweetwater Stagelines
1. Page 2 (Golden Retriever) Don Kirk/Sweetwater Stagelines
2. Page 4 (Borador) Don Kirk/Sweetwater Stagelines
2. Page 10 (Borador) Don Kirk/Sweetwater Stagelines
2. Page 17 (Borador) Don Kirk/Sweetwater Stagelines
2. Page 21 (Borador) Don Kirk/Sweetwater Stagelines
2. Page 29 (Borador) Don Kirk/Sweetwater Stagelines
2. Page 34 (Borador) Don Kirk/Sweetwater Stagelines
3. Page 38 (Yellow Lab Cat's Eyes) Don Kirk/Sweetwater Stagelines
3. Page 40 (Yelllow Labrador) Larisa Kursina/stock.adobe.com
4. Page 42 (Kookierhondje) Erik Lam/stock.adobe.com
4. Page 46 (Kookierhondje) Erik Lam/stock.adobe.com
5. Page 52 (Beagle) Eric Isselée/stock.adobe.com
5. Page 60 (Beagle) Flickr/pexels.com
5. Page 71 (Beagle) Tim Piredda/pexels.com
6. Page 72 (Great Dane) everydoghasastory/stock.adobe.com
6. Page 74 (Scottish Deerhound) Kim/stock.adobe.com
6. Page 77 (Bordeaux) seregraff/stock.adobe.com
7. Page 80 (Barberchair) Don Kirk/Sweetwater Stagelines
7. Page 83 (Boxer) Don Kirk/Sweetwater Stagelines
7. Page 86 (Boxer) Don Kirk/Sweetwater Stagelines
8. Page 88 (Australian Sheepdog) GlobalP/istockphoto.com
8. Page 92 (Australian Sheepdog) pawelprus/stock.adobe.com
9. Page 96 (Sternwheel) Don Kirk/Sweetwater Stagelines
9. Page 98 (German Schnauzer) nicholashan/ stock.adobe.com
9. Page 101 (Black Labrador Retriever) Pixabay/pexels.com
9. Page 103 (Life ring) Don Kirk/Sweetwater Stagelines
10. Page 104 (Boxer) Mindaugas/pexels.com
10. Page 107 (Wheaton Terrier) Adrianna Calvo/pexels.com
10. Page 117 (Parakeets) DymoTo/iStockphoto.com
11. Page 118 (Siberian Husky) Don Kirk/Sweetwater Stagelines
11. Page 124 (Siberian Husky) Don Kirk/Sweetwater Stagelines
11. Page 128 (Siberian Husky) Don Kirk/Sweetwater Stagelines
12. Page 130 (Dachshund) Don Kirk/Sweetwater Stagelines

12. Page 132 (Dachshund) Don Kirk/Sweetwater Stagelines

13. Page 134 (Pug) ClarkandCompany/iStockphoto.com

13. Page 141 (Pug) Steshka Willems/pexels.com

14. Page 144 (Yorkshire Terrier) zothen/stock.adobe.com

14. Page 149 (Yorkshire Terrier) zothen/stock.adobe.com

15. Page 152 (Redbone Coonhound) cunniff2011/stock.adobe.com

15. Page 159 (Redbone Coonhound) cunniff2011/stock.adobe.com

15. Page 164 (Chuckwagon) Don Kirk/Sweetwater Stagelines

16. Page 172 (German Shepherd) RichLegg/iStockphoto.com

16. Page 181 (German Shepherd) Eleanor/stock.adobe.com

17. Page 186 (Yorkshire Terrier) Pavel Hlystov/stock.adobe.com

17. Page 189 (Chihuahua) Quang Nguyen/pexels.com

17. Page 192 (Yorkshire Terrier)Pavel Hlystov/stock.adobe.com

17. Page 195 (Chihuahua) miraswonderland/stock.adobe.com

18. Page 198 (Dalmatian) funkyfrogstock/stock.adobe.com

18. Page 205 (Dalmatian) funkyfrogstock/stock.adobe.com

19. Page 214 (Russell Terrier) Viktoria B./pexels.com

19. Page 216 (Bulldog) Chris Shafer/pexels.com

20. Page 218 (Shih Poo) Don Kirk/Sweetwater Stagelines

20. Page 221 (Boston Terrier) Sharon/stock.adobe.com

20. Page 222 (Pug) Jesse Kunerth/stock.adobe.com

21. Page 230 (Beagle) Artem Beliaikin/pexels.com

21. Page 233 (Beagle Puppies) Master1305/stock.adobe.com

22. Page 242 (Maltese) Kang Sunghee/stock.adobe.com

22. Page 246 (Maltese) Kang Sunghee/stock.adobe.com

23. Page 248 (Pitbull) Don Kirk/Sweetwater Stagelines

24. Page 250 (Chihuahua) Don Kirk/Sweetwater Stagelines

24. Page 252 (Chihuahua) adogslifephoto/stock.adobe.com

24. Page 255 (Chihuahua) Don Kirk/Sweetwater Stagelines

24. Page 261 (Chihuahua) Don Kirk/Sweetwater Stagelines

25. Page 268 (Cat) Pixabay/pexels.com

25. Page 270 (German Shepherd) Don Kirk/Sweetwater Stagelines

25. Page 272 (Irish Wolfhound) foaloce/iStockphoto.com

25. Page 274 (Bull Mastiff) Pixabay/pexels.com

26. Page 280 (Boxer) Don Kirk/Sweetwater Stagelines

27. Page 286 (Rhodesian Ridgeback) Julia/pexels.com

28. Page 298 (Pomeranian) dimedrol68/stock.adobe.com

28. Page 305 (Pomeranian) ValerieMak/iStockphoto.com

RATE THESE STORIES

		WORST	BEST

1. The Dog Nanny (Ballad) 1 2 3 4 5 6 7 8 9 10
2. A Hound Dog At Heart 1 2 3 4 5 6 7 8 9 10
3. The Lab And The Cat (Ballad) 1 2 3 4 5 6 7 8 9 10
4. Buddy and Baby Girl 1 2 3 4 5 6 7 8 9 10
5. Lead Detective 1 2 3 4 5 6 7 8 9 10
6. Special Victims 1 2 3 4 5 6 7 8 9 10
7. Clancy's Barbershop 1 2 3 4 5 6 7 8 9 10
8. Aaron And His Dog Aussie 1 2 3 4 5 6 7 8 9 10
9. Dog Heroes 1 2 3 4 5 6 7 8 9 10
10. The Adventures of Shag & Slugger 1 2 3 4 5 6 7 8 9 10
11. A Boy And His Dog 1 2 3 4 5 6 7 8 9 10
12. Dog Gone It 1 2 3 4 5 6 7 8 9 10
13. A Courthouse Case 1 2 3 4 5 6 7 8 9 10
14. Scene Three Take One 1 2 3 4 5 6 7 8 9 10
15. Charlie Chuckwagon 1 2 3 4 5 6 7 8 9 10
16. Der Deutsche Polizist 1 2 3 4 5 6 7 8 9 10
17. Two Talking Toys 1 2 3 4 5 6 7 8 9 10
18. Firehouse #9 .... 1 2 3 4 5 6 7 8 9 10
19. Get Me An Old Bulldog (Ballad) ... 1 2 3 4 5 6 7 8 9 10
20. Moe, Larry, & Curley 1 2 3 4 5 6 7 8 9 10
21. Dog Lessons 1 2 3 4 5 6 7 8 9 10
22. Mario & Frida 1 2 3 4 5 6 7 8 9 10
23. Always With Me (Ballad) 1 2 3 4 5 6 7 8 9 10
24. Gran Chico 1 2 3 4 5 6 7 8 9 10
25. Showdown 1 2 3 4 5 6 7 8 9 10
26. The Incredible Hulk 1 2 3 4 5 6 7 8 9 10
27. The Brain Switch 1 2 3 4 5 6 7 8 9 10
28. Fluffy 1 2 3 4 5 6 7 8 9 10

Sweetwater Stagelines™
5118 Village Trail
San Antonio, Texas 78218

www.ingramcontent.com/pod-product-compliance
Lightning Source LLC
Chambersburg PA
CBHW022222010726
47493CB00002B/560